HOT KNOT SUMMER

A WHISPERING GROVE NOVEL

COZY OMEGAVERSE ROMANCE

HARLEY KNIGHT

Hot Knot Summer © Copyright 2025 Harley Knight

Cover Designer: Bookin It Designs

All rights reserved.

No part of this book may be reproduced or transmitted in any form or by any means, electronic or mechanical, including photocopying, recording, or by any information storage and retrieval system, without permission in writing of the author, except for use of brief quotations in a book review.

This is a work of fiction. Any resemblance to actual persons, living or dead, or actual events is purely coincidental.

CONTENTS

HOT KNOT SUMMER
A WHISPERING GROVE NOVEL

I came here to hide from heartbreak. Not fall straight into it again, times three.

One cheating ex, a million shattered promises, and a heat that decided to crash down weeks early. So yeah, I'm not exactly thriving.

My only plan? Hide out in a remote cabin, write my next book, and avoid Alphas forever.

Instead...

Boom. Fire. Cabin gone.

No explanation. No warning. Just smoke, ash, and the sinking feeling that maybe it wasn't an accident.

Enter three local firefighters who are way too hot, way too kind, and way too Alpha.

Atlas. River. Levi.

They offer me a place to stay. I should say no.

But with no other options, I'm stuck in their mountain home with questions burning hotter than my heat.

I don't know if I can trust them.

I don't know if the fire was an accident.

And I definitely don't know what scares me more... who lit the match, or what's about to ignite between us.

A standalone RH Omegaverse romance with three protective Alphas, one determined Omega, and a fire hot enough to melt every wall she's built. If you love steamy small-town chaos, primal heat, and the kind of chemistry that fogs up cabin windows, this one's for you.

One Omega. Three Alphas. A mountain full of desire, danger, and the kind of heartbreak you never forget.

1

EMMA

Crying in an airport bathroom is a special kind of pathetic. The harsh fluorescent lighting highlights every puffy feature, the automatic paper towel dispensers keep whirring judgmentally, and the parade of strangers giving sympathetic but please-don't-talk-to-me smiles is just the cherry on top of the humiliation sundae.

Yet here I am, Emma Collins, bestselling fantasy romance author and officially discarded Omega, doing exactly that.

I splash cold water on my face for the third time, willing the redness around my eyes to subside. The bathroom mirror doesn't sugarcoat things. I look like I've been hit by the sad train and dragged for several emotional miles.

"Get it together, Emma," I mutter, yanking another paper towel as the dispenser whirs to life. "You've written heroines who overcome way worse than some

Alpha asshole with the emotional depth of a kiddie pool."

My phone buzzes. Jess, of course.

Did you make it through security without committing justifiable homicide?

I manage a faint smile. My best friend since college practically shoved me out the door this morning, insisting I take this trip.

No casualties yet. Saving my energy for when I get back and burn all his stuff.

That's my girl. Remember, this vacation is officially a Fuck Chad holiday, and I don't mean literally. You've had enough of his mess... and Megan's.

Despite everything, I snort-laugh, earning a concerned glance from a woman joining me at the sink.

Boarding soon. Will text when I land.

You'd better. And Emma? He's the loser who couldn't recognize what he had. Not you.

I pocket my phone, grab my carry-on, and straighten my shoulders. Two weeks in Whispering Grove, the picturesque mountain town Chad and I booked for what I stupidly thought might be where he'd finally mark me as his. Two weeks of cozy cabin solitude I now get to enjoy alone. Two weeks to lick my wounds and maybe, just maybe, find the writing spark that's been missing since my fourth book hit the best-seller lists.

Two weeks to forget how completely, spectacularly wrong I was about everything.

The woman nearby is applying lipstick, catching my eye in the mirror. "You're too pretty to look so sad, honey," she says, capping her lipstick. "Whatever he did, he's not worth those tears."

I blink, startled by the unexpected kindness from a stranger. "That obvious, huh?"

She steps nearer, and her delicate Omega scent carries notes of cinnamon and aged paper.

"Honey, I know the 'my Alpha is trash' face when I see it." She glances around to make sure we're alone. "Listen, can I give you some advice? Not all of us Omegas need to fall into the perfect expected role of submitting to any Alpha who pays us attention. Our bodies betray us to them—that's biology—but it doesn't mean we should stop fighting until we find the right Alphas for us. The ones worth surrendering to." She tucks a lock of stray hair behind my ear in a motherly gesture that nearly makes me tear up again.

"Took me forty-seven years and three bad marriages to figure that out. Don't waste your youth like I did. Wait for the ones who earn your submission, not the ones who demand it."

"Thank you. Really appreciate it." My throat tightens up.

She gives me a wink and picks up her bag. "Now, go show him what he's missing."

With a final glance at my reflection, I wipe away the last tears from my face and force myself toward the boarding area. The concourse stretches before me, a gauntlet of overpriced food kiosks and duty-free shops

I have to navigate while looking like the poster child for *Omegas with Abandonment Issues*. People move in streams around me, couples holding hands, families corralling children, business travelers striding purposefully toward their gates. Normal people living normal lives who didn't have their partners suddenly decide their scent was *wrong*.

Chad seemed so different at first. I met him at a book signing event for my second novel, where he was working security. He approached me afterward with my book in hand, asking for an autograph with that easy, charming smile. Said he'd bought it for his niece but ended up reading it himself. I was flattered. An Alpha who wasn't embarrassed to read fantasy romance literature.

He was attentive and protective, everything an Omega is supposed to want from an Alpha. Brought me soup when I was sick. Remembered my favorite coffee order. Listened to me ramble about plot points and character arcs. For the first few months, I walked around in a daze, wondering how I'd gotten so lucky. Even when my friends pointed out little things like how he'd check my location a bit too often, how he'd dismiss my career as *cute*, how he'd subtly put down my friends, I made excuses for him.

What a cliché I was. The naive Omega so desperate for an Alpha's approval that she ignored every red flag waving frantically in her face. Stupid!

The boarding area comes into view, and I focus on the logistics of finding my gate, checking my boarding pass, and making sure I have my ID ready—anything to keep my mind off the humiliating train wreck of my love life. I'd rather think about the soul-crushing discomfort of economy seating than dwell on how spectacularly I misread everything about my relationship.

"Now boarding Zone 3 for Flight 1526 to Mistcrest Mountains," the gate agent announces.

I shuffle forward with my fellow travelers, feeling like I'm moving through molasses.

The tiny Mistcrest airfield is barely more than a glorified landing strip, with a log cabin pretending to be a terminal. It's the only way in or out of this corner of nowhere unless you're up for a six-hour drive on winding mountain roads. Whispering Grove is pretty much it as far as civilization goes around there—just a little town tucked into the valley, about thirty minutes from the airfield by car.

On the plane, I scan the row numbers.

I settle into the window seat, immediately popping in earbuds and turning to stare out at the tarmac.

My mind circles back to three days ago, the moment everything imploded.

"Your scent is wrong," Chad said.

I was standing in our kitchen—well, Chad's kitchen, but after a year together, it felt like ours—chopping vegetables for dinner, when he walked in and dropped the bomb with all the ceremony of commenting on the weather.

"What?" I turned, knife still in hand, something that would seem almost prophetic in retrospect.

"Your scent. It's wrong." Chad didn't even bother looking up from his phone as he said it, thumbs tapping away at some message. "Nothing draws me to you anymore."

The carrots lay forgotten as I stood there, stupidly mute with shock. "Is this... are you breaking up with me?"

"Look, Emma." He finally pocketed his phone; his handsome face arranged in that patronizing expression I'd somehow never noticed before. "We had fun, but let's be real. You knew this wasn't forever."

"I... what? We're leaving for Whispering Grove in three days! We've been planning this trip for months!" My voice rose with each word, disbelief quickly turning to anger. "You said... you literally said last week that maybe this trip would be 'the one.'"

Chad shrugged, actually shrugged, like we were discussing a canceled dinner reservation. "I was trying to let you down easy. You Omegas get so emotionally attached." His tone suggested this was somehow my biological failing rather than his colossal dick move. "I paid for the cabin already. You can still go if you want."

"Wow. So generous." The knife in my hand suddenly seemed very relevant to my interests.

"Look, you'll find someone else." He glanced at his watch. "I need to head out. Can we skip the dramatic Omega meltdown? You can get your stuff later this week while I'm at work."

And then he walked out. Just like that.

I stood frozen until his car pulled away, then sank to the kitchen floor, vegetables abandoned on the cutting board. An hour later, his iPad chimed with a message. Something in me, call it writer's intuition or just garden-variety suspicion, made me pick it up.

The text preview from Megan Sloane glowed on the screen. *Did you tell her yet? Can't wait to see you tonight, Alpha.* 🩶 *And you taste better when she's angry.*

Megan. My so-called friend from Omega Academy. The woman who'd hugged me last month and said Chad was "so lucky to have you."

That was when I started throwing things.

The memory makes my chest tighten all over again. A pathetic whimper escapes before I can trap it behind my teeth. God, I hate that he still has this power over me.

This wasn't even my first Alpha rejection. There was Jason in college, who said I was "too opinionated for an Omega" after three months of dating. Then Michael last year, who ghosted me after meeting my successful Beta friends at a dinner party. Now Chad, with his "Your scent is wrong" crap. Maybe there is something fundamentally broken in me, some Omega defect that makes me untouchable, unmarked, unwanted. And these three aren't the only ones who rejected me.

Maybe I'm cursed to always be almost enough but never quite right.

I hiccup a heavy breath, fighting back tears. Three

strikes. That's what my grandmother would have called it. *Three strikes and you're out, Emma: F.O.E. Failed Omega Extraordinaire.*

"Excuse me. I believe this is my seat," a deep male voice says, instantly raising delicious goose bumps down my arms.

Reluctantly, I glance up.

Oh.

Oh, no.

Standing in the aisle is six-plus feet of what can only be described as a walking Alpha fantasy. Dark brown hair with a perfect hint of dishevelment and sides trimmed shorter than the top. A jaw that could cut glass, sporting a meticulously maintained five-o'clock shadow. Shoulders that make the economy seat look like doll furniture, housed in a body that's clearly been forged through years of physical exertion, not pretentious gym sessions. And eyes... good Lord, they're not gray, as I first thought, but the deepest midnight blue, so dark they're almost black, like the ocean at its most fathomless point.

But what crashes into me the hardest is his scent. Woodsmoke that makes me think of controlled bonfires on autumn nights, toasted sugar with caramel, and rich maple that reminds me of Sunday mornings. It wraps around me with such intensity that my Omega hindbrain short-circuits momentarily, neurons firing in every direction while synapses melt like candle wax.

This is what a scent match is supposed to feel like.

This is what I've read about, what I've written about in my books. This is what I never felt with Chad, despite trying to convince myself otherwise for a whole damn year.

"That seat was supposed to be empty," I blurt out.

One perfect eyebrow arch slightly, amusement flickering across his face. "Sorry to disappoint." He gestures to the boarding pass in his hand. "Last-minute standby. They just called me."

Every other passenger waiting in the standby queue must have mysteriously vanished for this particular Alpha specimen to be assigned the seat next to the emotional wreck that is me. The universe is clearly running a special on cosmic jokes today.

"Great," I mutter, not even attempting to mask my sarcasm. I shift my bag from the spare seat next to me to allow him access to the row, pressing myself closer to the window like I might be able to phase through it if I try hard enough.

He settles beside me, and I'm immediately aware of three things. He smells even better up close, he's absolutely massive in a way that makes economy seating a special kind of torture, and there's something hanging from a leather cord around his neck, some kind of small wooden charm that disappears beneath his shirt before I can make it out. His broad shoulder and arm commandeer the armrest we're meant to share, his long legs clearly uncomfortable in the limited space.

I lean against the window, creating as much distance as physically possible. The last thing I need is an Alpha distraction, especially one whose mere proximity has my traitorous Omega senses perking up like a dog hearing the word *walk*.

The flight attendants begin their safety demonstration, but I notice that one blonde attendant keeps directing her spiel specifically toward my seatmate, her smile wide and flirtatious.

"...and if you need anything during our flight today, just press the call button," she concludes with a wink that's about as subtle as a neon sign.

I roll my eyes so hard I'm surprised they don't get stuck. The attendant catches my expression and narrows her gaze slightly before moving on. Great. Now, I'll probably get *accidentally* skipped during the beverage service.

My seatmate shifts, his arm brushing mine in the process. A jolt of awareness zips through me, irritating in its intensity. I shove my earbuds in deeper and crank up my *Men Are Trash* playlist, determined to maintain my emotional force field.

As we taxi toward the runway, I steal a glance at him. He's reading something on his tablet, his profile unfairly perfect. A little frown of concentration creases his brow, and his full mouth is set in a serious line. He looks like he could be on the cover of *Alpha Quarterly* or whatever ridiculous magazines perpetuate the stereotype that all Alphas are brooding sex gods with superhuman abilities and zero emotional baggage.

My grandmother's voice echoes in my head.

"The world will tell you that we Omegas can't run

our lives alone, that we need Alpha guidance, that we should focus on finding mates and making pups instead of competing in a world that wasn't built for us. Don't you believe it for a second." She'd lost her Alpha at thirty-five and never remated, building her own consulting firm from scratch instead. The business world still operates on the assumption that Omegas will eventually abandon their careers when the right Alpha comes along and biology takes over.

The thought makes my skin crawl. I've seen too many brilliant Omega colleagues reduced to shadows of themselves after being knotted and claimed. It's not that I don't understand the appeal; the biology is undeniable. That primal connection between Alphas and Omegas has shaped our society for millennia, leaving Betas to form the middle management of our social hierarchy. Betas date Alphas too, of course, for the status and intensity, but without the biological imperative of knotting, that final, unbreakable physical bond that drives Alphas to near madness if denied. It's why so many Alphas treat us like walking possessions. Because, obviously, that's all we Omegas think about —finding mates, making babies, and being good little breeders.

At least more of us are venturing out on our own these days, carving paths through boardrooms instead of nurseries, even as society watches with its collective breath held, waiting for us to fail.

The plane accelerates down the runway, and I close my eyes, partially because I'm not crazy about takeoffs, but mostly to avoid acknowledging the living temptation beside me. I've sworn off Alphas. All Alphas. Forever. Or at least for the duration of this trip.

I will not be distracted by spectacular cheekbones and a scent that makes my inner Omega want to purr. I will not.

The plane levels off, and I force myself to relax. Two hours and forty-seven minutes. That's all I have to endure before I can escape this flying metal tube and the disconcerting Alpha beside me. I can manage that. I've survived worse this week.

"First time flying?" his voice breaks through my music, which has apparently ended without me noticing.

I pull out an earbud. "What?"

"You seem nervous. I wondered if this was your first flight."

"No," I respond, more curtly than necessary. "I've flown plenty of times."

He nods, and a smile plays at the corners of his mouth. It transforms his serious face, softening the hard edges and making him look younger, more approachable, and infinitely more dangerous to my emotional stability.

"I'm Atlas Wood," he adds, extending a hand that could probably engulf mine completely.

Of course he's named Atlas. Of course the universe would put me next to an Alpha named after a literal Titan who held up the world.

I hesitate before placing my much smaller hand in his. "Emma."

His large hand envelops mine, and another jolt of awareness shoots up my arm. I withdraw quickly, hoping he doesn't notice the slight tremor in my fingers.

"Nice to meet you, Emma." His voice sounds like he's savoring having my name in his mouth, testing the feel of it on his tongue, and something warm and unwelcome flutters in my stomach. "Heading to Whispering Grove for *vacation?*"

I tense. "How did you know that?"

He nods toward the paperback peeking from my bag—a guidebook on things to do in Whispering Grove. "Lucky guess."

"Oh." I feel foolish for my defensive reaction. "Yeah. Supposed to be with my boyfriend, but that's..." I trail off, not sure why I'm offering this information to a complete stranger. "Anyway. What about you? Business or pleasure?" The question comes out sounding unintentionally flirtatious, and I mentally kick myself.

"Let's just say it's complicated." He answers with a small smile that does absolutely nothing to minimize his appeal. "But I live in Whispering Grove."

"Oh," I say again, eloquent as ever. I want to ask what he does, but that would suggest I'm interested in conversation, which I'm definitely not. Instead, I reach for my water bottle, unscrewing the cap with perhaps more force than necessary.

"So, what's your story?" he asks, ignoring my

obvious attempts to end the conversation. "You don't seem like the typical tourist heading to Whispering Grove."

"What's a typical tourist?" I counter.

"Retirees, honeymooning couples, outdoor enthusiasts with more gear than sense," he lists, that almost smile playing at his lips again. "You don't fit the profile."

"Maybe I'm an axe murderer scouting the area," I suggest dryly.

His mention of honeymooners twists something in my chest. This trip wasn't supposed to be solo.

A full smile breaks across his face, and it's like watching the sun emerge from behind storm clouds, sudden, dazzling, and slightly disorienting.

"If you are, you might want to work on your cover story. The puffy eyes and general aura of heartbreak aren't very intimidating."

I blink, caught between offense at his directness and surprise at his perception. "I could be devastated about all the people I've murdered."

He chuckles, a rich sound that seems to reverberate in my chest. "Fair point. I'll sleep with one eye open once we reach Whispering Grove."

The plane suddenly drops, my stomach lurching as we hit an air pocket. I gasp, both hands immediately white-knuckling the armrests, including the one his arm occupies. My fingers inadvertently dig into his forearm, and I feel solid muscle beneath my panicked grip.

"Sorry about that, folks," the captain's voice comes over the intercom. "We're experiencing some light turbulence. Please return to your seats and fasten your seat belts."

Another stomach-dropping lurch, and I squeeze my eyes shut, trying to control my breathing. I hate turbulence. Absolutely hate it. It's irrational but persistent, this fear that the plane is seconds from plummeting from the sky.

"Hey," Atlas's voice is low and steady near my ear. "It's just air currents. Think of it like driving over small bumps on a road."

"Small bumps don't drop you a hundred feet in half a second," I mutter through clenched teeth, eyes still firmly shut as the plane shakes once more.

"Look at me, Emma."

It's a gentle command that bypasses my brain and speaks directly to my Omega instincts, making me open my eyes.

His face is closer than I expected, that midnight gaze holding mine with calm assurance. "Breathe with me. In"—he takes a deliberate breath—"and out." He exhales slowly.

I find myself mimicking him, my breathing syncing with his without conscious thought. His scent envelops me, somehow both stimulating and calming, and I feel my death grip on his arm loosen slightly.

"There you go," he murmurs. "The plane is designed to handle turbulence much worse than this. We're completely safe."

The rational part of me knows he's right, but another part, the part currently drowning in woodsmoke and maple, is just responding to the steady confidence in his voice. It's infuriating how effective it is, how quickly my panic recedes under his attention.

I become acutely aware that I'm still clutching his arm and force myself to let go. "Sorry," I mumble, embarrassed by my overreaction.

"Don't be." He grins. "You can use me as a stress ball anytime."

There's a subtle flirtation behind his words that sends a completely inappropriate tingle through me. I narrow my gaze.

"Do you practice that in the mirror? The whole calm, reassuring Alpha routine?"

Instead of being offended, he laughs, a sound so genuine it takes me by surprise. "Is it working?"

Despite myself, I feel a reluctant smile tugging at my lips. "A little too well. It's annoying."

"I'll try to be less effective next time," he promises solemnly, but his gaze is dancing with amusement.

God, he's charming. And that makes him dangerous. Chad had been charming too, at first. All sweet words and attentive gestures until he secured me. Then came the subtle undermining, the casual dismissals of my work, the not-so-subtle hints that I should be grateful an Alpha like him was interested in an Omega like me. Classic manipulation that I, with all my education and supposed intelligence, had fallen for hook, line, and sinker.

The memory of Chad's betrayal is like a bucket of cold water, dousing the warmth that had begun to build. I turn away, pulling out my notebook again.

"Sorry," I say, not looking at him. "I should really use this time to work."

I sense his slight surprise at my abrupt shift, but he simply nods. "Of course."

The turbulence gradually subsides as I pretend to write, pen hovering over paper without producing anything coherent. It's how I brainstorm ideas—old-school pen and paper—but right now, I can't concentrate. My mind keeps circling back to the Alpha beside me, to the ease with which he'd calmed me, to the way his scent seems to bypass all my defenses.

A week after discovering my boyfriend of a year had been cheating on me with my friend, I'm sitting next to an Alpha who embodies everything I've ever written into my fictional heroes. It's not fair that his scent makes me want to lean closer while my brain screams to keep my distance. It's not fair that men like Chad exist in the world, pretending to be decent until they get what they want, while men like Atlas probably do the exact same thing but are just better at disguising it.

"Would you like something to drink?"

I jolt back to awareness, realizing the flight attendant, a different one, thankfully, is looking at me expectantly.

"Um, water, please," I manage, and she gives me a small bottle and a few napkins.

"And for you, sir?" She's practically batting her eyelashes at Atlas.

"Coffee, black. Thank you."

Once the attendant leaves, I check the time. We've been in the air for nearly an hour, which means we're almost halfway through this ordeal.

"So, what do you do for a job?" Atlas asks, catching me off guard.

"Oh." I tap my pen against the page. "I write fantasy books. Nothing you'd have heard of."

"Try me." There's a challenge in his tone.

I sigh, relenting, deciding to select my young adult series, as I find men react strangely when I say I write romance books. "The Moonlight Chronicles? It's about a young Omega who discovers a hidden magical world and—" I stop as recognition flares in his expression. "Wait, you know it?"

"Emma Collins," he says, his expression shifting. "You're that Emma Collins?"

I blink, startled. "You've heard of my books?"

"One of my colleagues' daughters is obsessed with them. She made me read the first one so I could understand her world," he admits, and a reluctant smile tugs at my lips despite myself. "I ended up reading all four. They're good. Really good."

A warm flush of pleasure courses through me at the unexpected compliment. Having a guy like Atlas admit to reading and enjoying my books is... disarming.

"Thanks," I mumble, suddenly shy, my cheeks burning up. "The fifth one is giving me trouble."

"Writer's block?"

"Something like that." I don't mention that my creativity has been strangled by Chad's constant and subtle undermining of my career, his dismissal of my books as cute little stories despite their commercial success.

Atlas studies me with those perceptive eyes. "Your protagonist, Brienne, she reminds me of you."

"How would you know?" I challenge. "You've known me for all of an hour."

His mouth quirks up at one corner. "Strong-willed. Brave. Protective of others, despite her own vulnerability. Am I close?"

I stare at him, unsettled by how accurately he's described not just my character but also the parts of me I try to channel when writing her. "Lucky guess," I mutter.

He shrugs those impressive shoulders. "Maybe. Or maybe you're easier to read than you think."

Before I can formulate a response that doesn't involve telling him exactly where he can put his insights, the plane drops again, harder this time. My water sloshes dangerously in its bottle, and Atlas's coffee nearly spills before he steadies it.

"Ladies and gentlemen, we're experiencing some moderate turbulence," the captain announces. "Please remain in your seats with your seat belts fastened."

My heart rate immediately spikes, and I grip one

armrest again, knuckles white, while setting the water bottle on the open tray in front of me. I know turbulence is normal, but my fight-or-flight instincts don't care about statistics.

Atlas sets his coffee down and, without asking permission, places his large hand over mine on the armrest.

"Focus on my voice," he says quietly. "Tell me about the fifth book. What's giving you trouble?"

I shoot him a glare, knowing exactly what he's doing—distracting me from my fear—but I'm desperate enough to play along.

"My editor wants more romance," I say through gritted teeth as the plane shudders again. "But I don't feel like writing about love when it's all a lie anyway."

His eyebrows rise slightly. "All of it?"

"The magical connection, the perfect understanding, the happily-ever-after," I list, my voice bitter even to my own ears. "It's all fantasy, and not the good kind."

"Sounds like someone did a number on you," he observes, his thumb absently stroking the back of my hand, sending warmth spiraling up my arm.

"Someone always does," I reply, trying to ignore how comforting his touch is. "Alphas are great at promising the world and then taking everything."

Instead of defending his designation as most Alphas would, Atlas nods thoughtfully. "There are certainly enough bad examples to justify your cynicism. But dismissing an entire designation based on one person's actions seems a bit..." He pauses, searching for the word.

"Rational?" I supply. "Self-protective? Completely justified?"

His lips twitch. "I was going to say *limiting*."

"Let me guess... You're not like other Alphas, right? You're one of the good ones?"

To my surprise, he laughs. "I wouldn't presume to classify myself. I just think people are individuals first, designations second."

"That's exactly what a privileged Alpha would say," I point out.

"Probably," he concedes with a good-natured shrug. "But it doesn't make it less true."

I'm suddenly aware that the plane has stabilized, the turbulence passing while I was distracted by our conversation. Atlas's hand still covers mine, large, warm, and far too comforting. I pull away, tucking my hands into my lap.

"Thank you," I say stiffly. "For the distraction."

A slow smile spreads across his face, transforming those serious features again. "Anytime, Emma."

"Listen," I say, more sharply than intended. "I'm not... I'm not looking for anything, okay? I'm just trying to get through this flight and this vacation without any more complications. So maybe we could just..." I gesture vaguely between us. "Not."

Atlas studies me for a long moment, his expression thoughtful rather than offended. "Not what, exactly?"

"Not... this." I wave my hand again, accidentally

knocking over my half-empty water bottle. I lunge to catch it, somehow managing to bash my elbow against the armrest in the process. Perfect. Real smooth. I right the bottle with as much dignity as I can muster while my funny bone screams in protest.

"The whole Alpha-Omega chemistry thing," I continue, rubbing my elbow. "The scent thing. The... whatever this is. I'm not interested."

His mouth curves into a smile that makes my stomach flip traitorously. "Are you sure about that?" he asks, his voice dropping a register. "Because your scent tells a different story."

Heat floods my face. "That's... that's biological. It doesn't mean anything."

"If you say so." His tone is light, teasing, but there's something in his eyes, a knowing look that makes me want to simultaneously slap him and drag him into the tiny airplane bathroom for entirely different reasons.

"I do say so," I insist, leaning against the window. "Trust me, you're doing yourself a favor. I'm pretty sure I'm cursed when it comes to..." I trail off, suddenly aware I'm veering into overshare territory. "Let's just say my track record isn't great. So, really, this is for your benefit."

His expression softens, curiosity replacing the teasing light in his eyes. "A curse, huh?"

The simple question catches me off guard. Once again, he's zigged where I expected him to zag, showing genuine interest rather than pressing his advantage.

"We can just be two strangers sharing a row, if that's what you need," he offers, and this time there's no hidden challenge or flirtation in his tone.

The kindness in his voice makes my eyes sting traitorously. I blink rapidly and turn back to the window. "Thank you."

We fall into silence, but it's somehow less tense than before. I glance down at my notebook in my hand, flipping to a blank page and attempting to channel my emotional turmoil into something useful for my next book. My pen hovers over the paper as inspiration strikes.

Dark-haired Alpha hero. Mysterious summer job. Eyes like midnight over the ocean. Voice like velvet-wrapped steel, smooth but unyielding...

I frown at the page. Too safe. Too bland. My publisher is always pushing me to turn up the heat in my romance novels. Well, fine. Let's see where this goes.

Alpha businessman meets Omega on a crowded flight. Cramped seating leads to accidental touches. Turbulence throws them together. His scent overwhelms her suppressed instincts. Bathroom small but not impossible. Mile-High Knot Club definitely not going to happen in real life, but makes for excellent fiction...

My cheeks are burning as I scribble frantically, aware that I'm channeling my inconvenient attraction into increasingly explicit scenarios. I shift in my seat, hoping he can't somehow read my thoughts, or worse, catch a whiff of my changing scent as my imagination runs wild.

I sneak another glance at Atlas, only to find him watching me with that maddeningly knowing look. I slam my notebook closed so fast I nearly catch my fingers in it and clutch it to my chest. Now, I'm writing airplane smut about the stranger sitting next to me. This trip is already a disaster, and we haven't even landed yet.

"Working on something interesting?" His voice slides over me like warm honey.

"Just... notes." I tuck the notebook firmly into the seat pocket in front of me, as if putting physical distance between us and my inappropriate fantasies might somehow neutralize them. "Nothing worth reading."

"I doubt that." There's genuine interest in his tone, not just Alpha flirtation. "I've always admired people who can create something from nothing. Just... pull worlds out of thin air."

I risk looking at him again. He's watching me with something that feels uncomfortably like respect. Great. I feel guilty about mentally undressing him.

"It's not as magical as it sounds. Mostly, it's staring at blank pages and stress-eating snacks."

He laughs, and the sound vibrates through me, setting off little tremors of pleasure that have no business existing between strangers.

A flight attendant interrupts, leaning over with a trash bag. "Any garbage to collect before landing?"

I fumble with my empty bottle and napkins, somehow managing to drop half of them on the floor between us. Atlas and I both reach down at the same time, our heads bumping with a dull thud that sends my already scrambled thoughts into complete disarray.

"Sorry!" I gasp.

His pupils dilate slightly, midnight eyes growing darker as he hands me the fallen napkins, our fingers brushing with deliberate slowness. "No harm done," he murmurs.

My skin prickles. Every nerve on high alert. I'm drowning in the quiet, aching awareness between us.

"Deep inhales and exhales. It helps with the pressure change."

But it's not the altitude making my ears ring or my pulse race. It's him. His proximity. The subtle notes of his Alpha scent.

The captain's voice crackles overhead, announcing our descent. I almost jump, my breath catching in my throat. I've never been so grateful for an interruption in my life.

I find myself oddly reluctant for the flight to end. Despite my initial hostility, Atlas's calm presence has been strangely comforting. He hasn't tried to hit on me, fix my problems, or mansplain anything. He's just... been there. A solid, steady presence that somehow makes the jagged edges of my pain a little less sharp.

"Ladies and gentlemen, we are beginning our final

descent into Mistcrest Regional Airfield," the captain announces. "Local time is 2:17 p.m., and the temperature is a pleasant seventy-four degrees. Flight attendants, please prepare the cabin for arrival."

I gather my scattered belongings, tucking my notebook back into my bag. The notion that I'll never see Atlas again after we land creates an unexpected pang in my chest. Which is ridiculous. I don't know this man, and I certainly don't need another Alpha complication in my life.

"Do you have plans for your stay in Whispering Grove?" Atlas asks.

"Solitude, wine, and possibly some angry writing," I reply honestly, and we fall silent.

Finally, the plane touches down with a slight bump, tires screeching against the runway. We've arrived, and with that, my brief interlude with a captivating Alpha is coming to an end.

When the seat belt sign dings off, Atlas stands and retrieves his bag from the overhead compartment. Then, without being asked, he gets mine too.

"Thanks," I say, accepting my carry-on.

"You're welcome." His eyes meet mine, and for one disorienting moment, I feel like I'm falling into them. "I hope you find what you're looking for in Whispering Grove."

Something about the way he says it feels significant, weighted with meaning I can't quite grasp. Then he's moving down the aisle, his height making him easy to track as he exits the plane.

I wait until most passengers have deplaned before standing. As I make my way toward the exit, one of the flight attendants, the blonde from earlier, gives me a knowing smile.

"Lucky you," she says with a sigh. "If an Alpha like that sat next to me, I would have been all over him."

I open my mouth to say something but decide it's not worth the effort. Instead, I offer a noncommittal smile and continue into the terminal.

Whispering Grove awaits, and with it, two weeks of solitude, healing, and, hopefully, inspiration. I've survived a heartbreak, a betrayal, and a flight seated next to the most distractingly attractive Alpha I've ever encountered.

Whatever this small mountain town throws at me next, I can handle it.

2

EMMA

Mistcrest Regional Airport is smaller than my former apartment back home. The entire arrivals area consists of one sad baggage carousel, a rental-car desk with precisely zero people staffing it, and a coffee kiosk that looks like it might serve motor oil instead of caffeine.

Welcome to my two-week exile.

I grab my black duffel bag on wheels and head toward the exit. The terminal is surprisingly crowded for such a tiny airport, a testament to the region's popularity as a summer escape. Families juggle luggage and excited children, couples lean into each other with vacation anticipation, and I'm suddenly, painfully aware of my solo status.

My phone pings with a notification from my rideshare app. Twelve minutes until my driver arrives. Good timing, especially because of the storm building in the sky over the mountains.

I make my way to the coffee kiosk, where a bored-looking teenager is scrolling through his phone. He looks up when I approach.

"What can I get you?" he asks, slipping his phone into his pocket.

"Largest coffee you have, black as my soul."

His mouth quirks. "Rough flight?"

"Rough week," I correct, sliding my card across the counter.

"One soul-black coffee coming up."

While he prepares my drink, I scan the crowd, a writer's habit. I love people-watching. My gaze snags on a familiar broad-shouldered silhouette near the exit. Atlas stands with a small group of people, all wearing similar practical clothing. Co-workers, maybe? I duck my head when he glances in my direction, pretending to be fascinated by the napkin dispenser.

"Here you go," the barista says, sliding a cup toward me. "Hope your week improves."

"Thanks," I mutter, grabbing the coffee and my luggage and making a beeline for the exit, carefully avoiding Atlas's general vicinity.

Stepping outside, the wave of humidity that hits me is like walking into a steam room. June in Whispering Grove means temperatures in the high eighties with humidity to match. My thin cotton sundress suddenly feels like too much fabric, and I regret ordering hot coffee despite my emotional need for bitterness.

My phone pings again. My driver has arrived, a blue sedan pulling up to the curb. I wave to catch his attention and roll my bag toward him.

"Emma Collins?" the driver confirms as he pops the trunk.

"That's me," I say and climb into the back seat while he stows my luggage.

"I'm Bob, your driver. So, is this your first time in Whispering Grove?" he asks as we drive away from the airport.

"Is it that obvious?"

He chuckles. "Nah, just making conversation. Here for the Founders Festival?"

"There's a festival?"

"Starts this weekend. Biggest event of the year for crafts, food, music. Whole town gets involved. Hotels book up months in advance."

"Great," I mutter and sip at my coffee. Not only am I nursing a broken heart in a strange town, but I'll be doing it surrounded by festivalgoers having the time of their lives. Perfect.

"Where you headed?" he asks.

"I'm staying at a rental cabin," I explain, rattling off the address. "I just need to drop off my duffel bag first. Then, if it's not too much trouble, would you mind taking me back to town? I need to pick up some supplies before heading back, and I'd rather not lug the bag around with me."

"No problem. Town's gonna be packed, though. Brace yourself."

Forty-five minutes later, my coffee cup is empty, and I've dropped off my duffel bag at the rental cabin. Now we're back in town. I see what the driver means. Whispering Grove's Main Street looks like it was plucked straight from a Hallmark movie—charming storefronts with colorful awnings, hanging flower baskets, old-fashioned lampposts—and currently, it's swarming with people. Every sidewalk cafe is filled, people window-shop in groups, and there's a line outside an ice cream parlor despite the early hour. In truth, it's beautiful.

"You can let me out here," I tell him, spotting a grocery store. "I'll call another ride when I'm ready to head to the cabin."

He wishes me luck before pulling away. I stand on the sidewalk for a moment, overwhelmed by the sheer humanity around me. So much for my peaceful mountain getaway.

The grocery store is blessedly air-conditioned, and I take a moment to cool down before grabbing a basket. I mentally run through my list, essentials for a two-week stay, plus comfort food. Heartbreak demands chocolate and wine in medically inadvisable quantities.

I'm debating between cheap wine in large quantities and good wine in smaller amounts when I hear it, a laugh that stops me cold, a sound that featured in countless brunches and girls' nights before it became the soundtrack to my nightmares.

No. It can't be.

But it is.

Megan stands at the end of the aisle, examining a bottle of sparkling water like it's a fascinating artifact. She looks precisely as she always does, sleek dark hair falling in a perfect curtain, designer jeans, and not a drop of sweat despite the heat outside. A silk scarf is wrapped loosely around her neck, the fabric printed with a pattern of tiny gold moths swirling through inky blue. Her scent, jasmine and leather with that underlying sour grape note I never quite liked, drifts toward me.

For a moment, I contemplate retreating. I could abandon my basket, duck out the back, and avoid this confrontation entirely. But then I remember her text on Chad's iPad, and white-hot anger surges through me, overpowering any instinct for self-preservation.

Before I can reconsider, I'm marching down the aisle, my basket swinging dangerously from my arm.

"Fancy meeting you here," I blurt out, my voice sharper than the expensive cheese knife Megan got me for my last birthday. "Small world. Or should I say, small bed?"

Megan's head whips around, her eyes widening in genuine shock. "Emma? Oh, what are you—"

"Doing here? Funny, I was about to ask you the same thing." I step closer, noticing with vicious satisfaction how she takes a small step back. "Were you going to meet Chad here? Was that the plan? A romantic getaway while he was supposed to be in the cabin he booked with me?"

Her perfectly contoured face pales. "I don't know what you're talking about."

"Really? Because Chad's iPad knows. It knows all about how you can't wait to see him, Alpha." I mimic her breathy, syrupy tone I imagined from the text I saw.

Megan glances around nervously. We're attracting curious stares from other shoppers, including an elderly woman who has abandoned all pretense of shopping to watch our drama unfold.

"Emma, please," Megan hisses, lowering her voice. "This isn't the place."

"I'm sorry; is my public confrontation inconvenient for you? Next time I discover that my friend is sleeping with my boyfriend, I'll be sure to schedule it at a more appropriate venue."

Megan reaches for my arm, but I jerk away. "It's not what you think."

"Oh? So you weren't texting Chad about whether he'd broken up with me yet? You weren't planning to meet him?"

"I—" Megan falters, her calculated composure slipping. "It's complicated."

"It's really not." I laugh, a brittle sound that doesn't remotely resemble humor. "It's actually incredibly simple. You're a backstabbing, fake friend, and he's human garbage. See? Simple."

Megan's expression hardens. "You don't understand. You never saw what was right in front of you.

Chad and I... we have something special. A real scent bond. Something you and he never had."

The words are like a slap to the face. Chad said almost the exact same thing to me. To hear it echoed by someone I'd considered a friend twists the knife deeper.

"A real scent bond," I repeat flatly. "So special he couldn't tell me the truth about why? You two deserve each other." I'm fuming, my breaths coming fast.

"He was trying to spare your feelings," Megan insists. "He cares about you, just not... not like that."

"Oh, please," I snap. "If either of you cared about my feelings, you wouldn't have been sneaking around behind my back. How long has this been going on?"

Megan at least has the decency to look uncomfortable. "Emma..."

"How. Long?" I push.

She drops her gaze. "Three months."

Three months. I'm sick to my stomach. A quarter of my relationship with Chad was spent in complete ignorance while my supposed friend was with him behind my back. Every girls' night when she asked about him, every sympathetic nod when I confessed my concerns, every "You two are so cute together"—all lies. The shop is spinning with me.

"Were you ever actually my friend?" I ask, hating the catch in my voice, and I feel my chest tightening.

Something flickers across her face. "Of course I was. I am. This... it just happened."

"Things don't just happen, Megan. You make choices. Both of you made choices."

"Like you've never made a mistake," she snaps, her own anger finally surfacing. "You've always been so perfect, so special. Emma, the successful author. Emma, with her talent, her career, and her life together. Maybe if you'd paid more attention to Chad instead of your precious books, he wouldn't have looked elsewhere."

My mouth drops open.

The old woman watching us gasps audibly. I'm momentarily speechless, blindsided by the venom in her words.

"So, it's my fault," I say slowly. "I was too successful, too focused on my career, so naturally, the appropriate response was for him to cheat with my friend."

"That's not what I—"

"No, I think that's exactly what you meant." I set my basket on the floor, suddenly exhausted. "You know what? Have him. Have this trip. Have all of it. I don't need either of you in my life."

I turn to leave, but Megan grabs my arm. "Emma, wait. I didn't come here to meet Chad. I'm here for work. *The Tideline Tribune* sent me to cover the literary panel at the festival for the local paper. I had no idea you'd be here."

I blink at her, ripping my arm free while processing this new information. Megan has been the features editor at our hometown magazine in Moonshell Bay for three years now. It's the kind of publication that covers artisanal coffee shops and beach cleanups with equal enthusiasm, quintessentially small-town vibes but with aspirations of cosmopolitan relevance. Moonshell Bay is exactly the sort of place where everyone knows everyone's business, which is why I'd been so careful to keep my breakup quiet.

"It doesn't matter," I tell her, feeling myself shaking, and I'm surprised to realize I mean it. "Even if you're telling the truth, it doesn't change what you did. What you both did."

Her expression shifts to something almost pleading. "Can we at least talk? Properly? Maybe over coffee?"

"Fuck no." The words come out firm and final. "I don't have anything else to say to you."

I walk away, leaving my abandoned basket and a speechless Megan behind. The elderly woman who's been watching our exchange gives me an approving nod as I pass. My hands are trembling, and my chest feels tight, as though I might either cry or scream, possibly both.

Outside the grocery store, the cheerful bustle of Main Street is jarring against my inner turmoil. I need somewhere quiet, somewhere I can process what just happened. And I need sugar to drown in, immediately, in whatever form I can get it.

Across the street, a storefront catches my eye. A cozy-looking bakery with an old-fashioned sign reading FLOUR & FABLE BAKERY. Perfect. If I can't drown my sorrows in wine yet, cake is an acceptable substitute.

The bell above the door chimes as I enter, and the scent of sugar, butter, and vanilla wraps around me like a hug. The bakery is busy but not packed. A long glass case displays an array of pastries and cakes.

I stop dead in my tracks. This place is nothing like the chain bakeries back home. Copper pendant lights hang from exposed wooden beams, causing everything to glow with a warm, honey-colored light that makes even the most decadent pastries look somehow healthy. The entire shop is smaller than I expected, with just the counter and display cases taking up most of the space, clearly designed for grab-and-go rather than lingering.

Behind the counter stands an Alpha who could double as a surfing magazine cover model, his tanned forearms flexing as he boxes up pastries. Two women work alongside him, one piping something that looks like edible art onto a wedding cake and a younger woman ringing up customers, smiling despite the busy crowd.

I clutch my purse a little tighter as I join the line, suddenly self-conscious about the wrinkled state of my travel dress. Nothing in Moonshell Bay comes close to this level of Instagram-worthy perfection, not the bakery and definitely not the staff.

The entire left wall of the bakery is hidden behind a floor-to-ceiling tarp, with the words *Expanding Our Story, New Chapter Coming Soon!* painted in whimsical lettering across it. The occasional muffled thump and drill whir suggest active renovations happening just out of sight, though somehow the construction noise only adds to the charm rather than disrupting it.

I've never seen anything like this place. It's as if someone reached into my imagination and built my perfect escape. Even the pastries seem a little magical. I eye the chocolate cake that's basically calling my name with siren-like intensity.

When it's my turn, the young woman behind the counter looks up with a smile that dims just a little when she catches my face. She's shorter than me, with soft curves and dark curls that frame her face. Her golden-brown eyes flick over me like she's used to reading people before they speak.

"How can I help you?" she asks, her voice warm and slightly husky.

"I need to drown in cake," I reply honestly. "Preferably chocolate. And maybe a coffee chaser."

Her mouth quirks in understanding. "Bad day or bad breakup?"

"Both. Plus, I just ran into the friend who was sleeping with my ex behind my back. So, essentially, I've hit the trifecta of awful." The words just pour past my lips.

Instead of the awkward sympathy I'm expecting, she grimaces. "Oh, that calls for the Emergency Chocolate Situation." She turns and selects an enormous slice of triple-layer chocolate cake. "This has ganache between the layers, dark chocolate buttercream, and espresso in the batter. It's basically therapy in cake form."

"I'll take two," I decide aloud. "One for now and one for later when I have to face my empty rental cabin."

"Visiting for the festival?" she asks as she boxes the cake slices.

"Not intentionally. I was supposed to be on a romantic getaway, but that plan imploded rather spectacularly."

She slides the boxes across the counter. "On the house."

"What? No, I couldn't—"

"Cheating exes and backstabbing friends unlock the emergency cake protocol." She waves away my protest. "I'm Lily, by the way. Co-owner of this sugar palace."

"Emma," I reply, touched by the unexpected kindness. "And thank you. Seriously."

"Don't mention it. Want that coffee too?"

"Please, I need it." I have at least four a day.

She laughs, a bright sound that momentarily lifts my mood. "Coming right up."

While she prepares my coffee, I settle at a small table in the corner, opening one of the cake boxes. The slice is enormous, easily enough for two people, and looks like something from a food magazine. I take a bite and make an involuntary sound of pleasure that's probably inappropriate for public spaces.

Lily brings my coffee over. "Good, right?"

"If this is what heartbreak gets me, maybe it's not so bad," I admit, taking another bite.

She glances at the clock. "My shift ends in ten minutes. Want company? I'm an excellent listener, and I know all the town gossip if you need a distraction."

The offer is tempting. Normally, I'd decline—I came here to be alone, after all—but after seeing Megan, I feel shaky and raw. "I'd like that," I hear myself say.

Lily grins. "Perfect. Let me just hand things over to my sister."

She returns to the counter, speaking briefly to another woman who shares her curly, yet darker, hair but looks more polished, less flour-dusted. Then she comes back with her own coffee and sits across from me.

"So," she says, settling in. "Tell me everything."

Surprisingly, I do. I tell her about Chad, about our year together, about the breakup and discovering the texts. Then I mention Megan and our confrontation in the grocery store. I even tell her about my book series, which she recognizes with delighted surprise. I can't believe I just blurted it all out to a complete stranger.

Lily whistles low. "Well, congratulations! You've just won the Worst Alpha Boyfriend Olympics. Gold medal for Chad the Cheater, silver for his terrible lack of scent skills." She raises her coffee cup in a mock toast. "I mean, seriously? 'Your scent is wrong'? That's like rejecting someone because their elbow isn't pointy enough." She rolls her eyes dramatically. "And Megan?

With friends like that, who needs enemies? She's what we call a *small-town piranha* around here, smiles while she's eating you alive."

I grin, appreciating her words more than she realizes.

"The bakery is beautiful," I say, suddenly embarrassed by my outburst and desperate to change the subject.

"Thanks. My sister, Hannah, and I opened it when we lost our mom." Lily's expression softens with memory. "She would have loved seeing so many people enjoying her recipes." She snaps back to her energetic self, pointing her fork at me.

"Listen, I've dated enough Alphas to start my own reality show, *The Alpha-chelor: Who'll Knot Be Eliminated?*" She snorts at her own joke. "Trust me, the universe isn't cursing you; it's doing you a solid. Better to find out Chad's a walking red-flag factory now than after you've picked out matching towels."

"That's a good way of looking at it."

She leans in conspiratorially. "Between us Omegas, I used to be the poster child for terrible Alpha choices. My dating history was so bad that my friends started a betting pool on my next disaster." She winks. "But then I hit the Alpha jackpot... times three."

"Oh, you're one of the lucky ones." I try to keep my tone light, but the words stick a little in my throat. It's hard not to wonder if that kind of happy ending is something people like me get... or if it's just the kind of story you hear from someone else's life.

"What can I say?" She grins wickedly. "I'm an over-achiever. And let me tell you, it wasn't on my vision board—more like my When Hell Freezes Over list." She waves her hand dismissively. "But that's not the point. The point is, you're not broken because some knothead Alpha couldn't appreciate you. That's like blaming the sunset for someone being color-blind."

Her words stay with me, striking something raw and vulnerable beneath her humor. "How do I move past it?"

"Step one: Eat more cake. Step two: Remember you're Emma first, Omega second." She takes a sip of her coffee. "And step three: Accept that your biology is just one chapter in your story, not the whole damn book. You just told me you literally write romance novels, so you know the good ones are worth wading through the Chad-infested waters to find."

I instantly move to hug her. "You have no idea how good it feels to hear this."

We chat until I've demolished the entire cake slice and drained my coffee. Lily is funny with a sarcastic edge I immediately appreciate. She tells me about growing up in Whispering Grove, about the festival I've unknowingly arrived for, and about her ridiculous obsession with true crime shows.

"I basically think I'm a detective now," she admits with a laugh. "My sister says I see conspiracies everywhere."

"Are there many murders in Whispering Grove to solve?" I ask, amused.

"Sadly, no. But Mrs. Abernathy's prize-winning petunias were suspiciously trampled last month, and I have theories."

I laugh, surprised at how much better I feel after an hour in Lily's company. "This was what I needed. Thank you."

"Anytime. Seriously, stop by whenever." She glances at her watch. "I hate to cut this short, but I'm meeting my friend Ruby for a drink. You should join us."

I hesitate. "I should probably get to my cabin and get settled..."

"Come on," she wheedles. "Just for a bit. We're just going across the street to Winterscape. Ruby owns it, best bar in town. You said yourself that you need something stronger than coffee."

The thought of facing my rental cabin alone, with all its romantic getaway trappings, is suddenly unbearable. "Okay," I agree. "One drink."

"That's the spirit!" Lily stands, gathering our empty cups. "Let me change out of my flour-coated clothes, and we'll head over."

Twenty minutes later, we cross Main Street to a building with a sleek, modern facade that stands out from the rest of the quaint storefronts. A minimalist sign reads *Winterscape*.

"Don't let the name fool you," Lily says as we approach. "Ruby actually hates winter and all things Christmas with a passion. The name is ironic."

Inside, Winterscape is surprisingly cozy despite its

modern exterior. Warm wood, comfortable seating, and subtle lighting create an intimate atmosphere. The bar itself is a magnificent piece of polished wood, behind which stands a woman with reddish-blonde hair pulled into a messy bun and amber eyes that assess us as we enter.

"You're late," she calls to Lily as we approach.

"I made a friend," Lily replies, unperturbed. "Ruby, this is Emma. Emma, this is Ruby, owner of this fine establishment and collector of random bar coasters."

Ruby's sharp gaze softens slightly as it lands on me. "Nice to meet you. Any friend of Lily's is welcome here."

"Emma needs a drink," Lily announces. "She caught her Alpha cheating with her friend."

"Jesus, Lily," I mutter. "Tell the whole town, why don't you?"

"Ruby isn't the whole town," Lily says cheerfully. "Just the part of it that serves alcohol."

Ruby doesn't miss a beat. "Cheating Alpha, huh? I know just the thing." She pulls three glasses from under the bar. "Join me?"

Before I can answer, she's pouring amber liquid into the glasses and sliding them across the bar.

"What is it?" I ask, sniffing cautiously.

"Whiskey. Good whiskey." Ruby, who I'm convinced is closer to my age of twenty-four, raises her glass. "To men being disappointments and women being resilient."

"I'll drink to that," Lily agrees, lifting her glass.

I raise mine, clinking it against theirs before taking a sip. The whiskey burns pleasantly down my throat, warming me from the inside.

"So," Ruby says, leaning on the bar. "How bad was it?"

I give her the condensed version of my saga, which she listens to with an increasingly disgusted expression.

"What a complete waste of genetic material," she declares when I finish. "And the friend? Almost worse."

"Almost?" I raise an eyebrow.

"Alphas being trash is practically expected, but another Omega betraying you?" Ruby shakes her head. "That's some next-level betrayal."

"Tell me about it," I mutter, the words rougher than I meant them to be as I take another sip of whiskey. The burn is nothing compared to the twist in my chest, but at least it gives me something else to focus on.

"Listen," Ruby says, her amber eyes serious. "Men are like buses. Miss one, there's always another coming. And sometimes the next one is nicer, cleaner, and doesn't smell like someone died in it."

I choke on my whiskey, laughing despite myself. "That's... weirdly specific."

"I have a lot of bus-related trauma," she says with a straight face before breaking into a grin. "But the point stands. This Alpha wasn't your last chance at happiness. He was just a stop on the route."

"God, now you're getting metaphorical," Lily

groans. "Next, she'll be telling you about the transfer tickets of life."

Ruby swats her with a bar towel. "My metaphors are excellent, thank you very much."

Their banter makes me smile. Looking at these two women, so comfortable with each other, so genuine, it has me realizing how superficial my friendship with Megan had been. There was always a level of competition that I'd ignored, always a sense that she was measuring herself against me.

"So, where are you staying while you're in town?" Ruby asks, refilling our glasses with water.

"I rented a cabin a few miles outside town. The Pinecrest property?" I check my phone, realizing with a start that it's almost 6:00 p.m. "Actually, I should probably head there soon."

Ruby's eyebrows rise. "Isolated place. Beautiful, though."

"Good for writing your stories," Lily adds. "Oh, you should totally set your next book here in Whispering Grove! We could be characters."

"I write fantasy, not small-town romance," I say, but even as the words leave my mouth, I feel the tiniest tug. I've always craved the escape of far-off worlds, monsters, magic, battles bigger than real life, in my books. It's easier than facing the mess of the everyday. Still... there's something about this place, as though it has its own kind of magic. The kind that sneaks up on you with front porches, good coffee, and people who might just want you to stay.

"Even better. Make me a witch. I've always wanted magic powers, especially when dealing with difficult customers." Lily wiggles her fingers like she's casting a spell. "I'd turn rude people into toads. Or maybe just make them compulsively overtip."

I laugh. "I'll consider it."

"Ooh! And I could solve magical mysteries!" Lily's eyes light up. "Like, 'The Case of the Cursed Cupcakes' or 'Who Hexed the Honey Buns?'"

Ruby grins. "If Lily gets to be a witch, I want to be a werewolf. I already work nights at the bar, and I'm grumpy during full moons anyway."

"Perfect!" Lily claps her hands. "We could be a supernatural crime-solving duo. Ruby sniffs out the clues with her wolf senses, and I cast spells to trap the culprits."

"I'd read that," I admit, surprised by how much I'm enjoying this ridiculous conversation.

"What about Hannah?" Ruby asks. "Your sister's too sweet to be anything scary."

Lily taps her chin thoughtfully. "Fairy, definitely. Looks innocent but actually has ancient, terrifying power. Like, she smiles at you while simultaneously commanding an army of bespelled bees."

We're all giggling now as we build this absurd, magical version of Whispering Grove.

The door behind the counter swings open, and a young, handsome, tall man with sleeve tattoos of nautical scenes steps through, carrying a box of supplies. "Did I miss something?" he asks, eyeing our laughter.

"We're casting Emma's next fantasy novel," Ruby explains. "I'm a werewolf, Lily's a witch, and Hannah's a fairy queen." She glances at me. "This is Ash, my bar hand and sometimes bodyguard for the place. Ash, this is Emma. She's in town for vacation."

Ash sets the box down, revealing the charming gap between his front teeth when he smiles. "What about me appearing in the story?"

"Hmm." I study him, getting into the spirit. "Maybe a selkie? You've got the whole Navy vibe, nautical tattoos..."

"Nah," Ruby cuts in. "He's obviously a guardian griffin. Protector type with sharp eyes who can spot trouble from a mile away."

"I like that." Ash nods appreciatively. "Do I get to fly?"

"And tear apart bad guys with your talons," Lily adds cheerfully. Then, at my raised eyebrow, she says, "What? Every good fantasy needs some violence."

"You all are too much fun," I say, yet I'm smiling.

"But you'll write us into your book, right?" Lily presses, eyes sparkling.

"Maybe I will," I answer, surprising myself. "A witch, a werewolf, a fairy, and a griffin walk into a magical bakery..."

"...and solve magical crimes while eating supernatural pastries," Lily finishes.

As we dissolve into another round of laughter, I

realize I haven't thought about Chad or Megan in over an hour. Maybe Whispering Grove is exactly what I needed after all.

After promising to return to the bakery, I call a rideshare to take me to the cabin just as it starts to sprinkle outside, darkening the sky fast. The driver is less chatty than the first, which suits my increasingly tired state.

As we leave the main part of town, the road winds upward through a thick forest. The trees grow denser, the houses sparser, until finally, we turn onto a private drive marked *Pinecrest Cabin.*

"Pretty remote," the driver comments as we approach. "You staying here alone?"

"Oh... yeah, I've got friends meeting me later tonight," I say, forcing a smile. No way am I about to admit to a complete stranger that I'm here alone.

The cabin itself is beautiful. A classic wooden building nestled among towering pines with a wide deck and large windows. In other circumstances, I'd be thrilled by the romantic seclusion. Now, I just hope the Wi-Fi is strong enough for streaming sad movies.

The driver leaves me alone in the darkening storm. I punch in the four-digit code Chad gave me, back when we were still supposed to vacation here together, then step inside. My duffel bag sits just where I left it earlier, dropped off with the rideshare. The cabin is just as charming inside as it is out: knotty pine walls, a stone fireplace, a cozy seating area, and a kitchen that opens into a small dining nook. From the living area a short hallway leads off towards the bedroom.

I reach for a light switch. Nothing happens.

"You've got to be kidding me," I mutter, trying another switch. Still nothing.

I pull out my phone, relieved to see I have one bar of service, and call the number for the rental agency.

"Whispering Grove Rentals, this is Donna," a cheerful voice answers.

"Hi, I'm staying in the Pinecrest Cabin, and there's no power," I explain.

"Oh dear. There was a storm last night that knocked out some lines in that area. The electric company is working on it, but they're backed up with the festival preparations."

"So, when will it be fixed?" I almost gasp the words.

"They're hoping by tonight." Her voice is apologetic. "There are flashlights in the kitchen drawers, and the water should still work since it's on a well with a backup generator."

"Great," I say, not bothering to hide my sarcasm. "Anything else I should know about? Bears? Axe murderers? Alien abductions scheduled for tonight?"

She laughs nervously. "No, nothing like that. With the festival, most places are booked solid, or I would offer to find you another temporary location to stay."

"It's fine." I sigh, remembering what both my rideshare drivers had said about accommodations. "I'll manage."

"I'll have someone out first thing tomorrow to check if the power hasn't returned. And I'll give a small refund for the inconvenience, of course."

"Thanks," I say and end the call.

I find the mentioned flashlights and even some candles in the kitchen drawers and set about making the place habitable. Thankfully, the refrigerator isn't fully stocked yet, so there's nothing to spoil. The stove is gas, at least, and there's a small packet of ground beans so I can make coffee in the morning with the French press I spot on the counter.

As I light candles, the romantic atmosphere they create feels like a cruel joke. This is where Chad and I were supposed to spend two weeks together, where I thought he might finally mark me as his Omega with his bite. Instead, I'm alone with flickering shadows and a growing sense of ridiculousness.

I heave my duffel bag upstairs and onto the bed, unzipping it, and I freeze. The scent that wafts up isn't mine. It's Chad's, that familiar blend of sandalwood and citrus that used to make my heart race and now makes my stomach clench.

"What the hell?" I mutter, digging through the contents. Men's clothes. Chad's favorite designer shirts meticulously folded. His expensive toiletry kit. His stupid protein powder.

Wait! This isn't my bag. It's Chad's. Our duffels are identical, both black with tan leather trim. We'd bought them as a set last Christmas, laughing about how it was our first "couple purchase." Now, I'm standing here holding his packed bag, not mine.

"Why the hell would he have his bag packed?" The answer follows immediately, stealing my breath. He was planning to leave his place until I relocated, considering I moved across the country to live with him. His decision wasn't spontaneous.

I sink down onto the edge of the bed, a shirt clutched in my hands. The one I bought him for his birthday last month. He must have decided to end things days, maybe weeks, ago and was just waiting for the right moment. All those late nights at the office, the distracted conversations, the way he'd stopped scenting me in the mornings before work—it hadn't been stress or tiredness. He'd been mentally checking out of our relationship while I was still planning our future.

"God, I'm such an idiot," I whisper, my voice catching. Despite everything, despite telling myself I hate him, his scent still calls to something primal in me. My Omega biology responds to the Alpha pheromones embedded in his clothes, making me ache for the security I thought I had with him.

I hate that my body betrays me like this. Hate that I can hate him and miss him simultaneously. Hate that he's somehow managed to ruin even this, my escape, my chance to start fresh, by literally forcing me to sit in a cabin surrounded by his scent with none of my own things.

In a sudden burst of fury, I grab the duffel and

upend it, scattering his belongings across the bed, including a plastic folder of documents inside, because, of course, he packs work stuff whenever he travels. He's always been a workaholic.

I gather his things roughly, shoving them back into the duffel with none of the care he'd taken in packing. The zipper catches on a sleeve, and I yank it so hard the fabric tears. Good. Let something of his be damaged too.

My phone vibrates with a text. For one pathetic heartbeat, I hope it's him, realizing the bag mix-up, concerned about me. But it's just my service provider welcoming me to Whispering Grove with a notification about roaming charges.

I wash my face with cold water from the tap, using one of Chad's T-shirts as a towel out of spite. Without any of my own clothes, I'm forced to borrow one of his shirts to sleep in. The soft material feels like a betrayal against my skin, but it's either that or sleep in my travel-worn clothes. With a sigh, I head downstairs to blow out the scattered candles, their flames guttering in protest before the room falls into darkness, and then climb back upstairs and go to bed.

I place my second slice of Lily's Emergency Chocolate Situation cake on a napkin and settle onto the bed, using my phone flashlight to illuminate my impromptu dinner.

"Happy vacation to me," I mutter, taking a bite of cake, and before I know it, I've finished the whole slice.

Outside, the forest sounds are punctuated by

distant rumbles of thunder that seem to draw closer with each passing minute. A flash of lightning briefly illuminates the trees, their shadows dancing across the cabin wall like restless spirits. Night falls completely as the patter of rain begins—soft at first, then growing steadily more insistent against the roof and windows. Under different circumstances, a summer storm in the mountains would be peaceful. Now, it just underscores how utterly alone I am.

As I settle under the covers, my phone chimes with a text from my bestie, Jess.

How's the Fuck Chad vacation going? Drowning in wine yet?

I smile despite myself and type a response.

Currently holed up in a cabin with no electricity, eating emergency chocolate cake for dinner. Ran into Megan—yes, that Megan—at the grocery store. That was... fun. On the upside, made two new friends and tried some really good whiskey. So, yeah, calling it a mixed bag.

Her reply comes quickly.

NO ELECTRICITY? And you MET Megan there? I need details! Call me tomorrow!

Will do. If I survive the night without being eaten by bears.

Bears are the least of your worries. Watch out for hot forest rangers instead. More dangerous to your sworn-off-Alphas plan.

Snorting, I set my phone aside. The idea of meeting any Alpha, hot or otherwise, is the furthest thing from my mind. One day of emotional upheaval is quite enough.

I think about Atlas from the plane, of his woodsmoke scent and midnight eyes, and quickly shut down that train of thought. The last thing I need is to start romanticizing every Alpha who crosses my path.

Tomorrow, I'll get groceries properly, and some clothes too. I'll charge my devices and start working on my book. I'll take back control of this vacation and my life.

But for now, I let the exhaustion pull me under, thunder rumbling in my ears as sleep drags me down.

3

ATLAS

Thunder rumbles in the distance as I drive my truck through the winding roads of Whispering Grove. The massive pines lining the route to the station sway in the growing wind, their needles hissing warnings of the coming storm. At least the rain will help with the dry conditions we've been facing all month.

In the distance, a spark of lightning flashes over the mountains. It reminds me of the turbulence during the flight home, the same turbulence that sent that gorgeous Omega, Emma, practically into my lap when the plane dropped a hundred feet without warning.

Fuck.

My chest tightens at the memory of her scent—old books, honey, and vanilla—wrapping around me like a drug made specifically for an Alpha. Even now, hours later, I swear I can still catch traces of it on my jacket. I inhale deeply, chasing the ghost of that perfect Omega sweetness.

She was beautiful in a way that snuck up on you, honey-blonde hair escaping from a messy bun, large hazel eyes that widened when she realized I'd caught her writing about me. The blush that crept up her neck and stained her cheeks when I leaned over to read what was unmistakably a romance scene. The way she clutched her notebook to her chest as if I might steal it, chin raised defiantly even as her scent betrayed her attraction.

"Fuck," I mutter, slamming my palm against the steering wheel. I should have gotten her number. Should have pushed just a little harder to see her again. But the moment she threw up those walls, all cool politeness and firm boundaries, I backed off. The last thing I needed was to come across like another Alpha asshole who couldn't take no for an answer.

Still, I can't shake the feeling that I've missed something important. My knee bounces with restless energy as I take the turn onto Station Road.

I pull into the parking lot of Whispering Grove Fire Department. The station sits on the edge of town, a sprawling single-story building of red brick and reinforced concrete that we've expanded twice in the years since I took over as chief. Usually, the sight of it settles something in my chest, the closest thing to home I've known since I was thirteen, but today, my skin feels too tight, like I'm buzzing with an electric current I can't ground.

The garage doors stand open, revealing our main engine, the brush truck, and our newest acquisition, a specialty rescue vehicle we'd fought the town council for three years to get approved. Beyond them, I spot the training yard, where several volunteers are hastily packing up.

I grab my backpack from the passenger seat and march indoors.

The main bay smells of diesel, metal polish, and the sweat of honest work. Three volunteers, Kai, Dana, and Miguel, are meticulously checking the breathing apparatus. They glance up as I enter, and the familiar routine of the station begins to work its steady magic on my agitated nerves.

"Chief's back," Miguel calls out, his stocky frame straightening as his face breaks into a grin. He's one of our best, a former military medic who moved to Whispering Grove five years ago and has been an essential part of our team ever since. "Station's still standing, sir."

"Apparently." I nod, a ghost of a smile touching my lips. "Training going well?"

"Station record on the hose deployment," Dana says proudly, pushing her braids back from her face. At twenty-two, she's our youngest volunteer, but what she lacks in experience, she makes up for in sheer determination. "River's been drilling us like we're heading to the Olympics."

I glance at the polished equipment and immaculate bay. "Good. Summer tourist season is about to hit hard, and we're already getting dry conditions up in the north valley." A flash of lightning illuminates in the distance through the window. "Though that might help for a day or two."

"Storm's rolling," Kai confirms, his calm voice carrying the slight accent of his Japanese heritage. "River and Levi are in the office."

I nod my thanks and head down the hallway, my boots echoing on the polished concrete. Our department is small but efficient, twenty-three volunteers total, with just the three of us as full-time staff. We rotate shifts, so there's always one of us on duty, with at least three or four volunteers per shift. It works because we've built something special here—not just colleagues, but a pack comprising River, Levi, and me.

The office door is open, and I pause for a moment to watch them before they notice me. River is stretched out in my chair, my fucking chair, boots propped up on my desk, animatedly gesturing while recounting some story that has Levi shaking his head in disbelief.

River looks like he belongs on the cover of one of those firefighter calendars that suburban moms secretly collect. Tall and lean-muscled with golden-blond hair that falls to just below his ears, usually pushed back. Today he's wearing a faded WGFD T-shirt stretched tight across his shoulders and worn jeans with a hole in one knee. The braided leather bracelet he never takes off encircles his right wrist.

Levi stands by the window, arms crossed over his chest, watching River with that silent, assessing gaze that misses nothing. He's taller than River by an inch, with a leaner build that disguises surprising strength. His straight black hair is longer on top, where it often falls across his forehead in a way that softens his sharp, angular features. Today he's dressed all in black, jeans and a button-up with the sleeves rolled precisely to mid-forearm. The silver watch that belonged to his father gleams on his wrist as he gestures to whatever point River is making.

"...then she says, 'I thought firefighters were supposed to be good with their hands,' and I tell her —" River catches sight of me, and his face lights up, teal-blue eyes smiling. "Well, fuck me sideways! Look what the cat dragged in!"

"Get your ass out of my chair," I growl with a smirk. River is the only person I know who can lift my mood no matter how dark it gets. He's on his feet in an instant, crossing the room in three long strides to pull me into a rough embrace, slapping my back hard enough to make me grunt. His cinnamon scent wraps around me, warming with genuine happiness at my return.

Levi pushes away from the window, a rare smile transforming his serious face. "Welcome back." He clasps my shoulder, his amber-gold eyes searching my face. "You look like shit. How'd it goes?"

"It's done," I say, dropping my bag by the door and rolling my shoulders to release the tension that's been building since I left three days ago. "Easier than I thought it would be." That's not entirely true, but they don't need to know how I'd stood frozen on the porch for twenty minutes before I could make myself turn the key to my parents' home or how the emptiness of the rooms echoed with memories I'd spent years trying to bury.

"Told you it'd be easy," Levi states.

"And the plane didn't crash like you were convinced it would," River adds, throwing himself into the chair opposite mine, one leg slung over the armrest. "Atlas Wood, fearless fire chief, afraid of a little turbulence."

I snort, reclaiming my rightful place behind the desk. The chair is still warm from River. "I made one comment. Once."

"One comment, six times," River corrects, dimples appearing as he grins. "I counted. You texted me before take-off, during the flight, and after landing. Both ways."

"Fuck off." I can't help the small smile that breaks through. "Some of us have seen what happens when machines fall from thirty thousand feet."

"Yeah, yeah, we've all watched *Air Crash Investigation*." River waves a dismissive hand, his fingers tapping a restless rhythm on the armrest. "More importantly, did you bring us anything? Tell me you at least got those maple cookies from that bakery near the airport."

"In the truck," I admit, and River pumps his fist triumphantly, making Levi roll his eyes. "By the way," I add, running a hand through my hair. "I bumped into

Caroline and Mark at the airport. They were heading back from Hawaii. Lucky bastards looked like they'd spent the entire week on the beach."

"So, it's really done, then? The house, the estate, all of it?" Levi asks, perching on the edge of the desk. As the pack's most analytical mind, he's always focused on closure, on tying up loose ends.

"All of it. Sold the house to a pediatrician and her wife." Something eases in my chest slightly as I say it out loud, making it real. "They've got twins on the way. Place will be filled with kids' crap instead of dust and ghosts."

"Good." Levi nods decisively, amber eyes warm with approval. "It was time."

"Speaking of time," River interjects, leaning forward with a predatory gleam in his eye that immediately puts me on guard. "You seem different. Distracted." He taps his nose significantly. "And you smell... interesting."

I shift in my chair. As pack leader, I'm not used to being the one under scrutiny. "Had a long flight. Probably just tired."

"Bullshit," River says cheerfully. "You've got that look. The one where you're trying not to think about something, which means you're thinking about nothing else." His eyes widen suddenly. "Did you meet someone?"

Damn him.

"It was nothing," I say, but even I can smell the lie in my scent. Despite my best efforts, my mind drifts back to the plane, to Emma's startled gasp when the turbulence threw her against me, to the way her eyes had darkened when our gazes locked.

"Holy shit, you did!" River crows, sitting up straight. "Who is she? Details, Chief!"

I sigh, knowing I won't get any peace until I give them something. "Just sat next to an Omega, who's a writer, on the flight back. We talked a bit."

"An Omega writer?" River's interest visibly sharpens, and even Levi leans forward slightly. They know I've avoided Omegas since Caitlin cleaned out my bank account and disappeared a year ago.

"It was nothing," I repeat more firmly. "Just a conversation."

"Yeah? Then why does your scent spike every time you mention her?" River challenges, a knowing smirk on his face.

"Because..." I run a hand through my hair again, frustration bubbling up. "Fuck. She smelled incredible, all right? Like old books and honey and vanilla. And she was writing what looked like a romance novel about an Alpha who sounded suspiciously like me."

"She was writing about you?" River's eyes go wide with delight. "On the plane? While sitting next to you?"

"It wasn't like that," I mutter. "She's in Whispering Grove, but she made it very clear she wants nothing to do with me."

"Wait, she's in town?" Levi straightens, suddenly more interested. "For how long?"

"I don't know. She mentioned being here as if it was supposed to be a vacation, then talked about finishing her book." The thought that Emma might be somewhere in Whispering Grove right now makes my skin prickle with awareness. "But like I said, she wasn't interested."

"Bullshit again," River scoffs. "If she was writing sexy Alpha fiction inspired by you, she was definitely interested. What did you do to scare her off?"

"Nothing!" I protest, then sigh. "I might have been reading over her shoulder. She didn't appreciate that."

River throws his head back and laughs, the sound filling the office. "You nosy bastard! No wonder she shut down."

"It doesn't matter," I insist, though the words taste like a lie. "I'm going to respect her boundaries. We've got a station to run and a town to protect."

But hell, it's going to be damn hard not to check in on her. She's in my head constantly, like a song I can't turn off, a scent I keep chasing even when I know I shouldn't. Every hour I'm not seeing her, I'm thinking about where she is.

"Atlas," River blurts, suddenly serious, his teasing tone gone. "You've been saying for months that the pack feels unbalanced. That we need an Omega to complete us. And now you happen to sit next to one who smells right and is already writing fictional versions of you? That's not nothing."

I stare at him, momentarily caught off guard by his insight. It's easy to forget sometimes, with all his joking and flirting, that River has depths that rival the mountain lakes surrounding our town.

"I never said she was 'the one,'" I argue, but it sounds weak even to my ears.

Levi pushes off the desk, shaking his head at both of us. "Well, better get changed and settled in. We're on high alert with potential fires and the town full of tourists." His lips quirk in a smirk. "You can moon over your plane Omega later."

"I'm not mooning—" I start, but I'm cut off by an especially loud crack of thunder. I glance out the window at the darkening sky, the first sprinkles of rain on the glass.

The phone on my desk rings. I reach for it automatically, but River beats me to it, snatching up the receiver with a wink.

"Whispering Grove Fire Department," he answers, instantly professional despite the teasing glint still in his eyes. His expression sobers as he listens, reaching for the notepad. "Location? Uh-huh. How many? Right. We're on it."

He hangs up, and we're already moving before he speaks, reading his body language. "Climbing accident at Thunder Rock. Two hikers stranded on the north face. Storm's coming in."

"Rock rescue in a thunderstorm. Fucking perfect," I mutter, but we're all grabbing gear.

"Welcome home, Chief," River says, slapping my shoulder as we head for the rescue truck.

Lightning illuminates the bay as we load the last of

the equipment, and for a moment, I catch Levi watching me.

"What?" I ask.

"Nothing," he says mildly. "Just thinking this Omega must have made quite an impression." He adds, "You know, the universe doesn't often give second chances. If you meet her again, maybe don't fuck it up this time."

"Eight calls," River announces, dropping into a chair in the station's common room with exaggerated exhaustion. "Eight fucking calls in seven hours. I'm telling you, Chief, you're bad luck. We had zero emergencies while you were gone, and now we're running ourselves ragged."

It's well past dark now, nearly eleven, and the storm has intensified to a full-blown deluge. Rain pounds against the windows in waves driven by howling wind, and lightning flashes nearly continuously, turning night to strobing day.

After the rock rescue, which had been harrowing enough with the rain making the cliff face slick as glass, we'd barely caught our breath before the calls started rolling in. A downed power line that had us coordinating with the electric company while keeping sightseers at bay. A tree that fell and crushed someone's shed. More minor accidents caused by the increasingly hazardous road conditions.

"Might be a record for a rainy evening," Levi agrees, running a towel over his hair. He'd been the one to climb the tree in the Hendersons' yard to rescue their cat, which had rewarded him with three deep scratches across his forearm.

I lean against the doorframe, nursing a cup of coffee that's strong enough to strip paint. The station is quiet now except for the skeleton crew, just the three of us and Kai, who's monitoring the radios while doing inventory in the supply room.

"Could be worse," I point out. "At least we're not dealing with a structure fire in this mess."

River groans, throwing an empty protein bar wrapper at me. "Don't jinx it, for fuck's sake. I want to actually sleep tonight."

"You're getting soft in your old age," I taunt. We're all exhausted, and I'm still not fully recovered from three days of dealing with my parents' estate.

"I'm younger than you," River shoots back. "And prettier."

"Keep telling yourself that," I mutter, but I'm fighting a smile.

Levi ignores our bickering, focused on bandaging his scratched arm. "Weather report says the storm should pass in a few hours. Flash flood warnings are in effect for the lower valley. We might need to assist with evacuations if the river overflows."

I nod, making a mental note to check the emergency protocols. The Whispering River can rise dangerously fast during heavy rains, threatening the older cabins built too close to its banks. "We'll set up cots in the community center if needed."

River yawns widely, not bothering to cover his mouth. "Well, I'm hitting the shower, then crashing for as long as the universe allows." He stretches, joints popping audibly, before fixing me with a suddenly serious look. "And tomorrow, we're revisiting this Omega writer situation. Because if she really is in town for a while, you need to at least try to apologize for being a creep."

"I wasn't—" I start to protest, but he's already sauntering out of the room, whistling some pop song I don't recognize.

Levi finishes with his bandage and levels me with one of his assessing gazes. "He's not wrong, you know."

"About me being a creep?" I scowl.

"About you needing to try again." He stands, methodically packing away the first aid kit. "You've been off-balance since your ex left you. We all have. The pack needs... something." He chooses his words carefully, never one to speak without consideration. "Or someone."

I don't answer immediately, staring into my coffee as if it might contain solutions to problems I'm not even sure how to articulate. The truth is, our pack does feel incomplete. Has for a long time. Three Alphas make for a strange dynamic, too much dominance, not enough softness. We make it work because we each fill different roles, but there's always been a sense that something—or someone—is missing.

"I don't even know where she's staying," I finally say, which isn't a denial.

"We know all the hotels, motels, cabins, and even the Airbnbs in Whispering Grove," Levi points out with his usual practicality. "How hard could it be to find her?"

"Stalking. That's your suggestion?" I raise an eyebrow.

A ghost of a smile passes over his face. "Information gathering. There's a difference."

Before I can respond, the radio on my belt crackles to life, and Kai's voice comes through, tense and urgent. "Chief? We've got a call. Residential structure fire at 1247 Pinecrest Lane. Multiple reports coming in. It's bad."

Time seems to slow down for a heartbeat, then speeds up double. I'm already moving, Levi right behind me, as I respond. "Copy that. Full response. Wake the volunteers on the roster and get dispatch to send out the alert."

The alarm blares through the station a moment later, the automated system activating as we hit the bay floor at a run. River emerges from the locker room, hair still wet but all signs of exhaustion gone from his face.

"Structure fire," I call out as he jogs over, already reaching for his turnout gear. "Pinecrest Lane."

"Fuck," he mutters. We all know what that means. Pinecrest Lane is a winding road that leads up the eastern slope, lined with expensive vacation homes built primarily of wood. But in this storm, the situation might be in our favor, with the rain battling the fire alongside us.

Kai bursts into the bay, followed by the two volunteers who were sleeping in the bunk room. "Police are en route, but they're coming from the south side. Roads are starting to flood in places."

I nod sharply. "Engine one, Rescue one," I bark. "Kai, Dana, Miguel, you're with me on engine. River, take Rescue with Levi and Terry. We roll in sixty seconds."

The rain is coming down in sheets as we tear out of the station, lights flashing and sirens wailing.

"Dispatch, this is Chief Wood," I radio in as we speed through the deserted streets. "En route to Pinecrest Lane. What's the situation?"

"Chief, we have multiple nine-one-one calls reporting a house fire," the dispatcher responds, her voice steady despite the urgency. "Callers indicate the vacation rental is occupied. Unknown number inside. Police are ten minutes out."

"Copy that." I glance in the rearview at my team, all grim determination now. "Engine one ETA four minutes. Rescue right behind us."

The wipers struggle against the torrent, and I grip the wheel tighter as we navigate the winding road leading up to the eastern slope. The higher we climb, the stronger the glow becomes, a malevolent orange beacon cutting through the night. Beside me, Kai checks his breathing apparatus one last time, his usually jovial face set in hard lines.

As we round the final bend on Pinecrest Lane, the full scene comes into view, and my breath catches in my throat. A large A-frame cabin is half engulfed in flames that the downpour is doing little to douse, fire licking up the wooden siding and punching through the roof in multiple places.

"Jesus Christ," Miguel breathes from behind me.

The radio crackles with River's voice from the rescue truck behind us.

I pull to a stop at a safe distance and throw the engine into park. "Establish water supply. Primary search is priority one. River, circle around back when you arrive. Levi, I want a structural assessment before we commit to an interior attack."

We hit the ground running, rain pelting us as we don our masks and gear up. The storm has turned the ground to mud, making every movement more diffi-cult, but we maneuver with the efficiency of a team that's faced hell together before.

"Ready?" I ask, adjusting my mask as the rest of the team forms up.

I'm met with curt nods, and I feel the weight of leadership settle onto my shoulders. This is what I was made for, this moment, this purpose. Everything else, houses full of ghosts, plane rides with intoxicating

Omegas, the weight of the past, it all burns away in the face of the flames.

"Let's move," I order. With Kai and Miguel flanking me, we charge toward the inferno, ready to tear through fire and wood and whatever else stands between us and anyone trapped inside.

Then I hear it—a scream piercing through the roar of flames and pounding rain. Desperate. Terrified. Coming from somewhere inside the burning house.

"Someone's in there!" Miguel shouts.

The wind shifts, and for just a moment, the flames part enough to see a figure in an upstairs window.

A woman. Trapped.

4

EMMA

My eyes snap open to a darkness thick with gray haze. For one disorienting moment, I think I'm still dreaming, until the acrid burn hits my lungs, and I erupt into violent coughing. It rips through my chest, each spasm painful and tight. I bolt upright, heart hammering against my ribs as adrenaline floods my system.

Fire. The cabin is on fire. Fuck!

The thought crashes through me with brutal clarity. The air tastes wrong—toxic, metallic, deadly. My eyes water instantly, stinging tears tracking down my cheeks. Through the blur, I make out wisps of smoke slithering under the bedroom door like searching fingers.

"Shit," I whisper, the word catching in my throat. I cough again, doubling over as my body tries desperately to expel the poison I'm breathing.

Survival instinct kicks in. I fumble for my phone on

the nightstand, knocking it to the floor in my panic. When I scurry out of bed and onto my hands and knees to retrieve it, the screen shows 1:47 a.m. and barely any signal—one bar flickering in and out. I try to call 911 anyway, my trembling fingers slipping on the screen, but the call fails to connect. The sound that escapes me is half sob, half cough.

Lightning from outside flashes, briefly illuminating the smoke-filled room in stark white before plunging it back into shadow. Shit... I need to get out.

Coughing, I push up from the floor and stumble toward the bedroom window. I grab the latch and yank. Nothing. I wrench harder, both hands now, but it won't budge. Jammed.

Panic claws up my throat, but I bite it down.

I drop to my knees, pressing close to the floor. What do they say about fires? Stay low. Get out. Don't try to save possessions.

But my laptop is in my backpack by the dresser. I can't leave it.

On all fours, I crawl across the floor, where the air is marginally clearer. The summer dress I left draped over the chair is within reach. I drag it on over Chad's T-shirt, not caring that it's inside out, needing to cover myself. Every movement sends me into another coughing fit, each one more violent than the last.

My backpack. I lunge for it, clutching it to my chest like a lifeline. The hard edge of my laptop presses against me through the fabric. I shove the charger in blindly, then grab Chad's jacket from where I threw it earlier to cover myself with. The irony of needing something of his to survive isn't lost on me, even as I'm choking on smoke and terror.

The temperature in the room is rising rapidly. Sweat beads on my forehead, mixing with tears as I struggle to see through stinging eyes. A horrific groan from above drives a spike of pure fear through my chest. I look up as a spiderweb of cracks appears in the ceiling, glowing orange at the edges.

"Oh God," I whimper, scrabbling backward as embers begin to rain down. My throat feels raw from coughing.

A deafening crack explodes as part of the ceiling gives way, showering the room with burning debris. The heat is sudden and overwhelming, a sensation of standing too close to a bonfire multiplied tenfold. I can feel my skin tightening, my exposed arms prickling with pain.

I scream.

Dread becomes a living thing inside me, clawing at my insides, stealing what little breath I have left. My heart pounds so hard I can feel it in my fingertips, in my temples. My thoughts fracture, splinter. I don't want to die, not like this, not here, not alone.

I press Chad's sleeve over my nose and mouth, hating that his scent might be the last thing I ever smell, and scramble toward the door on hands and knees.

My fingers close around the doorknob, and it's hot but not unbearable yet. I twist it, yanking the door open, and the rush of oxygen creates a whoosh behind me that sends me tumbling into the hallway. The fire roars louder, as if angry I've escaped its first attempt to claim me.

From here, I find the full extent of the nightmare. The back half of the cabin is ablaze. Flames climb the walls in rippling waves of orange and gold, beautiful in their terrible hunger. The wooden staircase at the end of the hall is already partially consumed.

I have to get downstairs. I have to get out before the whole place collapses.

Every survival instinct screams at me to run, but I force myself to stay low, crawling toward the stairs as quickly as I can. The smoke is thicker here, forming a choking blanket that hovers about three feet from the floor. I pull the jacket tighter around my face, but it does little to filter the poisonous air. Each breath feels like inhaling sandpaper, my lungs protesting with every shallow gasp.

Halfway to the stairs, I'm overcome by another coughing fit so violent that I collapse fully, my forehead pressed against the scorching-hot hardwood. Black spots dance in my vision. My backpack suddenly feels impossibly heavy, but I clutch it tighter. If I die here, at least my words will die with me.

Get up. MOVE.

The voice in my head sounds like my grandmother's, the same steel-spined woman who taught me that Omegas weren't just soft things to be protected but survivors. Drawing on some reserve of strength I didn't know I possessed, I push myself forward.

The staircase looms ahead, partially obscured by billowing smoke. Parts of it are already burning, the lowest section completely engulfed in flames. There's no way down, the path is blocked by a wall of fire that seems to taunt me with its bright, dancing light.

I back away from the burning staircase, mind racing. Is there another way down? A fire escape? I didn't notice one when I arrived, too busy wallowing in self-pity over Chad and Megan to pay attention to emergency exits.

Through the smoke and chaos, I hear the distinct sound of the front door being kicked in. Then voices, shouting commands I can't quite make out.

Someone is here. "Help m—" I cough out of control.

I turn to see a massive figure forcing a path through the flames, trampling over burning debris, creating a pathway where there was none.

The firefighter is huge, wearing bulky protective gear, face covered by a mask and helmet. There's something almost supernatural about the way he moves through the fire with such purpose, such power.

I wave my arms frantically to draw his attention, my throat ravaged by coughing.

The firefighter's helmet swings in my direction. Even through the mask, I feel the intensity of his gaze locking on to me. He gestures sharply, pointing at me, then at the floor—*stay down*—before resuming his determined advance.

With one powerful leap, he vaults over the most damaged section of stairs, landing with a solid thud on the upper hallway floor. The move is so athletic, so unexpected, that for a moment, I forget the danger we're in. Who is this person? How can he move like that in all that heavy gear?

The firefighter reaches me in several long strides, dropping to a crouch beside me. Up close, he's even more imposing—broad-shouldered and solid, radiating strength and calm that make something inside me unclench slightly.

"We need to get out now," his voice comes through the mask, deep and commanding. "This whole place could go at any minute."

I nod frantically, another coughing spasm preventing speech. The firefighter's gloved hands move quickly over me, checking for obvious injuries.

"We're going back down," he states.

I shake my head, pointing toward the burning staircase. The firefighter follows my gesture, then looks back at me.

"Trust me," he says simply.

And strangely, inexplicably, I do. Something in that voice, in the sure way he moves, makes me believe he can get us out of this nightmare. I nod, clutching my backpack tighter to my chest.

Without warning, the firefighter scoops me up as if I weigh nothing, one arm under my knees, the other supporting my back. I gasp at the sudden motion, instinctively wrapping my free arm around his neck for support.

"Keep your face covered," he instructs, already moving toward the stairs. "And hold on tight."

I press Chad's jacket sleeve over my nose and mouth again, burying my face against the firefighter's shoulder as much as possible. Even through the protective gear, I feel the solid strength of the body holding mine.

We reach the top of the stairs, and the firefighter pauses, assessing the burning path below. The lowest section is completely engulfed, but he seems undeterred.

"Taking the express route," he announces, and already we're moving, not down the stairs, but toward the banister. With one fluid motion, the firefighter kicks over the railing and leaps off the stairs. Both of us are hanging for a brief moment before dropping the eight feet or so to the ground floor, landing with a controlled thud that jars but doesn't injure.

The impact forces another coughing fit from me. The ground floor is a maze of flame and fallen debris, the heat so intense it feels like my skin might blister despite the brief exposure. The firefighter navigates it easily, sidestepping burning furniture and ducking under a beam that threatens to fall.

"Almost there," he assures me even as the cabin groans and pops around us, wood splintering.

A crash from our right, part of the wall collapsing

inward, sends a shower of flaming debris across our path. I can't help the scream that tears from my ravaged throat, pressing myself closer to my rescuer's chest in instinctive terror.

The firefighter doesn't hesitate, changing direction and finding another path through the burning maze. The open front door appears through the smoke—a rectangle of darkness promising safety beyond.

As we near it, the ceiling above us gives an ominous crack. The firefighter reacts instantly, surging forward with a burst of speed that leaves me breathless. We clear the doorway as a section of the roof collapses behind us, sending a blast of superheated air against our backs.

Then we're outside.

The rain is torrential, soaking me instantly as the firefighter carries me away from the burning cabin. The contrast between the infernal heat we escaped and the cool downpour is shocking, making me gasp and triggering yet another round of painful coughing.

My rescuer doesn't stop until we're well clear of the house, across the street from it, finally setting me down gently on what feels like the tailgate of a fire truck. Emergency lights pulse in alternating strokes of red and white, cutting through the darkness. Through watering eyes, I watch other firefighters attacking the blaze with hoses, shouting to each other over the combined roar of fire and rain.

The storm continues, wind driving the rain in sheets that should be dousing the flames, but somehow, the fire rages on, as if fueled by something impervious to water. Lightning flashes overhead, briefly turning night to day, followed by a rumble of thunder that vibrates in my chest.

"Just breathe," my rescuer instructs, pulling something from a nearby compartment. It's an oxygen mask, which he places over my face with surprising gentleness for such large hands. "This will help."

The rush of clean oxygen is immediate relief, easing the burning sensation in my lungs. I close my eyes briefly, focusing on taking slow breaths despite the coughing fits that still rack my body.

"Is there anyone else who might have been in the house?" the firefighter asks, words clearer now that we're away from the roar of the fire.

I pull the mask away momentarily. "No," I manage to rasp. "Only me."

The firefighter nods, then begins checking me over more thoroughly, examining my arms and neck for burns or injuries. "You got out mostly unscathed," he says. "But we need to have the paramedics treat you for smoke inhalation."

I nod, unable to stop staring at the massive figure before me. Even knowing he saved my life, there's something intimidating about his size. I can't see any features past the mask, just a powerful presence that radiates authority.

"Thank you," I whisper, the words inadequate for what he's done but all I can manage through my raw throat.

The firefighter pauses, then reaches up to remove his helmet. Dark hair is plastered to a strong forehead, damp with sweat despite the rain. Next comes the mask, pulled away to reveal a face that makes my breath catch for reasons entirely unrelated to smoke inhalation.

Sharp jawline, straight nose, and those midnight-blue eyes that locked with mine on the plane. Atlas. The Alpha whose scent wrapped around me in the cramped airplane seat, whose penetrating gaze caught me writing about him.

"You," I breathe, the word barely audible, even to my own ears. My brain struggles to connect the dots, to make sense of this impossibly coincidental rescue. "You're... a firefighter?"

"Fire Chief," he corrects, his deep voice no longer muffled by the mask. Rain streams down his face, catching in his long eyelashes and dripping from his strong chin.

I stare at him, my mind spinning. The odds against this are astronomical. To be rescued from a burning building by the very man I'd been fantasizing about in my writing?

"Emma," he says, and the sound of my name in his mouth sends a strange shiver through me despite everything. "Seems like you can't stay out of trouble for even a day in Whispering Grove." He grins.

Our gazes lock, and for a breath-stopping moment, the world narrows to just us, me sitting on the tailgate, him standing close enough that the heat radiating from his body, even through his protective gear, pours over me.

My skin tingles with awareness despite the trauma of the fire.

I should look away. Should focus on the fact that I nearly died, that my temporary home is currently burning to the ground, or that I'm sitting here in a rain-soaked summer dress and Chad's oversized jacket. Instead, I'm transfixed by the way Atlas's eyes seem to darken as they hold mine, by the subtle shift in his scent that finds me even through the smoke clinging to both of us.

He reaches out, his thumb gently wiping a smudge of soot from my cheek. The brief contact sends a jolt through me as if I've touched a live wire, and I can't contain the small gasp that escapes me. His gaze widens slightly at my reaction, his pupils dilating in a way that makes my toes curl inside my shoes.

"When I saw you through that smoke," he says quietly, "I thought I was seeing things. Couldn't believe it was really you."

I swallow hard, wincing at the pain in my throat. "Seems the universe has a strange sense of humor," I manage through my oxygen mask.

"Or fate," he suggests, his gaze so intense I can almost feel it like a physical touch. "Maybe there's a reason—"

The moment shatters as another firefighter approaches, this one tall and lean with golden-blond hair visible beneath his helmet. He's grinning despite the situation, dimples appearing in his cheeks as he glances between Atlas and me.

"Chief," he says, a hint of teasing in his tone. "The west side is contained, and we should be able to salvage the front side." His teal-blue eyes flick to me with undisguised curiosity. "Good to see you found a survivor."

Atlas straightens, instantly shifting back to professional mode, though his hand lingers near my shoulder a moment longer than necessary. "Go help Kai with the north exposure. Looks like it's trying to jump to those pine trees."

The blond firefighter nods, but his knowing smile doesn't fade as he heads back toward the blaze. I watch him go, noting the confident, almost swaggering way he moves, even in his bulky gear. When I stare back at Atlas, he's looking at me with an unreadable expression.

"My second-in-command," he explains briefly. "River Graham."

Suddenly, the wail of another siren cuts through the storm as an ambulance pulls up, followed closely by a police cruiser. Atlas steps back, his professional mask firmly in place now.

"You need to get checked out properly," he says, his tone all business again. "Smoke inhalation can be serious."

I nod, suddenly exhausted beyond words. The adrenaline that kept me going is crashing, leaving me shaky and weak. As a female paramedic with short-cropped hair approaches, Atlas gives my shoulder a brief, reassuring squeeze before turning away to direct his crew.

He strides toward the burning cabin, powerful and commanding, rain streaming off his gear. He joins several other firefighters wielding hoses, pointing and shouting directions that are instantly obeyed. Even from this distance, there's no mistaking his authority, the natural Alpha leadership that seems to radiate from him.

"Ma'am?" The paramedic gently reclaims my attention. "I'm Sara. Let's get you checked out, okay?"

She guides me to the back of the vehicle, out of the worst of the rain, and replaces the firefighter's oxygen mask with her own, then begins examining me methodically. Blood pressure, pulse, oxygen levels, pupil response. I submit to it all in a daze, answering her questions about my symptoms automatically while my mind circles back to Atlas's rescue, to the way he looked at me, to the electric shock of his touch.

"Your oxygen levels are lower than I'd like," Sara informs me. "But not dangerously so. Any pain when you breathe deeply? Dizziness? Nausea?"

"Just my throat," I rasp. "And my chest hurts from coughing."

"That's normal. We'll still need to take you in for observation," she says kindly. "Smoke inhalation effects can sometimes be delayed."

A police officer approaches next, middle-aged with salt-and-pepper hair and lines around his eyes that deepen as he smiles at me. "Officer Brennan. I know this isn't a great time, but I need to ask you a few questions if you're up to it."

I nod, pulling the oxygen mask away from my face. "Of course."

He settles beside me on the ambulance tailgate, rain dripping from his police cap. "Nasty business, house fires," he says conversationally, flipping open a small notebook. "Especially in weather like this. You'd think all this rain would keep things from burning, wouldn't you?"

There's something comforting about his casual approach, as though we're two people having a chat on a porch somewhere.

"I thought the same thing," I admit. "I kept hoping the rain would help, but it seems like the fire... ignored it."

Officer Brennan nods thoughtfully. "Fires can be strange that way. Once they get hot enough, they create their own weather systems, in a manner of speaking." He meets my gaze. "Were you alone in the cabin tonight, Ms....?"

"Emma Collins. And yes," I confirm, another coughing fit interrupting me briefly. "I arrived today... yesterday, I mean."

"Any candles burning? Fireplace? Kitchen appliances left on?"

"I had some candles lit earlier, but I'm positive I blew them all out before going upstairs to bed. I remember doing it one by one." My brow furrows as I try to think if I'd missed anything. "The fireplace wasn't lit, and I didn't use the stove or oven."

He makes notes, his expression thoughtful rather than suspicious. "Any electrical issues you noticed? Lights flickering? Circuit breakers tripping?"

"There was no electricity when I arrived at the cabin. Everything else seemed fine."

"We'll have the fire investigator look into it once it's safe to enter the structure." He glances up at the still-burning cabin.

He asks a few more routine questions. How long I plan to stay in Whispering Grove, where I'm from, if I'd noticed anything unusual before going to bed. I answer as best I can through my increasingly sore throat, growing more exhausted with each passing minute.

"I'll need your phone number and contact details," he says finally. "Also, I have to ask you not to leave Whispering Grove while this fire is being investigated."

My heart sinks. "I'm a suspect?"

Officer Brennan's expression softens. "Standard procedure, Ms. Collins. We can't rule anything out at this stage, but between you and me, accidental causes are far more common than deliberate ones. Especially in rental properties where maintenance might not be up to code."

His kindness eases my anxiety somewhat. Still, the thought of being considered even a potential arsonist is distressing. As if sensing my unease, he pats my arm lightly.

"Try not to worry too much," he advises. "Focus on getting checked out medically for now."

Sara, the paramedic, returns. "We need to transport you to the hospital now," she says firmly. "Standard protocol for smoke inhalation cases."

Officer Brennan stands, tipping his hat slightly. "We'll continue this conversation later, Ms. Collins. Take care of yourself first."

As the paramedics prepare to load me into the ambulance, I look over at the firefighting operation once more. The cabin fire is close to being put out now, the combined efforts of the firefighters and the relentless rain finally gaining ground. Through the chaos, I spot Atlas chatting with two other men at the edge of the property.

One is the blond firefighter from earlier, River. The second man is tall and built, with dark hair, clearly explaining something technical to the others.

All three are soaking wet, their gear steaming slightly. Despite the grim circumstances, I can't help noticing what an imposing trio they make, three powerful Alphas working together.

They turn to look in my direction. I flush instantly, embarrassed at being caught staring. My stomach flutters. Just then, Sara and her partner are helping me into the ambulance. As I settle onto the stretcher, I catch one last glimpse of Atlas through the closing doors, rain streaming down his face, his midnight eyes fixed intently on mine until the doors shut completely.

The ambulance pulls away, sirens blaring despite

the late hour. I slump against the stretcher, physically and emotionally drained by everything that's happened. In less than twenty-four hours, I've been dumped by my boyfriend, discovered he was cheating with my friend, flown to a strange town, survived a fire, and been rescued by possibly the most attractive and unsettling Alpha I've ever encountered.

As Sara adjusts my oxygen mask and starts an IV line just as a precaution, I stare at the ceiling, trying to make sense of the bizarre turn my life has taken.

One troubling thought rises above the chaos of everything else: What if the fire wasn't an accident? What if someone set it deliberately?

And if they did, what if they try again?

5

EMMA

The antiseptic smell of the hospital finally fades as the automatic doors slide open, releasing me into the bright morning sunshine that instantly makes me squint. After a night of poking, prodding, and oxygen checks every hour—seriously, do they think oxygen levels dramatically change while you're unconscious?—I'm finally free. Well, *free* might be a relative term.

I pause on the sidewalk, clutching my backpack to my chest like it contains the last remnants of my dignity. Which, considering I'm still wearing yesterday's smoke-infused summer dress and Chad's jacket, the ultimate walk of shame outfit minus the fun part that usually precedes it, isn't far off.

Where the hell am I supposed to go now? Hotel, if I can find a room.

The cop's words echo in my head about not leaving town until their investigation is complete. *Right.*

Because apparently, I've graduated from Failed Omega Extraordinaire to Suspected Arsonist in the span of twenty-four hours. Talk about career advancement.

I run through the events of last night for the millionth time, a mental checklist I've been obsessively ticking off. Candles, extinguished before going to sleep. Fireplace, never even lit it. My battery-operated emergency reading lamp. I definitely switched off and stowed in my bag. I did everything right. I always do everything right. That's part of my problem.

My phone buzzes with a text from Jess after I messaged her early this morning. *Still alive? Hospital update?*

I quickly type back. *Discharged. Clean bill of health except for my pride and vacation plans.*

The universe clearly has it out for me. Though if there's one silver lining to the entire fiasco, it's that Chad's duffel bag, filled with his precious designer clothes and that ridiculous cologne he practically bathed in, is now a pile of designer ash. The thought pulls a somewhat vindictive smile from me.

"What's with that mischievous smirk? You look like you just figured out the perfect plot twist for your next villain," a male says, drawing my attention.

Startled, I glance, and there he is. Atlas, leaning against a massive black pickup truck that's parked super close to the hospital entrance. The morning sun hits him in a way that should be illegal, casting golden highlights through his dark hair and accentuating the sharp angles of his face. His uniform shirt is partially unbuttoned at the collar, sleeves rolled up to his elbows, revealing tantalizing tanned skin.

Great. Just what I need. Alpha McHotterson, here to witness the continuation of my humiliation tour.

"Not murder," I say automatically. "Arson, apparently. Might as well perfect my technique since I'm already a suspect."

One corner of his mouth quirks up. "That's not funny."

"Yet you're almost smiling," I counter, shifting my backpack to my other arm. The weight of it suddenly feels like it contains bricks rather than the few possessions that survived the fire. "What are you doing here, anyway? Don't you have fires to fight? Cats to rescue from trees? Calendar photo shoots to pose for?"

His eyebrow lifts at that last one, and I immediately want to melt into the pavement. Why do I always default to sarcasm when I'm uncomfortable? And why does he smell so impossibly good even from ten feet away? Woodsmoke and sweetness that make my stupid Omega brain sit up and take notice, completely ignoring the *Not Interested in Alphas* memo I've been trying to circulate.

"I came to check on you," he says simply.

"You did?" The softness in my voice betrays me, and I immediately straighten my spine. "I mean, that's... unnecessary. I'm fine. All good. Shipshape and Bristol fashion, as my grandmother used to say."

I can almost hear Gran's words in my head, the way she'd use that phrase whenever I'd come downstairs for school with my uniform perfectly pressed. She learned it from my grandfather, who'd spent years working on fishing vessels before settling down. It was her highest form of approval—nothing was better than being *shipshape and Bristol fashion* in Gran's world. The memory brings a pang of longing; she'd know exactly what to say right now to make this disaster seem manageable. She's been gone for three years, and I miss her terribly.

I try to step past him but realize I have absolutely no idea where I'm going. I'm in a town where apparently every accommodation is booked. I stop, pivot awkwardly, then stop again, resembling a malfunctioning windup toy.

"Where are you heading?" he asks, pushing off from his truck.

"That's a little creepy," I blurt out. "Like, serial killer level of interest in my whereabouts."

Instead of being offended, he actually laughs. "I spoke with your real estate contact this morning."

"You did what?" I stare at him.

"And a few other rental agencies in town," he continues, as if invading my privacy is completely normal. "I wanted to make sure you had options, considering you need to stay in town until the investigation is complete."

My mouth falls open, stunned, unable to believe his thoughtfulness. "I... you... why would you do that?"

"Because it's tourist season, and the town is at capacity." He crosses his arms over his chest, and I absolutely do not notice how it makes his biceps flex against the fabric of his shirt. "And because the cabin you were staying in belongs to Martin Greene, who isn't exactly known for his customer service skills."

"So, you're what? The town welcome committee?" I tease. "Firefighter by night, fairy godfather by day?"

"Just trying to help." He shrugs those ridiculous shoulders. "Plus, you still smell like smoke."

I self-consciously tug at Chad's jacket. "Not all of us can roll out of bed looking and smelling like we just stepped out of a cologne commercial," I mutter.

His mouth twitches again. "You think I look like a cologne model?"

"That is not what I said." I push a strand of hair behind my ear, a nervous habit I've never been able to break. "I'm just saying some of us had our possessions incinerated last night and haven't had a chance to freshen up."

"So, where are you going now?" he asks again, more gently this time.

"To see Martin Greene and figure out my options," I say with far more confidence than I feel. "I'm sure there's been some mistake about me needing to stay in town. I mean, it's obvious I didn't start that fire."

Atlas's expression shifts slightly. "The investigation is standard procedure. And trust me, you don't want to deal with Martin right now."

"Why not?"

"Because he's already telling everyone in town that

his *nightmare Omega tenant* burned down his best rental cabin."

My stomach drops through the pavement. "He's what?"

"I tried to set him straight, but he's..." Atlas trails off.

"A misogynistic asshole?" I supply.

"I was going to say 'upset about the property damage,' but your description works too."

I groan, pressing the heels of my palms against my eyes. "This is unbelievable. I've been in this town for less than twenty-four hours, and I'm already the local pariah."

"Let them talk," he says, his voice deepening with a hint of that commanding Alpha tone. "Anyone who matters will see exactly who you really are. The rest?" He shrugs those broad shoulders. "They don't deserve your concern."

The way he's looking at me creates a swarm of butterflies in my stomach that I have no business feeling. It reminds me of how my characters look at each other in my books, as though they're seeing something precious and rare, not how people look at me in real life.

"Let me give you a lift to Martin's office," he offers. "At least then you'll have backup when you talk to him."

I narrow my eyes. "And I should trust you, why exactly?"

"I've saved you twice so far." He holds up two fingers. "That's a pretty good track record."

"Twice?"

"The fire. And the turbulence on the plane." He grins, and it transforms his serious face into something so devastatingly attractive that I have to physically lock my knees to keep from swaying toward him.

"That doesn't count," I argue, even as my traitorous body remembers the feeling of his arm anchoring me during that terrifying drop.

"Three times if you count making sure you got medical attention," he adds, looking entirely too pleased with himself.

"Fine," I sigh, pulling out my phone. "But just so you know, I'm texting my friend your details right now so she has a record of who I was last seen with if I disappear."

"Smart," he says approvingly, which is not the reaction I expected. He actually steps closer and poses next to his truck. "Make sure you get the license plate in the picture."

I blink at him, then snap the photo, capturing him with the truck in the background. "You're very accommodating for a potential axe murderer."

"I prefer fire, actually. More dramatic." He winks and opens the passenger door for me.

As I climb up—this truck is ridiculous—I send the picture to Jess with a message. *If I go missing, this Alpha firefighter did it. Name: Atlas Wood. Currently driving me to real estate office. If no update in 1 hour, call authorities.*

I settle into the passenger seat as Atlas walks around to the driver's side. The interior of the truck is surprisingly neat and smells like him, that intoxicating blend of woodsmoke and sweetness that makes me want to lean closer and inhale deeply. Which would be extremely creepy and completely inappropriate.

As he starts the engine, my phone buzzes with Jess's reply. *OMG WHO IS THAT?!!! Is he single? If you don't climb him like a tree, I will personally disown you.*

I quickly angle my phone away as Atlas glances over, heat flooding my cheeks.

"Everything okay?" he asks.

"Just a funny meme," I lie, shoving my phone into my backpack. "So, um, how long have you lived in Whispering Grove?"

"Born and raised," he says, pulling out of the hospital parking lot. "Left for a few years, but came back when..." He hesitates briefly. "When the position at the fire station opened up."

There's a story there, but I don't press. We all have our sore spots.

Atlas glances at my backpack, where the corner of my laptop is just visible. "You managed to save the most important thing, I see."

My hand instinctively touches the backpack. "Yeah. Grabbed it in a panic before running out. Thank God for that automatic backup reflex. Five years of writing habits drilled into me after losing half a manuscript once to a power surge."

"That sounds terrifying," he says, keeping his eyes on the road.

"It was. Just like my current writer's block. I need to kill off a character that readers love, and I've been procrastinating for weeks."

"The solo retreat should help," he says with understanding.

"Hopefully. No distractions, just me and the inevitable fictional heartbreak I have to cause." I sigh dramatically. "Instead, I got an actual fire. The universe has a twisted sense of irony."

"Maybe it's research," he suggests, a smile playing on his lips. "Nothing like real-life experience for authenticity."

"If I include a cabin fire in my book now, critics will call it *too convenient* or *unrealistic*," I say, making air quotes. "Fiction has to make more sense than reality."

"Is that why you write fantasy? More control over the rules?"

The question surprises me with its insight. "Partly. Also because I grew up escaping into those worlds when real life got too..." I trail off, suddenly aware I'm revealing more than I intended.

"Too much?" he offers quietly.

Our gazes meet briefly, and I have the unsettling feeling he sees more than I want him to.

"Something like that," I murmur, turning to look out the window.

We fall into a surprisingly comfortable silence for a few moments. I catch myself inhaling deeply, trying to separate the lingering smoke smell on my clothes from his natural scent. Then I realize what I'm doing and wrinkle my nose.

"God, I really do stink," I mutter.

"It's not that bad," he says unconvincingly.

"You're a terrible liar." I laugh despite myself. "I smell like I've been hanging out in a chimney."

"We have facilities at the station," he says casually. "Showers, washing machines. You're welcome to use them if you need to freshen up."

"I'm good," I say automatically, though the thought of clean clothes and washing away the smoke smell is incredibly tempting. "I'm sure I'll find a place soon. It can't be that hard."

"In Whispering Grove? During the summer festival season?" He raises an eyebrow. "There's a reason we had to convert the station's old storage room into extra bunks. The population triples this time of year."

"Great," I sigh. "So I'm homeless, suspected of arson, and smell like a campfire. This vacation is officially a disaster of epic proportions."

"Could be worse," he offers.

"How, exactly?"

"You could be trapped in a car with someone who doesn't appreciate sarcasm."

I burst out laughing. He joins me, and the sound of his deep laugh does strange things to my insides. For a brief moment, I forget about the disaster my life has become. It feels good, too good, as though I'm connecting with him on a level I never reached with Chad, despite trying.

"Seriously, though," I say, sobering. "Do you think I could actually be blamed for the fire? Because I swear I didn't do anything to cause it."

His expression turns serious. "We'll figure out what happened. Between my team and the police, we'll find the cause."

"How long will that take?"

"Hard to say. Town's running at capacity, so both departments are stretched thin. Could be days or weeks."

"Weeks?" I groan. "What am I supposed to do in a town where everyone thinks I'm an arsonist and there's nowhere to stay?"

"Not everyone thinks that." His voice is soft but certain. "And we'll figure something out about a place for you to stay."

"We?" I echo.

"Force of habit." He shrugs. "I'm used to looking out for people."

"Is that an Alpha thing or a firefighter thing?"

"Just an Atlas thing," he says simply, and I can't believe this guy is real.

Something warm unfurls in my chest at his words, something dangerous that I need to squash immediately. I've made the mistake of falling for Alpha charm before, and I'm not about to do it again, especially not with one who smells like everything I've ever wanted and looks like he stepped out of one of my novels.

We pull up to a small office building with *Greene Properties* on a weathered sign out front. My stomach clenches with anxiety.

"Ready?" Atlas asks, turning off the engine.

"No, but let's do this anyway." I take a deep breath and push open the door, nearly falling out of the truck in my haste to get out. Atlas is there in an instant, steadying me with a hand on my elbow that sends electricity shooting up my arm.

"Careful," he murmurs, his face close enough that I can see flecks of lighter blue in his dark eyes.

"I'm fine," I say quickly, stepping back. "Just... gravity and I have a complicated relationship."

His lips quirk. "I've noticed."

We walk side by side into the office. A bell jingles overhead, announcing our arrival. Behind a cluttered desk sits a balding man with ruddy cheeks and a permanent scowl that deepens when he looks up and sees me.

"Hello, I'm Emma Collins. I'm looking for Mr. Greene," I say, figuring I should come across as civil.

"You," he spits, jabbing a finger in my direction. "You've got some nerve showing up here after what you did to my property!"

"Mr. Greene," Atlas commands, his voice taking on an authoritative tone I haven't heard before, but I like it more than I should. "I believe there's been a misunderstanding."

"No misunderstanding," Martin Greene snaps. "I

rented my best cabin to her and her boyfriend, and twelve hours later, it's a pile of ashes!"

I cringe. "Ex, he's my ex-boyfriend. And I didn't start that fire," I say, stepping forward. "And I nearly died in it, in case you forgot that part."

"Convenient story," he sneers.

"Excuse me?" My voice rises an octave. "You think I what? Deliberately set fire to your cabin while I was inside it? For what possible reason?"

"Insurance scam," he suggests immediately. "Looking for a payout."

"On a rental cabin?" I laugh incredulously. "That's not how insurance works. And I'm a writer, not a con artist."

"Same thing, if you ask me," he mutters.

"No one asked you," I snap, my patience evaporating. "Look, I understand that you're upset about your property—"

"Upset?" He stands up, face flushing darker. "That cabin brings in six thousand dollars a week during festival season! Do you have any idea how much money I'm losing while it's being rebuilt?"

"Again, not my fault," I say through gritted teeth. "And I almost died. You know, just for perspective on what's really important here."

"All I know is I've got a cabin in ashes and probably from something you did!" He jabs his finger toward me again.

My blood runs cold. "What?"

Atlas places a hand on my shoulder. "The investigation is still ongoing, Martin. No one is making any accusations yet."

"I am," Martin says to me. "And I've told everyone in town to steer clear of renting to you. One business burned down is enough."

"Are you kidding me?" I practically shriek. "You're blacklisting me based on what? A hunch? Your expert opinion as an amateur fire investigator?"

"Based on protecting my colleagues' properties," he retorts. "Now, if you'll excuse me, I have actual paying customers to help. Ones who don't have a habit of leaving smoldering ruins in their wake."

"This is ridiculous," I sputter. "I need a place to stay, and the police have told me not to leave town."

"Not my problem." He sits back down and pointedly opens a folder, ignoring me.

"It will be your problem when the investigation proves I had nothing to do with it," I say, leaning forward on his desk. "Because then I'll be having a very interesting conversation with my lawyer about slander and defamation."

It's a complete bluff. I don't have a lawyer on retainer, and the most legal experience I have is researching contract law for my third book, but he doesn't need to know that.

"Get out of my office," he barks coldly.

"Gladly." I spin around so fast I nearly collide with Atlas's chest. He steadies me again, his hands warm on my upper arms, and guides me out of the building.

The moment we're outside, hot tears prick at the

corners of my eyes. I blink them back furiously, refusing to cry in front of Atlas.

"That absolute bastard," I hiss, stalking toward his truck. "Did you hear him? He's sabotaged any chance I had of finding a place to stay!"

Atlas unlocks the truck but doesn't immediately open the door. "Sometimes what seems like the worst thing can turn out to be a blessing in disguise."

"That's your takeaway from this? Fortune cookie philosophy?"

"What I mean is," he says patiently, "now you don't have to waste time checking other rental places. We can move straight to finding you an alternative."

"There is no alternative," I say, throwing up my hands. "You heard him—the town is full, and he's told everyone I'm an arson risk!"

"Not everyone listens to Martin Greene," Atlas says calmly. "Come on, let's get you back to the station. You can clean up, get some rest, and then we'll figure this out."

Too exhausted and frustrated to argue, I climb back into his truck, slamming the door with more force than necessary. Atlas slides in behind the wheel, seemingly unfazed by my outburst.

As we pull away from Greene Properties, my phone buzzes with a text from Jess.

Wait, back up. You ALMOST DIED last night in a FIRE, and this hunky firefighter SAVED YOU, and you're sending me his info in case he MURDERS you? Girl, take your blinders off and see what's right in front of you. The universe is finally giving you an alternative to Chad's cheating ass.

I glance at Atlas from the corner of my eye. The sunlight catches on his profile, highlighting the strong jaw and the focused intensity in his eyes as he drives. His scent, even mixed with the lingering smoke on my clothes, calls to something primal in me, something I've read about in books but never truly experienced.

Is Jess right? Is the universe trying to tell me something?

Or am I about to make the same mistake again— falling for an Alpha who will eventually decide I'm too much, too independent, too something to be what he wants?

As if sensing my scrutiny, Atlas glances my way, an electric moment, before he returns his attention to the road.

"What?" he asks.

I quickly glance away, mortified at being caught staring. "Nothing. Just... thanks for the ride, I guess."

My phone buzzes in my hand, and I glance down at Jess's latest message. *Girl, he's gorgeous, AND he saved your life? This is literally the plot of the new book you need to write! Give the guy a chance!*

I hurriedly type back. *It ALWAYS starts this way— they rescue you, they're charming, then they decide you're too opinionated for an Omega, or your scent isn't right, or whatever new excuse they'll invent. Three strikes, remember? I'm done with Alphas.*

The truth is that Atlas's scent makes my entire

body hum like a tuning fork that's found its perfect pitch. But that scent compatibility didn't save me from Jason's criticism or Chad's betrayal. If anything, it just makes the inevitable disappointment more painful when it comes.

No, I need to focus on finding temporary housing, clearing my name, and getting back to my manuscript. That's the only relationship I can trust right now. The one between me and my words.

Besides, firefighters are probably the worst category of Alpha to fall for. All that heroic energy and protective instinct? Recipe for disaster for an independent Omega like me. Been there, burned the T-shirt, bought the heartbreak.

"We're almost at the station," Atlas explains, interrupting my thoughts. "You'll feel better after a shower and some food."

Despite all my mental warnings, a traitorous part of me already feels better just being near him.

6

RIVER

I'm leaning against the back of Levi's chair, watching him organize his meticulously labeled folder system for the third time this week. The guy is a certified genius with structural engineering, but sometimes I wonder if he's got a touch of that obsessive-compulsive thing going on. His amber eyes narrow in concentration as he aligns each tab to perfect precision, the overhead lights catching the sharp angles of his cheekbones and that always flawless undercut he maintains.

"You know," I say, flicking one of his perfectly aligned tabs, "I bet you color-code your underwear drawer too."

Levi doesn't even look up, just bats my hand away without missing a beat. "Better than having to smell-test like you probably do."

"Harsh, man." I clutch my chest in mock offense.

"And here I was going to share my secret stash of those spicy chips you pretend not to like."

A ghost of a smile crosses his face. "The ones from that place in Portland?"

"The very same," I confirm, reaching into my bag to pull out the contraband. Levi's amber eyes light up for a millisecond before he schools his expression. I've known this guy long enough to recognize his tells.

"Fine," he says, taking the bag and carefully opening it along the seam. Such a fucking perfection-ist. "But if Atlas asks where they came from—"

"You know nothing," I finish, grinning. "Speaking of our fearless leader..."

My eyes catch movement through the station window. I jump up from where I'm lounging and rush over for a better view. Atlas's heavy-duty truck is pulling into the parking space marked *Chief*. Even from here, I can see his broad silhouette behind the wheel. But it's the passenger that makes me press closer to the glass.

"Holy shit," I mutter. "He actually brought her."

Levi is suddenly at my side, folders forgotten as he peers through the window. "The Omega author?"

"In the flesh," I confirm, watching as Atlas exits the truck and circles around to open her door. Such a gentleman, our Atlas. "Damn, she looks even better in daylight than she did covered in soot and ash last night."

We watch as she steps out, all curves and honey-blonde hair. She's shorter than I expected, delicate next to Atlas's hulking frame. She's wearing a simple sundress, and it hugs her in all the right places. I feel a tug low in my gut.

"She's pretty," Levi murmurs, his usually softer tone infused with something I rarely hear from him—genuine interest.

"Pretty?" I scoff, bumping his shoulder with mine. "Dude, she's fucking gorgeous. Look at those legs. And that ass... you could bounce a quarter off it."

"Must you be so crude?" Levi sighs, but he doesn't deny it or look away.

"You're not disagreeing," I point out, watching as Atlas guides her toward the station entrance, his hand hovering near the small of her back but not quite touching. Always so careful, our chief. "Ten bucks says you've already imagined what she'd look like spread out on your sheets."

"Shut up," Levi hisses. "Atlas will hear you."

"Atlas will smell it on you anyway," I tease. "You're practically broadcasting 'interested Alpha' right now."

It's true—there's a shift in Levi's usually controlled scent. That clean, tea-and-smoke smell has deepened, taking on notes that make my own Alpha instincts stir in response. It's been happening more between the three of us lately, this strange synchronization of reactions.

"Like you're any better," Levi mutters.

He's got me there. I can feel my own scent sharpening, that cinnamon-spice intensity that always gives me away.

"Can you blame me? First Omega to catch my attention in months," I admit, watching as they disappear from view. "She's something special. You felt it too, last night at the fire."

Levi's gaze flicks to mine, a moment of silent communication passing between us. Yeah, we both noticed her, even in the chaos of that house fire. There was something about her that made all three of us hyperaware of her presence.

"Come on," I say, pulling back from the window. "Let's not be creeps staring through the glass. Time to turn on my famous charm."

"God help us all," Levi mutters but follows me toward the main entrance.

The station's common area is empty when we enter, but I can hear Atlas's deep voice coming from down the hall. We follow the sound to the east wing, where our spare quarters are located. As we approach, I catch fragments of their conversation.

"...should be comfortable enough for however long you need to stay," Atlas is saying.

"I really don't want to impose," she replies.

"After what happened at your place last night, I'm offering you a place to stay," Atlas insists. "Could be a day, could be a month. However long you want."

I round the corner, Levi close behind, just as she's stepping into the doorway. Atlas stands beside her, looking like a damn mountain next to her petite frame.

His dark blue eyes flick to us, a silent warning evident in them that I cheerfully ignore.

"And this will be your room while you're with us," Atlas continues as we approach. It's the best room in the station.

She stands in the doorway, taking in the surprisingly spacious accommodation. There's a comfortable queen bed with actual decent linens, a private bathroom, a small desk, and even a little sitting area with a reading lamp. Homey, by firehouse standards.

"This is... way nicer than I expected," she says. She turns to Atlas. "I really appreciate this. You didn't have to do all this."

"We take care of our own in Whispering Grove," Atlas replies, his deep voice rumbling in that way that makes even me want to stand at attention sometimes.

I can't help myself. "What the chief means is, we don't often get beautiful Omegas gracing our humble station, so we're pulling out all the stops."

Three pairs of eyes turn to me. Atlas's midnight blues narrowing in warning, Levi's amber ones communicating exasperation, and her hazel ones widening slightly. Up close, with the morning light streaming through the station windows, I can see flecks of gold in those hazel eyes. Goddamn captivating.

"River Graham," I introduce myself, stepping forward with my hand extended and my most winning smile in place. "Wildfire specialist and second-in-command around here. The pleasure is absolutely mine."

Her hand feels small in mine, but there's surprising strength in her grip. Up close, her scent hits me like a sucker punch—old books and honey and something warm that coils around my senses like a vise. Something primal in me wants to bury my face in her neck and breathe her in until I'm drunk on it.

"Emma," she replies, a slight flush coloring her cheeks. "Though I guess you already know that from last night."

I hold her hand a beat longer than strictly necessary. "I mostly saw you from a distance while this big guy played hero." I jerk my thumb toward Atlas, who doesn't quite manage to hide his eye roll.

"You're the one who kept the neighbor's tree from catching fire and spreading to the rest of the block," she counters, surprising me with her observation. "I noticed."

"She's observant," I say to my packmates, impressed.

"I'm Levi Wolfe, fire prevention and structural engineering specialist."

Emma takes his offered hand, and I don't miss how Levi's nostrils flare subtly as they touch. The corner of her mouth quirks up, suggesting she didn't miss it either.

"Nice to meet you," she says, and there's a slight crack in her composure as she takes in all three of us standing there. Can't blame her—three Alphas in close quarters is a lot for anyone, let alone an Omega who's been through what Atlas told us she has.

"Do you all live here?" she asks, gesturing around the station.

"Might as well, considering how much time we spend here," Atlas replies. "But no, we have a place just outside town, in the woods."

"Kitchen's fully stocked," Levi states, gesturing down the hall. "Dining area is communal. We usually eat dinner together around seven when we're not on a call. You're welcome to join us or eat in your room if you prefer."

"We won't bite," I add with a wink. "Unless specifically requested."

"River," Atlas growls.

I throw up my hands in surrender, though I don't miss the way Emma's pulse jumps in her throat. Interesting.

"Ignore him," Levi advises her. "We all do."

"Wound me, why don't you?" I clutch my heart dramatically.

A small laugh escapes Emma, and it's like music, slightly husky and genuine. "It's kind of amazing how well you play off each other. How long have you been a pack?"

"Five years, officially," Atlas answers. "Though we worked together for a while before that."

"It's nice," she says, and there's a wistfulness in her tone that tugs at something deep in my chest. "Having people who just... get you. Who fit with you."

The observation is unexpected, and for a moment, none of us seem to know how to respond. There's a heaviness in the air suddenly.

"It is," Levi adds finally.

Atlas glances at his watch. "I have to make some calls. Emma, get settled in. Anything you need, these two can help you. Or if they're being pains in the ass, which is likely, any of the other crew members can assist."

"Actually"—Levi looks at a notification on his sleek watch—"I have that video conference with the county board about the new fire prevention protocols in five minutes."

"Guess that leaves me as your welcoming committee," I say to Emma, unable to keep the pleasure from my voice. "Lucky you."

"Lucky me," she echoes, but there's a wariness in her eyes that makes me wonder if she doesn't feel particularly lucky at all. That's fine. I've always enjoyed a challenge.

Atlas gives me one last warning look before he and Levi head out, leaving Emma and me alone in the doorway of her temporary room. She shifts her small backpack from one hand to the other, looking momentarily lost.

"Need help unpacking?" I offer.

"Not much to unpack," she admits. "I grabbed what I could when I escaped the fire." She winces slightly. "Still feels surreal. Yesterday, I was just checked into the cabin for a vacation, and today, I'm basically a refugee."

"A very welcome refugee," I assure her. "Come on, I'll give you the grand tour while those two handle their important business." I wait as she sets her bag on the bed, then lead her out into the corridor. "So, emergency exit that way," I point to the right. "Main bay that way, and kitchen and common areas to the left. Anything in particular you'd like to see first?"

"Kitchen would be good," she says. "I haven't had coffee yet, and I'm basically useless without it."

"A woman after my own heart," I declare. "Atlas is a tea guy, if you can believe it. And Levi drinks these disgusting green health shakes he makes in the blender at unholy hours of the morning."

That gets another smile from her, and I find myself cataloging the microexpressions that cross her face. The slight crease at the corners of her mouth when she grins, the way her bottom lip curves just a fraction more on the right side. There's something almost addictive about making her smile, about watching the subtle play of emotions on her expressive face.

"Your pack is... not what I expected," she says as we walk.

"How so?" I ask, genuinely curious.

"You're all so different. Most packs I've encountered tend to be more... uniform. Similar types, similar personalities."

I consider this as we enter the kitchen, a well-equipped space with industrial-sized appliances and a large island in the center. "I think that's why we work.

Atlas is the leader, the protector. Levi is the brain, the planner. And I'm—"

"The heart," she finishes for me, then looks embarrassed. "Sorry. That was presumptuous."

Something warm unfurls in my chest at her assessment. "Most people just say I'm the comic relief."

"You're more than that," she says with a certainty that catches me off guard. "I can tell."

For once, I don't have a clever response ready. Instead, I busy myself with the coffee maker, pulling out cups and grounds. "How do you take it?"

"Black, two sugars," she replies, hopping up to sit on one of the barstools at the island. She looks around the kitchen appreciatively. "This place is seriously nice for a fire station."

"Atlas has been upgrading it piece by piece since he took over as chief," I explain, measuring coffee. "Says if we're going to spend half our lives here, it should feel like someplace worth being."

"He seems like a good leader," she observes.

"The best," I agree without hesitation. "Saved my ass more times than I can count... literally and figuratively."

The coffee maker gurgles to life, and the rich aroma starts to fill the kitchen. Emma inhales appreciatively.

"So," I say, leaning against the counter while we wait for the coffee. "What's your story, Emma? Besides being a successful author whose cabin just got torched." She tenses slightly, and I realize I've pushed her too far, too fast. "Sorry," I say, backtracking. "Professional hazard. We firefighters tend to skip the small talk."

"It's okay," she murmurs, though her posture remains guarded. "Not much to tell, really. I write fantasy romance books. They've done... unexpectedly well. Enough that I had to get an agent to handle the business side."

I'm pouring the now-ready coffee into two mugs—a novelty one with *Too Hot To Handle* emblazoned on it for her and my personal fire-engine red one for me.

She accepts the mug with a grateful smile, adding sugar from the bowl I slide her way. She takes a sip of her coffee, her expression thoughtful.

"Anyway," she says. "What about you? How does one become a wildfire specialist?"

I debate whether to give her the sanitized version I tell most people, but something about her makes me want to be honest.

"Got caught in a forest fire when I was seventeen. Ran away from home, well, from the corrections facility my parents sent me to. Was living rough in the woods when a wildfire started. Fire crew found me, saved me. Figured I'd pay it forward."

I don't know why I'm telling her these bits of myself I usually keep locked down tight, but there's something about her that draws the truth out, as natural as breathing.

Her eyes soften with understanding rather than pity, which I appreciate. "Corrections facility?"

"My pheromone patterns are slightly atypical," I

explain, surprised that I'm willing to share this so soon. "Not enough to prevent me from being an Alpha, but enough that my perfect, wealthy parents decided I needed to be fixed. Turns out you can't beat biological quirks out of someone, though they sure as hell tried."

"That's terrible," she says with a gasp, and the genuine outrage in her words is oddly comforting. "I'm so sorry you went through that."

I shrug, uncomfortable with the direction I've taken our conversation. "Ancient history. Made me who I am, right? And now I get to play with fire for a living, so who's the real winner here?"

She smiles, but it's softer now, as if she sees through my attempt to lighten the mood. "Still. Parents are supposed to protect you, not hurt you."

"Speaking from experience?" I ask, catching something in her tone.

She looks down at her coffee. "My parents died when I was sixteen. Boating accident."

"Shit. I'm sorry," I say, mentally kicking myself. "Me and my big mouth."

"It's fine. It was a long time ago," she says, but her knuckles have gone white around her mug. "My grandmother raised me after. She was the one who encouraged my writing."

"She sounds like a smart lady."

"She was," Emma says, and the past tense tells me all I need to know. "She passed just as my first book was accepted for publication three years ago."

The raw hurt in her tone makes something feral stir in my chest, a desire to shelter, to protect, to ensure nothing else hurts her ever again. It's disturbing in its intensity, far beyond what I should be feeling for someone I've just met.

"So," I say, trying to pull us back to safer ground. "What does a bestselling author do for fun when she's not fleeing burning buildings?"

That gets a genuine laugh out of her, and the sound of it eases something tight in my chest.

"Not much, lately. Writing takes up most of my time. I used to love swimming, grew up on the coast. Moonshell Bay has some decent lakes and rivers, though."

"We've got a lake about twenty minutes from here," I offer. "The water is clean, and there's a nice little beach area."

"Sounds nice," she says, but there's a hesitancy in her voice. Is she not planning on sticking around long enough to see it?

She finishes her coffee, and an hour passes before I realize it, her company making time slip by unnoticed. I'm about to tell her about the time Atlas had to rescue a raccoon family from the station's chimney when she glances at her phone.

"I should probably get settled in," she says, though she sounds reluctant. "And I'm sure you have actual work to do instead of entertaining me."

"Entertaining beautiful women is my specialty," I say with a wink, though in truth, I've enjoyed our conversation more than I expected. It's comfortable, yet exciting at the same time.

"I bet it is," she says dryly, sliding off the barstool. "Is there somewhere I could wash some clothes? Everything I grabbed smells like smoke."

"Laundry room is this way," I say, taking our empty mugs to the sink. "Come on, I'll show you."

I lead her down a hallway to the facilities room. It's nothing elaborate. Three industrial washers and dryers lined against one wall, shelves of supplies on the other.

"Fancy," she teases.

"Only the best for Whispering Grove's finest," I reply with a grin. "You should see our gym. State-of-the-art equipment from at least 2015."

That gets a laugh out of her. Something twists in my gut at the sound, a possessive feeling I haven't experienced in a long, long time.

"Why don't you get your clothes, and I'll meet you back here?" I suggest. "I can show you how these temperamental beasts work."

"Sounds good," she agrees, heading back toward her room.

I find myself watching her walk away, the sway of her hips in that simple sundress making my mouth go dry. *Get it together, Graham,* I scold myself. She's under our protection, for fuck's sake. But my traitorous head is already cataloging the curve of her waist, the smooth skin of her bare shoulders, and the way her hair falls in waves down her back.

She returns about thirty minutes later, now

dressed in what looks like our spare station clothes—an oversized T-shirt and sweatpants rolled at the waist and ankles. The shirt is tucked in but still big on her, emphasizing how tiny she is compared to us. Her arms are holding a small bundle of clothes, and her damp hair is slicked back from her face, emphasizing those high cheekbones and full lips.

No bra, my gaze points out before I can shut that thought down. Focus.

"Found the shower, I see."

"Hope that's okay," she says. "Atlas said to make myself at home, and I really needed to get the smoke smell off me."

"Of course," I assure her, tearing my gaze away from the way the damp shirt clings to certain parts of her body. "This one works best," I say, patting the middle washer. "The one on the left eats socks, and the one on the right makes this concerning grinding noise that Levi keeps promising to investigate."

I watch as Emma dumps the few clothes she'd been wearing during the fire into the washing machine. She's frowning slightly, probably thinking about everything she lost.

"So, have you heard about the festival happening this weekend?" I ask, trying to lighten the mood as I grab the detergent from the metal supply cabinet.

Her expression shifts, curiosity replacing the momentary melancholy. "Oh, yeah, the rideshare driver told me."

"Founders Festival," I say, unscrewing the cap with

a flourish. "Big event in our little slice of nowhere. Three days of small-town chaos that you absolutely have to experience."

"What's it like?" she asks, leaning against the dryer while I take over the washing duties.

I start pouring detergent directly into the machine. "Picture this: an entire town collectively losing its mind in the name of tradition. There's a parade with the world's most underwhelming floats, but everyone acts like they're watching the Macy's Thanksgiving spectacle."

She laughs, the sound hitting something warm in my chest. "Sounds charming, actually."

"Oh, it gets better," I continue. "The food stands are run by the same five families who've been having the same argument about whose corn dog recipe is superior since 1952. The rides are all probably older than we are, but somehow, they pass inspection every year."

"Now I'm definitely intrigued," she says.

"Last year was epic," I tell her. "Atlas got roped into judging the pie contest because Mrs. Henderson, the mayor's wife, has had a crush on him since he carried her cat out of a tree three years ago."

"No!" Emma is covering her mouth, but I can see the smile behind her hand.

"Oh, yeah. There he was, Mr. Serious Fire Chief, having to taste twenty-seven different pies while Mrs. Henderson kept *accidentally* touching his biceps." I demonstrate, making an exaggerated swooning motion that has Emma laughing outright now.

"What about Levi? He seems quiet," she says, clearly enjoying this peek into our world.

"Levi is the farthest thing from quiet," I sigh dramatically. "At the last festival, he made the mistake of mentioning once—ONCE—that he understood the physics behind the dunk tank. Next thing we knew, he was sitting on the platform in shorts, explaining to anyone who would listen about the optimal trajectory needed to hit the target while some eight-year-old with freakishly good aim kept sending him into the water."

"And you?" she challenges, eyebrow raised. "What disaster were you causing?"

"Me? I was the model of decorum and restraint," I declare with mock offense.

She just looks at me, disbelief written all over her face.

"Fine," I concede, turning to the washing machine control to select a cycle. "I might have gotten carried away at the charity auction. Bid way too much on a quilt because Mrs. Finch made it, and she's this sweet little grandmother who's been stitching quilts for the auction for forty years. Nobody was bidding high enough, and her face just fell, and I couldn't—"

"That's actually really sweet," Emma interrupts, looking at me with something new in her expression.

I feel my neck heat up. "Yeah, well, don't tell anyone. I have a reputation as an irredeemable troublemaker to maintain." I hit the start button on the washer with more force than necessary. "Anyway, you should check it out. They've got these caramel apples that'll change your life."

"Another reason to attend this festival," she says.

When she catches me staring, I don't look away. Let her see. Let her know exactly what's running through my mind.

"How about some hot chocolate? I make the best in town."

"Lead the way," she says, and there's a huskiness to her voice that wasn't there before.

As we walk down the corridor, I'm hyperaware of her presence beside me, the way she keeps a careful distance, not quite close enough to touch. Smart Omega. But it doesn't matter how careful she is. I can still catch the edges of her scent, still feel the heat of her body like a phantom caress against my skin.

In the kitchen, I throw myself into making the hot chocolate, needing the distraction. I use the good stuff—whole milk, real chocolate that I melt slowly, and a touch of cinnamon and nutmeg. From the back of the pantry, I unearth Levi's hidden stash of mini marshmallows. He'll be pissed, but right now, I don't care.

Emma perches on a stool at the counter, one bare foot tucked under her, the other swinging slightly. Her hair has mostly dried now, falling in soft waves around her face. She's absently twirling one strand around her finger as she watches me work.

"You seem to know your way around a kitchen," she observes.

"I'm a man of many talents," I reply, unable to keep the suggestive edge from my voice. Her cheeks flush slightly, and satisfaction curls through me like smoke.

I place a steaming mug in front of her, heaped with marshmallows, and lean against the counter opposite her, cradling my own. The kitchen feels smaller somehow, the air between us charged.

"So..." she says after taking a sip, leaving a small chocolate mustache that I want to lick away. "Is cooking one of your hidden talents?"

"Not so hidden. I do most of the cooking at our place." I take a deliberate drink, watching her over the rim of my mug. "Levi can barely boil water, and Atlas burns toast. Someone has to keep us from starving."

"Wouldn't have pegged you as the domestic type," she says, and there's a new curiosity in her gaze as it travels over me, lingering a beat too long on my arms, my chest.

"There's a lot you don't know about me," I say softly. "Yet."

Her pupils dilate slightly, the hazel of her eyes darkening. She licks the chocolate from her upper lip, and the simple gesture sends a jolt of heat straight through me.

"You're very sure of yourself," she murmurs, but there's no conviction behind it. Just a token resistance.

"I'm sure of what I want," I correct her. "There's a difference."

She glances away, but not before I catch the shiver that runs through her. "And what is it you want, exactly?"

The question is quiet, almost reluctant, as if she's afraid of the answer. As she should be.

I set my mug down, the ceramic making a decisive click against the countertop. "Right now? I want to stop pretending there isn't something happening here."

Her gaze snaps back to mine, startled by my directness. "I don't know what you mean."

"Yes, you do." I hold her gaze, refusing to let her look away again. "I felt it the moment I saw you. You felt it too."

"You don't know what I feel," she says, a defensive edge creeping into her words.

"Your body gives you away, Emma." I step closer, not touching her but near enough that her scent intensifies—honey and books and woman. "Your pulse speeds up when I get close. Your pupils dilate. Your scent changes."

Her hand tightens around her mug. "That's just biology. Omega responding to Alpha. It doesn't mean anything."

"Lie to yourself if you want, but don't lie to me." I lean in. "This isn't just any Omega responding to any Alpha. This is you responding to me. To us."

She's breathing faster now, her chest rising and falling in a rhythm that makes me want to press my hand there, feel her heartbeat racing under my palm.

"I barely know you," she whispers, but she doesn't move away.

"And yet you know exactly who I am," I counter. "The same way I know you. The same way Atlas knew you the moment he sat next to you on the plane and later pulled you from that fire. The same way Levi knew you when you shook his hand."

A flush spreads across her cheeks, down her neck, disappearing beneath the collar of the borrowed shirt. I wonder how far down it goes, how much of her skin turns that delicious pink when she's aroused.

"Stop looking at me like that," she says, but there's no force behind it.

"Like what?"

"Like you want to devour me."

I smile, slow and deliberate.

Her sharp intake of breath is the sweetest sound I've ever heard. For a moment, we're frozen, her seated on the stool, me leaning against the counter, gazes locked.

Then I pull back slightly, giving her space to breathe, to think. Atlas always tells me I can come off a bit pushy.

"Don't worry. I won't touch you until you ask me to," I say, straightening up and retrieving my mug. The certainty in my voice isn't bravado. It's bone-deep knowledge. She's ours. She just doesn't know it yet.

She stares at me, lips parted slightly, a war of emotions playing across her expressive face. Desire, frustration, fear, intrigue.

"You're very confident," she says finally.

"I know what I want," I repeat simply. "And I'm patient enough to wait for it."

"What if I never ask?" she challenges, a spark of defiance in her eyes.

She won't be easy to tame. Good. I don't want easy.

"Then I'll have to live with that." I shrug, though we both know it's a lie. "But you will."

She stands abruptly, nearly knocking over her stool. "You're infuriating."

"So I've been told." I smile, not bothered by her anger. It's just another form of passion, after all.

She looks like she wants to say something else—something cutting—then clears her throat. "Look, you seem great, all three of you do, but I should probably make something clear. I'm not looking for an Alpha. Just so you know."

"Oh?" I raise an eyebrow. "You already have one?"

"Hell no," she blurts out. "Had one, then didn't, and every one I've ever encountered has eventually broken my heart. Now, I think I have no heart left, and I can't do it again. I just... can't."

The pain behind her voice is raw, real. It hits something in me, that part that understands what it means to be rejected, to be told you're not good enough, not right. The clinical reports describing me as *defective*.

"Who was it?" I demand. "These Alphas who hurt you."

She blinks at the sudden shift in my tone. "It doesn't matter. Ancient history."

"It matters," I insist, and I'm surprised by the ferocity I feel. I want names. I want to hunt down every Alpha who ever made her feel less than treasured and show them exactly what happens to those who misuse what's *mine*.

Wait. *Mine*? Where the hell did that come from?

I force myself to dial it back when I see her tense.

"But I get it. Not pushing."

Before she can respond, there's a loud clunk from down the hall, followed by an ominous gurgling sound. We both freeze, staring at each other.

"Please tell me that's not—" she starts.

"The washing machine," I finish, already moving.

We race down the hall to find suds creeping out from under the laundry room door. I push it open to reveal a scene straight out of a sitcom—the middle washing machine convulsing as foam spills from under the lid and around the seal, forming a growing mountain of bubbles on the floor.

"Shit!" I lunge for the controls, hitting the emergency stop. "What the hell happened?"

Emma is right behind me, grabbing towels from the shelf. "I don't know! Did we put in too much detergent?"

I wrench the lid open, releasing another wave of bubbles that splatters us both. Emma lets out a startled laugh, and despite the mess, I can't help joining in. There's something absurdly hilarious about standing ankle-deep in soap suds with a beautiful woman.

"So much for making a good impression." She

giggles, wiping foam from her face. There's a streak of bubbles across her cheek, and without thinking, I reach out to brush it away.

My thumb grazes her soft skin, and the laughter dies in my throat. We're standing close, too close, her face upturned to mine, eyes wide. The world narrows to just the two of us, time suspended in the small space between our bodies. Her lips part slightly, and for a wild moment, I think she might be leaning in.

I'm not sure who moves first, but suddenly, my hand is cupping the back of her neck, fingers tangling in her loose hair. My body crowds hers against the edge of the machine, not quite touching but close enough to feel the heat radiating from her. Her pulse races beneath my fingers, a frantic beating that matches my own.

"This is a mistake," she whispers, but her eyes drop to my mouth, contradicting her words.

"Probably," I agree. "Should I stop?"

Her hands come up to rest on my chest, and I can't tell if she's about to push me away or pull me closer. The scent of her surrounds me, honey and books, and a part of me has already decided she belongs to me... to us.

"You should," she says but makes no move to increase the distance between us. "I told you I'm not looking for an Alpha."

"And I'm not asking you to look," I murmur, thumb brushing the line of her jaw. "Just to see what's already in front of you."

Her breath catches, a small sound that shoots straight through me. I lean in closer, drawn by an instinct more powerful than reason or propriety. I want to taste her, to claim her, to make her forget every Alpha who came before me.

"What the hell's happening here?" Levi's words cut through the moment like a bucket of ice water.

Emma jerks back as if burned, nearly slipping on the sudsy floor. I catch her elbow to steady her, and the brief contact sends another jolt of electricity up my arm.

"Laundry disaster," I explain, letting go of her reluctantly and gesturing vaguely at the foam still seeping across the floor. "Minor setback."

Atlas appears behind Levi, taking in the situation with a single sweep of his gaze. His eyes narrow when they land on me, and I know he's reading the scene. "Seriously, River?"

"Hey, this was a team effort," I protest, shooting a conspiratorial look at Emma.

"Entirely my fault," Emma jumps in, wringing out a soaked towel over a bucket. Her cheeks are flushed, and she won't meet Atlas's eyes. "I told you I was cursed. Everything I touch somehow breaks."

"Not your fault," I counter. "I wasn't paying attention to how much detergent went in."

"Because you were too busy flirting," Levi mutters, rolling up his sleeves and joining the cleanup effort.

"I can neither confirm nor deny these allegations," I say loftily, though my insides are craving this Omega.

The want. The possessiveness. The soul-deep certainty that just slammed into me moments ago.

Emma, looking mortified, addresses Atlas directly. "I'm so sorry about this mess. I should have been more careful."

"It's fine," Atlas says, his expression softening as he looks at her. "Not the first disaster this place has seen. Won't be the last."

The radio on Atlas's belt crackles to life, and the four of us freeze instinctively. Dispatch's voice comes through, calling all available units to a fire downtown.

"Duty calls," Atlas states grimly. "Emma, get yourself dry and comfortable. The volunteers will be in soon, so they can help finish cleaning this up."

"I can handle it," she insists.

"That address is the old Miller warehouse—lots of chemicals stored there," Levi states, staring at his phone.

Atlas nods, all business now. "Gear up. We roll in two minutes."

I hesitate for a split second, glancing back at Emma. She's standing amid the chaos of bubbles, looking small in our oversized station clothes yet somehow not out of place. As though she belongs here, with us.

"Go," she urges. "I've got this. Save the day, wildfire guy."

I give her a quick salute, then sprint after my pack-mates. As I'm pulling on my gear, I catch Atlas watching me with that penetrating gaze that always feels like he's reading my mind.

"What?" I challenge, securing my helmet.

"You know what," he rumbles softly. "I saw that little scene with Emma. What were you thinking exactly?"

"Wasn't exactly planned," I mutter, checking my equipment. "There's something about her, Atlas. Something that just…" I trail off, not having the words to explain the magnetic pull I felt toward her.

"I know," he admits quietly, surprising me. "I feel it too."

I look up sharply, meeting his midnight-blue eyes. There's an understanding there, a shared recognition of something none of us expected to find.

"We all do," Levi adds from behind us. "But that doesn't mean we get to claim her."

"But what if she's—" I start.

"Later," Atlas cuts me off, all chief again. "Our help is needed first. Omega complications second."

He's right, of course. But as we climb into the truck, my mind keeps circling back to that moment in the laundry room, to the way Emma felt close to me, to the look in her eyes that suggested she felt this inexplicable connection too.

Mine, that primal part of me growls again. *Ours*.

And this time, I don't try to silence it. Because for the first time in my life, I'm absolutely certain of something: Emma belongs with us. And I'm going to make damn sure she knows it, whether she's ready to admit it or not.

As the sirens wail and we speed toward the fire, I can't help the dangerous smile that spreads across my face. I've always loved a challenge, and Emma is the most enticing one I've ever encountered. She thinks she's not looking for an Alpha? Fine. But she's about to discover that sometimes what you need finds you, whether you're looking or not.

And once I decide something is mine, I don't let go. Ever.

7

ATLAS

I grip the steering wheel a little tighter than necessary as we head to yet another crisis point. The day has been nonstop. First, the fire caused by the downed power line at the old Miller warehouse. We contained it quickly, but not before it took out electricity to half the town. Then, straight to the main intersection where the traffic lights went dark—directing angry drivers and keeping pedestrians from wandering into danger zones. Now, dispatch is sending us to the other end of town, where some kind of crowd situation is developing during the festival. The police are stretched thin with multiple incidents, so once again, we're stepping in. My shoulders ache from the tension of the day, but there's no time to rest. Not yet.

"That woman in the red Subaru was about to run you over, Levi," River declares from the passenger seat, still buzzing with the restless energy that never seems to leave him. "I swear she gunned the engine when you turned your back."

"I noticed," Levi replies dryly from the back seat. "That's why I moved."

"Should've written down her license plate," River continues, drumming his fingers on his thigh. "Could look her up, leave some flaming dog shit on her porch—"

"We're not doing that," I cut in, though the corner of my mouth twitches despite myself. "That's called arson, and we're supposed to prevent that, not cause it."

"Spoilsport," River grumbles, but I catch his grin in my peripheral vision. "I was thinking of it more as a public service. A little warning to the community about a menace on the roads."

"Your civic dedication is touching," Levi deadpans.

"Speaking of touching," River says, pivoting, and I immediately tense, sensing where this is going. "I had an interesting moment with our guest before we left."

"Is that what we're calling the soap explosion?" I ask, trying to divert what I know is coming.

"A minor mishap." River waves dismissively. "But before that... Atlas, I'm telling you, she's my scent match."

I nearly miss the turn onto Main Street, my hands tightening on the wheel. "River—"

"Don't," he snaps, suddenly serious. "You felt it too... I know you did. When you carried her out of that house last night? Your scent changed. You're usually all toasted sugar and woodsmoke. She's vanilla and honey. But together?" He exhales sharply. "You smelled like the perfect toasted marshmallow. Like you blended. I noticed. Levi noticed. Hell, she noticed too. She's just too scared to admit it."

"We barely know her," I counter, but even to my own ears, it sounds weak.

"You don't need to know someone to recognize a scent match," River argues. "That's the whole point. It's biological. Primal." He turns to look at Levi in the back seat. "Back me up here, Mr. Science."

Levi shifts uncomfortably. "Scent compatibility is a documented phenomenon. The research suggests it relates to genetic diversity and complementary immune systems."

"See?" River points triumphantly. "Levi agrees with me."

"I didn't say I do," Levi corrects. "I simply stated biological facts."

"Your scent changed too, when you shook her hand," River counters. "Don't think I didn't notice that little inhale you did, the way your pupils dilated. Classic Alpha response to a compatible Omega."

"Are you done with your little biology lesson?" I interject, annoyed at how accurately River has pinpointed what I've been trying to ignore.

"Not even close." River grins, undeterred. "Because here's my proposal... We ask her to move in with us at the cabin."

I nearly swerve the truck. "What?"

"In the woods," he clarifies, as if that was the part I found confusing. "She should move in with us at the cabin. She's my scent match, almost certainly yours too, and probably Levi's, by the way he's been pretending not to stare at her all day."

"I don't stare," Levi protests weakly.

"You absolutely do," River shoots back. "Like you're trying to solve a particularly challenging equation and she's the answer."

Levi falls silent, which is as good as an admission from him.

"You can't be serious," I say, though I know he is. River doesn't joke about pack matters, despite his generally lighthearted approach to life.

"Dead serious," he confirms. "Look, the cops are swamped. You heard what the chief said tonight. They've got their hands full with three separate arson investigations plus that string of break-ins on the east side. They're not going to resolve Emma's case anytime soon."

"So, she stays at the station a bit longer," I counter. "It's secure, comfortable enough—"

"For a few days, sure," River interrupts. "But we're talking weeks, maybe months. You want her living in that spare room that long? With volunteers and shift workers coming and going at all hours? Especially when she's a perfect match for us?"

Fuck, I hate that he has a point, but I'm not ready to concede it.

"She made it pretty clear she's not interested in

Alphas, River. *Any* Alphas. Inviting her to live with three of us is hardly going to make her feel safer."

"She said the same to me," River admits, surprising me with his honesty. "But she's afraid. Someone she trusted betrayed her. Of course she's wary."

"All the more reason not to push," Levi interjects, ever the voice of reason.

"I'm not saying we force her," River argues, twisting in his seat to look at both of us. "I'm saying we offer a safer alternative. Where is she going to go otherwise when there are no accommodations left in town? At least at the cabin, we'd know she's protected. I sure as fuck don't want her at the station unless one of us is there all the time," he continues, passion bleeding into his voice. "And we can't guarantee that with our schedules. The cabin is isolated, secure, and we'd always know who's coming and going.

"Plus," he adds with a mischievous grin, "I could cook for her. You know my chili is amazing."

"Your chili could be classified as a chemical weapon," Levi mutters.

"You ate three bowls last time!" River exclaims, indignant.

"And regretted it for days afterward," Levi replies.

"Lies and slander," River sniffs.

I shake my head at their familiar bickering, but it doesn't distract me from the real issue at hand. "We're getting off topic."

"Right," River agrees, sobering. "Emma. Cabin. Protection. Scent match. All good reasons for her to stay with us instead of at the station. Plus, we were talking about taking a bit more time off... What better reason?"

A heavy silence falls in the truck as we consider his words. I hate to admit it, but River is making sense. The thought of Emma alone at the station with just the volunteers for company unsettles something deep in my Alpha instincts. The thought of her somewhere else, somewhere I can't be certain of her safety, is even worse.

"He makes a good argument," Levi says quietly, surprising me. He's usually the most cautious of us three.

"Hell yeah, I do," River says, satisfaction evident in his voice. "This is the most sense I've made all year. Mark the date."

"It's not a high bar to clear," Levi deadpans.

"Ouch." River clutches his chest. "Mr. Precise lands a direct hit. But seriously, Atlas, you know I'm right about this."

I grind my teeth, thinking through the complications. "And what happens when she realizes we're not just offering protection? That we're all... reacting to her?"

"You don't think she's noticed already?" River scoffs. "She's observant. She's just choosing to ignore it because she's scared."

Levi makes a scoffing sound.

"You didn't think an Omega was going to just be easy, did you?" River challenges. "Omegas are all afraid of us Alphas to some degree, especially if they've been hurt before. So we have to show her she's safe with us. That we're angels."

Levi bursts out laughing, the sound echoing in the confined space of the truck. "We are the farthest thing from angels, and you know it."

"Then, for her, we try," River states with such conviction that I find myself glancing over at him. "I mean, what's more angelic than saving a damsel in distress from her burning tower? You've already got that part down, Chief," River continues. "Levi can be the brainy angel with his calculations and safety protocols. I'll be the charming, devastatingly handsome angel who makes her laugh and feeds her excellent food that definitely won't cause intestinal distress, no matter what certain killjoys might claim."

He shoots a pointed look at Levi, who rolls his eyes but doesn't hide his smile.

"You've already named yourself the handsome one? That's a bit presumptuous," Levi remarks.

"I didn't hear you volunteering for the position," River shoots back. "Besides, we all know you're the brainy one with those intense eyes and that whole 'I could dismantle and rebuild this entire truck while explaining fluid dynamics' vibe you've got going on."

"I don't have a vibe," Levi protests.

"You absolutely do," River insists. "A very specific, very strong vibe that some people find extremely appealing. Right, Atlas?"

"Leave me out of this," I mutter, but I can't help the

amusement that creeps into my voice. These two idiots are my pack, my family, and despite the seriousness of the situation, they still manage to make me feel lighter.

"The point," I redirect, "is that we need to consider Emma's feelings in all this. Not just our own instincts or preferences."

"Absolutely," River agrees, too quickly. "Her comfort, her safety, her happiness... all priorities."

I eye him suspiciously. "You're being very accommodating."

"That's me," River murmurs innocently. "Just ask that family we rescued from the mudslide last spring. I carried their Yorkie five miles while telling it bedtime stories."

"You told that dog dirty jokes," Levi corrects. "I heard you."

"It was an adult dog." River shrugs. "And it laughed."

"It was whimpering in terror," Levi sighs.

"Agree to disagree." River waves dismissively. "The point is, I can be sensitive to others' needs. And Emma needs us, whether she's ready to admit it or not."

I've known River for years, seen him through countless fires, pack formation, the worst and best of times. He's always been passionate, but there's something different in his voice now—a certainty, a determination I've rarely heard from him.

"You're serious about this," I say quietly, realization dawning. "This isn't just about protection for you."

River meets my gaze steadily, no trace of his usual flippant manner. "No, it's not. There's something about her, Atlas. Something that calls to me. To all of us, if you'd just admit it."

I focus back on the road, unwilling to confirm or deny his assertion, but the truth is, he's right. From the moment I sat next to Emma on the plane, something clicked into place, a recognition that went beyond simple attraction or protective instinct. I just hadn't expected River to feel it so strongly too. Or to act on it so quickly.

"Even if I agreed," I say carefully, "how would we approach this? We can't just say, 'Hey, come live with three Alphas you barely know in an isolated cabin in the woods.' That sounds like the setup for a horror movie, not a safety plan."

"Or the beginning of a very different kind of movie," River suggests with a waggle of his eyebrows.

"River," I warn.

"Sorry, sorry," he says, backpedaling, though he doesn't look sorry at all. "It doesn't have to be creepy. We just present it as a practical solution. Better security, more comfortable living arrangements, home-cooked meals... Who could resist?"

"We tell her it's a temporary situation," Levi suggests, always thinking three steps ahead. "Until we can find her an alternative accommodation that's secure. Frame it as practical, not personal."

"Exactly!" River points at Levi triumphantly.

"We'd need to set boundaries," I continue, finding

myself oddly engaged with the logistics now that we're discussing it as a real possibility. "Clear rules. Her own space that's completely private."

"The east bedroom has its own bathroom," River says quickly. "And there's that small sitting area attached. It would be perfect, like a mini-suite. We could clear our stuff out of there in an hour."

I shoot him a suspicious look. "You've thought about this in detail already, haven't you?"

"Maybe," he admits with a shameless grin. "What can I say? I'm a planner."

"Since when?" Levi snorts.

"Since about six hours ago," River replies cheerfully. "I think fast. Especially when beautiful Omegas with book scents and honey eyes are involved."

"Hazel eyes," Levi corrects automatically.

"Hazel with gold flecks when the light hits them just right," River counters. "I was paying very close attention."

"We noticed," I say dryly.

"Like you weren't," River challenges. "I saw how you looked at her when you thought no one was watching, Chief. That protective Alpha stance whenever anyone else came near her."

I don't bother denying it. River knows me too well.

"Let's say, hypothetically, we offer her this arrangement," I say instead. "What if she says no?"

"Then she says no." River shrugs, though the tightness around his eyes says otherwise. "We don't force it.

We figure out something else. But we have to at least offer her the option."

"He's right," Levi says, surprising me again. "Security-wise, it makes the most sense. And she'd be more comfortable in a real home than at the station long-term."

I consider their words as we turn onto the road that leads back to the station. Part of me, the cautious, responsible part that's kept us all alive through countless dangerous situations, is screaming that this is a mistake. That bringing an unknown Omega into our space, especially one that triggers such intense responses in all of us, is asking for trouble.

But another part, the Alpha, the protector, can't stand the thought of Emma vulnerable, alone, at risk from whoever burned her house down.

"Fine," I relent eventually. "We can broach it with her gently. As a temporary solution only until we find her a more permanent safe situation."

"Yes!" River pumps his fist in triumph. "You won't regret this, Chief."

"I already regret it," I mutter, but there's no real conviction behind the words. "And you're not going to be the one to ask her. You have all the subtlety of a sledgehammer."

"Hey!" River protests. "I can be subtle."

"You once tried to announce a surprise birthday party for Levi by setting off the station alarm," I remind him dryly.

"It got everyone's attention, didn't it?" he grins

unrepentantly. "And the look on his face was priceless. Total shock."

"That was horror, not surprise," Levi clarifies. "I thought the station was on fire while I was in the shower."

"Details." River waves dismissively. "The point is, it was memorable."

"My point exactly," I say. "I'll talk to her. Calmly and rationally, with no pressure."

"Fine, but I get to help set up her room," River negotiates.

"We'll all help," Levi interjects. "If she agrees."

"She will," River says with that same strange certainty. "She belongs with us, even if she doesn't know it yet."

The intensity of his conviction makes me glance at him again. "Don't push her, River. I mean it. She's been through enough."

"I wouldn't," he admits, suddenly serious. "I know what it's like to be pushed into something against your will. I'd never do that to her. But I also know what it's like to find where you belong after thinking you never would. She deserves that chance."

The reference to his past, to the corrections facility his parents sent him to, makes me soften. For all his bravado, River knows pain intimately. It's easy to forget that sometimes, behind his perpetual good humor.

"Okay." I nod. "I'll talk to her tonight, but we're

presenting this as a practical, temporary solution, not some pack-bonding opportunity. Clear?"

"Crystal," River agrees, a little too quickly for my comfort. "Though I can't promise I won't charm her with my culinary skills and winning personality in the process."

"I mean it," I insist, pinning him with my gaze at a stop sign. "No pressuring, no... whatever it was you were doing in the laundry room earlier."

River has the grace to look slightly abashed. "That was... unplanned. But noted. I'll be on my best behavior."

"For what it's worth," Levi offers quietly, "I think this could be good. For all of us."

His unexpected support makes me pause. Levi isn't given to impulsive decisions. If he sees merit in this plan, perhaps I should trust it more than I do.

8

EMMA

I sit on the edge of the bed in my temporary room, staring at the wall without really seeing it. The nest of blankets behind me is still rumpled from where I'd created a makeshift cocoon after scrounging every spare blanket I could find in the room and in the cupboard. It had taken that fortress of fabric wrapped around me before I'd felt secure enough to curl into it to stop the panic from taking over.

The station is quieter, seeing that the guys left on their call, but my mind is anything but calm.

"Get it together, Emma," I mutter to myself, rubbing my temples.

The problem is, I can't stop thinking about them. All three of them. It's crazy. I've known these men for less than twenty-four hours, yet I can't get them out of my thoughts, especially after that moment with River in the laundry room.

I glance back at the rumpled blanket nest. I told

myself it was just because the station was cold, the bed unfamiliar. Just a comfort thing.

But here I am, twenty-four hours in this town, and suddenly, I'm exhibiting behaviors I've successfully suppressed for years.

It must be stress. The fire. The displacement. It has nothing to do with three pairs of eyes that follow my movements, three distinct scents that somehow complement each other perfectly and, horrifyingly, seem to complement mine as well.

It hadn't really worked anyway. Even in my mind, I can't stop fantasizing made-up stories about them.

Atlas's hands lock around my waist, unbreakable. "Found you," he growls, his breath hot against the curve of my shoulder. His presence engulfs me completely as he pulls me hard against his chest, one hand splaying possessively across my stomach.

"No more running, Emma." River appears before me, blue eyes darkened to midnight, that dangerous smile cutting across his face. He traces the outline of my lips with his fingertip, a touch so light, yet commanding my full attention. "We always claim what belongs to us."

Levi materializes at my side, studying me as his fingers trail down my arm, raising goose bumps in their wake. "Your body betrays you," he observes. "Every reaction tells a story you're trying to deny."

Atlas's lips brush the sensitive skin behind my ear. "She's afraid of how perfectly she fits with us."

"How completely she'll surrender to us," River adds, leaning close enough that I can feel the heat radiating from

him. His fingers tangle in my hair, tugging gently to tilt my face up to his. "Tell us what you've never told anyone else," he whispers. "Tell us what you truly crave."

Words fail me, but Levi leans in. "She wants what her previous Alpha denied her," he murmurs, fingers brushing my collarbone. "The claiming. The bond. The mark that announces to the world that she belongs to someone."

"Not someone," Atlas corrects, his hold tightening possessively. "Us."

They close in, their heat surrounding me, imprisoning me, and I'm breathless. The pressure of their bodies, hard muscle against my softness, makes me feel small yet powerful in the way they respond to every tiny movement I make.

"Please," I whisper, not even sure what I'm begging for.

River's lips capture mine in a kiss that starts as gentle but quickly turns demanding, consuming. When he pulls back, his eyes are wild. "Tell us you're ours."

Levi's mouth finds the pulse point at my throat, his tongue tasting my skin with deliberate precision. "Say the words, Emma."

Atlas's teeth graze my earlobe. "Submit to us."

"Yes," I hear myself gasp as some final barrier crumbles inside me. "I'm yours... please..."

As if orchestrated, they move as one. Three sets of teeth find different points on my body—Atlas at the junction of my neck and shoulder, River at my wrist over my racing pulse, and Levi at the sensitive spot just below my ear. The pressure builds, the promise of what I've secretly wanted for so long, what Chad always refused to give me—a true claiming. A mark that would bond me forever.

Just as their teeth break skin—

I gasp for breath, my fingers flying to my neck, my wrist, behind my ear, searching for marks that aren't there.

God, why do they smell so good? It's not fair. My stomach flips every time they get close.

"Please, no," I groan, falling against the mattress, flashing back on my fantasy, the nest behind me. "Not a scent match. That can't be."

Except I know the signs. My grandmother taught me all about them when I presented as an Omega. The inexplicable pull, the way their scents seem designed specifically to appeal to my most primal urges, the heightened awareness whenever they're nearby.

"A true scent match is rare, Emma," she'd told me, running a brush through my hair as we sat on her porch swing, watching the lake. "So rare that many Omegas never find it. And that's okay. You can still have a good relationship with an Alpha without it. It'll still work out."

I never felt anything close to a scent match with Chad. His smell was pleasant enough, sandalwood and citrus, but it never made my knees weak or my heart race. I thought that was normal. That my grandmother's stories of overwhelming attraction were just romantic exaggerations from a different generation.

I didn't realize how intense a fragrance match could actually be. How different my body's response would feel compared to Chad. The way my skin tingles when Atlas is near, how my pulse jumps when River looks at me, the strange calm that settles over me when Levi speaks, it's nothing like what I felt with Chad. Nothing like any attraction I've experienced before.

Gah, fucking Chad. I wish I could stop thinking about him and the situation he's put me in. The betrayal, the mess, the fire, all because of him rejecting me.

If I ignore the attraction, then nothing will happen between me and the firefighter Alphas. I mean, I can try to suppress my Omega response, right? I can handle this. I have to. Getting tangled up with one Alpha nearly destroyed me. Three would be suicide.

I push myself up, determined to distract myself with something productive. I've got soggy, soapy clothes to deal with, and sitting here obsessing over three Alphas I have no intention of getting involved with isn't going to solve that problem.

As I make my way back to the laundry room, I catch the faint trace of their combined scents lingering in the hallway. My knees actually weaken for a second, and I have to steady myself against the wall.

"Pathetic," I scold myself. "Pull it together."

The laundry room is still a disaster zone, with foam coating every surface. I grab a mop from the supply closet and get to work, trying to focus on the task rather than the memory of River standing too close, his touch on my face, the heat of his body nearly pressed against mine.

"Need a hand with that?" a female voice asks.

I whirl around to find a young woman, maybe in her early twenties, a similar age to me, in a uniform, standing in the doorway, eyebrows raised at the sudsy carnage.

"I'm Claire," she says, already grabbing a bucket. "Volunteer firefighter and, apparently, now a janitor."

"Emma," I reply, feeling heat rise to my cheeks. "This is... kind of my fault."

"I heard." She grins, filling the bucket with water. "The soap monster strikes again. Happens at least once a month around here."

"Really?" I ask, relieved I'm not uniquely disaster-prone.

"Nope." She laughs. "But it makes you feel better, right?"

Despite myself, I laugh too. "Not particularly."

"So, you're the author they rescued last night?" Claire asks, efficiently mopping a section of the floor. She's petite with short-cropped dark hair and friendly brown eyes. Her scent is mild, distinctly Beta.

"That's me," I confirm. "Though I'm hoping that doesn't become my permanent identity. 'The author who needed rescuing' doesn't exactly scream competent adult."

"Could be worse." Claire shrugs. "Could be 'the volunteer who set the training dummy on fire trying to demonstrate proper extinguisher technique.'"

"Oh..."

"In my defense, it was my first day," she says with a mock-serious expression. "And in my further defense, Chief Wood looked really hot putting it out."

I nearly drop my mop. "You and the chief..."

"Gosh, no." She laughs, waving dismissively. "Not for lack of trying on my part, but those three are notoriously difficult to pin down."

"Really?" I ask, trying to sound casual while my heart does a strange little skip. "They seem so... I don't know. Solid."

"Oh, they're solid with each other," Claire says, wringing out her mop. "That's the problem. They've got their little pack, and nobody else seems to fit into it for long."

I focus on scrubbing a particularly stubborn patch of foam, pointedly not looking at her. "What do you mean?"

"Just that they don't have the best track record with relationships," she explains. "River will flirt with anything that moves, and I do mean anything. I once caught him winking at a mannequin in a store window."

That sounds like him, and I can't help the small smile that tugs at my lips.

"Levi's the ghost, here one minute, vanished the next. He once left mid-date because he had an epiphany about flame-retardant chemical compositions," Claire continues, making air quotes.

"And Atlas?" I ask, surprised by how much I want to know.

"Atlas is..." She pauses, considering. "Complicated. Too responsible for his own good. He takes care of everyone except himself."

"They all sound kind of... damaged," I observe, wringing out my mop.

"Aren't we all?" Claire points out. "But yeah, they've got their issues. River had some family stuff, never talks about it, but apparently, it was bad. Levi lost his parents in a fire when he was a teenager. After Atlas lost his parents, the relatives who took over the family home made it clear he wasn't welcome. With nowhere else to go, he followed a friend back to Whispering Grove, hoping for something better, but ended up on the streets as a teen until the old fire chief stepped in."

I remember what bits Atlas told me about his past. Despite my determination to keep my distance, my heart aches a little at the thought of them struggling.

"Anyway," Claire continues. "They're good guys. Great firefighters. Just not exactly relationship material. They never can hold on to anyone for long."

"Maybe they don't want to," I suggest, uncomfortably aware that I'm defending men I barely know.

"Could be."

There's something in her tone that makes me wonder if she's speaking from personal experience. Whether she tried to get close to one of them, or all of them, and was rebuffed.

"So, what about you?" she asks, clearly wanting to change the subject. "Staying with us long?"

"I don't know," I admit. "Until they work out how the cabin I was in got torched and, hopefully, not implicate me, I guess. Or until I find somewhere else."

"Well, the station's not bad as temporary housing goes," she says, sweeping the last of the suds into a drain. "Just... be careful, okay? Alphas have this way of making you feel special, as if you're the only one who understands them, but at the end of the day, they always choose each other."

Her words settle uncomfortably in my stomach. Of course it was too good to be true—the immediate connection I felt, the way they all seemed so attentive, so interested. It wasn't special. It was just what they did.

"Thanks for the warning," I say, gathering up our cleaning supplies. "And for helping with this mess."

"Anytime," she says easily. "Us girls have to stick together in this testosterone-fueled environment."

We finish the cleanup in silence, but my mind is racing. I can't deny the pull I feel toward all three of them, but Claire's words have planted a seed of doubt. Were they just being nice because they felt responsible for me? Was River's flirting just his default setting, not specific to me at all?

And more importantly, why do I care so much after less than a day?

By the time the guys return from their call, I've managed to dry my clothes and am now back in my summer dress. I've also decided to be polite but distant, to not give in to whatever this bizarre attraction is. I have enough complications in my life without adding three Alphas to the mix.

Then they walk through the door, all broad shoulders and easy confidence.

I can't stop staring at them.

"Dinner's ready!" Hendricks calls. The volunteer has been cooking up a storm for the past hour. The dining area is set up with large round tables, surprisingly cozy for a fire station. The smell of chili con carne fills the air, along with rice and tortilla chips.

I take a seat, determined to keep my composure. River immediately heads toward me, but Levi slides into the chair beside me first, his gaze meeting mine briefly before he focuses on serving food. Another volunteer is on my other side.

"Hungry?" Levi asks, ladling a generous portion of chili into a bowl.

"Starving," I admit. Stress always increases my appetite, and between the house fire, the move to the station, and my confusing reactions to these men, I've been nothing but stressed.

He hands me the bowl along with a smaller plate of

tortilla chips and nudges the rice toward me too. I help myself, then sprinkle it all with cheese.

"Hendricks makes the best chili in three counties. Not too spicy, but flavorful."

"Thanks," I say, surprised by his thoughtfulness. Levi has been the quietest of the three, more reserved than the overtly protective Atlas or the flirtatious River, but there's something about Levi's calm presence that puts me at ease.

"How was the power outage situation?" I ask, taking a mouthful of the chili. It's delicious—rich, savory, and with just enough heat to warm without overwhelming.

"Resolved," Levi replies. "Though River nearly caused a second incident by antagonizing an irate driver."

"I did not," River protests from across the table. "I simply suggested, very politely, that perhaps running over emergency personnel was not the best way to expedite her journey."

"You told her if she was in such a hurry, you'd be happy to call her an ambulance preemptively," Atlas corrects, shaking his head.

"Customer service," River insists, loading his bread with butter. "I was anticipating her needs."

The chatter continues, and despite my intention to keep my distance, I find myself smiling, then laughing, at their easy rapport. There's something comfortable about sitting here with them, as though I've found a place where I fit without even looking for it.

Dangerous thoughts, Emma.

I catch Claire watching us from another table, her expression unreadable. Her warning echoes in my mind, tempering my enjoyment of the moment.

"So, Emma," River says suddenly, fixing me with that bright, focused gaze that makes me feel like I'm the only person in the room. "About your living situation."

"River," Atlas warns, his deep voice cutting through the chatter around the table.

"What?" River asks innocently. "I'm just making conversation."

"Subtle as a sledgehammer," Levi mutters beside me.

"I don't know what you're talking about," River continues blithely. "I was simply going to mention that staying in a fire station long-term might not be ideal. The sirens alone would drive anyone crazy."

"My living situation is temporary," I say carefully. "Until I figure out my next steps."

"Exactly," River nods enthusiastically. "And in the meantime, you need somewhere comfortable. Somewhere safe."

Atlas pinches the bridge of his nose while Levi smothers what might be a laugh behind his hand.

"The station is safe," I counter.

"But is it comfortable?" River challenges. "Do you really want to live in a place where the alarm could go off at three a.m.? Where there are people constantly coming and going? Where privacy is, at best, a theoretical concept?"

"River," Atlas says, his tone making it clear this is the final warning.

"Fine, fine," River relents, raising his hands in surrender. "I'll stop. But the offer stands."

"What offer?" I ask, though I have a sinking feeling I already know.

"Our cabin at the edge of town," River says simply. "It's private, secure, and much more comfortable than the station. Plus, no sirens."

"You want me to move into your cabin," I say flatly, glancing at Claire, who raises her eyebrows in an "I told you so" expression.

"Temporarily," Atlas interjects, shooting River a look that would make most people wither. River just grins back, unrepentant. "Until we can find a more permanent solution for you."

"That's... very generous," I say carefully. "But I don't think it's a good idea."

"Why not?" River challenges.

"Because I barely know you?" I reply, my voice rising slightly. "Because three Alphas and one Omega living together is a recipe for disaster? Because I'm not looking for complications right now?"

The table falls silent, and I realize I was louder than I'd intended. A flush creeps up my neck as several heads turn our way.

"Sorry," I mutter, pushing my chair back. "I need some air."

Before anyone can respond, I'm up and moving toward the door that leads to the small patio area outside. The cool evening air hits my heated skin, and I take a deep breath, trying to calm my racing heart.

What is wrong with me? I'm not usually this reactive, this emotional, but something about these three men pushes all my buttons—good and bad.

I hear the door open behind me, and I tense, expecting River with more of his persuasive arguments. Instead, it's Levi who steps out, and my breath catches involuntarily.

There's something about him in the evening light that highlights those high cheekbones and the line of his jaw. Levi's appeal is more subtle, more dangerous for how quietly it sneaks up on you.

His dark hair is swept back from his forehead, revealing more of those unusual amber eyes, which seem almost backlit from within.

"I apologize for River," he says simply. "He can be... overwhelming."

My gaze drops traitorously to his mouth—the surprisingly full lower lip that calls to me.

"It's fine," I sigh, leaning against the railing to steady myself. "I overreacted."

"Your reaction was perfectly reasonable," Levi counters, coming to stand beside me but maintaining a respectful distance.

The sleeve of his dark T-shirt rides up slightly, revealing a powerfully strong bicep. When he places his hands on the railing, I notice small, silvery scars across his knuckles.

"We're asking you to trust us with your safety when you have very little reason to do so."

There's a slight roughness to his voice that wasn't there yesterday, as if he's been up all night thinking about this, about me. His throat works as he swallows, and I find myself mesmerized by the movement.

My heart stutters in my chest.

"Then why ask?" I manage, struggling to keep my voice even.

When he turns to face me fully, I'm reminded that his lean frame hides considerable strength. The T-shirt stretches across his shoulders, revealing the outline of so many muscles.

He touches the bridge of his nose briefly, a thinking gesture I've noticed before, and despite everything, I start wondering what it would be like to feel those hands moving over my skin with that same attention to detail.

He draws a breath to answer, and I realize I'm holding mine, suddenly aware of how much I care about what he's about to say.

"Because it makes sense," he replies after a moment. "The station isn't designed for anyone to live here long-term. There's no privacy, sirens going off at all hours, volunteers and shift workers constantly coming and going; it could be dangerous."

I bite my lip, thinking about the unfinished manuscript saved on my laptop. The deadline is looming. The fact that returning to Moonshell Bay is impossible with the authorities still investigating the fire at the cabin… and right now, I technically don't have a place to live back home, with Chad most likely having packed up my stuff. Bastard hasn't even called me…

Regardless, I need to start writing for my deadline, as everything has derailed my work completely.

"Besides," Levi continues more gently. "Wouldn't you rather spend that time somewhere with actual decent water pressure, a kitchen that doesn't smell like firefighter boots, and the best view in town?"

Despite myself, I smile a little. "The shower pressure here is pretty terrible."

"The cabin has the best shower," he says, a hint of his usual charm returning.

"You're really selling this hard," I observe, studying him. "Why?"

He looks at me for a long moment, all pretense falling away. "Because none of us like the idea of you being alone right now. Not after everything you've been through."

I wrap my arms around myself, suddenly feeling exposed despite the station walls surrounding us. "You don't even know me."

Levi shrugs. "It's our job to help people in danger, but that wouldn't be entirely truthful."

"Then what's the truth?" I ask eagerly.

Before Levi can respond, the door opens again, and Atlas and River step out.

"Everything okay out here?" Atlas asks, his deep voice rumbling in the quiet night.

"Just getting some air," I reply, straightening up. "And listening to Levi's perspective on your... offer."

"And?" River prompts, looking unreasonably hopeful.

"And I still think it's a bad idea," I say firmly. "Look, I appreciate everything you've done for me, but I can't just move in with three Alphas I barely know."

"Is it because of what Claire told you?" River asks.

I blink, caught off guard. "How did you—"

"You've been different since we got back," River says. "And you kept looking at her during dinner. Doesn't take a genius to figure out she said something."

"It wasn't just that," I hedge, though it was a significant factor.

"What did she say?" Atlas asks, his voice carefully neutral.

I hesitate, not wanting to create drama. But they're watching me with such intensity that I find myself answering.

"She said you three can never hold on to anyone for long. That you... have a pattern of not committing."

The three exchange glances, having one of those silent conversations that close-knit groups can manage without words.

"Did she happen to mention that she asked River out six months ago and he said no?" Levi asks mildly.

My eyebrows shoot up. "No."

"Or that she then asked Levi right after that, then Atlas out three months ago, and got the same answer?" River adds, crossing his arms.

"She left that part out," I admit, feeling a twinge of sympathy for Claire. Rejection is never easy.

"She's not wrong that we've had our issues with relationships," Atlas says carefully. "But her perspective is... biased."

"The point is," River says, jumping in, "we're not asking you to date us. We're offering you a safe place to stay while you sort out your situation."

"With separate rooms," Levi adds. "Clear boundaries. And one of us would always be at the station."

I look at each of them in turn. All watching me closely.

"I don't really have a place to go right now," I admit finally.

"So that's a yes?" River asks eagerly.

"It's an 'I'll try it temporarily,'" I clarify. "With conditions."

"Name them," Atlas says immediately.

"I need my own space. Complete privacy when I want it," I begin, thinking rapidly. "I need to be able to leave whenever I choose. No Alpha posturing or... or territorial behavior. And I help with expenses, food, utilities, whatever."

"Done," Atlas agrees without hesitation. "Anything else?"

I consider for a moment. "If at any point I feel uncomfortable, I leave. No questions asked."

"Absolutely," Levi nods.

"And no funny business," I add, looking directly at River.

He places a hand over his heart. "I am the very soul of propriety."

Atlas snorts, and even Levi rolls his eyes.

"I mean it," I insist. "This is about safety and practicality. Nothing else."

"Of course," Atlas assures me, though there's something in his eyes that makes me doubt he believes it any more than I do.

"Fine," I sigh, wondering if I'm making a huge mistake. "When do we do this?"

"Tomorrow?" River suggests eagerly. "We're all off rotation until tomorrow night."

"Tomorrow," I agree, already questioning my sanity.

"You won't regret this," River says, his grin wide and genuine.

But as the three of them stand there, their scents mingling in the night air, wrapping around me like an invisible embrace, I'm not so sure. Because despite all my conditions and barriers, I can feel myself being drawn to them. All of them.

And that terrifies me more than being homeless ever could.

L ater that night, I'm packing my few belongings when there's a soft knock at my door. Expecting one of the volunteers, I'm surprised to find all three men standing in the hallway.

"Everything okay?" I ask, suddenly self-conscious in my borrowed pajamas.

"Just wanted to check if you need anything for tomorrow," Atlas says.

"And to give you this," River adds, holding out a small box. "A welcome gift."

I accept it warily. "What is it?"

"Open it," he urges, bouncing slightly on his toes like an eager child.

Inside is a small key attached to a wooden tag carved with a crescent moon, the same design as the tattoo on my wrist.

"It's to the cabin," Levi explains. "Your own key. So you know you can come and go as you please."

"How did you...?" I gesture to the moon design, matching my tattoo perfectly.

"I noticed it earlier," River admits. "I'm observant about things that matter."

The simple statement, delivered without his usual teasing tone, catches me off guard. I look up to find all three watching me.

"Thank you," I say softly, closing my fingers around the key. "This was thoughtful."

"We want you to feel safe with us, Emma," Atlas says, his deep voice sincere. "To know that you have control in this situation."

"I appreciate that," I reply, and I mean it.

There's a moment of silence, the four of us standing there, an invisible current seeming to flow between us. Atlas inhales slightly, his pupils dilating. Levi's posture stiffens, and River's perpetual smile fades, replaced by something hungrier.

"We should let you rest," Atlas states finally, his voice rougher than before. "Big day tomorrow."

"Right," I agree, though rest is the last thing on my mind with them standing so close.

"Good night, Emma," Levi says softly.

"Sweet dreams," River adds, his usual smile returning but with an edge I hadn't noticed before.

They turn to leave. "Good night," I manage, closing the door before I can do something stupid like ask them to stay.

I lean back against the door, heart racing, body burning up from the inside. This isn't normal. This level of reaction to three Alphas I barely know isn't just attraction; it's something more primal, more fundamental.

What am I doing?

I've spent years carefully avoiding entanglements, protecting myself. And now I'm voluntarily moving into a remote cabin with three Alphas who make my body react like it's been struck by lightning?

I'm either making the biggest mistake of my life or, somehow, impossibly, finding where I belong.

I'm terrified it might be both.

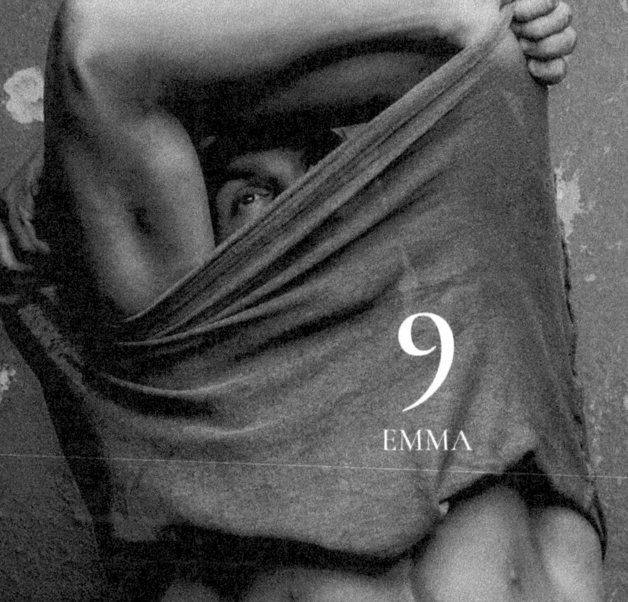

9

EMMA

"I'm sorry, ma'am, but we're completely booked through the next three weeks."

"Nothing?" I press my phone harder against my ear, as if that might somehow change the answer. "Not even a janitor's closet with a cot?" I joke.

The woman on the other end of the line clears her throat. "We have a waiting list I could add you to, but I should warn you that there are already twenty-seven names ahead of yours."

"Right. Of course there are." I blow a strand of hair from my face, squinting against the morning sun. "Thanks anyway."

I hang up and add Pine Valley Inn to my mental graveyard of lodging options. That makes six motels, three B and Bs, and two hotels that have slammed their metaphorical doors in my face. Each conversation follows the same depressing script—complete disbelief that I'd dare to seek accommodation without a reservation during Whispering Grove's peak season.

An involuntary shudder ripples through me as fragments of last night's dream claw their way into my thoughts. I was back in the rental cabin, but the windows had disappeared, replaced by solid walls of crackling timber. The smoke had a voice, whispering, taunting, as it curled around my throat. I'd woken up gasping, sheets damp with sweat, convinced for five terrifying seconds that I could smell burning wood. Even now, in broad daylight, the memory makes my pulse skip erratically. I shake my head, forcing the images back into whatever dark corner of my mind spawned them. I can't afford to fall apart now. Compartmentalize. That's what I'm good at. File the trauma away like an overdue bill—something to deal with later or, preferably, never.

I peer at my watch, 8:37 a.m. Atlas should be here in about twenty minutes to pick me up, as he had a morning call. My backpack sits loyally at my feet, stuffed with my laptop and the few pitiful items I managed to rescue from the cabin blaze. The morning breeze carries the scent of coffee from somewhere nearby, taunting me with its promises of caffeine and normalcy.

My phone buzzes against my palm. Jess's face, tongue out, eyes crossed, from our college graduation, fills the screen. I smile despite myself and answer.

"Please tell me you have a spare bedroom I can teleport into," I say by way of greeting.

"Hello to you too, sunshine." Jess laughs. "That bad, huh?"

"I've called almost every establishment with a roof in this town. Unless I want to pitch a tent in someone's backyard or sleep in a rental car, which, by the way, would also require a miracle to obtain, I'm officially homeless."

"What about Mr. Hot Firefighter? The one from the photo you sent?"

I feel heat rush to my cheeks that has nothing to do with the morning sun. "Atlas."

"Ooh, yes. Mm-hmm. And his biceps just happened to be in that selfie, and I can't unsee them."

"Anyway, I might be staying with him and the two guys in his pack. Temporarily."

The silence on the other end lasts precisely three seconds before Jess's screech nearly ruptures my eardrum.

"EMMA COLLINS! You've been in Whispering Grove for LESS THAN A WEEK!"

"It's not like that," I hiss, feeling my face flame hotter. "He offered his guest room. And they have this cabin in the woods—"

"Three Alphas, hey!"

"They're firefighters," I insist. "They rescued me. They're good guys."

"Okay, okay." Jess's voice softens. "Text me their full names and address. And maybe set up one of those 'if I don't check in, call the police' apps."

"You've been watching too many true crime documentaries."

"And you're an Omega moving in with three strange Alphas in the middle of nowhere. One of us is being sensible, and it's not you."

I sigh, knowing she's not entirely wrong. "I'll send you their details, but honestly, Jess, they've been nothing but respectful."

"Mmm, that doesn't make you sound smitten at all."

"I'm not—"

"Em, boo." Her interruption is gentle. "I know you're not over Chad yet, but—"

"I am so over Chad," I interject, perhaps too forcefully.

"Really?"

I kick at a pebble near my foot, watching it skitter across the pavement.

"Have you told him about the fire?"

"God, no. And he hasn't bothered to ask how I am." The familiar ache throbs dully in my chest. Not for Chad himself, but for what I thought we had. For being a fool and believing he would finally mark me as his with his bite. To make me feel like I truly belonged to him...

"Well, he betrayed you, then dumped you. Fuck him, but just be careful."

I let out a laugh that's more air than sound. "Thanks for the permission."

"Look, all I'm saying is I'm all for not pushing away

potential good things because one Alpha-hole hurt you. Just be careful not to rush into another relationship too quickly."

A pickup truck turns onto the street, and my heart does an embarrassing little flip when I recognize Atlas behind the wheel.

"Speaking of which, my ride is here. I should go."

"Send me those details! And call me after you've seen their place. I want to know if it's a palace or a murder shack."

"Will do. Love you."

"Love you too."

I hang up just as my phone starts vibrating again. Chad's name flashes on the screen, accompanied by a photo I now regret not deleting—his arm slung possessively around my shoulders at last year's Christmas party. My thumb hovers over the decline button when a text message preview appears...

Your stuff's packed in garbage bags. When are you coming back to get it? Also, pretty sure you took my gym duffel by mistake. Need it back.

A startled laugh escapes me. Of course he's worried about his precious bag while my entire life is in shambles. I type back.

Nice to see you got over me so quickly that you don't even care I nearly died in a cabin fire the other night... asshole!

I hit Send with vicious satisfaction, then immediately regret engaging at all. I should be better than this.

Shouldn't give him the satisfaction of knowing he can still affect me.

His response comes fast.

Are you ok?

For a split second, I feel a twinge of validation when the phone dings with his next message.

My bag ok? Call me!

Fire races through my veins, and I type back so forcefully I'm surprised my screen doesn't crack.

Fuck you!

I mute the conversation and shove my phone into my pocket as Atlas's truck pulls up to the curb.

The driver's-side window rolls down, revealing Atlas's strong profile. The morning light catches on his dark hair. His five-o'clock shadow has progressed to what I'd call seven-thirty stubble, and somehow, it makes him look even more ruggedly appealing.

"Morning," he calls, his deep voice sending an unwelcome shiver down my spine. "Ready to see your temporary home?"

I hoist my backpack and approach the truck, trying to appear more confident than I feel. "Ready as I'll ever be."

He leans across to push open the passenger door, and I climb in, immediately enveloped by the smell of woodsmoke and his masculine scent, which makes me sit up and take notice.

"Everything okay?" Atlas asks as I buckle my seat belt. "You looked like you were having quite the conversation with your phone back there."

Heat creeps up my neck. "You saw that?"

"Hard to miss someone trying to shove their fingers through the phone angrily." His lips quirk up at the corners.

"Ex," I admit, then immediately regret it when his expression shifts to something unreadable. "He's demanding the return of his bag, the one that's now a pile of designer ash in the burned-down cabin."

"He doesn't know about the fire?" Atlas pulls away from the curb, his large hands confident on the steering wheel. We turn onto the main street, which is already full of cars and people.

"He does now." I stare out the window at the bustling town.

"Still thinking about him? The ex who had you stabbing your phone with murderous thumbs moments earlier," Atlas asks.

I tear my gaze from the window and the decorations of the Founders Festival that's overtaken Whispering Grove. "I wasn't—" I stop myself. No point in denying it. "He has a way of burrowing under my skin, even from hundreds of miles away."

Atlas's hands flex on the steering wheel, the movement subtle but impossible to miss. "Some men think the world owes them something. That biology makes them entitled to whatever they want." He glances over. "I'll be the first to admit our kind can be absolute pricks."

"Understatement of the century," I mutter.

"If you ever need someone to put him in his

place…" The sentence hangs in the air, unfinished but crystal clear.

I study his profile, the strong line of his jaw, the tension in his shoulders. "Are you offering to be my personal bodyguard, Fire Chief?"

A half smile plays at his lips, softening the edge of whatever emotion had momentarily darkened his features. "Maybe I just don't like the idea of someone making you look at your phone like it personally betrayed you."

"That's dangerously close to protective Alpha behavior," I tease, though something warm flutters in my chest.

"Guilty as charged." He slows as we pass through the center of town, where a group of volunteers is hoisting an enormous banner across Main Street. "Though I suspect you're perfectly capable of handling yourself."

"You'd be right. I once shattered a guy's windshield with a baseball bat after he spread rumors about me." I pause. "I've matured since then."

His laugh is unexpectedly deep and genuine. "Remind me to keep all sporting equipment away from you when I'm on your bad side."

"Bold of you to assume I need equipment to cause damage," I counter.

"Hey, but seriously," he says, voice gentler, "you okay?"

"Fine." I brush it off automatically, then reconsider. "Actually, I'm not sure. Not really. I feel like I'm drowning in a way, and last night in my dream, I kept hearing this cracking sound... you know, right before the roof started to collapse when the cabin was on fire? It's like it's stuck in my head on repeat."

He nods, understanding without pity. "That's normal. The brain doesn't just let go of trauma, especially the sensory impressions."

"Is that your professional firefighter opinion?"

"That, and personal experience." He falls silent for a moment, negotiating a tricky turn as we begin to climb into the foothills, leaving the town behind. "After my first big fire, I couldn't wash the smell out of my nose for weeks. Thought I was going crazy."

I study his face, the way the morning light carves shadows beneath his cheekbones. God, this man is crazy handsome, but I school my expression.

"How did you make it stop?"

"I didn't, exactly." His voice drops lower, more intimate somehow. "You just make room for it. Acknowledge it. Eventually, it becomes a part of you instead of something consuming you."

Silence falls between us as I digest his words. The truck climbs higher into the mountains, and I watch as the town recedes in the side mirror, the buildings growing smaller until they're just a colorful speck in the valley below.

"Your town really goes all out for this festival," I comment, thinking of the decorations and the buzz of excited energy that seemed to permeate the streets.

"The rideshare driver wouldn't stop talking about it when he brought me to the cabin."

Atlas smiles. "It's the one time of year we're actually on the map. Tourism keeps half the businesses afloat."

"We don't have anything like that back in Moonshell Bay. Small town but none of the charm."

"Heard it's a beautiful town."

"Mostly," I admit. "After my parents died, so much still reminds me of them. Don't get me wrong, I love it, but it's also heartbreaking." The words escape before I can catch them, and I mentally curse my runaway mouth.

"How long ago?"

"I was sixteen, so about eight years ago." I twist my grandmother's wave pendant between my fingers. "Boating accident."

He nods, his eyes briefly meeting mine before returning to the winding road. "That's young to lose both parents."

I stare out at the passing trees, their shadows dappling the sunlit road. "So, what's your backstory?" I ask, wanting the conversation off me. "How does someone so young end up as fire chief of a town like Whispering Grove?" Claire had told me a bit about his past, but after realizing last night that she might have been gaslighting me about the men, I'm not sure how much I can believe.

A shadow crosses his face. "I'm not that young. I'm thirty-two. And I got the position the hard way."

"Meaning?" But I can't stop thinking about his age. Eight years older than me. Chad was only three years older, and even then, I thought that was something. This... this is different. I can see it in the way Atlas holds himself, in the way he looks at me, as though he already knows how this ends. And maybe that's exactly why I can't look away.

"That my mentor, the previous chief, died in a fire. I was next in line."

"Oh, shit, I'm sorry," I say, suddenly regretting my question.

"Tom was more father than mentor." His jaw tightens, the words rough like they cost him to say. His knuckles go white on the steering wheel. "He took me in when I was about sixteen. Caught me stealing food from the fire station."

I blink, surprised by the revelation. "What happened?"

"Instead of calling the cops, he gave me a job. Then a room when he found out I was living on the streets." Atlas's voice remains steady. "Taught me everything I know about firefighting. About being a man worth something."

The vulnerability in his admission catches me off guard. It's so at odds with the confident, commanding Alpha I've seen these past few days. Something inside me softens, dangerous as that feels.

"He sounds incredible," I say gently.

"He was." The simple declaration speaks volumes. "He'd like you, I think."

"Yeah, why's that?"

Atlas's mouth quirks up at one corner. "He always said people who survived something hard had the best stories to tell."

The sentiment steals my breath for a moment. "And do I have good stories?"

His eyes meet mine. "I think you've barely started telling them."

The weight of his gaze makes my skin prickle. I force myself to glance away, out the window at the thickening forest. Away from the pull I feel toward him, a sensation that terrifies me.

We crest a hill, and suddenly, the road opens onto a clearing.

"How much farther?" I ask, eager to see his place.

"We're almost there," Atlas says, putting the truck in park. He shifts in his seat to face me more directly. "Emma..."

Something in his tone makes my pulse quicken. "Yes?"

"I need you to know something before we get there." His eyes hold mine, intense and unreadable. "The past couple of days, since you entered our lives... it's been..." He trails off, seemingly struggling with words.

"Been what?" I prompt, my voice embarrassingly breathless.

"Distracting," he finally says. "In ways I wasn't prepared for."

The admission hangs between us. My throat goes dry.

"Atlas—"

"You don't need to say anything," he cuts in gently. "I know you've been through hell recently. The ex, the cabin fire, being stranded here. The last thing you need is another Alpha complicating things."

"Is that what you'd be?" The words escape before I can trap them behind my teeth.

His gaze darkens, pupils expanding until the blue is just a thin ring around bottomless black. "I'd be a fucking disaster for you right now, Emma. And you know it."

The raw honesty of his statement hits me with almost physical force. I should be grateful for his restraint. Should be relieved he's acknowledging the terrible timing, the impossibility of whatever this electricity between us might ignite.

Instead, I feel robbed of something I hadn't even admitted I wanted.

"Right," I manage, looking away. "Of course."

"That doesn't mean I don't—" He stops and exhales slowly. "Look, I just want you to feel safe with us. No pressure. No expectations."

I force a smile I don't feel. "Message received, Chief. You're offering sanctuary, not seduction. Exactly what I was asking for, right?"

A muscle in his jaw flexes. "Emma."

I gesture toward the road ahead. "Shall we? I'm dying to see your home."

For a moment, I think he might press further, might crack open this tension between us and examine what lies beneath. Instead, he puts the truck back in gear and continues up the winding path.

"You won't be disappointed," he states, and I'm not sure if he's talking about the cabin or something else entirely.

Either way, as we approach what will be my temporary home, I have the sinking feeling that disappointment is the least of my worries.

The truck rounds a bend, and the trees part to reveal our destination. I forget whatever clever retort I was forming as I stare up, mouth slightly agape.

"That's... You live there?"

The building before us rises like something from a fantasy novel. A large rustic cabin forms the base, all golden wood and stone, with large windows reflecting the morning light. But what makes it truly spectacular is the fire watchtower that extends from its center, reaching skyward on sturdy supports. The tower is crowned with a glass-enclosed observation room, surrounded by a wraparound deck that offers what must be breathtaking 360-degree views of wilderness.

"Home sweet home," Atlas states, but there's a hint of pride in his voice as he watches my reaction.

"It's incredible," I breathe as he parks beside a sleek black SUV that must belong to one of his packmates. "How did you even—"

"Lots of work," he says, cutting the engine. "We've been building it ourselves over the last few years. The tower was decommissioned decades ago, but the structure was still sound."

I climb out of the truck, tilting my head back to take in the full height of the tower. A hawk circles lazily above, as if completing the picturesque scene.

"The stairs look much more daunting from down here," I mutter, eyeing the wooden staircase that spirals around the exterior of the tower.

"They're worth the climb," Atlas assures me, retrieving my backpack from the truck before I can protest. "The view from up top will make you forget all about your burning cabin."

"That's a pretty high bar," I quip. "I was rather attached to that smoke inhalation."

He chuckles, gesturing for me to follow him. "Let's get you settled. Levi should be inside, but River got called to assist with a hiker rescue this morning."

The front door opens into a space that simultaneously makes me want to gasp and curl up with a good book. The interior is exactly what you'd expect from three Alphas with excellent taste, or at least one with excellent taste who bullied the others into submission. Wide-plank hardwood floors stretch throughout an open floor plan, with a massive stone fireplace in a living area furnished with deep leather couches that look sinfully comfortable.

The kitchen along the far wall is rustic and modern, with butcher block countertops, a farmhouse sink, and high-end appliances. Windows everywhere frame the forest views, like living artwork. I'm suddenly envious of having such a gorgeous home.

"This is..." I struggle to find words adequate for the space.

"Acceptable?" Atlas suggests with a smile.

"It's like someone took the coziest cabin Pinterest board and made it real," I admit, wandering into the living room. "Please tell me you didn't design this yourself, or I'll have to hate you on principle."

"Levi is the design genius. River and I just provide the muscle and occasional veto power."

I run my fingers along the back of a butter-soft leather couch. "Well, it's obscenely perfect."

"Atlas?" Levi calls from somewhere deeper in the house. "Is that you?"

"Yeah," Atlas calls back. "Got Emma with me."

A moment later, Levi appears from a hallway, and I have to consciously remember to keep my mouth closed. If Atlas is rugged, masculine beauty, Levi is his refined counterpart. Tall and muscular, with straight black hair falling across his forehead and cheekbones that could cut glass. His eyes, startlingly bright against his olive complexion, assess me with quiet curiosity.

"Emma," he says with a nod, his voice softer than I expected. "How are you feeling this morning?"

"Less smoky, but currently in awe of this place," I reply, then mentally kick myself. *Less smoky? Real witty, Emma.*

But Levi's mouth curves slightly. "That's generally the preferred state of being around here."

Atlas sets my backpack on the couch. "I was going to show Emma around before I head out to meet River. Is the guest room ready?"

"Almost," Levi says. "Just putting fresh sheets on the bed."

"I can help," I offer quickly, not wanting to be more of a burden than I already am.

Levi shakes his head. "No need. Why don't you show her the tower first? I'll finish up."

Atlas's face brightens. "Good idea." He turns to me. "You up for a climb?"

"Are there coffee and views at the top of this climb?" I ask.

"Views, definitely. Coffee, we can arrange."

"Then lead on, Chief."

Atlas guides me back outside to the base of the wooden stairs that spiral around the exterior of the tower. "Watch your step," he warns as we begin to climb. "The wood can be slick in the morning dew."

Naturally, my foot slips on the very next step, sending me lurching sideways with a startled yelp. Atlas's hand shoots out, catching my elbow and steadying me with seemingly effortless strength.

"Sorry," I mutter, heat rushing to my face. "I come with a warning label: Coordination not included."

His hand lingers a beat longer than it should, warmth rushing up my arm, and suddenly, all I can think about is his touch, right there between us.

"I'll keep that in mind."

We continue our ascent, and thankfully, it's not

one of those super lofty towers. But I'm painfully aware of how close Atlas stays behind me, as if expecting me to tumble backward at any moment. Given my track record, it's not an unreasonable concern.

The stairs terminate at a wooden deck that wraps entirely around the glass-enclosed tower room. I step onto it and immediately freeze, momentarily dizzy with the sudden expanse of view.

Miles of forest stretch below us in every direction, a rippling sea of green broken only by the occasional rocky outcrop or clearing. To the east, Whispering Grove nestles in the valley, looking like a model village from this height. Beyond that, mountain ranges rise in hazy layers against the horizon.

"Oh," I breathe, the syllable inadequate for the panorama before me.

"Worth the climb?" Atlas asks softly, coming to stand beside me. Too close, leaving me breathless.

"Worth burning down a cabin for," I admit, then glance at him. "Not that I did that."

"Good to know." His smile is warm, his eyes reflecting the endless sky. "I was starting to wonder if you were some sort of chaos agent sent to keep fire-fighters employed."

"If I were, I'd be doing a terrible job. One cabin fire in over twenty-four hours? Amateur hour."

He laughs, and the sound seems to expand in the open air around us. "Come inside. The view is just as good indoors."

The interior of the tower is a single square room with windows on all sides, making it feel like we're suspended in the sky. A central fireplace with a copper hood provides the only interruption to the glass, with comfortable seating arranged to take advantage of every possible view. A telescope stands in one corner, and built-in bookshelves occupy the space below the windows.

"This is where I'd live if I were here," I say, turning slowly to take it all in. "I'd never leave."

"We spend a lot of evenings up here," Atlas admits. "Especially during storms or meteor showers."

I stroll over to the eastern windows, resting my fingertips against the cool glass. "I can't imagine how beautiful it must be during a thunderstorm."

"Like being inside the storm itself," he says, coming to stand beside me. "The lightning illuminates the entire valley. You can watch it roll in from miles away."

"And during winter?"

"Even better. The silence after a snowfall is like nothing else."

I turn to find him watching me rather than the view, his expression unreadable. We're standing close enough that I can feel the heat radiating from his body and smell the now-familiar scent of woodsmoke and maple that clings to him. Something electric crackles in the space between us.

"It's wonderful to have you here," he says quietly. "I hope you'll feel at home while you stay."

"It would be hard not to," I reply, surprised by the huskiness in my voice. "This place is magical."

His gaze drops briefly to my lips, and for one heart-stopping second, I think he might lean in. Instead, he takes a small step back, breaking whatever spell had momentarily enveloped us.

"I can see myself setting up here and writing," I explain quickly, moving toward one of the comfortable chairs. "Best inspiration ever."

"You're welcome to use this space whenever you want," he offers. "No one will disturb you up here."

The silence that follows hits like a lightning strike, intense, electric, and awkward in a way our earlier banter wasn't. It crackles between us, heavy with things neither of us is saying.

I drag in a breath, reminding myself again that, as attractive as Atlas is, and God, he's devastating in that quietly dangerous way that gets under your skin, getting involved with anyone right now would be catastrophically stupid.

My heart is already broken. I don't need to hand the shattered pieces to someone new, least of all someone who pretty much admitted we shouldn't give in to our temptation.

His phone chirps, breaking the moment. He checks it and sighs.

"Duty calls," he murmurs, returning the phone to his pocket. "River needs backup with the hiker rescue."

"Go save lives," I tell him with a smile I hope looks

more confident than it feels. "I'll be fine. I mean… how could I not be? I'm in this, you know, sky palace. Pretty sure the couch alone is fancier than my entire former apartment." I shut my mouth before I make it worse, heat creeping up my neck.

"Levi will show you to your room and help you get settled." He hesitates, as if wanting to say more, then simply adds, "Make yourself at home, Emma. Really."

I watch him descend the stairs, taking them two at a time so easily that it makes my earlier stumble even more embarrassing in retrospect. Only when he disappears from view do I let out a long exhale.

What am I doing here? In this beautiful tower, in this magical place, with these impossibly perfect Alphas? This isn't my life. My life is tiny apartments and rejection letters and boyfriends who ruin my heart. Yet, here I stand, surrounded by breathtaking views and inexplicable kindness from strangers who owe me nothing.

I turn back to the panorama of mountains and forests, pressing my palm against the cool glass as if I could somehow absorb the serenity of the landscape. Maybe, just maybe, this unexpected detour is exactly what I need. A place to lick my wounds, finish my novel, and remember who Emma Collins is outside of Chad's shadow.

And if that process happens to include occasional moments of electricity with ridiculously attractive Alphas? Well, I'm only human. Or rather, only Omega.

Hopefully, I can manage not to fall down the tower or say something absurdly awkward.

But given my track record so far in Whispering Grove, I'm not betting on it.

10

The door leading to the watchtower stairs closes behind me with a soft click, leaving me alone in the main living area of what is apparently now my temporary home. The enormity of the space hits me all at once—this isn't just a cabin; it's practically a mansion disguised as rustic living.

"Damn," I whisper to nobody, turning in a slow circle. "And I thought Chad's two-bedroom apartment was fancy because it had a garbage disposal." This cabin, though, is the kind of place people post on Instagram with captions like "Just a little weekend getaway" while the rest of us contemplate murder.

I run my fingers over the polished edge of a wooden side table, half convinced I've stumbled into an alternate reality where firefighters moonlight as luxury real estate developers, when the creak of the floorboards comes from my left and nearly sends me jumping out of my skin.

"Like what you see?" Levi says.

I whirl around, clutching my chest. "Jesus! Shouldn't you be wearing a bell or something? Or do they teach ninja-level sneaking at firefighter school?"

He's leaning against the doorframe of a hallway. And honestly? The sight of him does nothing to convince me that I haven't fallen into some parallel universe where men like this actually exist outside of romance novel covers.

While Atlas gives off that whole rugged-lumberjack-who-could-bench-press-you vibe, Levi is... well, he's what would happen if someone gave a Renaissance sculptor permission to go absolutely feral. Dark hair falls across his forehead in that annoyingly perfect way that would take me forty-five minutes and three styling products to achieve. Cheekbones sharp enough to split shadows. And a body that's all muscle wrapped in a charcoal Henley and jeans that fit him like they were custom-made.

But it's his eyes that make my stomach do a weird flippy thing—amber gold and watching me with this little half smile that makes me wonder if he can read minds. God, I hope not. My thoughts right now aren't exactly PG-13. Like, if he told me to get on my knees, I don't think my brain would even put up an argument.

"I was coming to get you," he murmurs, pushing off from the doorframe with a graceful movement that has me mentally comparing him to a panther. A sexy panther. In people's clothes. My brain is a disaster zone.

"Atlas said you might be hungry," he continues, moving into the room with a casual confidence that somehow makes the space feel smaller.

I realize I'm staring when his lips twitch into a small smile. Not the polite customer-service smile he wore when Atlas introduced us yesterday. This one has an edge to it, as if he's enjoying a private joke.

"Sorry, what?" I manage, mortified to be caught ogling him like he's the last donut in the box.

His smile widens, revealing a small dimple in his right cheek. "You weren't listening to a word I said, were you?"

"I was"—my brain scrambles desperately—"honestly just having an existential crisis about how three bachelors live in a place this gorgeous, while my place had a suspicious stain on the ceiling that I'm pretty sure was forming its own ecosystem."

He laughs, and the sound is deeper than I expected, more genuine.

"So, you like the place?"

"*Like* is what I feel about pizza and puppies. This house is..." I gesture helplessly. "It's a palace."

"Thanks." He actually looks pleased, a hint of pride softening his sharp features. "I had a vision for it. The others helped execute it, but the design was my baby."

"Well, congratulations on your very attractive baby," I say, then immediately cringe. "That came out weird. Please ignore me. I'm still slightly traumatized from nearly becoming a human s'more the other day."

Instead of backing away slowly like any reasonable person would, Levi just grins wider. "So, hungry?"

My stomach answers before my mouth can, growling audibly in the quiet room.

"I'll take that as a yes," he answers, heading toward the kitchen. "Come on, let's raid the fridge before you start eyeing the furniture for edibility."

I follow him, oddly comforted by his lack of reaction to my awkwardness.

"So, this is how the other half lives," I mutter, perching on a barstool at the island.

Levi gives me a curious look as he opens the refrigerator. "Other half?"

"You know, the half that doesn't eat ramen three nights a week."

"Ah." He nods sagely. "The struggle between artistic integrity and capitalism's cold, unforgiving embrace."

I blink, surprised by the poetic phrasing. "Exactly that."

"Drink preference?" he asks, head still in the fridge. "We've got water, juice, beer—though it's probably too early for that."

"Do you have soda?" I ask, trying to appear casual while my internal organs are still doing the electric slide every time he moves.

He turns around, and the way his face lights up makes my heart do a stupid little stutter. In each hand, he holds a can of Dr. Pepper like he's presenting the crown jewels. "Would you believe this is my favorite? The others think I'm crazy."

"No way!" The genuine delight that bubbles up surprises even me. "It's my favorite too!"

"Atlas and River think it tastes like sweetened motor oil," he adds, sliding a can across the island to me. "Their loss."

Popping the tab, I take a grateful sip. "So good." I tap mine against his. "To temporary roommates who don't judge my questionable beverage choices."

"Speaking of your temporary residence," he says after taking a long drink. "Want to see where you'll be staying?"

"Lead the way," I reply, sliding off the stool and grabbing my backpack. "Fair warning, though—my standards are now impossibly high after seeing this kitchen."

Levi guides me down a hallway that branches off from the main living area. The walls are lined with framed photographs—mostly landscapes, a few of the three Alphas in firefighting gear, and some of spectacular thunderstorms.

"These are gorgeous," I comment, pausing to examine a shot of lightning illuminating a mountain range. "Local?"

"Mostly," he says, stopping beside me. "We picked some of them up at the art market during the summer festivals. The photographers around here are incredible. They capture the valley in all seasons."

He's standing close enough that I can feel the heat

radiating from him and smell the intoxicating blend that seems to cling to his skin. He doesn't touch me, but the way he angles his body makes it clear that he could, easily, if he wanted to. The realization sends a shiver down my spine.

"This one is my favorite," he begins, nodding to a photo of the watchtower silhouetted against a sunset. "Reminds me how lucky we are to call this place home."

There's something about the way he says "home" that makes my chest ache a little. It's been a long time since anywhere felt like that to me. I moved in with Chad about a year ago, but the apartment never felt like mine. More like I was borrowing someone else's life, and it never quite fit.

We continue down the hall, passing several closed doors. "Atlas's room," he explains, pointing to one, then another: "River's." And then a third: "Mine." Reaching the end, he pauses, hand on the doorknob of the final door.

"This is you," he says, then pushes it open.

I step past him, and the tiny gasp that escapes me is embarrassingly audible in the quiet room.

This isn't just a guest room. This is... it's like someone reached into my tired Omega brain, extracted all my secret comfort fantasies, and manifested them into physical form.

The room is bathed in a warm glow from bedside lamps, the harsh overhead light dimmed to almost nothing. A four-poster bed dominates the center, draped with gauzy fabric that creates a secluded cocoon. The bedding has a cloud-looking comforter. Plush blankets in jewel tones, throws that look butter-soft, and dear God, are those silk pillowcases? There must be a dozen pillows, all arranged in a way that practically screams *Dive into me.*

A small bookshelf holds what looks suspiciously like dog-eared romance novels, thrillers, and even a few literary fiction titles. Beside it stands a small table with—my heart actually skips—an arrangement of snacks that can only be described as a shrine to emotional eating. Chocolate in various forms, cheese crackers, trail mix, and even a thermos of what smells like herbal tea.

Near the window is a reading nook with an over-sized armchair and ottoman. The TV mounted on the wall is positioned perfectly for bed-viewing, with a remote already on the nightstand next to... are those mini chocolate bars?

But it's the smaller touches that utterly undo me. Slippers by the door. An oversized hoodie hanging from a hook. The subtle scent of lavender and vanilla permeates the air. This isn't just hospitality. This is an Omega nest. One created with deliberate, thoughtful care by an Alpha who... noticed.

Who saw me.

"You did this for me?" My voice comes out small, vulnerable in a way I hate.

Levi leans against the doorframe, watching me with an intensity that makes my skin prickle with awareness. "I noticed how you'd started to nest at the fire station last night. Figured you could use the real thing after what you've been through."

I circle the room slowly, touching everything with my fingertips, the soft edge of a blanket, the smooth cover of a book, the cool ceramic of a mug waiting beside the thermos. A lump forms in my throat, hot and tight.

"No one's ever done anything like this for me," I admit, the raw honesty hanging in the air between us.

Something fierce and possessive flares across his face. For a split second, he looks like he might cross the room to me, but instead, he simply says, "That's a damn shame, Emma."

The way he says my name sends heat spiraling through me.

"I stocked the snacks like it was an emergency shelter," he adds, nodding toward the table. "Chocolate for immediate crises, salty things for sustained energy, tea for comfort, backup treats in the drawer for when you inevitably demolish the visible supply."

I laugh despite the emotion still thick in my throat. "Planning for the snackalypse?"

"Always be prepared," he intones seriously, but his gaze is dancing. "There's also an electric blanket already set up, controller between the mattress and headboard. And a massage pad under it, instructions in the nightstand drawer."

I stare at him, genuinely speechless. "You thought of everything."

"I pay attention." He says it simply, but there's nothing straightforward about the way he's looking at me like I'm a treasure map he's memorizing.

Heat crawls up my neck, and I feel compelled to clarify. "I'm not, um, going into heat or anything, if that's what you're thinking."

His smile is slow, deliberate, transforming his serious face into something almost predatory. "I'm not worried," he says, voice dropping lower. "But nesting doesn't automatically mean heat."

He tilts his head slightly, and I watch with a mixture of alarm and arousal as his nostrils flare subtly. Is he... scenting me? The thought sends a jolt of electricity straight to places that have no business being electrified right now.

"Unless you are?" he adds.

"No!" I blurt, then scramble to recover. "Definitely not." I need to change the subject before I spontaneously combust. "I don't know how to thank you enough. This is seriously incredible."

I move toward the bed, pushing aside one of the gauzy curtains to sit on the edge. The mattress is perfect, supportive but plush, like sleeping on a soft cloud.

"I have to ask," I say, desperate to redirect the conversation. "What's with your Dr. Pepper love? Most people I know think it's the weird cousin of the soda family."

Levi hesitates for a moment, then comes to sit beside me on the bed. Not close enough to touch, but close enough that I'm acutely aware of every inch of him.

"Want to know a secret?" he asks, his voice lower, more intimate.

I nod, relieved by the conversational lifeline.

"My mom used to love it," he reveals, rolling his can between his palms. "When I was a kid, maybe six or seven, I'd sneak into the kitchen at night and steal sips from her stash in the back of the fridge." His expression softens with the memory, making him look younger and more open. "She always knew. Would complain to my dad about the mysteriously disappearing soda, and he'd get all defensive because he hated the stuff. Meanwhile, I'd be sitting there, trying not to giggle and give myself away." He shakes his head, a quiet laugh escaping. "Every single time, she'd wink at me when he wasn't looking. Our little conspiracy."

The image of a small, serious-faced Levi trying to suppress his giggles makes something warm unfurl in my chest. "That's adorable."

"Yeah, well." He shrugs, but I can tell the memory means more to him than he's letting on. "Now, it's just habit. Comfort in a can, I guess."

"The best traditions usually start as accidents," I tell him. "The ones that remind you of people you love."

His eyes meet mine, and something electric passes between us, a current that feels too dangerous to examine closely.

"You can stay here as long as you need, you know," he says, his gaze never leaving mine. "We've got plenty of space."

"Thanks, but hopefully, it won't be too long." I try to sound casual, like I'm not hyperaware of how close we're sitting, how his scent is wrapping around me. "Just until they figure out what caused the fire and I can sort out my next steps."

"About that." He leans back slightly, one arm braced behind him on the bed. The movement stretches his Henley across his chest in a way that should be illegal. "Atlas is heading out to the site tomorrow to start investigating with the police. He's been pushing them to prioritize it."

"Really?" I'm genuinely surprised. "That's... unexpectedly kind of him."

The smile that spreads across Levi's face is nothing short of sinful. "I don't see the rush. Do you?"

There's something in his tone, a dark undercurrent of suggestion that makes slick pool between my thighs ridiculously fast. It's the voice of an Alpha who knows exactly what he wants and is simply waiting for the right moment to take it.

And God help me, that voice does things to me that I should ignore.

"I—" My voice catches, and I have to take a sip of Dr. Pepper to cover the momentary lapse. "I suppose there's something to be said for taking one's time."

His eyes darken fractionally, and I watch, trans-fixed, as he stands smoothly and walks—no, prowls—

to the bookshelf. He trails his fingers along the spines of the books, the gesture somehow both casual and deliberately sensual.

"You're going to sleep better knowing I built this room for you," he says, glancing back at me. His voice is low, almost gravelly. "That's what matters to me." He moves away from the bookshelf and pauses beside me again, deliberately close. "Oh, I almost forgot. There are some clothes in the dresser for you. Nothing fancy, just basics—T-shirts, sweatpants, a couple of hoodies. Until we can get some clothes."

I blink up at him, momentarily thrown by this casual statement. "You... bought me clothes?"

"We all did," he says, but there's something in his expression that makes me think he was the driving force. "Figured you'd need more than what was in your backpack."

"Thank you," I manage, the words inadequate for the tightness in my chest. "That's incredibly thoughtful."

He smiles, that small dimple appearing again. "That's what a pack does, Emma. We take care of our own."

The implication that I might somehow be included in that "our own" category sends a confused, pleasant warmth through me. Before I can respond, his phone chirps in his pocket.

He checks it and sighs. "River. I need to take this."

I nod, strangely disappointed as he moves toward the door.

"I'll let you get settled," he says, pausing in the doorway. "Bathroom's directly across the hall if you need it. Towels are in the cabinet under the sink."

"Thanks," I say, forcing a casual smile. "For everything."

He nods, then disappears down the hallway, his soft "Hey, River" fading as he moves away.

I collapse backward onto the bed, staring at the ceiling through the gauzy canopy. What the hell am I doing? I've been in Whispering Grove for less than a week, and I'm already entertaining wildly inappropriate thoughts about not one but three of the Alphas who've generously offered me shelter.

Alphas who are packmates. Alphas who live in this isolated, beautiful tower in the woods. Alphas who have shown me nothing but kindness and respect, who created this perfect Omega nest for me without being asked.

I press my thighs together, suddenly aware of the insistent throb between them. Even to my own nose, I can detect the subtle shift in my scent—sweeter, more intense, embarrassingly revealing to anyone with Alpha senses.

God, I need to get a grip. Or a cold shower. Preferably both.

I sit up, resolute. A shower. That's what I need. To clear my head, to cool the fire that seems to have taken up permanent residence in my veins since arriving in this town.

I duck into the bathroom, closing the door perhaps

more firmly than necessary. As I turn on the shower, cranking the temperature dial toward the blue end of the spectrum, I catch sight of myself in the mirror. My cheeks are flushed, eyes too bright, lips slightly parted. I look... affected.

"Get it together, Emma," I mutter. "They're being nice. You're just traumatized and emotional and mistaking basic human kindness for... whatever this is."

But even as I say it, I know it's a lie. The way Levi looked at me wasn't just kindness. The energy between us wasn't my imagination. And if I'm honest with myself, the same charge has been building between Atlas and me since the moment he sat next to me on the plane.

And now I'm living under their roof. Surrounded by their scents. Sleeping in a nest one of them built for me with his own hands.

As steam begins to fill the bathroom, I force myself to face the unavoidable truth—I am in serious, serious trouble. How am I supposed to resist three gorgeous Alphas when just one of them makes my knees weak? How am I supposed to protect my already battered heart when they're all being so impossibly, irresistibly perfect?

The answer is simple: I can't.

That terrifies me more than any fire ever could.

11

LEVI

My head spins at River's rapid-fire questions about our new housemate. If I didn't know better, I'd think he was the one who'd spotted Emma first, not Atlas.

"Yes, she's settling in. No, she hasn't tried to escape yet. Yes, I gave her the nest room," I answer, barely getting a word in edgewise.

"The job's almost done," River explains. "We'll be back around lunch. We'll bring pizza. Sound good?" Before I can answer, he continues, "Atlas says hi. Well, he grunted, but in Atlas-speak, that's practically a sonnet. See you soon."

I slide my phone into my pocket, calculating angles and load-bearing considerations for the bookshelf I've been designing for the living room. Three days ago, my biggest concern was whether Baltic birch or walnut would better complement our existing furniture. Then a blonde Omega with haunted eyes and a smart mouth crash-landed into our lives, and suddenly, we're all circling like planets that have found a new sun.

I'm crossing through the living room when a high-pitched scream splits the quiet. Not just any scream, but the kind that freezes your blood, the kind that triggers every protective instinct in Alpha biology.

My body reacts before my brain can process, my heart rate spiking, muscles tensing. I'm halfway down the hall before the scream cuts off, only to start again, louder this time.

"Emma?" I call out, already knowing she's in the bathroom. Spatial awareness has always been my strong suit; I can map a building in my head after walking through it once and can pinpoint sound origins with near-perfect accuracy. "Are you all right?"

Another scream is my only answer. Not one of pain, as there's no underlying growl of someone truly hurt, but one of pure, unadulterated terror. The mathematics of the situation compute instantly: Emma + bathroom + terror - visible threat = something unanticipated frightening her, not an intruder or an injury.

"I'm coming in!" I shout, not bothering to knock as I throw open the bathroom door.

Steam billows out in a thick cloud, momentarily disorienting me. Through the fog, I can make out Emma's form behind the frosted glass of the shower, pressed into the corner. The sight triggers an unexpected pulse of desire that I ruthlessly suppress. Emergency first, inappropriate thoughts later.

"Get it out! GET IT OUT!" she shrieks, her voice pitching higher with each word.

I scan the bathroom for anything out of place. No structural damage, no visible source of water leakage, and no electrical malfunctions that might cause shock.

"What's happening?" I ask, moving closer to the shower. "Emma, what's wrong?"

"THERE!" She points frantically to the opposite corner of the shower. "Oh my God, it's coming closer! Please, please get it!"

I move toward the shower door, still trying to identify the threat. "I'm coming in, okay?"

"HURRY! Before it jumps!" The genuine terror in her voice has me sliding open the door without further hesitation.

A rush of steam escapes, then—

Oh.

Fuck.

My brain short-circuits for approximately two point seven seconds.

Emma stands before me, completely naked, water cascading down her body in rivulets that make my mouth go desert dry. Honey-blonde hair darkened by water plasters against her shoulders. Droplets cling to her skin like they're afraid to let go, and who could blame them?

Her breasts, which are perfect, rose-tipped handfuls that would fit in my palms exactly, heave with each panicked breath. My gaze tracks lower, over the gentle swell of her stomach to the curve of her hips, then to the apex of her thighs, where there's a thin strip of light hair. Fuck!

Focus. Threat assessment. Now.

With monumental effort, I force my gaze to follow where she's pointing.

And there it is.

Its front legs arch high, poised in a threat display, jagged edges silhouetted against the haze. A huge spider. Its body bloated and black, bulbous and slick, gleaming wet in the humidity.

Even I flinch slightly.

"Don't move," I tell her, keeping my voice calm despite the adrenaline. "That's a wolf spider. Their venom is quite ineffective against people, but they can grow big and look intimidating. I need you to very slowly move toward me."

"A what?" Emma squeaks, momentarily distracted from her terror by my terminology. "No, I'm not moving an inch. It'll jump. Spiders always jump."

"Actually, they rarely jump unless severely threatened," I explain automatically, my brain reverting to facts as a defense against the overwhelming sensory input of naked, wet Emma. "They prefer to retreat when confronted by something larger than—"

"If you're about to tell me spider facts while I'm naked and terrified, I swear to God, Levi—" She breaks off as the spider shifts position slightly. "OH MY GOD, IT MOVED!"

"Emma," I say firmly, using just enough Alpha tone

to cut through her panic. "I need you to trust me. Move toward me, slowly."

"I can't." She shakes her head, pressing herself further into the corner. "I literally can't make my legs work. I'm completely paralyzed." Her voice drops to a horrified whisper. "I have severe arachnophobia. Like, diagnosed, went-to-therapy-for-it arachnophobia."

That explains the intensity of her reaction. I reassess the situation, calculating a new approach while trying desperately to keep my eyes on her face and not on the water droplets sliding between her breasts.

"Okay, new plan," I say. "I'm going to grab something to—"

"Don't you DARE leave me alone with that monster!" She looks on the verge of tears now, her hazel eyes wide with genuine fear. "Please, Levi. Don't go."

The vulnerability in her voice hits me harder than I expect, awakening something fiercely protective that has nothing to do with Alpha biology and everything to do with... her. Just her.

"I'll be right back," I promise, softening my tone. "Five seconds. Count them out loud."

Before she can protest further, I move away from the shower to grab a towel from under the sink. I also push the door all the way open to create an escape route if she needs it.

"One... two... thr— Oh, thank God, you came back," she gasps, relief plain in her voice.

"I promised I would," I say simply. "Here's what we're going to do. I'm going to throw this at the spider. The second I do, you run to me. Got it?"

Emma nods frantically, still pressed against the far corner. Water continues to stream down her body, and I can't help but notice how her skin has pebbled with goose bumps despite the steam. My gaze drops involuntarily to her breasts, where her nipples have hardened to tight peaks, and a fresh wave of heat crashes through me.

Not the time, I remind myself harshly.

"On three," I say, forcing my attention back to the arachnid threat. "One... two... THREE!"

I fling the towel at the spider, but instead of staying put, the little nightmare leaps. Not toward Emma, thankfully, but directly at me. Pure reflex has me ducking, and the spider lands on the bathroom floor with a barely audible pat.

Before it can scurry away, I bring my boot down hard. There's a sickening crunch as eight legs' worth of menace meets its maker.

I've barely straightened when a wet, naked missile crashes into my chest. Emma throws herself against me, shaking violently, her arms locked around my waist like I'm the only solid thing in a collapsing world.

"Is it dead?" she gasps against my now-soaked shirt, face buried against my sternum. "Tell me it's gone, or we might need to burn this cabin and salt the earth afterward."

I can't help but grin, even as my body responds all too eagerly to her nakedness pressed against me. "It's been permanently relocated to the underside of my boot."

"Eek!" She flinches away from my boot, and in that moment of separation, her situation seems to dawn on her.

For one suspended moment, we just stare at each other. Her eyes widen, darting down to her completely exposed body, then back up to my face, which, I'm sure, is doing a poor job of hiding exactly how affected I am by the view.

And what a view it is. This close, I can see the freckles dusting across her shoulders, the small birthmark just below her left breast, and the gentle swell of her hips flaring out from a narrow waist. Her skin is flushed pink from the cold water, or perhaps embarrassment, and glistening with droplets I suddenly, desperately want to trace with my tongue. My hands actually twitch with the need to touch, to explore, to claim.

My jeans are tightening around me to the point of pain.

She snatches another towel from the rack with lightning speed, wrapping it around herself with a squeak of mortification. "Don't look!"

"Oh, I saw nothing," I lie, unable to keep the grin off my face.

"You are such a liar!" She swats my arm, leaving a

wet handprint on my sleeve. "Your eyes practically took measurements!"

I can't help it. I laugh. "Force of habit. I'm an engineer."

Her cheeks flame even redder. Before I can say anything else, she's darting past me into the hallway, leaving wet footprints on the hardwood as she practically sprints to her room. The door slams behind her with enough force to rattle the frame.

"You're welcome!" I call after her. "I saved your life!"

Her muffled "Shut UP!" is just audible through the door, followed by what sounds suspiciously like laughter.

I glance down at my thoroughly soaked shirt and jeans, then at the spider corpse still under my boot. For a moment, I consider collecting the specimen, as it's unusually large for the species and might be worth documenting, but decide Emma might actually commit homicide if she saw me preserving her nemesis.

With a sigh that's equal parts amusement and frustration, I clean up the bathroom, dispose of the arachnid remains in the outside trash, and head to my room to change.

As I peel off my wet clothes, the image of Emma, wide-eyed, water-slicked, and gloriously bare, replays in my mind like a torturous highlight reel. This living arrangement just got a whole lot more complicated.

And exponentially more interesting.

By the time Emma emerges from her room, I've changed into dry clothes and am lounging on the couch with a book. I glance up casually, as if I haven't been listening for her door for the past forty-two minutes.

She hovers at the edge of the living room, wearing a pair of gray sweatpants and an oversized Whispering Grove Fire Department hoodie—both items from the clothes we'd purchased for her, tags recently removed, judging by the tiny plastic thread clinging to the sleeve. Her hair is damp but combed, falling in waves around her shoulders, and her cheeks are still flushed.

For several seconds, she seems to debate whether to acknowledge me or retreat back to her room.

I decide to make it easy for her. "The enemy has been vanquished," I say, setting my book aside. "The cabin is now a certified arachnid-free zone."

She takes a few tentative steps into the room, and I notice she's carefully scanning the floor and corners as she moves. Her spider trauma runs deeper than just momentary fear.

"Arachnophobia, huh?"

"Clinically diagnosed," she confirms, sinking into the opposite end of the couch. "Since I was eight. A babysitter thought it would be funny to put a tarantula on my pillow while I was sleeping."

I wince. "That's... sadistic."

"She didn't work for our family again," Emma says darkly. "But the damage was done. One glimpse of those eight legs and I'm instantly eight years old again, waking up to fuzzy legs on my face."

"That explains the extreme reaction," I say. "The adrenaline spike from a phobia trigger can be comparable to actual life-threatening situations."

She eyes me curiously. "You sound like my therapist."

"I did a research project on fear responses during college," I explain. "Panic reactions to fire alarms versus actual fires. I had to study phobic responses as a comparison point."

"Of course you did," she says.

We sit in silence for a moment, the earlier awkwardness gradually dissolving into something more comfortable. Then she clears her throat.

"So," she begins, not quite meeting my eyes. "About... what happened..."

"The spider assassination has been classified as a top-secret operation," I say solemnly. "All details are strictly need-to-know."

Relief floods her expression. "Thank you. I'd rather not have the whole naked, screaming Omega story become pack dinner conversation."

"Your dignity is safe with me," I assure her. Then, I add, "Though the image itself... that might be permanently etched into my memory."

Her blush returns in full force. "Levi!"

I raise my hands in mock surrender. "I'm just being honest! I'm a visual person with an eidetic memory. It's both a blessing and a curse."

"Right now, it sounds like a curse for me," she mutters.

I can't help myself. Standing, I move closer to her, watching as her eyes widen slightly, pupils dilating as I approach. When I'm standing directly in front of her, close enough that she has to tilt her head back to maintain eye contact, I lean down slightly.

"I can make it up to you, you know," I say, my voice dropping lower.

"Make... what up to me?" she asks, her own voice barely above a whisper.

"The embarrassment," I clarify. "I can even the playing field."

Her eyebrows furrow in confusion. "How?"

I lean even closer, near enough to catch the subtle vanilla-and-old-books scent that clings to her skin even after her shower.

"I'll strip for you," I murmur. "Let you see me naked. Only fair, right? Because now I won't ever be able to sleep without seeing you so beautifully displayed in front of me."

For a moment, she just gapes at me, shock written across her features. Then something shifts in her expression.

"Are you seriously offering to get naked as some kind of... consolation prize?" she asks, her voice caught between incredulity and something darker, hungrier.

"I'm offering to restore cosmic balance," I say with exaggerated seriousness. "It's simple mathematics.

One naked Omega plus one naked Alpha equals equilibrium."

A startled laugh escapes her. "I never thought I'd hear someone use math as a seduction technique."

"Is it working?" I ask, genuinely curious.

She studies me for a long moment, her hazel eyes unreadable. "You're different when we're alone," she finally says. "Less..."

"Reserved?" I suggest.

"I was going to say 'buttoned-up,'" she admits. "When Atlas and River are around, you're so careful. Precise. Now, you're all..." She gestures vaguely at my current position, looming over her with clear intent.

"They know who I am," I explain simply. "I don't have to prove anything to them. But you..." I trail off, considering how to articulate the strange effect she has on me. "You make me want to show you more."

Something vulnerable flashes across her face. "Yeah, right," she scoffs, but there's a breathless quality to her voice that betrays her affected nonchalance. "Consider yourself lucky for a one-time look. It's not happening again."

I cock an eyebrow. "Are you sure about that?"

The front door opens before she can answer, and the scent of pizza fills the cabin. River enters first, balancing three large boxes, followed by Atlas with a paper bag that smells like garlic bread.

"Honeys, we're home!" River sings out. "And we bring offerings of cheesy goodness for our—" He stops mid-sentence, eyes darting between Emma and me, taking in our proximity and the charged atmosphere. "Are we interrupting something?"

Atlas's gaze zeroes in on us with laser focus as he sets the food on the coffee table. "Everything okay here?"

Emma jumps up from the couch, putting distance between us with near comical haste.

"I almost died this morning," she announces dramatically, clearly desperate to change the subject. "When you invited me to move in, you conveniently failed to mention this place is infested with mutant spider monsters from the ninth circle of hell!"

The three of us exchange glances, River's lips already twitching with poorly suppressed amusement.

"There was one in the shower with me," Emma continues, gesturing wildly. "With fangs like steak knives! And those creepy front legs that were all..." She mimics the spider's threatening posture, raising her hands and wiggling her fingers. "It could have bitten me! Or I could have slipped and cracked my head open trying to escape it! There would have been blood everywhere!"

River turns to me, eyes dancing with mischief. "So you saved her? While she was in the shower?"

Emma's cheeks flame. "He's under strict instructions to never speak of it again."

I draw an *X* over my heart with one finger, expression solemn. "A burden I alone must bear."

River clutches his chest in mock despair. "The injustice! The cruelty!"

"It wasn't a show," Emma protests.

Atlas, who's been silently observing our banter, approaches us. "So, our resident hero saved you from certain death?"

"Yep," Emma confirms resignedly.

"Sounds like our Levi," River says, flopping onto the couch and patting the space beside him invitingly. "He's always had a flair for dramatic rescues."

Emma hesitates, then sits beside River, tucking one leg beneath her. Atlas settles on her other side, leaving me to either take the armchair or join them on the sofa. I opt for the latter, claiming the space on River's other side.

"I'm starving," Emma declares, clearly trying to steer the conversation away from her shower adventure.

Atlas chuckles, opening the top pizza box. "Wasn't sure what you liked, so we got a variety. Pepperoni, supreme, and veggie."

Emma's eyes light up at the sight of the pepperoni. "You beautiful, beautiful men," she says fervently, grabbing a slice and folding it in half before taking a massive bite. The small moan of pleasure she makes has all three of us staring.

"We miss all the fun when we're gone." River sighs, reaching for a slice of supreme.

"Speaking of comfort," Atlas interjects, his gaze landing on Emma. "How's the room working out for you? Levi put a lot of thought into it."

The way he looks at her, like he's imagining exactly

how she'd look sprawled across that nest bed, sends a flare of possessive heat through me. We don't compete; we complement. It's what makes us work.

"It's perfect," she answers. "I really can't thank you all enough. The nest, the clothes… it's incredibly generous." Her gaze flickers to me, and the blush returns in full force.

"Want to try the supreme?" I ask her, selecting a slice and holding it out to her, just close enough that she'll need to lean in if she wants it.

She eyes me suspiciously, but her stomach apparently overrules her caution. She leans forward, reaching for the slice, but I pull it back slightly, just out of reach.

"Ah-ah," I tease. "Open up." I'm curious to see how she'll respond to this small assertion of dominance.

River snorts into his soda, and Atlas watches with undisguised interest as Emma debates her options.

After a moment's hesitation, she narrows her eyes at me, challenging, not submissive, then opens her mouth, allowing me to feed her the slice. Her lips brush my fingertips, the contact sending a jolt of electricity up my arm. I don't break eye contact, don't care that the others are watching. Let them see. Let her know exactly what she's doing to me.

"Good?" I ask, my voice deliberately lower.

She swallows, then nods. "Not bad." Her attempt at nonchalance might be more convincing if her pupils weren't blown wide, her scent shifting subtly to something sweeter, headier.

"So," River interjects, clearly enjoying the show. "Any other creatures we should warn you about in these woods? Bears? Mountain lions? Overly amorous squirrels with boundary issues?"

"Just us three," Atlas answers with a wicked grin before Emma can respond.

She nearly chokes on her pizza again. "Good to know," she manages after recovering. "Any of you happen to be venomous? Should I keep my distance? Sleep with one eye open?"

"Only if you're afraid of getting bitten," I say, earning a swift kick from River.

"Don't mind him," River stage-whispers to Emma. "He's all equations and precision until he sees something he wants. Then he's like a different person."

Emma raises an eyebrow, glancing between River and me. "And you know this from experience?"

"We've been packmates for many years," River says with a wink. "I know all his secrets."

We enjoy the pizza while Atlas turns on the television, flicking through channels until he stops on *Midnight Valley*.

"Stop here," Emma say, a bit too excited. "I love this show."

"You watch it too? I try to watch it at the station, as it only airs at midday!" I state.

"It's his obsession," Atlas confirms. "He makes us sit through it every week."

"You said you liked it last episode!" I protest.

Atlas shrugs. "I said the werewolf was decent. Not the same thing."

River nods solemnly, biting into his slice of supreme.

Emma laughs, the sound bright and unguarded, and something in my chest tightens. It's the first time I've heard her really laugh, not nervous or sarcastic, but genuinely amused.

I pull up the latest episode, resting back on the couch, and we all settle in to watch.

A short moment later, I notice Emma surreptitiously pull out her phone. At first, I think she's checking messages, but then I catch a glimpse of the screen—she's angling it to capture a photo of River, who's absorbed in the show.

I watch her for a moment, fascinated by this small, secretive action. Is she documenting her stay? Gathering images of us for her enjoyment later?

When the commercial break comes, I lean over River, bringing my face close to hers. "Are you collecting images of us for future research?" I murmur, nodding toward her phone.

She startles, nearly dropping the device. "What? No!"

River looks up, immediately interested. "You took a photo of me? Sweet, tell me and I'll pose." Without waiting for a response, he unbuttons the top of his shirt with a theatrical flourish, then throws himself into a ridiculous pin-up pose on the couch, complete with duck lips and bedroom eyes.

Emma bursts out laughing but lifts her phone to snap the picture anyway.

"It's for my friend Jess," she admits, the blush returning to her cheeks. "She insisted on knowing who I'm staying with, so if I go missing, she knows whose photos to give the cops."

"Oh, so we're potential criminals now?" I raise an eyebrow.

She shrugs. "An Omega's got to be safe. For all I know, you're all serial killers."

"I posed for mine back at the hospital," Atlas points out, a hint of smugness in his tone. "Full disclosure for the authorities."

"So, want me with or without my shirt?" I ask, already pulling the fabric over my head before she can answer. "Gotta make sure your friend has accurate identification materials."

The words die in Emma's throat as she takes in my bare chest. Her lips part slightly, eyes widening. It's gratifying, that look—a validation of the hours I spend training.

"You're drooling," River points out helpfully, nudging her with his elbow.

Atlas chuckles. "If you want to sit next to him, I'll take a photo of both of you. Then we could do all of us."

"Nope!" Emma squeaks, frantically snapping a picture of me anyway. "Got all I need, thanks!"

We all laugh, and as the show resumes, I make no move to put my shirt back on. Every few minutes, I catch her stealing glances at me, her eyes tracing the lines of my torso before darting away when caught.

I stretch deliberately, showcasing the muscles of my abdomen, and am rewarded with a sharp intake of breath from her direction.

Two can play at this game. If I'm never going to sleep again without a hard-on while she's in this house, then she deserves a little torture too.

Let the games begin, indeed.

12

"So, did her tits look as good as I'm imagining them?" I ask Levi, leaning against his desk with what I hope is casual nonchalance but is probably more like the desperation of a starving man outside a bakery.

Levi doesn't even look up from his paperwork, the corners of his mouth twitching upward. "I made a vow not to discuss it, and I keep my promises."

"Come on," I wheedle, perching on the edge of his desk and deliberately blocking his view of the evacuation plans he's drafting. "Just one detail. Carpet match the drapes? Any interesting tattoos?"

Finally, he gives me his full attention, that rare Levi smile spreading across his face—not the polite one he gives strangers, but the slightly wicked one that reminds me why he fits so perfectly in our pack.

"All I'll say is this," he offers, leaning back in his

chair. "Once you see her naked, you'll never be able to unsee it."

"You absolute bastard," I groan, flopping dramatically across his desk and scattering his meticulously organized papers. "You think I didn't hear you last night? The shower running at two a.m.? Don't pretend you weren't flogging the log after spending all evening eye-fucking her over pizza."

Levi chuckles, not even bothering to deny it. "Seriously, River, she's going to be the death of us. You have no idea what her scent can do when she's close."

"Oh, I have every damn idea," I reply, remembering our encounter in the laundry room.

"Don't let Atlas see you mooning over her like that," Levi warns, though his tone is more amused than concerned. "He's still pretending to be the responsible adult of this operation."

As if summoned by his name, Atlas charges into the office. The effect would be more intimidating if I hadn't seen him dancing in his boxers to '80s pop music just last week.

"While you two are drooling over Emma," he begins without preamble. "Remember she specifically told us she's not looking for an Alpha, let alone three."

I exchange a knowing glance with Levi. "Right, because you weren't flirting with her every second you were next to her."

Atlas runs his fingers through his already disheveled hair. "Fuck, okay," he concedes. "She's... affecting all of us, but we need to respect her boundaries. She just got out of a bad relationship, she was in a fire, and now she's living with three Alphas who are all..." He gestures vaguely.

"Who all want to bend her over the nearest flat surface?" I suggest helpfully.

The look Atlas gives me could wither plants.

"Who all need to remember she's not just some Omega. She's Emma. She deserves better than being treated like a piece of meat."

There's a moment of silence as his words sink in. He's right, of course. Emma isn't just any Omega. She's smart, talented, funny, vulnerable in ways that make my chest ache, and stronger than she gives herself credit for.

"You're right," I acknowledge. Though I can't resist adding, "But have you seen her ass in those sleep shorts? I caught a peek at it last night in the hallway. Because holy fu—"

"River," Atlas growls.

"Fine, fine," I concede with a grin. "So what's the plan for today? Besides all of us taking cold showers and practicing restraint?"

Atlas's posture relaxes slightly. "River, I need you to head out to the burned cabin on my behalf, as I have another call I have to attend. Police are meeting you there to go over the scene again. Use that eagle eye of yours for anything that might point to how the fire started."

I nod, already mentally shifting gears. Fire investigation has always been one of my strengths.

"Levi, you're with me," Atlas continues. "We've got a job about a strange chemical smell at the local post office. Probably nothing, but—"

"Better safe than sorry," Levi finishes for him.

Ten minutes later, I'm sliding into my Jeep Wrangler Rubicon—lifted, mud tires, light bar on top, the works. It's loud, impractical for anything, and drinks gas like I drink tequila, but I don't give a damn. After years of having nothing to call my own, I'd splurged on something that matched the wild energy I could never quite tame. Something that could take me deeper into the wilderness I loved, faster and rougher than anything sensible.

I'm backing out of the station parking lot when I spot Claire hustling toward me, clipboard in hand. Great. What did I forget this time?

Claire volunteers at the station three days a week, helping with administrative tasks. She's attractive in an obvious way, with careful makeup and expensive clothes that show just enough skin to be distracting without crossing into unprofessional territory. She's also had a transparent crush on all three of us since she started six months ago.

Under normal circumstances, I'd have no issue with the attention. She's pretty, available, and enthusiastic, but something about her has always felt... calculated. As if she's auditioning for a role rather than being genuinely interested in any of us as people.

I roll down my window as she approaches, pasting

on my professional smile. "Morning, Claire. What's up?"

"Hi, River," she chirps, leaning to rest her arms on my door, giving me a deliberate view down her blouse. "I was wondering how Emma's doing, seeing as she's moved in with you three. Is she planning to stay in town long?"

The fact that she's asking about Emma, again, sends a little warning flare up my spine.

"She's fine," I say, keeping my tone light but offering nothing more.

"Oh, good," Claire replies. "It must be nice having a female around your place. Bet she's making herself right at home, huh?"

There's something in her tone, a hint of jealousy poorly disguised as casual interest, that makes my protective instincts bristle.

"I should get going," I say instead of answering. "Police are waiting."

I start to roll up my window but pause it halfway. Something compels me to turn back to her.

"Claire," I say, all pretense of casualness gone from my voice. "You're an amazing volunteer here, and you've always had our backs, but don't think that makes it okay to try to scare Emma away from us. Be careful."

Her constructed facade slips for just a moment before she recovers.

"So you do like her," she says softly. "All of you."

I study her face, seeing the genuine hurt beneath

the calculation, and feel a twinge of sympathy. Claire isn't a bad person, just insecure and overly invested in a fantasy that was never going to materialize.

"Everyone will find their perfect match eventually," I tell her, gentling my tone. "It just takes time and patience to recognize them when they appear."

She nods, stepping back from my car with a forced smile. "Thanks for the fortune cookie wisdom, River."

As I drive away, I catch a final glimpse of her in my rearview mirror, standing alone in the parking lot, looking smaller than before.

"Fuck me, I sounded like damn Atlas," I mutter to myself, revving the engine as I hit the open road. "What is wrong with me?"

The answer comes immediately—Emma. She's what's wrong with me. Or right with me. After just a few days, she's managed to burrow under my skin in a way no one has in years. The way she laughs without restraint when something genuinely amuses her. How she gets this tiny crease between her eyebrows when she's concentrating. The steely backbone beneath her softness.

Twenty minutes later, I park down the road from the burned remains of Pinecrest Cabin #3. Yellow police tape surrounds the blackened skeleton of what was once a charming rental. Looking at it in daylight, Emma was lucky to get out alive. The damage is extensive, the structure nearly gutted, yet half the front wall and door remain almost intact, even if slightly charred.

I park and check my watch. The cops are, unsurprisingly, late. Again.

"They'd better not fucking stand me up," I grumble, drumming my fingers on the steering wheel. "Fourth time this month."

To kill time, I pull out my phone and scroll to Emma's name in my contacts. We exchanged numbers this morning—for emergencies, she insisted—though the way she'd programmed hers into my phone had been adorably telling.

I hesitate only a moment before hitting Call. It rings twice, and her voice comes through, slightly breathless.

"River? Is everything okay?"

"Everything's fine," I reassure her quickly. "Just checking in. How's life in the tower?"

"Amazing, actually," she explains, and I can hear the genuine enthusiasm in her voice. "I haven't been this productive in months. I've written almost three thousand words already this morning."

"Look at you, being all prolific and talented," I tease, settling back in my seat. "What's the secret? Our coffee? The mountain air? My devastating good looks inspiring your romantic hero?"

She snorts, a delightfully undignified sound. "Definitely the coffee. Though the view doesn't hurt."

"Which view are we talking about?" I ask suggestively. "The mountains or the one you got of Levi's abs last night?"

"River!" she gasps, but I can hear the amusement

beneath her feigned outrage. Then she's laughing. "I might need to stay until I finish this book," she muses after a moment. "I forgot what it feels like to write without constantly second-guessing myself."

"Done," I say immediately. "No backsies."

"Did you just say 'backsies'?" she asks, giggling. "What are you, twelve?"

"Mentally? Sometimes. Physically? I've been assured I'm very much a grown man."

"I bet you have," she mutters, and I grin at the flirtatious undercurrent in her voice. "Anyway, all good, as you called?"

"Yep, just checking in on you. That's all. Making sure there are no spiders coming after you for revenge."

"Oh God, don't even joke about that," she groans. "I'm going to have nightmares for weeks."

"You know," I say with deliberate casualness, "Levi's actually pretty good at handling spiders. You're lucky he was there. I would've probably just filmed the whole thing."

There's a moment of silence on her end, and I can practically hear her trying to decide if I'm joking.

"You wouldn't dare."

"Try me," I tease. "It would've gone viral. Hot Omega versus Killer Spider: The Showdown. We could've monetized it, split the profits."

"You're terrible," she says, but I can hear the laugh she's trying to suppress. "And I bet you hounded Levi for details when you two were alone, didn't you?" she asks abruptly.

"To be fair, the guy is solid and didn't spill," I admit, genuinely impressed by Levi's restraint. "What did you do to him? He's never kept a secret from me before."

Her laugh this time is more satisfied, almost smug. "I appealed to his sense of honor."

Still no sign of the police. "So, tell me about this book you're writing. I want to be able to brag that I knew you when."

There's a pause, and I can practically feel her considering how much to share. "It's a fantasy romance," she finally says. "The fifth in my series. This one has a bit more romance in addition to the adventure than the others—my heroine is on a quest to find a magical artifact that can save her kingdom."

"Oh, Atlas mentioned you were writing something about him. Same story or different?" I tease. "Can I be in your story too? I'd make an excellent roguish thief or charming prince."

She laughs. "Do you guys share and talk about everything?"

"Yes," I say, my tone shifting to something more serious. "Every single thing." I pause for effect. "Well, except for what Levi made a promise not to."

"You're so easy to talk to," she says after a moment, her voice softer. "I should probably let you go, though. These words won't write themselves."

"Go create worlds, wordsmith. I'll see you later."

After we hang up, I sit in my car, waiting for the damn cops and thinking about Emma. It's impossible not to imagine what she looks like naked now, especially after Levi's nonanswers and the way she blushed any time the shower incident was mentioned.

Her wet hair would fall down her back, darkened to a rich honey-gold. Water would bead on her skin, trailing down the generous curves. Her breasts would be larger than they appear, spilling over my hands when I cupped them, tipped with rosy nipples that would harden under my touch.

I imagine her on her knees in front of me, those big hazel eyes looking up as her pink lips parted. Or bent over the kitchen counter, her bare ass raised, begging for my hand to come down on it. Emma's legs wrapped around my waist as I fucked her against the wall of the shower, her head thrown back in pleasure, my name a breathless cry on her lips.

My cock throbs painfully against my pants at the mental images. Fuck, I'm getting hard just thinking about her, like some hormonal teenager. If the cops weren't due any minute, I'd seriously consider taking care of this uncomfortable situation right here.

The fantasy refuses to leave as I picture Emma spread across my bed, her hair a golden halo on my pillow. Or Emma riding me, her back arched, those perfect tits bouncing with every move. Emma on all fours, my hands gripping her hips hard enough to leave marks as I thrust into that sweet pussy from behind, claiming her with every inch of me.

Even more intoxicating is the idea of sharing her. Not just taking turns, but all of us together—Atlas holding her down, sucking on her nipples, while I fuck her mouth, Levi buried between her legs. The three of us worshipping every inch of her, driving her to the edge of pleasure over and over until she's limp and satisfied, marked by all of us, claimed completely.

Mine. Ours.

Movement in my peripheral vision jolts me from my increasingly deepening daydream. I lift my gaze toward the burned cabin, where a brunette figure is picking through the charred remains and partial structure of the house. She's slender, dressed in dark jeans and a fitted jacket, moving quickly as she sifts through debris.

I frown, straightening in my seat. That's definitely not a police officer, as there's no cruiser in sight, just a nondescript sedan parked near the cabin that wasn't there when I arrived.

Curiosity piqued, I exit my car, adjust my aching cock, and approach the scene, deliberately making enough noise with my boots on the gravel that I don't startle her. She doesn't notice me immediately, too focused on whatever she's searching for among the ashes.

"Find anything interesting?" I ask casually, keeping my tone friendly.

She jumps, spinning to face me with wide eyes. Up close, she's conventionally pretty, with minimal makeup applied, expensive clothes, and sleek brown hair pulled back in a ponytail.

"This is a closed site," she says, recovering quickly. "You shouldn't be here."

I raise an eyebrow at her audacity. She's the one clearly trespassing, yet she's trying to warn me off?

"I could say the same to you," I reply, gesturing to the police tape we've both ignored. "Looking for something specific?"

"Nothing," she says too quickly. "Just... searching. You should mind your business."

I study her, taking in the tense set of her shoulders and the way her eyes keep darting back to a particular section of the burned cabin. Subtly, I slip my phone from my pocket and snap a few photos of her while pretending to check messages.

"If you tell me what you're looking for, I might be able to help," I offer, stepping closer. "These fire scenes can be dangerous if you don't know what you're doing."

She gives me a more thorough assessment now, her gaze traveling from my boots to my face with growing interest. When she meets my eyes, her expression shifts, a calculated smile replacing her wariness.

"Well, I lost something," she explains, her voice suddenly softer, more inviting. "Dropped it here the other day, and I just need to find it. That's all." She takes a step toward me, head tilting flirtatiously. "But thanks for offering. Maybe we could catch up for a drink later if you're free?"

The transformation is jarring, from defensive to seductive in the span of seconds. It reminds me uncomfortably of myself in my younger years, when charm was a survival strategy rather than a natural expression of personality.

I shrug, noncommittal. Something about this woman makes my instincts flare with caution. "How about I help you first? Hate to see you going through these fire remains alone. Like I said, it can be dangerous."

She steps forward again, close enough now that I can smell her perfume, something expensive and over-powering that makes me want to step back.

"I know what I'm doing," she snaps, then immediately softens her tone, composing her features into something more pleasant. "I mean, I'm being careful."

An uncomfortable silence stretches between us as I study her. The calculation in her eyes, the slight tension in her posture. She's hiding something.

"My name's River," I finally offer, extending a hand.

She hesitates before taking it, her grip too firm, like she's trying to prove something. "Nice to meet you, but I am a bit busy." She withdraws her hand quickly. "So, either yes to drinks later, or please don't waste my time." She turns away, resuming her search by poking through the remains with a stick, deliberately ignoring the police tape that marks this as an active investigation site.

"I can't do that," I say, dropping all pretense of casualness. "Especially since I'm here to investigate what started this fire." I reach out, gently but firmly grasping her arm as she starts to move away. "Unless there's something you want to tell me about this cabin and the fire?"

She glances up, and I feel a slight tremor run through her arm before she controls it.

"I told you," she says, voice tight. "I dropped something here the other day. I know nothing about this stupid fire." She wrenches her arm free with more force than necessary.

"Fair enough," I say, unconvinced but unwilling to escalate the situation without backup. "You got a name? And number... for later, then?"

She stares at me for a long moment, calculation clear in her dark eyes. "Nah, you lost out on that, pretty boy," she finally says, turning away and marching toward her car with quick, angry steps.

I watch her go, memorizing the license plate of her sedan as she drives away. Something isn't right here, but I can't put my finger on exactly what.

Before I can dwell on it further, a police cruiser finally pulls up, nearly an hour late. I sigh, heading back to my car to retrieve my gloves and investigation kit. Whatever that woman was looking for, I intend to find it first.

"So far, we haven't pinpointed exactly where the fire started," I explain to Atlas and Levi back at the station later that afternoon. "Burn patterns give us some clues, but a lot of the structure's collapsed, especially around the eastern wall. We need more hands to move the fallen sections safely and check underneath. Once the cops get back to us and we've got access again with a bigger team, we'll head back out and take another run at it."

Atlas nods, his expression grave. "Any sign of deliberate tampering with the wiring?"

"Nothing obvious," I admit. "Old cabins with some signs of rodent wear on the wiring, as you'd expect in any place, but nothing to start a fire. So I doubt it was that. Something started the fire on the ground floor inside the cabin, I suspect, though. There was some evidence of soot buildup as if it was a candle, but she said she'd blown them all out, so unsure if that was from the fire just consuming candles left behind. But there could be more once we remove the fallen walls."

"Emma was convinced she hadn't left any candles lit," Levi suggests.

I sigh and lean back in my chair, throwing my feet up on the desk despite Atlas's disapproving glare.

"And then there was this woman poking around the scene before the police arrived. Brunette, about five foot six, expensive clothes, claiming she lost something at the cabin, which was super sus."

"Did she give a name?" Atlas asks, already reaching for his notepad.

"Nope. Got defensive when I pressed, then tried to flirt her way out of the situation. I got her license plate number." I ramble it off.

"I'll run the plates with my contact at the station," Levi says, already typing on his laptop. "Should have a name soon enough."

"The police want to talk to Emma again tomorrow morning," I add. "Ask her a few more questions about the night of the fire. I told them we'd bring her in."

Atlas nods. "We can take her to the festival afterward, maybe. Help take her mind off things if the interview stresses her out."

"Great plan," I agree. "Nothing helps you forget about a potentially suspicious fire like fried food and carnival games. Plus, I make it my mission every year to win at least one of those rigged shooting games. This year, I can win her one of those giant stuffed animals."

Atlas rolls his eyes, but there's fondness in the gesture. "You just like showing off."

"Damn right I do," I agree shamelessly. "And I'm good at it."

Levi looks up from his laptop suddenly, his expression uncharacteristically troubled. "What if she did accidentally start the fire?" he asks quietly. "A candle tipping over, or maybe something electrical she plugged in with hope that the power would come back on?"

The question lands like a stone in still water,

rippling through the room and changing the atmosphere instantly.

Atlas straightens, his protective instincts visibly kicking in. "If that's the case, we'll handle it. Accidents happen."

"But legally speaking," Levi continues, ever the logical one, "she could be facing serious liability issues. Property damage, insurance fraud accusations if they think she did it intentionally—"

"That's not going to happen," I interrupt, all traces of joking gone from my voice. "Even if it was an accident, we'll make sure she's protected."

Atlas nods firmly. "We have connections in this town. People trust our assessment. If we say it was an accident, they'll believe us."

"And if the evidence suggests otherwise?" Levi asks.

"Then we find other evidence," I say simply. "I'm not letting her get railroaded for a mistake anyone could make."

Atlas gives me a measuring look. "This isn't just about wanting to get her into bed, is it?"

I meet his gaze steadily. "No. It's not." And I'm surprised by how true that is. Yes, I want her, desperately, but it's more than that. I want to see her smile, hear her laugh, watch her face light up when she talks. I want to be the one she calls when she's scared or happy or just needs someone to listen.

"For any of us," Levi adds softly.

We fall silent, each lost in our own thoughts. The

only sound is the occasional tapping of Levi's fingers on his keyboard. Outside, the sun slants through the blinds, casting stripes of light across the floor.

Atlas leans back in his chair, staring at the ceiling. "Do you think we're moving too quickly with her?" he asks finally, voice quiet but intent. "It's only been a few days."

The question hangs in the air between us.

Levi stops typing, considering as he lifts his chin. "Depends on each individual."

"When it comes to Alphas finding their Omega mates, not really," I counter, spinning a pen between my fingers.

"She's different," Atlas says, not looking at either of us. "This feels... real." He's rubbing his hand over his face. "We're smitten with an Omega who explicitly told us she wants no Alphas." He looks between Levi and me, his expression troubled. "Are we setting ourselves up for something bad here? Heartbreak?"

I've never seen Atlas look so uncertain. Our natural leader, always so sure of every decision, now questioning if we're heading straight for disaster. Levi is quiet, but I can see the tension in his shoulders, the way his fingers tap a pattern only he understands against the table.

"Fuck that," I say, standing up abruptly. I can't sit still with this energy coursing through me. "We are going to make her ours, and she will see that soon enough."

Atlas raises an eyebrow. "River—"

"No," I cut him off. "I know what you're going to say. That we need to be patient, respectful, give her space. And yes, we do. But that doesn't mean we can't also show her exactly what she'd be getting with us."

"He's right," Levi says, surprising us both. "Emma's been hurt. She's guarding herself against more pain. But what if we could show her that what we're offering is nothing like what she's experienced before?"

I nod emphatically. "Exactly. We'll respect her boundaries while making it damn clear that when she's ready, we'll be waiting."

"All three of us," Atlas murmurs slowly.

"All three of us," Levi confirms.

"Together," I add, a wicked grin spreading across my face. "We'll show her what it means to be claimed by a pack who worships her."

Atlas and Levi exchange a look, and I know they're on board. Whatever it takes, however long it takes—Emma is going to be ours.

And God help anyone who tries to get in our way.

"I want this," I say simply, looking from Atlas to Levi. "I want her. I want us, all of us, together."

Levi nods, solemn but with that intensity that burns behind his careful facade. "So do I."

"Then we're agreed," Atlas says, a slow smile spreading across his face. "Now we just have to convince her."

I can't help but laugh. "Piece of fucking cake."

13

EMMA

The colors of the sunset outside the watchtower are almost unreal. Oranges and pinks bleeding into purples so deep that they look like bruises against the darkening sky. From the watchtower balcony, the view stretches for miles, forest rolling out like a dark green sea beneath us. As night creeps in, the shadows deepen between the trees.

I cradle my mug of hot chocolate between my palms, letting the heat seep into my fingers. The marshmallows have melted into a gooey cloud on top, just the way I like it. The iron stove in the tower room crackles and pops, throwing shadows across the faces of the three Alphas lounging around me.

It should feel awkward, this domestic scene with men I've known for less than a week. Instead, it feels disturbingly comfortable, as though I've somehow stumbled into a life that was waiting for me all along.

That thought alone is enough to send anxiety spiraling through my chest.

"So," I begin, trying to keep my voice casual despite the knot of dread in my stomach. "Should I be worried about this police interview tomorrow?"

My right knee bounces nervously. Atlas, sitting beside me on the oversized couch, places a warm hand on my bare knee, stilling it instantly. The weight of his palm sends an electric current up my thigh that I desperately try to ignore.

"Not at all," he says, voice steady and reassuring. "It's standard procedure for them to conduct follow-up interviews for any structural fire. They just want to go over your statement again, see if you remember any additional details now that you've had time to process."

Levi nods from his position by the window. "Police reports show a statistical increase in accurate recall after a seventy-two-hour buffer period following traumatic events."

"We'll drive you there and wait for you," River adds. "Support you no matter what happens."

"You can't come in with me?" The question slips out before I can stop it, revealing more vulnerability than I intended.

Atlas shakes his head. "They'll want to speak with you privately. Standard protocol."

My stomach clenches painfully. What if they twist my words around? What if they don't believe me?

What if I accidentally say something that makes me sound guilty?

"Hey," River says. "You look like someone just told you dragons are real and they're coming for your chocolate stash."

I force a smile that feels more like a grimace. "Just nervous about being interrogated. That's all."

"It's not an interrogation," Levi clarifies. "In cases like yours where there's no evidence of foul play, these follow-ups are merely formalities."

"Right," I say, though the reassurance does little to calm the riot of worst-case scenarios playing out in my head. What if they've found evidence that contradicts my statement? What if they think I deliberately set the fire for insurance money? What if I somehow left a candle lit? What if they arrest me on the spot?

God, I can't go to jail. I'd never survive it. I'd be the world's worst inmate—I can't even handle spiders in the shower, let alone whatever horrors prison holds.

"Emma," Atlas says quietly, somehow reading the spiral of my thoughts. "I promise you, there's nothing to worry about."

Easy for him to say. He's not the one whose entire life went up in flames, literally, and now has to convince the authorities he had nothing to do with it.

"On a scale of one to completely screwed," I ask, trying to inject some humor into my voice. "How bad would it be if I just skipped town tonight? I hear Canada is lovely this time of year."

River snorts. "About a twelve on your scale. Fleeing

before questioning tends to scream 'guilty as hell' to the authorities."

"Besides," Atlas adds, giving my knee a gentle squeeze. "We'd just have to come find you and bring you back."

The casual way he says it, as if it's a foregone conclusion that they would chase me down, sends an unexpected thrill through me. I push the feeling away, trying to focus on the actual issue at hand.

"We'll be right outside the whole time of your interview," Levi assures me. "And if there's any problem, which there won't be, my cousin works in the DA's office. We have connections."

The quiet confidence in his voice, the absolute certainty that they'll protect me, loosens something tight in my chest. It's been so long since I've had anyone in my corner like this, not since Gran died.

"Thanks," I say, looking down at my mug. "For everything. The room, the clothes, letting me stay here... especially after I barged into your lives like some disaster movie heroine."

"Best disaster we've ever had," River quips with a wink.

A comfortable silence falls, broken only by the crackling of the fire and the distant hooting of an owl. The last sliver of sun disappears beyond the horizon, leaving us in the warm glow of the iron stove and a few strategically placed lamps.

"Can I ask you something?" Levi says suddenly,

drawing all our attention, yet he's staring at me. "What happened to make you not want an Alpha? Not that we're pressuring you," he adds quickly. "I'm just curious."

The question catches me off guard, though I'm not sure why. I've been waiting for one of them to ask for more details since that first day when I'd made it clear I wasn't looking for any Alpha attachments. I shrug, nibbling on my lower lip as my mind spins through possible answers. I could deflect, make a joke, and change the subject. The guys are all watching me, but none of them push, which I appreciate more than they realize.

"Hey, it's all good," River says after a moment, clearly sensing my hesitation. "No deep, dark secrets required."

Something about his easy acceptance makes me want to answer truthfully. Maybe it's the hot chocolate warming my insides, the coziness of this tower sanctuary, or just the genuine kindness these three have shown me. Whatever it is, I find myself wanting to be honest, even if it makes me look pathetic.

"It's nothing exciting," I say finally. "Just... a pattern I'd rather not repeat." I pause, gathering my thoughts, and none of them rush to fill the silence.

"I don't want to be hurt again," I admit, my voice smaller than I intended. "Rejection just breaks you down after a while, and I'm tired of feeling less than. Of losing my self-confidence every time another Alpha tells me I'm not good enough."

The words flow like a dam breaking after years of pressure.

"My first boyfriend in college told me my scent was too bookish, and it wasn't sexy enough for him. The next one said I was too independent for an Omega and that Alphas want someone who needs them more." My laugh is hollow, even to my own ears. "Then there was the guy who said I was too passionate about my writing, and it made him feel secondary. Oh, and let's not forget the one who said I was pretty enough but not quite what he was looking for in a mate." I swallow hard, horrified to feel tears pricking at the corners of my eyes.

"The latest, my ex, Chad, told me he wasn't attracted to me anymore, and my scent was *wrong*. As if I'd somehow gone bad, like milk left out too long." I blink rapidly, refusing to let the tears fall.

"And I don't want you to tell me none of these things are true, because, trust me, I tell myself that. But that part of me inside still holds on to those damn words like a lifeline, and I hate it. Hate myself for it. Because I let them get under my skin."

The silence that follows my outburst feels heavy. I chance a glance up and find all three men watching me with almost frozen expressions.

"Well, those guys sound like complete assholes." River is the first to break the silence.

"Grade-A fuckheads," Levi blurts.

"Fucking idiots," Atlas growls, his hand on my knee tightening slightly. "Every last one of them."

I laugh, a watery sound that threatens to turn into a sob. "You don't have to say that. I know I'm a mess. Too emotional, too independent, too everything."

"No," Atlas says firmly. "They were wrong, Emma. All of them."

"You don't know that," I counter, my defenses rising automatically. "You barely know me."

"I know enough," he insists. "I know you're brave enough to survive a burning building. You're talented enough to have published multiple books. You're strong enough to stand on your own feet, even when you're still shaking inside."

I blink at him, surprised by the force in his voice.

"I know," River adds, "that you have the best laugh I've ever heard. And that you're smart enough to keep up with Levi's nerd talk, which is, frankly, impressive."

"And I know," Levi says quietly, "that your scent is the most perfectly balanced combination of components I've ever encountered. The precise ratio of honey to vanilla to paper creates an olfactory harmony that's mathematically elegant. You're perfect."

I stare at them, speechless. They all seem so sincere, so earnest in their defense of me. It would be easier if they were just being polite, offering empty reassurances. This genuine belief in me is harder to dismiss, harder to protect myself against.

"God," I say, forcing a laugh that sounds brittle, even to my own ears. "You must think I'm such a loser. See? Told you, Atlas. Something's wrong with me that everyone eventually sees." I shove the last of my s'more into my mouth, needing something to do. It's sweet and delicious.

"Emma—" Atlas begins.

"There's nothing wrong with you," River interrupts, leaning forward intently.

"Those Alphas were the problem," Levi states. "Not you."

Atlas shifts beside me, moving closer, but I can't handle whatever comfort he's about to offer. Not when my heart is hammering so painfully against my ribs, not when I feel like I might shatter if anyone speaks too loudly.

"It's okay," I say quickly, cutting them off before they can continue with their well-intentioned reassurances. "You don't need to say anything. I'm saving you all from me, from your future selves feeling like you're stuck with me."

My face burns with humiliation. Why did I say all that? Why did I lay myself bare to three men I hardly know, men who've shown me nothing but kindness and are now witnessing me at my most pathetic?

"Anyway," I say, standing abruptly. "I just need some fresh air."

I set my empty mug on the small table and head for the balcony door, desperate to escape the weight of their gazes. The night air hits me like a blessing, cool against my flushed skin. I move to the darkest part of the wraparound balcony, where the shadows are thickest, and lean against the railing.

Behind me, I can hear the murmur of male voices,

too low to make out words. Probably discussing what a disaster I am and how they can politely ask me to find other accommodation now that they've seen the emotional wreckage beneath my attempts at normalcy.

Great job, Emma. You couldn't hold it back just a bit longer while stuck in this town? I scrub a hand across my eyes, angry at the wetness I find there. And the pity is, I really like it here. The tower, the town, and yes, the three men who are growing on me in ways that terrify me to my core.

Which is dangerous. So dangerous. The path to getting hurt again is paved with thoughts exactly like these.

I stare out at the dark forest stretching before me. In the distance, a wolf howls, the sound echoed by others farther away. It's haunting and beautiful and somehow perfectly matches the ache in my chest.

A floorboard creaks behind me, and I stiffen, quickly wiping my eyes. *Be cool, Emma. Remember what Jason said—Alphas don't like emotional Omegas. Too needy. Too much work.*

I hear my grandmother's voice in my head, gentle but firm as always. "A true Alpha will want all sides of you, firefly. The laughter and the tears, the strength and the vulnerability. Don't settle for less."

Well, I clearly haven't met those Alphas in my past.

I turn, expecting to find all three, but it's only Atlas. Through the glass walls of the tower, I can see that the living area is empty now. Levi and River must have gone downstairs.

Atlas joins me at the railing, standing close but not touching, his gaze fixed on the forest below us. He says nothing for a long moment, and surprisingly, the silence isn't uncomfortable. The breeze ruffles his dark hair, carrying his scent.

"Did you know," he finally says, voice low and steady, "that there are three wolf packs living in these woods? In winter, when food is scarce, they sometimes come quite close to town. We've had to scare them away a few times."

I appreciate the neutral topic, the chance to gather myself. "Are they dangerous?"

"Not usually to humans. They're more interested in easier prey. But they're territorial with each other. Each pack has its own section of the forest, and they defend their boundaries fiercely." He points to the north. "The largest pack lives that way, near the ridge-line. Sometimes at night, you can hear them calling to each other."

As if on cue, another howl rises from the darkness, sending a shiver down my spine.

"They mate for life, you know," he continues, still not looking at me. "Once they choose, that's it. Even if something happens to their mate, some never choose another."

I'm not sure why he's telling me this, but I find myself oddly captivated by the low rumble of his voice, the way it seems to blend with the night sounds around us.

He turns to face me. "It's okay to be scared if you've been hurt."

The abrupt shift in topic catches me off guard.

"I've avoided Omegas since my ex, Caitlin, cleaned out my bank account and disappeared a year ago."

I blink in surprise. Of all the things I expected him to say, this wasn't it.

"I thought she was it for me," he continues, a muscle in his jaw clenching. "We were together for nearly a year. She was... everything I thought I wanted. Beautiful, sweet, seemed to understand me better than anyone had before."

"I'm so sorry," I murmur.

"Looking back, there were signs I should have seen. The way she never answered my calls but always expected me to answer hers. How she only seemed to call when she wanted something. The way she'd push for things, like a shared bank account to save for our future, but always had excuses for why she wasn't ready to move in together."

He laughs, a bitter sound I haven't heard from him before.

"I was so fucking blind. So desperate to believe I'd found my mate that I ignored every red flag. Then, one day, I came home to find her gone. No note, no explanation. Years of savings gone."

"Atlas, that's horrible," I whisper, genuinely horrified.

He shrugs, but I can see the tension in his shoulders.

"For months, I kept expecting her to come back. To explain that it was all a misunderstanding, that she needed the money for some emergency. Even after I knew better, even after I accepted that she'd played me for a fool, part of me still missed her. How fucked up is that?"

I reach out without thinking, placing my hand on his arm. "It's not fucked up. You loved her. That doesn't just disappear because she betrayed you."

He looks down at my hand on his arm and then back up to my face.

"My point is, I understand being wary. Being afraid to trust again. Being afraid to believe what's right in front of you because you've been burned before."

The sharpness in his blue eyes makes my breath catch.

"But I don't think you're cursed, Emma. I think you're incredible. Brave and brilliant and so goddamn beautiful that any Alpha who turns his back on you is a fucking idiot who deserves to have his knot shrivel up and fall off."

The fire in his voice startles a surprised laugh out of me.

"I'm serious," he continues, eyes flashing. "Those pathetic excuses for Alphas who hurt you? Those worthless pieces of shit who made you doubt yourself? I want names. Addresses. I'll find every last one of those cocksuckers and make them regret the day they made you feel less than the incredible Omega you are."

"Wow," I say, both alarmed and oddly touched by his ferocity. "I'm quite liking this side of you."

Something shifts between us then, the air suddenly heavy. My heart beats faster, and I know I should step back and put some distance between us before this goes somewhere I'm not ready for.

A sudden movement overhead makes me glance up just as a massive bat swoops low over the balcony. I let out a small shriek, not my finest moment, and instinctively leap forward. My hands land flat against Atlas's chest, his arms coming around me automatically, holding me steady against him.

For a moment, we're both frozen, staring at each other. I sense his heart pounding beneath my fingers, matching the frantic thump of my own.

"Just a bat," he murmurs, but he doesn't loosen his hold.

I should step back. I know I should. But the heat of him, the solid strength of his body against mine, makes it impossible to move away.

"Why do I always feel safe around you?" The question slips out.

"I'm a protector." One of his hands slides up my back, coming to rest at the nape of my neck. "Haven't you noticed?"

He slips his other hand under my chin, tilting my face up until our eyes meet. Something molten and dangerous flares in those midnight depths, something that makes my pulse race.

"Nothing's going to happen," I whisper, even as I sway closer to him.

"That so?" he murmurs, his thumb brushing across my lower lip in a touch so featherlight that it might be my imagination.

"We both know better," I continue, my voice betraying me by dropping to a husky whisper.

"Speak for yourself," he counters, his face dipping closer to mine. "I don't have that kind of willpower where you're concerned."

Then his mouth is on mine, and any pretense of restraint evaporates like morning mist under a blazing sun.

This isn't a gentle first kiss. It's ravenous, consuming, as if he's been starving for the taste of me. His lips claim mine with a possessive hunger that makes my knees buckle and my mind go blissfully blank. One hand cradles the back of my head, fingers tangling in my hair, while the other splays across my lower back, pressing me closer until there's not even air between us.

I should pull away, but my body rebels against all logic, my hands sliding up his chest to the back of his neck, holding him to me as if I'm afraid he'll vanish if I let go.

He tastes like chocolate, woodsmoke, and sin, a combination that makes my head spin and my body burn. His tongue traces the seam of my lips, seeking entrance, and I open to him with a soft whimper that would embarrass me if I had any capacity for shame left.

The kiss deepens and turns molten. His tongue strokes against mine in a way that has me moaning against him. I'm drowning in sensation, in the heat of his body against mine, in the way his hands seem to brand me through my clothes.

When we break apart, he doesn't go far. His forehead rests against mine, both of us breathing hard, his hands now framing my face as if I'm something precious he can't bear to release.

"That was…" I try to find words but fail spectacularly. "A mistake?" I suggest, pulse still racing.

He shakes his head, eyes locked on mine. "Not even close. That was inevitable. I've been fighting it since the moment I sat next to you on the plane."

"This is a bad idea," I say, though my body screams otherwise. "I'm not looking for—"

"An Alpha. I know." His thumbs stroke my cheekbones, gentle despite the hunger still evident in his gaze. "But sometimes, what we're not looking for is exactly what the universe gives us."

Before I can form a response, he backs me against the railing, caging me with his arms on either side. The position should make me feel trapped. Instead, I feel strangely protected, sheltered from everything but him.

"If you were mine," he says with an almost growl, "I would tear down the fucking world if it made you doubt yourself for even a second. Would brand my claim on every inch of you until you couldn't remember the names of any man who came before me. Would worship your body, your mind, until you never questioned your worth again."

His words send liquid heat coursing through me, pooling low in my belly and between my thighs, where I'm already embarrassingly wet. Every Omega instinct I possess is screaming at me to submit, to offer my throat, to let this powerful Alpha claim me completely.

I fight it, fight the pull of biology and desire alike.

"Big promises, Chief, but I've heard pretty words before."

His head tilts to the side at the challenge in my tone. "I don't make promises I can't keep, Emma. And I don't just use pretty words." He leans closer, his breath warm against my ear. "I use actions. Would you like me to show you?"

God help me, I would. Despite every warning bell clanging in my head, despite all my promises to myself, I rise up on my toes and press my mouth to his again.

This time, there's no hesitation on either side. His hands slide down to my hips, lifting me effortlessly until I'm sitting on the railing, my legs parting instinctively to make room for him between them. The position brings us perfectly aligned, his hardness pressing against the core of me through our clothes, and I can't suppress the moan that escapes me.

His mouth leaves mine to trail fire down my jaw to my neck, where my pulse hammers beneath my skin. When he nips gently, then soothes the sting with his tongue, I nearly combust on the spot.

"You taste even better than you smell," he murmurs against my throat, his stubble creating delicious friction against my sensitive skin. "And you smell like fucking heaven."

"Atlas," I gasp as his hands slide under my sweater, calloused palms skimming over my ribs, thumbs brushing the undersides of my breasts through my bra. "We shouldn't—"

"Tell me to stop," he challenges, pulling back just enough to meet my eyes. "Tell me you don't want this, and I'll walk away right now."

I open my mouth, but the lie won't come. I do want this. Desperate for him.

He seems to read the surrender in my eyes. With a growl, he captures my mouth again, kissing me until I'm dizzy with desire.

Then, to my shock, he pulls me off the railing and onto my feet. He drops to his knees before me, looking up with such naked hunger that I nearly come undone on the spot.

"Let me taste you," he says, hands sliding up my thighs, pushing my skirt higher. "Let me show you how an Alpha should adore his Omega."

The possessive growl in his voice should terrify me. Instead, it sends a fresh flood of wetness between my legs, my body betraying my mind's caution with enthusiastic abandon.

"Someone could see," I protest weakly, even as I lean back slightly, giving him better access.

His smile is pure sin. "We're in the middle of nowhere, surrounded by forest. But if the idea of being watched excites you..." He leaves the suggestion hanging, his eyes gleaming with wicked promise.

"You're incorrigible," I gasp.

"I'm thorough," he corrects, pressing a kiss to my inner thigh, just above my knee. "And attentive." Another kiss, higher. "And very, very determined to make you forget every Alpha who came before me."

His hands slide higher, thumbs tracing circles on my inner thighs, each pass bringing him closer to where I'm aching for his touch. My head falls back, a whimper escaping me as he teases, approaching but never quite reaching where I burn for him the most.

"Atlas," I plead, beyond pride now. "Please."

"Please what, Emma?" His breath is hot against my most intimate place, only the thin cotton of my underwear separating us. "Tell me what you need."

"You," I gasp, hands fisting in his hair. "Your mouth. Please, I can't... I need..."

He growls with satisfaction, hooking his fingers into the waistband of my underwear and drawing them down my legs with agonizing slowness. The cool night air against my heated flesh makes me gasp, but it's nothing compared to the shock of his mouth on me, bare and intimate and devastating in its skill.

"Oh God," I moan as his tongue pushes between my folds, flicking across my clit. "Atlas, that's... fuck..." I grasp the railing behind me with a death grip, holding on, my knees melting as he nudges my legs wider, pressing himself closer, deeper.

He hums against me, the vibration sending shock waves of arousal through my body. My thighs tremble, threatening to give out, but his strong hands hold me steady.

"So responsive," he murmurs, pulling back just enough to look up at me as he bunches up my skirt, driving it up to my waist and tucking it in at the band so he can see me. His lips glisten with evidence of my slickness. "So fucking perfect. You taste like honey and sin."

Before I can respond, his mouth is on me again, more insistent now. His tongue circles my clit while one thick finger teases my entrance before pushing inside.

The sensation is overwhelming. I bite my lip to keep from crying out, my hips moving of their own accord, seeking more.

"Don't hold back," Atlas commands, adding a second finger alongside the first, stretching me deliciously. "Let me hear you. I want to know exactly what you like."

"Everything," I gasp, beyond coherent thought now. "Fuck, you're doing everything right... Just don't stop. Please don't stop."

He increases his pace, crooking his fingers inside

me to hit the spot that makes stars explode behind my eyes while his tongue works relentlessly against my clit. The pressure builds, higher and higher, my body drawing tight as a bowstring.

"That's it," he encourages, his voice rough with desire. "Come all over my mouth, coat my hand in your sweet juices, Emma. Let go. Show me how good I make you feel."

His words, combined with the twist of his fingers and the firm press of his tongue, send me hurtling over the edge. I come with a cry that echoes across the night, my body convulsing around his fingers as the most incredible orgasm crashes through me in waves.

Almost immediately, a chorus of wolf howls rises from the distant forest, the wild sound mingling with my gasps as I ride out the aftershocks.

Atlas stays with me through every tremor, gentling his touch but not stopping until I'm a quivering, over-sensitive mess above him. Only then does he pull away, pressing one final kiss to my inner thigh before rising to his feet, snatching my underwear in the process, and shoving them into his pocket. His gaze meets mine, glittering in the darkness, pupils so wide there's only a thin ring of blue around them.

"That," he murmurs, tucking a strand of hair behind my ear with unexpected tenderness, "was the most magnificent fucking thing I've ever seen and tasted."

I stare at him, still trembling from the force of my

release, wondering how this man, this Alpha I've known for less than a week, has reduced me to my most elemental self with such ease. In his eyes, I see galaxies, universes.

The reality of what we've just done crashes over me suddenly, bringing with it a wave of panic. What am I doing? This is exactly how it starts... The intoxication, the feeling of being special, unique. And then, inevitably, comes the crash, the moment when they decide I'm not enough after all.

I can't do it again. I can't survive another rejection, especially not from him. Not from any of them. I push down my skirt.

"Hey," Atlas says softly, clearly reading the shift in my expression. "Stay with me."

"I-I can't," I stammer, though every cell in my body screams at me to do just that, to see where this could lead.

"Yes, you can," he counters, his hand cupping my face. "Whatever you're thinking right now, whatever doubts are creeping in, they're lying to you."

For one breathless moment, I consider believing him. Consider letting myself fall into whatever this is, consequences be damned.

But then I remember the hollow feeling in my chest after Chad, after Jason, after all the others. Remember how each rejection chipped away at something fundamental inside me until I barely recognized myself.

"If I stay," I whisper, the truth of it burning in my

throat. "If I let myself have this, have you… I'll never recover when it ends."

"Who says it has to end?" The certainty in his voice is almost enough to convince me.

Almost.

With a force of will I didn't know I possessed, I slip from the railing and step to the side, putting precious space between us.

"Good night, Atlas."

Before he can respond, before I can change my mind, I hurry around the balcony to the stairs. I take them carefully in the dim lighting, my legs still unsteady from what just happened.

I rush through the living area of the house, past Levi and River, who are chatting in the kitchen. They both look up as I enter, and something in my appearance—flushed cheeks, mussed hair, the scent of arousal I'm sure they can detect—makes their conversation halt abruptly.

"Everything okay?" River asks, concern evident in his voice.

"Fine," I manage, aiming for casual and missing by a mile. "Just tired. Good night, boys." I don't wait for their responses, just continue to my room on legs that still feel like jelly. Once inside, I close the door and lean against it, my heart hammering in my chest.

"Oh God," I whisper to the empty room. "What did I do? Why did I do that?"

But even as panic and regret swirl through me, I can't deny the truth—it was the most amazing thing

I've ever felt. His mouth, his tongue, the way he looked at me like I was something precious, something worthy.

I slide down the door until I'm sitting on the floor, knees pulled to my chest.

I'm in so much trouble.

14

EMMA

I step out of the police station into the blinding mid-morning sunshine, hands still shaking from the hour-long interview. The detective's questions loop through my mind like a broken record. "Did you leave any candles burning? Any electrical devices on? Could you have accidentally knocked something over? Did you have any visitors over?"

No. No. No. No.

At least, I don't think so. But now doubt has crept in, worming its way through my certainty. I'm almost positive I blew out the candles before bed. Almost.

God, what if this was all my fault?

"Emma."

I glance up to find Atlas, Levi, and River waiting at the bottom of the steps. The sight of them, these three Alphas who've inserted themselves into my life with alarming speed, sends a jolt of something hot and primal through me that I desperately try to ignore.

Except right now, I couldn't be more relieved that they are waiting for me and I'm not alone.

"Hey," I manage, forcing a smile as I descend the stairs. "You guys didn't have to wait. I feel bad. You must have work to do."

"We took the day off," Atlas admits, both hands tucked into the pockets of his jeans. He stands there so casually, as if he's stepped straight out of a men's fashion magazine, looking entirely too intoxicating for my peace of mind. After last night's... explosion between us on the balcony, I can barely look at him without blushing furiously.

"All of you?" I ask, surprised.

River shrugs, offering me an easy grin. "The town hasn't burned down yet. We figured it could survive one more day."

"We wanted you to know you're not alone," Levi adds, giving me a wicked grin.

Something tight in my chest loosens at their words. It's been so long since any guy has shown up for me like this, not just offering help but actually being present when I need it.

"How did it go?" Atlas asks.

I shrug, trying for nonchalance. "Fine, I think? They asked about a thousand questions, made me go through everything step by step."

River slings an arm around my shoulders. "And now that the boring police stuff is done, we have plans."

"You said yesterday that we're going to the

Founders Festival?" I'm aware of the heat pouring from him as he's pressed against my side. What's wrong with me today? It's like every nerve ending in my body is dialed up to eleven.

"Yep," Levi answers with a small smile. "Best event of the year. And you, Emma, are our guest of honor."

"I don't know..." I begin hesitantly. All I really want is to crawl back into my nest-bed and process everything—the interview, the growing suspicion that I might have caused the fire, and the increasingly urgent heat that's been building in my core since I woke up this morning, slick with sweat and aching with need.

"Not optional," River announces cheerfully, steering me toward Atlas's truck parked at the curb. "Doctor's orders."

"You're a wildfire specialist who did a first aid course, not a doctor," Levi points out.

"Close enough." River dismisses him with a wave. "The prescription is funnel cake, carnival games, and at least one ride that makes you question your life choices."

Despite my misgivings, I find myself laughing. "Fine. But if I throw up after whatever death trap you put me on, I'm aiming for your shoes."

"Fair enough," River agrees with a wink.

We pile into Atlas's truck, with me sandwiched between Levi and River in the back seat because of the equipment River insisted on shoving into the front seat. The close quarters mean I'm pressed against both of them from shoulder to knee, their combined body heat making me feel almost feverish. I try to focus on the scenery outside the window, but I'm acutely aware of every shift, every breath from the Alphas surrounding me.

The drive to the festival grounds is mercifully short. As we pull into the designated parking area, I catch a full glimpse of the Founders Festival, and despite everything, a childlike excitement bubbles up inside me.

The main street of Whispering Grove has been transformed into an explosion of color and activity. Banners and fairy lights stretch between lampposts, booths line both sides of the street, and the air is filled with the mingled scents of fried foods, sugar, and people everywhere. In the distance, I spot carnival rides rising above the buildings, a Ferris wheel slowly turning against the backdrop of mountains and forest.

"Wow," I breathe, genuinely impressed. "The town really goes all out."

"Told you," Atlas states. "This festival keeps most of the businesses in town afloat. We don't do anything halfway."

As soon as we're out of the truck, River grabs my hand, tugging me toward the main entrance. "Come on! If we time it right, we can hit all the best food stands before the lunch rush."

I let myself be pulled along, laughing at his enthusiasm. Levi and Atlas follow behind us.

The next few hours pass in a colorful blur. River insists we start with food, leading us on a tour of his favorite stands. We share paper boats of crispy fries topped with melted cheese, corn dogs dipped in honey mustard, and slices of pizza loaded with toppings I can't even identify.

"You have to try this," Levi says, holding out a lopsided funnel cake drowning in powdered sugar and strawberry sauce.

I take an obedient bite and nearly moan as the sweet, fried dough melts on my tongue. "Oh my God," I mumble around the mouthful. "That's dangerous."

"The best things usually are," he says with a wink, using his thumb to wipe away a smudge of powdered sugar from the corner of my mouth. The casual touch sends a spark of electricity through me.

What's going on with me? I've never been this sensitive, this reactive, to simple touches.

After food, Atlas leads us to a row of carnival booths.

"Prepare to be amazed," he tells me, rolling up his sleeves as he approaches the shooting gallery.

I try to focus on his words, but my brain short-circuits the second those sleeves go up. His forearms are all muscle and strength, the kind that makes you feel how capable he is. There's just something about a man with rolled-up sleeves that is captivating, casual, and cocky in all the right ways, and apparently, it's my fatal weakness. I'm gawking. Unashamed. Because honestly? A man with his sleeves rolled is a billion times hotter than one without. Don't ask me why. It's primal. It's powerful. And right now, it's all I can do not to drool.

"Humble, isn't he?" Levi murmurs close to my ear, his breath stirring the hair at my temple. I suppress a delicious shiver.

Atlas hands over some tickets and picks up the air rifle, his stance confident and way too damn sexy. I don't even try to hide it as my gaze drops to his ass, perfectly hugged by those tight blue jeans. I watch, oddly mesmerized, as he hits target after target, his focus incredible. There's something undeniably attractive about his concentration.

When he finishes, earning a perfect score, the booth operator grudgingly gestures to a row of over-sized stuffed animals hanging from the ceiling.

"Winner gets to pick a prize," Atlas states, turning to me with a satisfied grin. "Your choice."

I blink, surprised. "For me?"

"Who else?" he says as if it's obvious.

I scan the options, oddly touched by the gesture, and point to a plush wolf with impossibly soft-looking fur. "That one."

The booth operator hands it down, and Atlas presents it to me with a flourish. "Your wolf, my lady."

"Thank you," I say, hugging the silly thing to my chest. It's been years since anyone won me a carnival prize. The last time was probably with my grandmother when I was thirteen.

"My turn," River announces, dragging us toward a strength-test game with a hammer and bell. He makes a show of stretching before taking the hammer, winking at a small group of children watching nearby.

"Witness greatness, kids," he says with theatrical seriousness, then brings the hammer down with impressive force. The puck shoots up the tower and strikes the bell with a satisfying clang. The children cheer, and River takes a mock bow before selecting another stuffed animal, this one a tiger with an improbable purple stripe, and adding it to my collection.

"Not to be outdone," Levi says dryly, leading us to a game involving throwing baseballs at stacked milk bottles.

Unlike the others, Levi takes his time at the game, circling the booth to examine the setup from different angles. His gaze narrows slightly.

His first throw sails just past the edge of the pyramid, missing by mere inches.

"Ohhh, so close!" River calls out, hand cupped around his mouth like a megaphone. "The notorious Levi-first-throw curse strikes again!"

Atlas chuckles, crossing his arms. "Every time. You'd think after five years he'd have figured out he always throws too high on the first shot."

"Says the man who couldn't hit water if he fell out of a boat last year," Levi responds dryly, but there's a spark of competitive fire in his eyes I haven't seen before.

"That was because of the wind!" Atlas protests with mock outrage. "And I had the sun in my eyes."

"It was cloudy, and the booth was covered," River stage-whispers to me, earning a glare from Atlas.

"Twenty bucks says you can't knock them all down with your remaining throws," Atlas challenges, changing the subject.

Levi's mouth quirks up at one corner. "Make it fifty."

"You're on."

I watch, fascinated, as he adjusts his stance ever so slightly. The teasing seems to fuel him rather than throw him off. He takes a measured breath, then releases the second ball with a powerful throw. It connects with the bottom right bottle with a thwack, sending the entire structure wobbling, but three bottles remain standing.

"You got this, Levi," I encourage, bouncing on my toes and hugging the stuffed prizes in my arms.

"Last throw, Wolfe," River singsongs. "No pressure, but Emma needs that stuffed bear to complete her collection."

Levi's eyes flick to me, and I give him an encouraging smile.

"You are going to smash it," I tell him.

That earns me a full smile that transforms his entire face. He turns back to the booth, ball in hand, takes one more look, and then throws with ferocity. The ball hits the exact center of the remaining bottles, sending them flying with such force that one nearly takes out the booth operator's hat.

"Physics," Levi says simply, accepting a crisp fifty-dollar bill from Atlas with a satisfied nod and a stuffed bear wearing glasses and a bow tie from the impressed operator. He presents the bear to me with a small bow. "For you, my sweet thing. I believe the proper terminology is 'boom.'"

River howls with laughter, slapping Levi on the back. "Did you just trash-talk? Our Levi? Atlas, I think we're witnessing evolution in real time!"

I accept the bear, balancing the growing mountain of plushies in my arms. "Thank you," I murmur, rising on tiptoe to press a quick kiss to his cheek. His skin is warm against my lips, and I linger a moment longer, inhaling his clean, distinctive scent, loving how he smells. When I pull back, I feel a flush on my cheeks. And with each of the Alphas watching me, I say, "These are getting a bit unwieldy," as the wolf slides sideways, threatening to topple the entire stuffed animal tower in my arms. The carnival prizes are big, each nearly the size of my torso, and I'm starting to resemble a walking plushie shop.

"I've got it," Atlas states, plucking the wolf from my stack before it can fall.

"And I'll take this handsome fellow," River adds, rescuing his tiger. "Can't have him suffering the indignity of hitting the ground."

Levi carefully adjusts the bear remaining in my arm. "Better?"

"Perfect," I reply. "Though if you guys win me any more prizes, we might need to rent a van just for stuffed animals."

"Speaking of which, let's put these in the truck," River suggests, already cradling his tiger.

By the time we've put the gifts away, we start working our way through half the game booths. I'm smiling despite everything. It's been so long since I've just had fun, since I've let myself be silly and carefree without worrying about deadlines, relationships, or the constant pressure to be enough.

"Having a good time?" Atlas asks, his deep voice sending butterflies through my stomach as he steps close enough that our arms brush. The casual contact shouldn't affect me so strongly, but my skin prickles with awareness where we touch.

I nod, surprised to realize it's true. "Yeah, I am. Thanks for this. For all of it."

He studies me for a moment, his gaze lingering on my lips before returning to meet my eyes. It's the same hungry look from last night on the balcony.

"You deserve good things, Emma," he admits, voice dropping lower, for my ears only. His hand comes up to tuck a strand of hair behind my ear, fingertips grazing the sensitive skin of my neck. "You have no idea what it does to me, seeing you smile and laugh like this."

The heat of his palm lingers against my skin, and I find myself unconsciously leaning toward him like a flower seeking sunlight. My pulse quickens as he steps even closer. For a wild moment, I think he might kiss me right here, surrounded by carnival games and cotton candy stands.

"I keep thinking about last night," he murmurs, his

thumb tracing the curve of my jaw. "The taste of you. The sounds you made."

Heat floods my face, and lower, much lower, at the slick that seems to respond instantly at the first sign of an Alpha's attention. "Atlas," I whisper, not sure if I'm warning him off or begging for more.

A slow, predatory smile curves his lips. "Don't worry. I can be patient when the prize is worth waiting for."

Before I can come back with a response to that loaded statement, River calls us over, having apparently won the ride debate with Levi. Atlas's hand slides down my arm as he steps back, his fingers tangling briefly with mine in a touch that feels more intimate than it should.

"Coming?" he asks.

"Not yet," I tease sarcastically with a wink, enjoying the flash of surprise in his eyes.

The smirk on Atlas's face is wicked.

"The Scrambler, then we work our way up to the big stuff," River announces, already pulling me toward the carnival rides and breaking my hold with Atlas.

The Scrambler looks like a giant metal octopus, its long arms extending from a central hub, each tipped with a small two-person car painted in garish primary colors. As we approach, I watch the current riders shrieking with laughter as centrifugal force flings them outward while the entire structure spins, creating a dizzying double rotation. Looks exciting.

"Two per car," the operator announces as we reach the front of the line.

River immediately tightens his hold on my arm. "I call dibs on Emma for this one!" His possessive enthusiasm makes me laugh as he tugs me toward a red car.

"Try not to traumatize her with your screaming," Levi calls after him.

"That was *one* time," River protests over his shoulder. "And it was a wasp, not the ride."

We slide into the narrow seat, thigh to thigh. River practically vibrates with excitement, bouncing slightly in his seat as the safety bar lowers across our laps.

"Fair warning," he says with a mischievous grin. "I'm a bit of a Scrambler enthusiast. I know exactly how to maximize the spin."

"Why does that sound terrifying?" I ask, but I'm smiling.

"Trust me." He winks. "It'll be the most fun you've had with your clothes on."

I burst out laughing at his outrageous flirtation. Across the ride, I spot Atlas and Levi settling into a blue car, both looking amusingly oversized in the small space.

The ride lurches into motion, starting with a gentle spin that gradually increases in speed. River wasn't kidding; he seems to know exactly how to time his movements, leaning into the turns to amplify the force.

"The trick," he shouts over the ride's music, "is to work with the physics, not against it!"

"You sound like Levi!" I yell back, gripping the safety bar as we pick up speed.

River throws his head back with a laugh. "Don't tell Levi I understand physics. I've spent years cultivating my pretty-but-dumb persona!"

With the next turn, he demonstrates by pushing slightly against the outer edge of the car, causing us to spin more dramatically.

"Holy shit!" I shriek, half terrified and half exhilarated, as the world becomes a dizzying blur of colors and lights. "What did you do?"

"Magic!" River grins wickedly. "Want more?"

"You're insane!" I shout, but I'm laughing too hard to clearly sound convincing.

"That's not a no!" he calls back, timing another push perfectly with the ride's rotation.

This time, the force slams me against him with enough power to knock the breath from my lungs.

"If I throw up on you, it's your own fault!" I gasp, clinging to his arm as the ride whips us around again.

"Worth it!" he declares, his eyes bright with mischief. "Besides, you're having fun! Admit it!"

"I admit nothing!" I reply, even as another burst of laughter escapes me. "Except that you're trying to kill me!"

River's arm comes around my shoulders, his body warm and solid against mine. He laughs right along with me as we spin, his joy as infectious as his smile.

"Is this how you impress all the girls?" I demand as we careen around another turn. "Spin them until they can't tell if they're dizzy from the ride or your charm?"

"Only the special ones," he says with a wink, somehow managing to look roguishly handsome despite being flung around like a rag doll. "Is it working?"

"Ask me when the world stops spinning," I retort, but I can't keep the smile from my face. There's something freeing about River's enthusiasm, his ability to find joy in the moment without overthinking it.

As we spin faster, I surrender to the chaos, letting out a whoop that matches River's. For these few minutes, I forget everything—the fire, the police interview, my complicated feelings about three Alphas who shouldn't affect me this way. There's just the wind in my hair, the thrill of speed, and River's presence beside me.

"Look at those two!" he yells, nodding toward Atlas and Levi. Their car spins past ours, and I catch a glimpse of Levi's normally composed face transformed by laughter as Atlas, looking slightly green, grips the safety bar with white knuckles.

"Atlas hates spinning rides," River confides in my ear during a brief moment when our car slows. "But he refuses to admit it."

This new knowledge endears Atlas to me even more.

As the ride reaches its maximum speed, River pulls me closer, one hand protectively bracing me against the force of the spin. Despite his playful demeanor, there's strength in the arm around me, his body a solid presence in the spinning chaos.

When the ride finally slows, we're both breathless with laughter. River helps me out of the car with a theatrical bow, then turns to Atlas and Levi as they approach.

"Atlas, my friend, you're looking a little pale there," River teases. "Should we do the Tilt-A-Whirl next?"

Atlas glowers at him. "I'm ready. Let's do this."

"He once threw up on the Scrambler," Levi informs me quietly. "We've never let him forget it."

"Traitor," Atlas mutters.

By the time I stumble off more rides, dizzy and laughing, the sun is beginning to set. The festival transforms as darkness falls, strings of lights illuminating the pathways between booths and rides. The atmosphere shifts subtly, becoming more intimate, more magical. It's gorgeous, in truth, and I can't believe we've been here so long already.

Atlas seems equally hesitant to let me go, his hand lingering at my waist as we exit the ride on slightly wobbly legs.

"One more ride," River suggests, his eyes gleaming with mischief in the colorful lights. "Then we hit the food stands again."

He points to a structure set slightly apart from the main rides—a Tunnel of Love. It's charmingly retro, with oversized swan-shaped boats that disappear into a darkened building decorated with heart-shaped lights and cheesy cupid statues.

"Seriously?" I laugh. "That's so corny."

"Exactly," River agrees. "Which makes it perfect. Plus, it's air-conditioned in there."

The idea of cool air is actually appealing. I've been feeling increasingly overheated all day, and not just from the summer temperature or the proximity of three attractive Alphas.

"Fine," I concede. "Who's riding with me?"

"Me," Levi bellows first and loudly. "You are *mine*."

I shake my head, giggling at their enthusiasm, though secretly, I can't get enough of their closeness, their touches.

"Shall we?" Levi asks.

I take his arm, trying to ignore the flutter in my stomach at his touch. "Why do I feel like I'm being set up?"

"Because you're perceptive," he replies as we join the short line for the ride. Atlas and River are behind us.

When it's our turn, Levi helps me into one of the swan boats, then settles beside me. The seat is a decent size with lots of legroom, and security belts are required.

"Comfortable?" he asks as our boat starts to move, gliding smoothly into the dark tunnel river.

"Mmm," I reply noncommittally, aware of him pressed against my side. The darkness seems to amplify his presence.

As the ride progresses, we pass through different scenes—animatronic couples in different romantic settings from various fairy tales, twinkling lights meant to represent stars, papier-mâché trees with carved hearts. It's cheesy and ridiculous and should be making me laugh.

Instead, I'm increasingly distracted by the heat of Levi's body next to mine, the way his thumb absently strokes my shoulder, and the solid strength of his thigh against mine. My heart races, and there's a building pressure low in my belly that's becoming harder to ignore.

"Have you been to many summer festivals?" I ask, desperate for a distraction, his face covered in shadows from the dark ride.

"A few," he answers, his voice low. "This one is special, though."

"Why's that?"

"Because you're here."

The simple statement shouldn't affect me so strongly, not to mention it's super corny, yet it sends a wave of heat through me that settles between my thighs. It's not just attraction anymore; it's something more urgent, almost painful in its intensity.

I shift closer to him under the pretense of adjusting my position in the small boat. My hand lands on his thigh, and instead of removing it, I let my fingers trace small circles against the denim of his jeans. The muscle beneath tenses immediately.

His breath catches audibly. "Keep touching me like that," Levi murmurs, his voice dropping to a growl I've never heard from him before, "and I can't be responsible for what I'll do next."

The threat should frighten me. Instead, it sends another rush of heat straight to between my thighs, and my nipples tighten. My body is betraying me, responding to him with savagery. I look up at him through my lashes, feeling reckless, dangerous.

"Is that a promise?" I ask, my fingers continuing their teasing path higher up his thigh.

His expression is one of raw hunger.

His hand wraps around my wrist, stilling my fingers on his thigh. For a moment, I think he's going to push me away. Instead, he guides my hand higher, letting me feel exactly what I've been searching for beneath his jeans.

"This is what you're causing," he growls, his voice low and dangerous. "Is this what you want?"

"Yes," I breathe, the word escaping before I can stop it. My fingers curl around his hardness as much as his jeans will allow, and his jaw clenches at my touch.

Our boat rounds a bend, slipping into a darker section of the tunnel designed for the themed events. I turn toward him fully, my free hand finding the back of his neck, tugging him down to me. The swan-shaped seat is high enough to conceal us, and with River and Atlas behind us, I know they can't see us.

Our lips crash together, fierce, demanding, almost desperate. His lips burn with heat, his tongue claiming my mouth with a dominance that makes me whimper.

His hands find my waist, lifting me effortlessly

until I'm straddling his lap in the small boat, facing him. The position brings us intimately close, the hard length of him pressing against my drenched pussy through our clothes. I rock against him instinctively, seeking friction and relief from the burning need consuming me. The itch is so deep, so insistent, that I feel like I might scream out with frustration.

"Fuck," he growls against my mouth, the curse shocking from his usually considered lips. "You have no idea what you do to me."

"Show me," I challenge, nipping at his lower lip.

His hands tighten on my hips, guiding my movements against him as his mouth trails fire along my neck and farther down. He pulls my shirt lower, so he's just above my nipple, kissing me. Then he bites down, not hard enough to mark, but enough to send a jolt of pleasure-pain straight through me.

I gasp, my back arching, pressing my breasts against him. One of his hands slides up my side to cup the weight of my breast through my shirt, thumb brushing over the hardened peak. Even through layers of fabric, the touch is electric.

"I've thought about this since the moment I saw you," he confesses against my throat, voice rough with desire. "Wondered how you'd feel in my arms, how you'd taste on my tongue."

His words are as arousing as his touch. I rock harder against him, chasing the building pressure.

"Levi," I moan softly, ignoring the mechanical scenery we pass.

I feel his smile against my skin, predatory and pleased. "I love you begging."

His mouth finds mine, and we're kissing again like the world around us is on fire. Unlike Atlas's consuming passion, Levi's kiss is deliberate and almost planned out. It's devastatingly effective. Within moments, I'm melting against him, a whimper escaping me as his tongue slides against mine.

I'm on fire, every nerve ending screaming for more. I've never experienced a desire like I do with these Alphas, so overwhelming, so all-consuming.

Before I fully register what I'm doing, I slide from my seat to kneel on the floor where there's extra legroom of the boat, between Levi's legs. His sharp intake of breath is the only indication of surprise.

"Emma," he growls. "You don't have to—"

"I want to," I interrupt, my hands already working on his belt. "Please, Levi. Let me."

In the darkness, I can barely see his expression, but I feel the tension in his body, the rigid control he's maintaining.

"Are you sure?"

In answer, I slide my hand into his now-open pants and beneath his boxers, wrapping my fingers around the thick length I find waiting for me. He hisses in pleasure, the sound sending a thrill straight through me. He's impossibly hard, yet there's a velvety softness to him that makes my contact feel electric. As I stroke him, my fingers don't quite meet around his girth, and the sheer size of him makes my breath catch.

Then I feel that swollen bulge near the base of his shaft. The knot. Unique to Alphas, meant for one purpose, and definitely not something meant for a mouth. Still, it never fails to amaze me just how differently Alphas are built, how everything about them feels designed to claim, to mark, to keep. Even just touching it sends a fresh flush of heat through me, as if my body instinctively recognizes what that knot means.

"Fuck," he breathes, helping me pull his jeans and boxers down his hips. He's breathing quicker, beautiful with the thick and heavy offering in my hand. I tug him a few times, and he groans. His hand moves to the back of my head, nudging me closer. "You're going to ruin me, sweet thing."

I don't hesitate, leaning forward and pressing my mouth over his tip, tasting his saltiness, then slide him deeper past my lips. I moan around his length, feeling like I have power over him, adoring the way he shakes slightly and how he makes those growling sounds. I fall into a rhythm that has me taking him deep, then back out, while he's sucking in sharp breaths.

"Emma," he grunts as I take him deeper. "Your mouth... so perfect..."

I use every trick I know, every technique I've learned, determined to make this brilliant, reserved Alpha lose his mind for me.

When I hollow my cheeks and swirl my tongue around the sensitive head of his cock, he curses, his thighs tensing beneath my hands. I feel powerful, desirable, and essential in a way I've never experienced before.

I pull free, staring at him, my hand on the base of his cock, the other on his balls, cradling them. He looks like a man who has submitted, and fuck, I love the feral look in his eyes as he stares at me.

"You want me to lose control? You want to see what happens when I stop holding back? Keep teasing me like that, and I may not be gentle when I break."

I tighten my grip and stroke him, twisting my wrist at the top just the way his hips give small thrusts. I let my thumb drag over the slick head of his cock, circling it slowly, watching his jaw clench as he fights to keep his composure. He's trying so damn hard to stay in control, but I want him undone.

Leaning in, I press soft kisses against his abdomen, just above where my hand works him, my breath warm and deliberate. Every moan he swallows, every tremor that runs through him fuels me. This brilliant, reserved Alpha might be a master of restraint, but right now, I'm determined to make him lose it. For me.

So I take him into my mouth again until he hits the back of my throat. I pause, tears instantly pricking my eyes as I slowly work him deeper.

"Close," he warns, his voice rough with restraint. "Emma, I'm going to..."

I double my efforts in response, taking more of him, humming around his length in a way that sends vibrations through us both.

He growls my name with a tone that sounds almost

pained, his hand fisting in my hair, holding me down, as he pulses into my mouth. I swallow everything he gives me, working my throat, feeling strangely triumphant at having broken his careful control.

When I'm done, I ease back onto my heels and wipe my mouth with the back of my hand, staring up at the man above me, this Alpha who just came undone with my name on his lips. His chest rises and falls like he's been through war, and maybe he has. I didn't just please him; I broke his calm composure.

With hands that still shake, I tuck him back into his pants, and he zips himself up as I slide onto the swan ride seat beside him. The ache between my thighs throbs in protest, hungry and unrelieved, but I don't regret a second of it.

"That was..." Levi starts, but the words die in his throat. He looks at me as though he doesn't know whether to worship me or destroy me.

I smile into the darkness, smug and breathless. "I know."

He doesn't laugh. No soft chuckle. No returned smirk.

Instead, he leans closer toward me, slowly and deliberately. One arm drapes behind my seat, and the other lands heavily on my thigh, fingers pressing into my skin as if he owns it, owns me.

I gasp for air.

His hand moves higher now. Not teasing but claiming.

"You have no idea what you've woken up, sweet

thing." He leans in, his lips brushing the shell of my ear, his breath ragged. "Next time, I won't let you finish until you're shaking... and begging me to stop."

His grip tightens, and I shudder as a flare of pleasure pulses across the apex between my thighs.

His words linger and tease me deeply. Not just filthy, but feral. My breath stutters. Heat blooms under my skin, a flush that starts in my chest and spills upward until even the roots of my hair feel warm. My thighs instinctively press together, desperate for friction. My heart pounds, but it's not from fear. It's from want. Raw. Undeniable.

Then he moves even closer, drawing me against him.

"I'm going to make you mine, Emma," he murmurs, his voice low, reverent, and lethal all at once.

It shouldn't feel like a vow, but it does. I sense it in the way his fingers grip my waist like I might disappear if he lets go. In the way his gaze burns into me, not just seeing me but claiming me.

I swallow hard, my body thrumming with heat, my brain slow to catch up. I don't trust myself to speak, so I lean into him instead, my fingers curling in the fabric of his shirt like I need him.

The swan ride glides out of the tunnel, golden light washing over us once more. And just like that, the world feels too bright, too exposed. My cheeks are on fire. I must look wrecked, with everything I felt on my knees between his legs.

People mill around the boardwalk, unaware. But Levi? He hasn't taken his eyes off me.

And I know, without a doubt, he meant every word.

We step out of the boat, and Atlas and River climb off after us. The sudden light is disorienting after the darkness, and I blink rapidly, hoping my appearance doesn't broadcast what we've been doing.

"Enjoy the ride? Didn't realize there were so many growls in the ride's audio," River teases, raising an eyebrow.

I instantly blush, glancing away from him. God, they heard Levi.

"Very educational ride," Levi replies with remarkable composure, though there's a flush high on his cheekbones, and his normally neat hair is mussed.

Atlas's eyes meet mine, dark and knowing, and the heat in his gaze sends another pulse of need through me. What is happening to me? I've never been this wanton, this unable to control my desires.

As we walk away from the ride, Levi's hand at the small of my back, I catch a glimpse of our reflection in a game booth mirror. My lips are swollen, my cheeks flushed, my eyes bright with lingering arousal. I look... different. Wild, almost.

A terrible suspicion begins to form in my mind, a quiet dread curling at the edges of my thoughts. I've been brushing it off all day, blaming the heat, the adrenaline, and the relentless pull I feel toward the three Alphas shadowing my every step, but something's not right. My skin feels too hot. My scent is thickening. Every glance, every breath of their pheromones has my body reacting like it knows something I don't.

No. It can't be heat. That's not possible.

My heat isn't due for weeks. It's been regular, every six months like clockwork. I prepare for it. I have to be ready. Other Omegas are different. Some go years before their first heat, while others flare up unpredictably, especially after prolonged exposure to Alphas. But mine? Mine has always been stable. Predictable. Manageable.

Last time, Chad was there, and even if it was a hollow experience, at least it followed the usual pattern. He'd knotted me, sure, but with all the passion of a routine chore. No intimacy. No tenderness. Just... obligation. And even then, the symptoms had been mild. Controlled.

This, whatever this is, feels entirely different. My body is reacting too fast, too intensely. It has to be something else. The Alphas. Their pheromones. Their constant, overwhelming presence.

My grandmother used to say, "If you spend too long near Alphas, your body will start answering to them whether you want it to or not."

That must be what this is. A hormonal fluke. Proximity overload. A trick of my body responding to their dominance, not to the cycle.

That's all it is.

It's not heat.

It can't be.

15

EMMA

I rush down the stairs, drawn by a strange flickering light coming from the kitchen. Orange and yellow dance across the walls, casting ominous shadows that seem to reach for me with grasping fingers.

"Hello?" I call out, rounding the corner to find a small fire spreading across the kitchen counter. The flames lick at the cabinets, consuming dish towels and jumping to the wooden spice rack. Smoke reaches my nose, and I cough.

"About time you showed up," a male says from behind me.

I spin around, startled by the voice. Chad stands in the doorway, arms crossed over his chest, watching the growing blaze with detached interest. He looks exactly as I remember—expensive clothes, carefully styled hair, and a smile that reminds me of a shark.

"Chad? What are you doing here?" My mind spins in confusion. "Why is there a fire? We need to get out!"

"This was supposed to be our vacation," he says,

ignoring my panic. "Remember? The cabin I booked for us before you decided to go slumming with your firefighter toys."

The fire grows as he speaks, spreading across the ceiling now, crackling and popping as it consumes the wooden beams. The heat intensifies, sweat beading on my skin, but Chad seems unbothered.

"We need to leave," I insist, reaching for his arm and coughing. "Now!"

He shakes off my grip, his face twisting into something unfamiliar, something that makes my blood run cold. The carefully maintained charm falls away like a cheap mask, revealing what's always been lurking beneath—cold calculation and rage.

"You went behind my back with three fucking Alphas?" he snarls, advancing on me as the flames rise higher, circling us like hungry predators. "I always knew you were trash."

"Chad, please." I back away, but there's nowhere to go. The fire has surrounded us, closing in with unnatural speed. "I didn't—"

"Always knew you were worthless," he continues as if I hadn't spoken. "Just another desperate Omega pretending to be special. You're nothing without me."

His hands shoot out, grabbing my shoulders with bruising force. His pale blue eyes, always cold, even when he smiles, now gleam with malice that chills me despite the inferno around us.

"You belong in the fire," he hisses, shoving me backward. I stumble, falling into the wall of flames behind me.

The fire catches on my clothes, my hair, my skin, and I scream—

I jolt awake with a gasp, my heart pounding against my ribs like it's trying to escape. The sheets are tangled around my legs. For a disorienting moment, I can still feel the fire licking at my skin, can still see Chad's icy stare, watching me burn.

"Just a dream," I whisper into the darkness of my room. "Just a stupid dream."

But my body doesn't seem to have gotten the message. I'm burning up, skin flushed and covered in sweat. Between my thighs, I'm embarrassingly wet and throbbing with an insistent need that makes no sense, given the nightmare I just escaped.

I kick off the sheets, trying to cool down. The air on my overheated skin brings temporary relief, but the ache deep inside only intensifies. Something's wrong. I've never felt like this before, as though I'm being consumed from the inside out.

A terrible suspicion forms in my mind. No. It can't be. My heat isn't due for weeks, and it's never hit this suddenly before. There are always warning signs, a gradual buildup, not this freight train of sensation.

I press a hand between my legs, shocked at the slickness I find there. My fingers come away glistening in the faint moonlight filtering through my window.

"Shit," I mutter, panic rising. "Shit, shit, shit."

This can't be happening. Not now, not here, not

when I'm living with three Alphas who already make my pulse race.

I need a cold shower. Now. The deep, sharp pain of heat hasn't set in yet, so maybe this is just my body responding to the Alphas being so close to me.

Stumbling out of bed, I grab fresh pajamas from my dresser—the shortest shorts and thinnest tank top the guys bought me, because it feels like anything heavier would suffocate me right now. The room tilts alarmingly as I move, my balance off-kilter, my limbs heavy and uncooperative.

I make it to the door through sheer determination, easing it open as quietly as possible. The last thing I need is to wake one of them in this state. The hallway stretches before me, the bathroom door seeming impossibly far away. Gripping the wall for support, I make my way down the corridor on unsteady legs.

Left foot. Right foot. Don't fall. Don't make noise. Don't think about how good the cool wall feels against your overheated palm.

I reach the bathroom without incident. The face that greets me in the mirror is almost unrecognizable—cheeks flushed, pupils wide, and lips parted and swollen as if I've been kissed senseless. I look drugged or feverish, or both.

Turning the shower to its coldest setting, I strip off my sweat-soaked pajamas and step under the icy spray. The shock tears a gasp from my throat, but the relief is immediate and profound. The fire under my skin recedes, the fog in my brain clearing slightly.

I stand there until I'm shivering, letting the cold water wash away the slick between my thighs, the sweat from my skin, and the lingering tendrils of the nightmare. When I finally shut off the water, I feel almost normal again. Still warm, still on edge, but no longer desperate.

As I towel off, I catch myself thinking about the three Alphas sleeping just down the hall. Each is so different, yet all stir something in me I've tried desperately to ignore.

I can't keep doing this, can't keep letting my guard down around them. The balcony with Atlas, the Tunnel of Love with Levi, the way I find excuses to touch River whenever we're in the same room... It's like I've lost all self-preservation instinct.

"Get it together, Emma," I mutter to my reflection as I pull on my clean pajamas. "They're being kind. That's all. Don't make it weird. Don't get attached. And for God's sake, stop imagining them naked."

The last command is futile. I've already had Levi's cock in my mouth, had Atlas's face between my thighs, and watched River's muscles flex as he won carnival games. My mind has filled in the blanks quite vividly.

I gather my wet hair into a messy bun to keep it off my neck. Then I step back into the hallway, ready to return to my room and figure out what the hell I'm going to do if this really is an early heat. But as I turn toward my bedroom, a scent hits me, warm, rich, intoxicating.

Cinnamon, firewood, and brown sugar.

Something primal stirs in response. My head turns, seeking the source of that delicious smell, nostrils drawing more into my lungs. My feet follow, one step, then another, as if drawn by an invisible thread.

It's River. I know it with absolute certainty, though I can't explain how. The sweet, spicy scent is unmistakably his, and right now, it's the most delicious thing I've ever encountered. My body responds instantaneously, a fresh wave of slick soaking my clean pajama shorts as heat surges through me again.

A small, rational part of my brain screams warnings, telling me to return to my room, to lock the door, to put as much distance between me and the Alphas as possible. But that voice is drowned out by the overwhelming need to be closer to that scent, to wrap myself in it, to taste it.

I find myself outside his door without any memory of deciding to go there. My hand trembles as it reaches for the doorknob, turning it with exquisite slowness to avoid making noise. The door swings open, revealing a bedroom bathed in silver moonlight.

Slipping inside, I carefully close the door behind me with a soft click that sounds deafening in the quiet room. River is sprawled across his bed, one arm flung above his head and the sheets tangled around his waist, exposing the sculpted planes of his chest and abdomen. The sight makes my mouth water.

I should leave. I should open the door and run back to my room. I should...

I'm already crossing the room, drawn by the intensifying scent that fills the space. It's everywhere here, concentrated and pure, wrapping around me like an embrace. A small sound, half purr, half whimper, escapes me as I breathe it in.

The need to be closer overwhelms all rational thought. Before I know what I'm doing, I'm crawling onto the foot of his bed, sliding under the sheet, drinking in his scent with desperate gulps of air. Each breath makes the ache inside me worse and better simultaneously.

I can't stop myself from moving higher, drawn to the source of that intoxicating smell. I slide along his body until I'm face-to-face with him, only then realizing his eyes are open, bright teal gleaming in the darkness.

"Well, hello there, sugar cube," he murmurs, voice rough with sleep but amusement clear in his tone. "This is a pleasant surprise."

Despite my state, embarrassment floods me. "I-I'm sorry. I don't know what I'm—"

"Shh," he soothes, his arms coming around me as if it's the most natural thing in the world to find an Omega in his bed in the middle of the night. "No need to explain."

His skin against mine is electric, sending sparks dancing across my nerve endings. I shudder at the contact, unable to suppress the small moan that escapes me.

"Bad dream?" he asks, one hand gently stroking my back.

The simple touch shouldn't feel so good, but in my sensitized state, it's almost overwhelming.

"Yes," I manage, struggling to form coherent thoughts with him so close, his scent filling my lungs, his warmth seeping into my overheated skin. "And I don't feel right. I didn't want to be alone."

River shifts, pulling me closer until I'm tucked against his side. Only then do I register that he's completely naked under the sheets, his arousal evident against my hip. The realization sends another flood of heat through me.

"Well, you picked the right Alpha to cuddle with," he whispers. "I'm excellent at chasing away nightmares."

I turn away from him, needing a moment to collect myself, to try to regain some control over my runaway body. But the movement only makes things worse because now we're spooning, his chest pressed to my back, his arm wrapped around my waist, his breath warm against my neck.

"Mmm," he hums appreciatively, nose tracing the line of my throat. "Fuck, you smell delicious. Why do you smell so good? And you're so soft, like velvet."

The praise sends a shiver down my spine, and I arch back against him. My ass presses against his erection, drawing a sharp intake of breath from him.

I do it again, a deliberate roll of my hips this time, feeling him harden further against me. The friction is delicious, a small relief to the building pressure inside me, but nowhere near enough.

"Be careful, sugar cube," he warns, voice dropping to a growl that vibrates through me. "I'm not a man who can say no to someone like you."

The heat in my veins makes me reckless. "Who says I want you to say no?"

"Are you sure you know what you're asking for?" His hand tightens on my hip, fingers digging into my flesh in a way that's just shy of painful. "Because right now, you smell like an Omega on the edge of heat."

The words confirm my suspicion, sending a spike of panic through the haze of desire. "No, I'm not," I protest automatically. "It's just from being around you three so much... my body is just adjusting. My heat isn't due for another couple of weeks." Even as I say it, I know it's a lie, but admitting it makes it real, makes it something I have to deal with.

River's hand slides up to cup my face, turning me slightly so he can see my eyes. "I've been around enough Omegas in heat to recognize the signs. Your scent has been changing for days."

I close my eyes, not wanting to see the truth in his gaze.

"Sometimes being around compatible Alphas can trigger a heat," he explains gently. "Especially when..." He trails off, seemingly reconsidering his words.

"When what?" I press.

He hesitates, then says, "When there's a potential mate nearby."

The word *mate* sends another rush of heat through me, my body responding instinctively to the concept.

"That's ridiculous," I say, with less conviction than I'd like. "I've known you guys for less than a week."

"The body knows what it wants," River says simply. "And right now, yours seems to want me pretty badly."

I can't argue with that, not when I'm practically writhing against him, desperate for more contact. "This is insane," I mutter, more to myself than to him.

"Completely," he agrees cheerfully. "But here you are, in my bed, grinding that perfect little ass against me like you're trying to start a fire."

Despite everything, I laugh. "Since when are you a philosopher?"

"I have hidden depths," he retorts, nipping my earlobe. "Speaking of which... what other secrets are you keeping from me?"

The question is playful. His hand has resumed its maddening path along my side, up and down, each pass bringing him closer to where I'm aching for his touch.

"Wouldn't you like to know?" I tease, even as I arch into his touch.

"I would, actually," he says, voice dropping lower. "Tell me what turns you on. Just so a man knows how to bring you ultimate pleasure."

The request sends a thrill through me, both the words themselves and the power they give me. But I'm not ready to surrender all my secrets just yet.

"Why don't you find out for yourself?" I challenge,

reaching back to slide my fingers into his hair. "I'm right here."

"Mmm, playing hard to get even when you're practically melting for me?" His hand slides to my bare thigh. "I like a challenge."

His touch moves higher, skimming the edge of my sleep shorts, deliberately avoiding where I need him most. The teasing is exquisite torture, my body coiling tighter with each brush of his fingers.

"River," I whimper, unable to keep the need from my voice.

"Yes, sugar cube?" He sounds far too composed, too in control, while I'm falling apart.

"Touch me," I plead, past pride now. "Please."

His lips brush the edge of my ear. "Here?" His hand slides up to just below my breast. "Or maybe here?" Down to the outside of my thigh.

I groan in frustration, grabbing his wrist and trying to guide his hand where I need it between my thighs. He resists easily, chuckling at my impatience.

"Not so fast," he murmurs. "First, I want to know what my Omega likes. What fantasies keep you up at night? What makes you bite that pretty lower lip when you think no one's watching?"

The questions make me squirm, from both embarrassment and arousal. "Why are you teasing me?"

"Because you're magnificent when you're desperate," he admits, the honesty in his words surprising me. "And because when I finally give you what you need, it'll be that much better for the waiting."

His logic is infuriating and arousing in equal measure. "Fine," I huff. "What do you want to know?"

"Everything," he says simply. "But let's start with how you like to be touched. Soft and slow? Hard and fast? Do you like to be in control, or do you prefer to surrender?"

The questioning makes me blush, but the heat in my veins pushes me past shyness. "It depends on my mood," I hedge.

"And what mood are you in right now?" His hand has resumed its maddening journey up and down my side, each pass bringing him closer to my breast.

I consider lying, consider playing coy, but what's the point? My body is already betraying every secret. "I like it doggy style," I admit, voice barely above a whisper. "Something about it just... hits different."

"Is that what my sugar cube needs?"

"Is that a problem?" I ask, suddenly self-conscious despite the fire racing through my veins.

He laughs. "Oh, not at all. I just want to make sure this is what you really want."

"Does a girl have to beg for it?" I grind back against him for emphasis, more deliberately this time, drawing a hiss from between his teeth.

"Christ, Emma," he groans, his hand sliding down my side to grip my hip harder. "Keep that up, and this will be over embarrassingly quickly."

I do it again, relishing the power I have over him despite my desperate state. "Maybe that's the plan."

His responding growl is pure Alpha.

I reach back to run my fingers through his golden hair. "Especially with you."

In one fluid motion, he rolls me onto my back, looming over me with those bright eyes that seem to glow in the darkness. His hand comes up to brush my hair away from my face with surprising tenderness.

"Look at you," he whispers, gaze traveling over my flushed face, my heaving chest, my parted lips. "If you could see yourself right now, all blushing and wanting, those gorgeous eyes begging me for relief. You're a fucking vision."

My chest squeezes. "River," I breathe, only knowing that I need him with an intensity that frightens me.

"I've been dreaming about having you in my bed," he confesses as his thumb brushes my lower lip. "Imagining how your skin would feel against mine, how you'd sound when I make you come."

Before I can respond, his mouth is on mine, and all coherent thought dissolves. There's nothing hesitant or careful about his kiss; he claims my mouth, his tongue dominating, taking playful nips at my lower lip, with a hunger that matches my own.

His hand tangles in my hair and angles my head exactly how he wants it while his body presses me into the mattress with delicious weight.

I'm breathless within seconds, my body arching up to get closer, seeking so much more of him. A whimper escapes me when he sucks my bottom lip between his teeth, the slight sting followed by the soothing swipe of his tongue.

"God, you're intoxicating," he murmurs against my lips. "Could kiss you for hours."

His hands slide down my body, exploring the curve of my waist and the flare of my hip. When he reaches the hem of my tank top, he pauses, looking at me with a question in his eyes.

"Yes," I nod frantically. "Please."

He grins that wicked, boyish smile that first caught my attention. "So polite when you're horny."

In one smooth motion, he pulls the tank top up and over my head, tossing it aside. His starving stare takes in my bare breasts, my nipples hardening to tight peaks in the cool air.

"Gorgeous," he breathes, palming one breast with reverent care. "Absolutely fucking perfect."

The praise washes over me, heightening every sensation. When his thumb brushes across my nipple, a gasp escapes me.

"Sensitive," he notes. "I'm going to have so much fun with you."

He lowers his head, replacing his hand with his mouth, sucking one nipple between his lips while his fingers tease the other. The dual sensation sends lightning down my spine, pooling between my thighs, where I'm already embarrassingly wet.

"That's so good," I moan. My hands fist in his hair as he switches to the other breast, giving it the same thorough attention. "Please."

He trails kisses down the valley of my breasts, across my ribs, toward my navel.

"I need you to touch me," I manage. "Between my legs. I'm so empty, River. It hurts."

"Can't have that," he murmurs, hooking his fingers into the waistband of my shorts. "Lift your hips for me."

I comply immediately, and he draws the shorts down my legs with agonizing slowness, his eyes darkening as he takes in my nakedness.

"Christ," he mutters, tossing the shorts aside and spreading my bent knees. "You're trying to kill me."

I'm beyond self-consciousness now, naked before him in the moonlight, my need too urgent for modesty. "Touch me," I plead.

He settles between my thighs, pressing a slow kiss to the inside of my knee, then another, working his way higher with maddening deliberation. Each press of his lips sends sparks dancing across my skin, winding me tighter with anticipation until I'm trembling, breath shallow, pulse fluttering like a trapped bird in my throat.

"So impatient," he murmurs against my inner thigh, his breath hot and wicked, then pulls back up to sit on his heels. "Good things come to those who wait."

But I can't help it—I glance down, needing to see him, all of him.

And when I do, I freeze.

He's completely nude, gloriously so, muscles everywhere. But the thick length between his thighs catches my attention, and not just because of the size, though he's achingly hard and more than impressive. No, it's the piercings. A row of small, gleaming silver bars runs beneath the head of his cock, glinting softly in the moonlight.

A Jacob's ladder.

"Holy shit," I whisper, eyes wide. "How does that feel?"

River glances up at me through thick lashes, smirking like the devil himself. "You're about to find out, gorgeous."

My mouth goes dry. My pussy clenches. And still, all I can do is stare.

It looks wicked on him, dangerous and beautiful, like everything about him is designed to undo me. The smooth metal contrasts against the thick, flushed heat of him, and the thought of what it might feel like inside me sends a fresh rush of fire through my body.

He's still smirking as he leans back down and trails his mouth higher, eyes locked on mine.

And suddenly, waiting feels impossible.

I protest with a groan. His hand finally, *finally*, slides between my thighs, fingers parting my folds with gentle pressure. We both moan at the contact— me from relief, him from excitement.

"Fuck, you're drenched," he says with evident awe. "All this for me?"

"Yes," I gasp as he drags one finger through my wetness, gathering it before circling my entrance teasingly. "Only for you."

The first press of his finger inside me is both relief and torture—good, so good, but nowhere near enough to satisfy the emptiness. I buck against his hand, seeking more, and he obliges by adding a second finger, stretching me deliciously.

"More," I plead, my hands fisting in the sheets. "Please."

River's eyes, bright with desire, lock on mine as he adds a third finger, filling me more completely. The stretch burns slightly, but in the best possible way, my body adjusting quickly to accommodate him.

"Like this?" he asks, curling his fingers inside me and thrusting in and out, making my whole body shudder.

"Yes," I cry out, hips lifting off the bed. "Like that."

He never pauses, his thumb occasionally brushing my clit with just enough weight to drive me higher without pushing me over the edge. It's deliberate torture, and he knows it.

"You should see yourself," he murmurs, voice rough with desire. "Flushed and writhing on my fingers, so wet I can hear it every time I move inside you. So fucking beautiful."

I'm beyond words now, reduced to moans and gasps as he drives me closer to the edge. Just when I think I might finally tip over, he withdraws his fingers, drawing a cry of protest from me.

"Shh," he soothes, bringing his glistening fingers to his mouth. My eyes widen as he sucks them clean, an expression of pure bliss crossing his face. "Just as sweet as I imagined," he says with evident satis-faction.

The sight of him tasting me sends another rush of heat through my body.

"I need you inside me."

"I will be," he promises, pressing a quick, hard kiss to my lips, letting me taste myself on his tongue. "But first, I want you how you said you like it best." He gives me a wicked grin. "Turn over for me, Emma. Hands and knees."

The command sends a fresh wave of slick between my thighs. I comply immediately, rolling onto my stomach and pushing up onto all fours. Cool air hits my overheated skin as River moves behind me, and I resist the urge to look back at him to see what he's thinking.

"Goddamn," he finally says, voice rough with desire. "You're a fucking masterpiece. All spread out for me, waiting to be filled."

His hands come to rest on my hips, thumbs pressing into the dimples at the base of my spine. I feel him shift on the mattress, positioning himself behind me. The head of his cock pushes against my entrance, and I move back eagerly, drawing a chuckle from him.

"So greedy, and your pussy is already fluttering on my cock, sucking down on me," he murmurs, one hand sliding up my spine to tangle in my hair. "I need more."

He enters me slowly at first. The stretch is beauti-ful, sharp and deep, just this side of too much, but in the best possible way. And then I feel it. The piercings.

Oh God.

Each bar of metal drags over me with a distinct, delicious friction, catching on the most sensitive spots inside me, making me gasp. It's not just pressure; it's texture. Just the right amount. Unrelenting. Like he's lighting up nerves I didn't even know I had. My body clenches around him in reaction, already desperate for more.

It's unlike anything I've ever felt.

When he's finally fully buried inside me, we both pause, panting. My hands are gripping the sheets, my body singing with sensation.

"You okay?" he asks, his voice tight with restraint, like he's hanging on by a thread.

"Better than okay," I manage, my voice breathless. I wiggle my hips, testing how those metal bars feel when I move—damn—and his groan tells me exactly how much that affected him.

"Now," I say, glancing over my shoulder with a grin, "show me what an Alpha can do."

He doesn't need to be told twice. His hands return to my hips, holding me steady as he withdraws almost completely, then slams back in with enough force to drive me forward on the bed. The angle is perfect, hitting spots inside me that make my vision blur.

"Fuck," I gasp, dropping to my elbows, changing the angle to take him even deeper. "Yes, just like that."

River sets a punishing pattern, each thrust accompanied by the obscene sound of skin on skin and the creaking protest of the bed frame. The headboard slams against the wall with each powerful drive of his hips. He grabs me hard, moves faster, more brutally. I can't get enough of being fucked.

"This what you needed?" he growls, one hand sliding around to find my clit, adding another layer of sensation that has me seeing stars. "This what you've been aching for?"

"Yes," I cry, past caring who might hear us. "Yes. God, River, don't stop."

"Couldn't if I tried," he pants, slamming into me. "Feel too fucking incredible."

Sweat slicks my body as we move together, the room filling with the sounds of our pleasure, my desperate moans, his guttural groans, the wet slide of him inside me.

"Close," I gasp, pushing back to meet each of his thrusts, the beautiful ache of him shoving so deep into me that I can barely hold on. "So close."

"That's it," he encourages, fingers pinching my clit. "Let go for me. Show me how good I make you feel."

His words push me closer to the edge, the pressure building to an almost unbearable peak. Just when I think I can't take any more, he leans over me, chest against my back, and whispers in my ear, "You're mine now. Mine to please, mine to protect, mine to cherish."

The possessive claim, combined with a particularly deep thrust and a clever circle of his fingers, sends me hurtling over the edge. The orgasm crashes through me with the force of a tidal wave, tearing a scream from my throat as my body convulses around him.

Wave after wave of pleasure washes over me, each more intense than the last, leaving me trembling and gasping beneath him.

River growls, his thrusting becoming erratic as my inner walls pulse around him. "Fuck, Emma, I'm going to—"

Then I feel it—the base of his cock swelling, catching just inside my entrance. His knot.

"Yes," I pant, pushing back against him, wanting, needing to feel that final connection. "Please, River."

With a guttural shout, he drives deep one final time, his knot locking inside me as he begins to come. The sensation of being so completely filled, so thoroughly claimed, triggers another unexpected orgasm that tears through me with shocking intensity.

River's hips continue to move in small, grinding circles as he empties himself inside me, his cock pulsing with each wave of his release. It seems to go on forever, his fingers digging into my hips hard enough to leave marks, his breath harsh and ragged against my ear.

"Fuck," he groans as the initial intensity subsides, leaving us both gasping. "That was... damn, that was incredible."

I can only manage a weak sound of agreement, too thoroughly spent for words. My arms give out, and I start to collapse onto the mattress.

"Careful," River murmurs, his arms wrapping securely around my waist as he guides us onto our sides, still joined intimately by his knot. "There we go. Easy does it."

We lie spoon-fashion, his chest pressed to my back, his arm draped protectively over my waist. His breath gradually slows against my neck, though occasionally, his cock still pulses inside me, smaller aftershocks of his release that make me shiver with residual pleasure.

"You okay?" he asks softly, pressing a gentle kiss to my shoulder.

"Mmm," I manage, too boneless and sated to form actual words, but that was exactly what I craved.

He chuckles, the sound vibrating through his chest against my back. "I'll take that as a yes." His hand strokes idly up and down my side, soothing rather than sexual now.

"You're absolutely stunning," he murmurs against my shoulder, lips brushing sensitive skin. "Not just your body, though God knows that's perfection, but everything about you. The way your eyes light up when you're excited about something. The little crease between your eyebrows when you're concentrating. How fiercely you protect your independence even when you're scared."

The unexpected tenderness catches me off guard, making my throat tight with emotion.

"I love how you're not afraid to sass Atlas, even though he's twice your size," River continues, his voice a gentle rumble against my back. "And how you match Levi in all those verbal sparring games. And how you laugh at my stupid jokes, even the really bad ones."

Each word sinks into me, warming places inside that have nothing to do with physical pleasure. His knot keeps us connected, but it's these soft confessions in the dark that feel more intimate somehow.

"You don't have to say all that," I murmur, strangely shy now that the initial urgency has passed.

"I know," he says simply. "I want to. I've been thinking about it for days."

We fall silent for a while, our breathing gradually slowing.

"Let me hold you while you sleep." He tightens his arm around my waist. "I'll keep the nightmares away."

The offer touches me more deeply than it should, this simple bit of care and protection. "I would love that," I whisper, already drifting toward sleep, warm and safe in his embrace.

"Sweet dreams, my sugar cube," he murmurs, pressing one last kiss to the nape of my neck.

As consciousness slips away, I realize with distant alarm that my heat hasn't broken—it's merely receded temporarily. This respite won't last; the fever will return, stronger than before.

But wrapped in River's arms, his heartbeat steady against my back, I can't bring myself to worry about tomorrow, knowing it may not happen for another day or two, seeing as how normal I feel once more.

16

Sunlight warms my face. I blink awake slowly, momentarily disoriented by the room around me. This isn't my nest-bed. Memories of last night crash over me like a wave.

River. His hands. His mouth. His knot.

I groan, burying my face in his pillow. What have I done? I don't feel guilty, but scared that I've let myself trust and fall for these Alphas' charms.

The bed beside me is empty, the sheets cool to the touch. I'm alone, but evidence of last night's activities surrounds me—rumpled sheets, a lingering scent of sex in the air, the pleasant soreness between my thighs.

My clothes from yesterday lie scattered across the floor where River tossed them. I gather them up, wincing slightly at the tenderness between my legs as I dress. Somehow, the tank top and shorts feel inadequate to cover me.

Once dressed, I head to my room to retrieve my phone. The cabin is silent around me, no sounds of life coming from the kitchen or living room. I check my notifications, and there's nothing from the guys, but there's an email from my editor about the upcoming deadline. I push those thoughts aside; I can't deal with work right now.

Back in the main living area, I search for signs of the Alphas. A note on the table, held in place by a salt-shaker, catches my eye.

Sugar cube,

Had to run. Urgent call came in. Killed me to leave you sleeping in my bed, looking so breathtakingly beautiful, like some fantasy come to life. Last night was more than incredible; it was transformative. The way you came apart in my arms, the sounds you made, the feel of you around me... I'm getting distracted just writing this. There are fresh pancakes staying warm in the oven. Help yourself to anything else you find. Or just wait for me, and I'll give you everything you need.

Counting the minutes until I can hold you again,
River

PS: Emma, I've left coffee in the thermal carafe, the special blend I've been saving. One sip and you'll understand why I guard it so jealously. You're the only one I'd share it with. Take your time this morning. Can't wait to see you. —Levi

PPS: You're safe here, always. This is your space now too. We won't be long, and when we return, we can talk... or

*not talk. Whatever you need. You're not alone anymore. —
Atlas*

I trace my finger over their handwriting, a smile tugging at my lips despite the anxiety churning in my stomach. Three different men, three different ways of showing they care. Is this somehow my life? I want to say I got lucky, but I'm terrified that my life of rejection will just repeat itself when I let myself fall for anyone.

The thought of fresh pancakes makes my stomach growl fiercely. Despite all the carnival food I devoured yesterday, my body is ravenous, likely a side effect of last night's amazing sex. I find the promised breakfast keeping warm in the oven, a stack of fluffy pancakes that must have been made just before they left.

A quick search of the pantry reveals a bottle of maple syrup, the real stuff, not the artificial kind. I carry my bounty to the dining table, curling up in one of the chairs with my legs tucked beneath me.

I don't bother with a plate or a fork. Instead, I tear off pieces of pancake with my fingers, pouring syrup on them. It's childish and messy, but there's something freeing about it. No one here to judge me, no need to be proper or controlled.

As I eat, my mind circles back to last night. The way River touched me, fucked me. The things he whispered in my ear as he drove into me. The intensity of the pleasure he wrung from my body was unlike anything I'd experienced before.

Sex with Chad had been... fine. Adequate. Sometimes even good. But with River? It was like floating, like the difference between a candle and a supernova. Each touch electric, each kiss an exploration, each thrust pushing me to heights I didn't know existed.

Was it because of my approaching heat? The compatibility of our scents? Or something about the way he looked at me like I was precious, the care he took to ensure my pleasure before his own?

Whatever the reason, I can't deny that something has shifted inside me. A wall crumbling, a door opening.

I've known these men for less than a week. I'm still raw from Chad's rejection. And now I've complicated everything by giving in to this... whatever this is.

My phone rings on the table beside me, startling me from my spiral of thoughts. Jess. I answer immediately, grateful for the distraction.

"Bitch, you've been holding out on me!" she announces playfully.

I laugh, licking syrup from my thumb. "Hello to you too, Jess."

"Don't *hello* me. I was promised regular updates on your firefighter situation, and it's been radio silence. Have you climbed any of them like trees yet? I need details, Emma. DETAILS."

"Sorry," I say, unable to keep the smile from my voice. "Things have been a bit... chaotic."

"Chaotic good or chaotic evil? Because if any of them have turned out to be secret serial killers, cough twice, and I'll call for backup."

"Definitely good chaos," I assure her. "They're... they're really great, actually."

"Oh my God," Jess gasps dramatically. "You slept with one of them!"

I nearly choke on my pancake. "How could you possibly know that?"

"I've known you since freshman year of college. I can hear sex in your voice. Spill. Everything. Now."

Heat rushes to my cheeks despite being alone in the cabin. "It was last night. With River."

"And?" she demands when I don't continue.

"And it was... incredible," I admit, twirling a strand of hair around my finger nervously. "Jess, I've never experienced anything like it. He was so... attentive and passionate and just... I don't even have the words. I mean, he fucks like a damn monster, and I loved it too much."

"Holy shit, I'm jealous," she breathes. "And you're smitten."

"I'm not!" I protest automatically. "It was just sex."

"In all the years I've known you, I've never heard you describe sex as incredible or compare it to being ravaged by a monster. Usually, it's 'fine' or 'pretty good' or 'he tried, bless his heart.'"

She's right, and we both know it. I sigh, abandoning the pretense. "What am I doing, Jess? I barely know these guys."

"You're having fun, that's what. After the Chad disaster, you deserve some happiness. Even if it's just really great sex with a hot firefighter."

"It's not just River, though," I confess, the words tumbling out before I can stop them. "There's something about all three of them. They're so different, but they fit together somehow. And being around them feels... right."

Jess lets out an excited squeal. "Are you telling me you've found yourself in the middle of an Alpha pack? Because if so, I'm both insanely jealous and demanding more photographic evidence immediately."

I laugh despite myself. "I'm just... confused."

"Confused is a step up from heartbroken, which is where you were a week ago. I'd call that progress." She pauses. "How are you, really?"

"I'm okay," I say, surprised to find that I mean it. "Better than I expected to be, given everything."

"Good. You deserve good things, Em."

"Enough about my disaster of a love life," I deflect. "How are you? How's work?"

Jess groans dramatically. "Don't even ask. Three double shifts this week, and the ER has been an absolute nightmare. Some virus going around that has everyone projectile vomiting. I've gone through six sets of scrubs."

"Gross." I laugh. "Anything exciting happening outside of work?"

"Oh God," she moans. "I wasn't going to tell you because it's too mortifying, but since you've already embraced chaos by sleeping with a hot firefighter, I might as well join you in the land of questionable life choices."

"Now you have to tell me," I insist, leaning forward eagerly.

"So there's this new guy who moved in next door," she begins. "Absolutely gorgeous. Like, illegal levels of attractive. The kind of face that will get me in trouble."

"And?" I prompt when she pauses.

"And I may have accidentally traumatized him for life by showing up almost naked on his doorstep at midnight."

I burst out laughing. "You WHAT?"

"It wasn't my fault!" she protested. "My demon cat locked me out! I'd left a window open because of the heat wave, and the little monster slipped out. Then, as I went after him, the door swung shut behind me. Then he somehow got back in through the window—evil thing."

"Oh, no."

"You see, recently, there were two stray dogs wandering the street, and I didn't want Lord Murderfloof to get hurt. And naturally, it had to be the one night I decided to sleep in the nude."

"Oh my God." I wheeze, trying to catch my breath. "What did you do?"

"What could I do? I grabbed old Mr. Rosenberg's faded Panama shirt from the clothesline. The thing barely covered me and made me look like someone's retired grandmother, and here I am knocking on the hot new neighbor's door, praying he still had the spare key my old roommate used to leave with the previous tenant next door."

I'm laughing so hard now. "Please tell me he was home."

"Oh, he was," Jess confirms grimly. "Opened the door in his boxers, took one look at me standing there, and just... froze. Like, blue screen of death froze."

"What did you say?" I manage between gasps of laughter.

"'Hi, I'm your neighbor, and I'm locked out, and I know this is weird, but do you have my spare key?' All in one breath while trying to look dignified."

"And did he have the key?"

"Eventually, he unfroze enough to let me in while he looked for it. Gave me his robe, which I still have because I'm too mortified to return it. And get this, I'm pretty sure I saw him through his window the next day, walking around his apartment completely naked. So, now we're even, I guess?"

"Jess," I say solemnly. "This is the beginning of a beautiful love story."

"Or the beginning of me changing my name and moving to a different country," she retorts. "I can't even look him in the eye when we pass in the yard now. And he's so hot, Emma. Like, unfairly hot. Tall, dark, just the right amount of scruff, arms that could— Wait, I'm getting distracted.

"Nah, I'm traumatized. There's a difference." She sighs. "Anyway, gotta run. They just paged me for another shift because Anderson called in sick. Again. I swear that man has the immune system of a newborn mouse."

"Go save lives," I tell her. "And maybe invest in some emergency pajamas for your midnight adventures."

"Hardy har," she deadpans. "Love you, disaster queen. Call me when you've figured out which fire-fighter you're keeping. Or if you're keeping all three, in which case I demand full details."

"Goodbye, Jess." I laugh, hanging up before she can make any more outrageous demands.

I'm still smiling as I finish the last of the pancakes, licking syrup from my fingers. Talking to Jess always helps put things into perspective. Maybe she's right and I don't need to overthink this. Maybe I can just... experience it. See where it leads.

But my body feels... different. There's a lingering warmth under my skin, not the desperate fever of last night, but something subtler, waiting. The calm before the storm.

I need a shower, I decide. Maybe that will help clear my head.

I make it halfway to the bathroom when a sharp, twisting pain hits in my lower abdomen. I drop to my knees with a gasp. It's followed immediately by a rush of heat so intense it feels like I'm being consumed from the inside out by flames.

"No," I whimper, clutching the wall for support. "Not now. Not alone."

But my body doesn't care about convenient timing. The fever surges through me in waves, each more powerful than the last. Between my thighs, I'm suddenly soaking wet, slick coating my inner thighs as my core pulses with urgency.

I try to stand, but another wave of pain and heat crashes through me, driving me back to the floor. This isn't like any heat I've experienced before. It's faster, stronger, and overwhelming in its demands. And way too early.

With a monumental effort, I crawl to my bedroom, thinking my nest might provide some relief. But the carefully arranged blankets and pillows that usually soothe me during my heats feel wrong—sterile, empty, missing something essential.

Missing them.

"Fuck," I groan, curling into a ball as another spike of pain lances through me. My hands shake as I press them against my stomach, trying to alleviate the cramping ache, but nothing helps.

On instinct, I drag myself back to River's room, drawn by the lingering scent of him on his sheets. I collapse onto his bed, burying my face in his pillow and inhaling deeply. The familiar notes of cinnamon and brown sugar wrap around me, providing momentary relief from the white-hot need consuming me.

I roll across his bed, trying to surround myself with his scent, but it's not enough. It's a pale shadow of what I really need—him, his touch, his knot. My knees curl up to my chest as another wave of pain racks me, a whimper escaping my clenched teeth.

This isn't just desire or lust. It's an agonizing emptiness, a void that demands to be filled. My body knows what it needs, and it's not satisfied with substitutes or memories.

My phone. I need to call them.

I reach for it with trembling fingers, nearly dropping it twice before managing to grip it properly. Just as I unlock the screen, it lights up with an incoming call.

Chad.

"You've got to be fucking kidding me," I mutter, tempted to ignore it, but the pain clouds my judgment, and I find myself swiping to answer. "What do you want?"

"Emma." Chad's voice, once so appealing, now grates on my nerves. "Finally. I've been trying to reach you for days."

"What do you want?" I repeat, unable to keep a groan from escaping as another wave of heat rolls through me.

There's a pause on the other end. "What's wrong with you? You sound weird."

"Nothing," I grit out, sweat beading on my forehead as I fight to keep my voice steady. "If you don't have anything important to say, I'm hanging up."

"Shit," he says suddenly, realization dawning. "Emma, are you in heat? Where the fuck are you? Want me to come help?"

The audacity of his offer sends a spike of anger through the haze of pain. "Fuck no," I snarl. "Why would you say that when you're with Megan, you asshole?"

"Megan's not what you think," he says defensively. "Look, we had a thing, but it's over. She turned out to be... complicated."

"Complicated," I repeat flatly. "Is that what we're calling it now? You rejected me during my heat, told me my scent was 'wrong,' then hooked up with my so-called friend behind my back. But sure, she's the complicated one."

"I made a mistake, okay?" He sounds frustrated now. "People make mistakes. I just... I don't know. I panicked. Your scent changed, and I freaked out. But I've been thinking about it, and I think I overreacted."

"How magnanimous of you," I say, sarcasm dripping from every syllable.

"Can we just talk?" he pleads, ignoring the barb. "Please? At least let me know you're safe during your heat. Like the old times. They were good times, right?"

For a brief, weak moment, I remember how it used to be. Chad taking care of me during my heats, attentive and passionate in a way he rarely was otherwise. But then I remember his coldness before he dumped me, how he'd turned away from me with a grimace, claiming my scent had changed, become unappealing.

"The good times are over," I tell him flatly. "You made sure of that when you rejected me at my most vulnerable. When you looked at me like I disgusted you."

"Emma, please—"

"No," I cut him off. "I want nothing to do with you. Not now, not ever again."

"I'm coming to Whispering Grove," he declares suddenly. "I'm going to find you, okay? We need to talk face-to-face."

Panic surges through me at the thought of him here, in this place that's become a sanctuary of sorts. "Stay away from me, Chad. I mean it."

"You're not thinking clearly right now. Once your heat passes—"

"Fuck off," I snap, ending the call before he can say anything else.

I toss the phone aside, curling tighter around myself as another wave of pain and need washes over me. The conversation with Chad has only intensified my distress, memories of his rejection compounding the physical agony of being alone during this heat.

What am I going to do? My heat has never hit this suddenly before, never been this intense. I didn't bring any emergency suppressants with me. Why would I when my cycle wasn't due for weeks?

But there's nothing manageable about this consuming fire in my veins, this desperate emptiness that feels like it might tear me apart.

Maybe I can take the edge off myself. It's not ideal, but it might provide some relief until the Alphas return.

With shaking hands, I slide my shorts down my legs, gasping as the cool air hits my overheated skin. I'm embarrassingly wet, thighs slick with evidence of my arousal. I close my eyes, trying to summon the memory of River's touch as I slide my fingers through my folds.

The first touch sends a jolt of pleasure through me, but it's immediately apparent that it's not enough. My fingers feel too small compared to what my body is demanding. Still, I persist, circling my clit with increasing pressure, desperately seeking release.

When the orgasm finally comes, it's a pale imitation of what I experienced with River. A momentary spike of pleasure that does nothing to ease the aching emptiness inside me. If anything, it makes it worse, highlighting exactly what I'm missing.

I need a knot. I need an Alpha. I need my Alphas.

With shaking hands, I reach for my phone again, scrolling to Atlas's number. It rings several times before going to voicemail.

"H-hey," I stammer when the tone sounds. "It's me. I kinda need to speak to you urgently. Please call me. I just..." I trail off, unsure of what to say without sounding pathetic. "Just call me."

I hang up, cursing under my breath. Next, I try River, hoping he might be more likely to answer, given what happened between us last night. Again, the call goes to voicemail.

"River," I say, my voice betraying more of my distress this time. "I need—" A particularly sharp cramp cuts me off, a grunt of pain escaping before I can stop it. "Please call me as soon as you can. It's important."

Levi is my last hope. I dial his number, my vision

blurring with unshed tears of frustration and pain as I listen to it ring endlessly. When his voicemail prompts me to leave a message, something in me breaks.

"Oh God, where are you all?" I sniff, unable to keep the desperation from my voice as another wave of heat crashes through me. "I'm in heat. Please, I need help."

After hanging up, I curl around River's pillow, trying to find comfort in his lingering scent, but it's fading, a poor substitute for what I truly need. Tears of frustration leak from the corners of my eyes.

As the minutes tick by with no response, my desperation grows. Maybe they're truly unreachable. What if they're in danger?

With trembling fingers, I dial the fire station, praying someone there can at least tell me when they might return.

"Whispering Grove Fire Department," a familiar female voice answers. "Claire speaking."

Of all the people to answer, it had to be her, the volunteer I met on my first day, who looked at me like I was an intruder even then.

"Hi," I manage, trying to keep my voice steady. "I'm trying to reach Atlas, or River, or Levi. It's urgent."

"They're at the elementary school," Claire replies, her tone coolly professional. "Gas leak situation. Is everything okay? You sound... distressed."

So that's the emergency call. At least now I know where they are. "Do you know when they'll be back? I really need to speak with them."

There's a pause, then Claire's voice takes on a

different quality, less professional, more personal. "You know, they're working right now. Saving lives. They don't really appreciate being... bothered while on duty."

"I wouldn't call if it weren't important," I say, gritting my teeth against both pain and irritation.

"Mmm," she hums, unconvinced. "Don't we all think our problems are important? But some of us manage without monopolizing all three of them, while others can't even get one."

The pettiness in her tone would be laughable if I weren't in such distress. "This isn't a competition, Claire."

"Isn't it?" She laughs, the sound brittle and forced. "You've been in town, what, a week? And somehow, you've got all three of them wrapped around your finger. Must be some kind of trick."

Another cramp hits me, this one so intense I can't suppress a gasp of pain. "I can't do this right now," I manage. "Just... tell them to check their messages if you see them."

I hang up before she can respond, tossing the phone aside with a frustrated growl. Great. Now, not only am I alone and in agony, but I've also apparently made an enemy of the one person who might have been able to help me reach the Alphas.

Curling into a tighter ball, I press my face into River's pillow as tears leak from the corners of my eyes. The pain is getting worse, the empty ache spreading from my core to encompass my entire body. Each wave brings with it memories of last night, River's hands, his mouth, his knot filling me so perfectly.

But it's not just River I crave. Images of Atlas on the balcony, of Levi in the Tunnel of Love, flicker through my mind. All three of them so different yet equally compelling, equally necessary somehow.

When did that happen? When did they become so essential to me?

The last few months flash through my mind—the growing restlessness in my relationship with Chad, the subtle signs of disconnection I ignored because it was easier than starting over. Then the brutal shock of his rejection, followed by learning of his thing with Megan,. I'd fled to Whispering Grove, seeking solitude, a chance to lick my wounds in private.

Instead, I found them. Three Alphas who, in less than a week, have made me feel more seen, more understood, more wanted than Chad did in our entire relationship.

And now, curled in agony on an Alpha's bed, soaked in my own slick and tears. My body was designed to seek connection, to crave compatible partners. Fighting that biological imperative has only led me here, alone, when I need support the most.

The worst part isn't even the physical pain, though that's excruciating. It's the fear. The vulnerability. The terrifying realization that I've come to depend on three men I barely know, that my body has recognized something in them my mind is still struggling to accept.

What if they don't come back soon? What if this

gets worse? Horror stories of Omegas driven to madness by untreated heats flash through my mind, tales whispered among friends of hospitalizations and permanent damage.

Is that my fate? After everything I've survived—losing my parents, my grandmother, Chad's betrayal—is this how I finally break? Alone in a strange town, consumed by an unexpected heat with no one to help me through it?

I reach for my phone again, sending desperate text messages to all three Alphas.

Please call me. In heat. Need help.

It's bad. Really bad. Please.

I'm sorry to bother you at work, but I don't know what to do.

The messages stare back at me, unread. Unseen. Unanswered.

Another wave of heat crashes over me, this one so intense that I cry out, clutching at the sheets as my back arches involuntarily. The emptiness inside me is a physical pain now, a hollow ache that nothing can fill.

I try pleasuring myself again, fingers working desperately between my thighs, but it's useless. The orgasm that ripples through me is weak, unsatisfying, serving only to highlight what I'm missing.

"Please," I sob, face pressed into River's pillow as another contraction of need twists through me. "Please come back."

Only silence answers me. I'm truly alone, at the

mercy of my biology and the cruel timing of an unexpected heat.

The minutes stretch into hours, each one an eternity of alternating waves of need and pain. I drift in and out of lucidity, the fever taking a greater toll with each passing moment. At some point, I stripped completely naked, the fabric of my clothes too abrasive against my hypersensitive skin.

In a moment of clarity, I remember something from an Omega health class. Water can sometimes help regulate body temperature during heat. With trembling limbs, I drag myself to the bathroom, every movement an exercise in agony as my body protests being pulled away from the Alpha scents in River's room.

I manage to turn on the shower, collapsing under the spray without bothering to adjust the temperature. The cool water provides momentary relief, washing away the slick from my thighs and the sweat from my skin, but it does nothing for the internal burn, the desperate emptiness that feels like it's consuming me from the inside out.

How long can I endure this? How long before this heat causes real damage? The rational part of my brain knows I should call for medical help, but the thought of strangers touching me during heat, of clinical hands and dispassionate faces, fills me with a different kind of terror.

I want them. My Alphas. No one else.

Eventually, the water runs cold enough to make me

shiver despite the fever raging through me. I turn it off with clumsy fingers and stumble back to River's room, leaving wet footprints in my wake.

I collapse onto his bed, not bothering to dry off or dress. The sheets soak through immediately, but I don't care. I curl around his pillow, inhaling deeply, searching for any trace of his scent that might provide even the smallest comfort.

Another wave of heat crashes over me, drawing a whimper from my parched throat. My body is on fire, burning, every nerve ending raw and screaming. The slick between my thighs is almost constant now, my core clenching rhythmically around nothing, seeking what it needs.

How ironic that after years of insisting I need no one, of building my identity around my independence, I'm reduced to this—an Omega in desperate need of her Alphas.

The realization should terrify me more than it does. Instead, there's a strange peace in finally admitting the truth—I need them. All three of them. In a way I've never needed anyone before.

The heat builds again, a tidal wave of need and pain that tears a broken sob from my throat. I press my face into River's pillow, inhaling desperately for any trace of his scent, any whisper of comfort in this torment.

"Please," I whisper, the word a prayer to deities I don't believe in. "Please help me."

17

ATLAS

"All clear, Chief Wood. Final readings show no trace of gas."

I nod at the technician, relief washing through me after three grueling hours containing what could have been a catastrophic situation. The elementary school's ancient gas system had finally given out, sending dangerous levels of methane through the entire east wing. Evacuating three hundred children and staff without causing panic had been a challenge, but one my team handled with practiced efficiency.

"Good work," I tell him, rolling my shoulders to release some of the tension that's been building since the emergency call came in early this morning. "Have your team do one more sweep of the classrooms before the technicians clear the building for reentry."

"Yes, sir."

I turn to find River helping the maintenance staff secure the newly repaired valve while Levi meticulously documents the entire incident for his safety report. My pack. My team. Pride swells in my chest, watching them work so seamlessly together.

With the immediate danger passed, I start removing my gear, the heavy jacket first, then the breathing apparatus we'd worn as a precaution while working near the leak. The weight of responsibility lifts from my shoulders with each piece I shed. No injuries, no structural damage, crisis averted.

My thoughts drift to Emma as I pack away the equipment. How is she doing back at the cabin? I hated leaving her this morning, especially after what River shared about their night together. She'd looked so peaceful sleeping in his bed, that cascade of honey-blonde hair spread across his pillow, her face relaxed in a way I'd rarely seen since meeting her.

The memory of our time on the watchtower balcony surfaces—her taste, her sounds, the way she came apart under my mouth. The attraction between us has been undeniable. And now, she'd formed similar bonds with both River and Levi.

In my many years as an Alpha, I've never felt this kind of immediate, powerful pull toward an Omega, especially not one who simultaneously connects with my entire pack.

I reach for my phone in the truck to check the time, seeing as I left it behind during the emergency response, as per protocol. The screen lights up, revealing missed calls and urgent text messages.

All from Emma.

"Shit," I mutter, quickly opening the first voice-mail. Her voice comes through, strained and uncertain.

"H-hey. It's me. I kinda need to speak to you urgently. Please call me. I just... Just call me."

My blood runs cold. Did something happen to her?

"River! Levi!" I call, urgency sharpening my words to a command. They both look up instantly, responding to the Alpha tone. "We need to go. Now."

They're at my side in seconds.

"What's wrong?" Levi demands, already packing up his documentation.

I hold up my phone, showing them Emma's message. "Emma's been trying to reach us."

Both of them suddenly scramble to grab their phones from the truck and listen to their messages.

I check the time stamp. "First one came in over an hour ago."

"Shit, shit, shit, she just said she's in full heat," Levi mutters, already moving toward the exit. "We need to go. Right now."

Fuck! An Omega in heat, alone, with no Alpha support, is more than uncomfortable; it's dangerous. The pain can become excruciating and the fever dangerously high without intervention.

Levi is already on his phone, calling in an additional team to help the technicians with final checks.

"It's bad if she called all three of us," I mutter grimly as we all get ready. "You know how independent she is. If she's asking for help..."

I don't need to finish the thought. We all know

what it means for an Omega as fiercely self-reliant as Emma to reach out in distress.

We move as one unit, abandoning the last of the cleanup to the technicians, throwing our gear haphazardly into the truck. I take the driver's seat while River and Levi pile in beside me. The engine roars to life as I floor the accelerator, sirens blaring to clear a path through town.

"Can't this thing go any faster?" Levi demands.

"Not without breaking several laws," I reply, though I push the speed a little higher anyway. Some rules matter less than others in an emergency.

"I knew something was different about her scent yesterday," River murmurs quietly. "She just calmed down so quickly last night, and I assumed it was her coming close to her heat... not that it was already here."

"We all should have noticed," I say, taking a corner perhaps too sharply.

River runs a hand through his already disheveled hair. "It's us," Levi explains. "Compatible Alphas can trigger early heats in Omegas. All three of us together... we probably accelerated her cycle without realizing it."

The weight of responsibility settles heavily on my shoulders. We have to make this right.

We reach the station in record time, the fire station vehicle barely coming to a stop before we jump out, heading for my pickup truck.

Claire meets us at the entrance, clipboard in hand.

"Everything go okay with the gas leak?" she asks, her gaze lingering on our obvious hurry.

"Fine," I reply curtly, handing off my equipment to one of the volunteers. "We've got an emergency at home. We'll be unreachable for the next day or two, but I'll check in when I can."

Her eyes narrow slightly. "What's going on? All okay?"

"Yep," I snap, not elaborating. Emma's condition is private, not something to be discussed with station volunteers, especially one who's made her interest in me uncomfortably clear over the past few months.

"Let's go," Levi states quietly over my shoulder. We all get into the truck.

We leave without further explanation. The drive to the cabin seems like an eternity, though it can't be more than twenty minutes from town.

"Drive faster," River urges as if that might somehow speed our journey.

"I'm already doing ninety," I growl, tension making my voice harsher than intended. "We'll be there in five minutes."

"I expect she's been with each of us, then," Levi observes. "I noticed something different about her after your time together on the watchtower, Atlas. Then there was our encounter at the Tunnel of Love ride yesterday."

"I knew it!" River's head snaps toward Levi. "Thought I heard you growling in the tunnel."

A hint of color touches Levi's cheekbones. "Says

you, who was so vocal with her last night. My bedroom shares a wall with yours."

River doesn't have the grace to look embarrassed. "Guilty as charged. But, Atlas, you sly bastard. When did you and Emma...?"

"Nights ago," I admit, keeping my eyes fixed on the winding mountain road. "Up in the watchtower after you two went back to the cabin."

"And you didn't think to share this information?" River demands.

"Nope," I reply simply.

"She's been with all of us," Levi says, voicing what we're all thinking. "Separately, but within days of each other, which would have influenced her hormones for her heat."

"She's ours," I say. "All of ours. And we've left her alone during her first heat with us."

None of us dispute it, but guilt chews me up on the inside.

We arrive at the cabin in tense silence. I park wildly in the driveway, then we're out of the truck, moving as one toward the door.

The scent hits us the moment we enter, sweet vanilla and honey, intensified tenfold and laced with distress pheromones that trigger every protective instinct I possess. River actually growls beside me, the sound low and primal in his throat.

"Emma?" I call out, already moving through the main living area, following the concentrated trail of her scent.

A faint whimper answers me, coming from the direction of River's room. We cross the space in long strides, pushing open the door to find her on his bed.

The sight has me pausing. Emma lies naked and shivering despite the obvious fever flushing her skin, her face streaked with tears, her body curled protectively around itself. The sheets beneath her are soaked with sweat and slick, evidence of how long she's been suffering alone. My heart shudders.

"Emma," I breathe, moving to her side immediately.

Her eyes flutter open, glassy with fever but focusing on me with visible effort. "You came back," she whispers, her voice cracked and raw. "I called... No one answered..."

"We're here now," I assure her, sitting on the edge of the bed, brushing sweat-dampened hair from her forehead. Her skin burns against my palm, the fever dangerously high. "We're so sorry, sweetheart. There's no excuse for making you suffer."

"Had our phones in the truck," River adds, kneeling beside the bed, taking one of her hands in his. "Couldn't hear them ring."

"We came as soon as we got your messages," Levi says. "How long have you been like this?"

"Feels like forever," she manages, another shiver racking her frame despite the heat pouring off her skin. "It hit so fast... Never been this bad before..."

My jaw clenches at the thought of her suffering alone for hours while we were unreachable. "We need to get her temperature down," I say, making the decision quickly. "She's burning up."

"Cool shower. I'll get it started," Levi agrees, already moving toward the bathroom.

"Can you stand, sugar cube?" River asks gently, his nickname for her softer than I've ever heard from him.

Emma tries to sit up, only to collapse back with a whimper of pain. "Hurts," she whispers. "Everything does. I just need you three."

"We're here now. Let's cool you down, then we are yours for however long you need us. We're not going anywhere." Without hesitation, I gather her into my arms, lifting her effortlessly against my chest. She feels smaller than she should, fragile in a way that contradicts the fierce, independent woman I've come to know. Her arms loop weakly around my neck, her face pressing into my shoulder as if seeking comfort in my scent.

"I've got you," I murmur, carrying her toward the bathroom where Levi has the shower running. "We've got you now."

River follows close behind, already stripping off his clothes, ready for what needs to happen next. Levi tests the water temperature with his hand, adjusting it to lukewarm—cool enough to bring down her fever but not so cold as to shock her system.

"All of you," Emma mumbles against my neck, her words slurring slightly with fever. "Need all of you."

"You have us," I assure her, setting her carefully on

her feet but keeping an arm around her waist to support her. "We're not going anywhere."

Levi is already undressing. His eyes are glossing over. The heat from Omegas impacts Alphas just as much, putting them into a wild, feral state with the urgency to rut, to knot. But beneath it all also comes care, helping an Omega in distress. *Our* Omega.

I keep one arm around Emma while removing my own clothes with my free hand, not willing to let her go even for a moment. She sways against me, weak from fighting the heat alone. That thought is torture to know she suffered.

Once we're all naked, I guide her under the spray, stepping in behind her, while River and Levi join us. Our shower is oversized, designed to accommodate multiple people.

The water sluices over her feverish skin, drawing a gasp from her lips that transforms into a moan of relief. We surround her, our hands moving over her in gentle, soothing patterns, helping the water cool her overheated body.

"I tried to call," she whispers again, breathing heavily, holding on to us, her voice stronger now as the water cools her down somewhat. "No one answered. I even called the station."

"Claire answered?" Levi asks, his clever fingers massaging shampoo into her hair, careful to keep the suds from her eyes.

Emma nods weakly, then breaks out into a moan, her body shuddering. She grasps more for Levi and

River, drawing them closer. I press up against her back, my cock already painfully hard from her ass, from her body against mine, her perfume drowning me.

"We're here," River purrs, his hands sliding soap across her shoulders, down her chest, and cupping her breasts. "You're so fucking beautiful."

Her eyes flutter closed as our hands work over her gorgeous, soft body, washing away the hours of suffering, replacing pain with something gentler, slower, barely contained tenderness beneath the heat.

"Emma," Levi murmurs. "How are you feeling now?"

She leans into him, her cheek pressed to his chest, and for a moment, I think she's too far gone to answer.

"Still... empty. Aching."

Her body shifts again, draping across all of us—desperate, clinging. Her arms curl around River's neck, her side arches into Levi's touch, and her leg slides between mine as if she's trying to get closer to all of us at once.

"I'm trying so hard to resist," she whispers, lips brushing against River's collarbone. "But you have no idea how much I need you all." Her voice cracks with the effort it takes to hold back. "It's like my body is screaming for you."

The cool water helps, but not enough. Her skin is still burning under our hands, sweat and scent mixing with the steam, sweet and feral and overwhelming. My instincts claw at me to take her, to ease her, to claim what's already ours. I see the same war in Levi's eyes, and River's jaw is clenched so tight I swear it might crack.

She turns to me now, eyes glassy. "Fuck me, please," she whispers almost innocently, and I might laugh if she weren't in so much pain. "Being near you helps, but it's not enough. I can't think. I can't breathe. Please..."

Even though we're all trying to be careful, I feel that the line between patience and primal has been crossed.

None of us are unaffected.

She cries out, clutching onto us, reaching down for Levi's cock, and I quickly turn off the shower.

"Okay, enough of the shower. Take her to her nest. We are going to claim our sweet Omega all fucking day and night, all week, if that's what she needs."

"Please, I can't hold on anymore. I need all your cocks inside me," she groans while River and Levi grin.

My dick is throbbing with the ache for her sweet hole.

I hold her close, not trusting her still-shaky legs, while River and Levi grab towels. We dry her quickly, and she pushes my hand between her thighs. I don't hold back... I crave all of her, so I press my fingers between her folds and push two digits into her. She arches against my chest, crying out, shaking, her nipples so tight that I'm drooling, staring at them.

"You are so perfect, so wet for us," I whisper in her ear as I finger her, loving seeing her come undone.

River and Levi are watching, mesmerized, hands palming their own cocks.

"I'm going to carry you to bed, okay?"

I pull my fingers out, drenched in her slick, but she whines in pain. Rapidly, I lift her into my arms and rush her out, River and Levi on my heels.

Her nest is in the largest bedroom with the biggest bed, designed to accommodate all of us comfortably. The sheets are cool and clean against my skin as I lay her down, her hair fanning out across the pillow like spilled honey.

For a moment, we simply look at this remarkable woman who has somehow become essential to all of us in such a short time. Her skin glows with lingering heat flush, her eyes dark with desire, her lips parted in anticipation. *Beautiful* doesn't begin to cover it.

"What are you waiting for?" she asks, a hint of her usual sass returning despite the need evident in every line of her body.

River laughs, breaking the tension as he stretches out beside her. "Just admiring the view."

"Admire later," she says, reaching for him with one hand while extending her other toward Levi. "Touch now."

We need no further invitation. The bed dips as we join her. River on her left, Levi on her right, me settling between her thighs at the foot of the bed. Three Alphas surrounding one beautiful Omega, balanced and feeling so perfectly right in a way I've never experienced before.

"So beautiful," Levi murmurs, tracing the curve of her breast with gentle fingers before leaning down to claim her mouth in a kiss.

River's lips find her other nipple.

My hands slide up her thighs, gently pressing them wider as I settle between them and display the most gorgeous pussy.

"Tell us if anything becomes too much," I instruct, my voice rougher than intended as her scent hits me with full force. Sweet honey and vanilla, intensified by heat and arousal—it's the most intoxicating thing I've ever experienced.

Emma's response is to arch her back, a silent plea for more contact, more touch, more everything.

I lower my head before tasting her for the second time. The flavor explodes across my tongue—sweeter, more intense than before, enhanced by her heat.

Her reaction is immediate and visceral, a moan torn from her throat as her hips buck against me. Levi holds the sound with his lips, kissing her deeply while River tugs her nipples, pinching and rolling.

"Please," she gasps when Levi finally releases her mouth. Her head thrashes on the pillow as I suck firmly on her clit, my fingers spreading her lips open. I want her exposed, stretched, sated. "I need... I need..."

"We know what you need," Levi murmurs, his voice a low rumble against her ear, hand braced beside her head. "Trust us to take care of you, Emma."

And she nods, smiling. "Thank you."

She lets go, breath hitching as her thighs part

wider for me. Her body trembles, flushed and slick with heat, her scent so potent now that it's like breathing her in is enough to make me lose control. But I toe the line—for now.

I hold her steady, drawing slow, deliberate strokes through her folds. She's soaked and swollen, and the taste of her on my tongue is pure fucking heaven—sweet and sharp and everything I've ever craved.

She moans, helpless against the way we're touching her, claiming her, unraveling her.

Her legs tense around my shoulders, her hips rolling now with desperation. She's close. I can feel it in the way she clenches, the way her breath stutters, the helpless little whimpers she makes when I suck her clit between my lips and flick it with my tongue. I slide two fingers into her, thrusting fast.

"Fuck... please... don't stop," she begs, her eyes glazed and wide, locked on mine.

"Not stopping," I promise, voice rough with need. "Come for us, Emma. Let go."

Her body bows, spine arched, thighs shaking around me as the orgasm tears through her. She sobs out a sound, and her hands grasp blindly at the sheets, at skin, at anything she can anchor herself to as the wave crashes over her.

It's not just pleasure. It's release. Relief. As if her body has been screaming for this, and finally, *finally*, we've answered.

She falls back against the bed, chest heaving, lips

parted, every inch of her trembling. And still, she's glowing. Ours.

And we're only just getting started.

My cock throbs almost painfully, demanding I fuck her. A glance at River and Levi shows they're similarly affected, their cocks hard.

Emma's heat is nowhere close to being satisfied.

Even as the last of her orgasm trembles through her body, I can see it, *feel* it—that pulse of arousal building again in her scent, the way her thighs press together, her hips rocking, the way she reaches for us with shaking hands, as if she's starving and we're the only thing that can sate her.

"Inside," she gasps. "Fuck me hard."

Her voice is raw. Wrecked. Pleading.

The moment had started slowly. Controlled. We'd tried to be gentle, careful, for her sake. But that restraint is hanging by threads now, snapping one by one under the weight of her heat and the way she smells—sweet and slick and meant for us.

Levi growls low, dragging a hand down his face like he's trying to center himself, and failing. "Fuck. I need a taste," he snarls, already moving.

We don't argue.

He switches places with me, settling between her thighs like he was born to belong there, his broad shoulders pushing her knees wide. The second his mouth touches her, Emma jerks violently, a whimper breaking from her lips.

I stretch out beside her, catching her mouth in a

kiss that's all teeth and heat, grounding her even as she shakes.

"You're so fucking good for us, baby," I whisper between kisses. "So sweet. So wet. Let us ruin you."

On her other side, River strokes a hand down her belly, his cock hard and flushed, the head leaking against her skin.

"Look at her," he murmurs, dragging his length slowly across her chest, smearing precum over her breasts. "Our perfect little Omega. You like how that feels, sugar cube?" His voice turns molten. "Wanna feel it everywhere?"

Emma nods desperately, completely lost in the sensations. Levi's tongue works her open below, I'm on her neck, sucking and licking, and River is rubbing himself over her as if he owns her. She's trembling, moaning, panting our names like prayers, grasping for his cock.

But it's more than just names now.

"That's it, good girl," Levi rasps against her pussy, his voice thick with hunger. "Taste so fucking good."

Emma sobs, her hands flying out to grasp at anything—my arm, River's cock, the twisted sheets beneath her. She's shaking, barely able to stay grounded.

"She's close," I warn, my voice tight, my teeth sinking into her bottom lip. "Fuck, Levi, don't stop."

He doesn't.

He groans low, feral, as Emma breaks apart again, her thighs clamping around his head, her back arching like a bowstring. She chants his name, wrecked and breathless, until she collapses with a shudder.

Levi finally rises, dragging his mouth across the back of his hand like he's tasted something sacred. His eyes are wild.

"Still not enough," he mutters, voice hoarse. "Not for her. Not for me."

I meet their eyes, every muscle in my body strung tight with restraint.

"Put her on me."

They don't hesitate. I lie flat on my back while Levi and River move fast, strong hands lifting her. She's limp, gasping softly and trembling again from the aftershocks. They ease her back onto me, her spine pressing to my chest, my cock already nudging against her slick rear entrance.

She gasps, her head falling back against my shoulder. "Atlas—"

"I've got you," I growl, wrapping an arm around her waist. "Let me fuck that sweet ass, baby."

She nods while Levi says, "Gonna help."

She tenses against me, and I feel his hand at her rear. I appreciate him fingering her there to help loosen her, prepare her.

"Why does it feel so good?" she purrs, shuddering all over.

"Because your body craves us."

"Doing so good," River growls against her skin.

Levi pulls back and gives me a nod, so I grip her

hips and push into her, slowly at first. She's hissing as I sink fully inside her.

"Taking all of me... fuck, you feel incredible."

She moans, her whole body trembling against me, caught in that razor-thin edge of too much and not enough.

Beside me, River lets out a low whistle. "You always gotta narrate like a porn star, Atlas?"

I glance back at him, smirking. "Sorry, would you rather I sing about how tight and perfect she feels?"

Levi chuckles from where he's stroking his cock, his other hand resting possessively on her thigh. "Honestly? I'd pay to hear that. Drop the bass and serenade her ass."

Emma lets out a shaky laugh through a moan, her head falling back. "You're all insane."

"Insanely obsessed with you," River replies, leaning in to kiss the corner of her mouth. "And you love it."

She doesn't deny it. She can't, not with the way she's clenching around me, her body practically begging for more.

"All right, all right," Levi says, rolling his eyes and sitting back on his heels. "You done showing off yet, Atlas? Some of us are still waiting to join in."

I snort, slowly easing out and then thrusting back in, watching Emma's eyelids flutter. "She doesn't seem to be complaining."

River runs a finger along her jaw, tilting her face to his. "You want a taste of me now, baby?"

Emma nods, dazed and breathless. "Yes. I want all of you."

Levi groans. "There they are. The magic words."

"Fuck, I love her voice when she begs," I mutter, pressing another kiss to her shoulder. "Makes me want to ruin her again and again."

"We will," Levi promises, his voice turning rough again as he moves to take position and sinks his cock into her.

Emma cries out, panting for breath.

"You're taking us so well," I whisper in her ear.

River strokes her cheek, smirking down at her like he wants to devour her whole. "One more hole, sweetheart," he murmurs, sliding two fingers across her parted lips. "Think you can take us all?"

Emma moans around his fingers, eyes wide, glassy with heat and need. She nods, and fuck, I feel her body clench in anticipation. I hiss, as does Levi.

"So full, huh?" he mutters, voice ragged. "Taking us so fucking well."

River cups her jaw, tilting her face up to his. "Open," he breathes, voice like velvet and smoke.

She parts her lips for him without hesitation, eyes hazy.

He guides his cock to her mouth, dragging the flushed tip slowly across her bottom lip first, smearing a bead of precum there like a promise. "That's it," he murmurs. "Let me feel that sweet mouth."

She moans as he slides in, her lips stretching to

take him, inch by inch. River lets out a low, wrecked sound, his hand tightening in her hair.

"Fuck, you were made for this," River groans. "So soft... so fucking eager."

And just like that, we're all inside her, filling in every way, surrounded by our touch, claimed completely. There's no hesitation, no patience left. We find our rhythm fast, thrusting in tandem, lost in the heat of her and the pressure building between us.

She arches, a soundless scream caught in her throat, trembling between us. Every moan vibrates, every flutter of her muscles around me makes it damn near impossible to hold back.

"Look at her," I groan, dragging my hand across her lower belly, feeling the tight pull of her body. "So fucking full. I can feel myself inside her, every goddamn inch. She's taking us like she was built for it."

"She is," Levi snarls, snapping his hips harder. "Our perfect Omega."

River smirks, cupping her cheek while her mouth is still wrapped around him. "You're gonna ruin us, you know that, Emma?"

She moans a knowing sound.

"She already has," I mutter. Then add with a strained laugh, "Not that either of you assholes is complaining."

"Not when she moans like that," Levi growls. "Fuck, do it again, sweetheart. Let them hear how good we make you feel."

Emma lets out a desperate, muffled whimper around River's cock, and it nearly wrecks me.

River strokes her hair back, voice softer now but still rough with need. "So fucking perfect, taking so much of my cock in that sweet mouth."

"She's cryin' again," Levi says with a grin, breathless. "Tears and drool—look at that. River, she's fucking messy for you."

"I like her messy," River says with a wicked grin, thrusting a little deeper, slow and controlled. "Don't pretend you don't, Levi."

"I'm counting on it," Levi grunts, his thrusts getting harder, more erratic. "She's gonna fall apart, and I want to watch every second of it."

Emma trembles, caught in the storm of us, her eyes wet and glassy, body overwhelmed but never pulling away. She takes every inch, every command.

And still, even in her bliss-drunk state, her hips rock back into us, desperate for more.

Our girl. Our Omega.

And we're not stopping until she forgets her own name.

Our pace grows ragged, frenzied.

The slick sounds of our bodies fill the room—the slap of skin, the wet heat of her breathless moans around River's cock. My grip tightens on her waist, holding her still against me, my chest slick with sweat as I thrust harder, deeper, chasing the edge like it's oxygen.

She tenses in my arms, the first ripple of her

orgasm tightening through her body, a whimper catching in her throat. I feel that unmistakable shift in her muscles, the way her body begins to seize around us.

"She's close," I pant, my voice raw. "Fuck, she's squeezing me... hard."

"Yeah, no shit," Levi growls through clenched teeth. "She's milking me like she wants every last drop."

Emma arches, her entire body trembling, every part of her locked tightly around us. Her ass grips me like a vise as her mouth goes slack around River for just a moment before she sucks him deeper again with a hungry moan.

She cries out around River's cock, the sound vibrating through him as her orgasm rips through her like lightning. Her body clenches, locking us inside her, holding us there like she owns us.

And that's all it takes.

Levi lets out a brutal, strangled sound. "Fuck... knot..." he chokes out, thrusting hard once, twice, then locking in place, his knot no doubt swelling as he empties himself deep inside her with a groan that borders on a growl.

My own knot swells in perfect sync, locking me inside with her tight grip, the pressure fiercely pulsing my cum into her. I curse, burying my face in her neck as I break, my release coming hard and fast, deep and endless.

"Shit. Emma. Fuck!" River's hips jerk as he spills

into her mouth, his hands cradling her face like she's something precious, even as he shudders through it.

It takes a while, with all of us breathless.

River finally slips free from her mouth, breathing like he just ran a marathon. Emma lets out a long, blissed-out moan and licks her lips with a smirk.

For a moment, there's only the sound of harsh breathing as the four of us recover.

"Still with us?" Levi asks her softly, brushing sweat-dampened hair from her flushed face.

She nods, her eyes glazed but aware, her smile tired but genuine.

"Well," she pants, voice raspy. "For a bunch of guys who talk a lot of shit, you sure managed to keep that going pretty impressively."

River snorts. "Sorry, sugar cube... didn't realize you were taking performance notes between orgasms."

"Someone's gotta keep track," she says, laughing breathlessly.

I'm too busy holding her, feeling the way her body pulses around my still-swollen knot, to say much—just pressing kisses to her shoulder, her neck, anywhere I can reach.

Eventually, we collapse.

Levi and I, still knotted deep inside her, lie on either side of her. Our arms are tangled across her belly and hips, caging her in the best kind of way. River flops down across the top of us like a lazy, satisfied wolf, his head beside hers, thumb tracing lazy circles over her brow.

She's glowing. Wrecked. Smiling as though it were the stars that just destroyed her.

"That was... insane. Incredible," she murmurs, breathless.

Then her smile falters. Just slightly. Her eyes flick from River to Levi to me. Her fingers toy with the edge of the pillow, a nervous energy creeping in.

"I might be asking too much," she says softly, barely above a whisper. "And you can tell me no. I just... I don't know."

I tense. "What is it?" I ask.

River lifts his head, brushing a kiss to her temple. "Anything you want, we'll give it to you."

"You're ours now," Levi adds, no hesitation in his tone.

Her eyes widen. "You mean that?"

I nod. "Of course. You really think we'd just walk away after you gave yourself to us in your heat?"

"I'm feeling this deep... pull. This urgency that's just... needling at me. I've never had a mating bite. But I... I want it. I want yours."

"You want us to claim you?" I murmur. "To make it official? Bond you to us?"

She hesitates. "It's stupid. I know. I always say the most embarrassing things when I'm emotional or overwhelmed or—"

"Hey," River cuts in gently, brushing her hair back from her face. "You think we don't want this? Fuck, Emma, this is everything." His voice drops, and he bares his teeth just a little, tongue grazing one of his canines. "I ache to mark you. To taste you like that. To make sure no one else ever touches what's ours."

Levi presses a kiss to her hand, more tender than I've ever seen him. "You want a bond? I want forever. With you. No questions asked."

I lean in, my lips brushing her ear. "This is all I've wanted for too long, Emma," I whisper. "To have an Omega to adore, to protect, to fucking worship. You. Only you. Let me love you the way you deserve."

Her eyes well with tears as she twists her head to look at me, a single drop slipping down her cheek.

"God," she breathes. "You guys are going to destroy me."

River chuckles. "That's kind of the plan."

Levi grins. "Ruin you, claim you, love you. In that order."

Levi lies in front of her, one arm wrapped around her waist, his mouth brushing reverent kisses across her breast. River shifts down to her hip, pressing slow kisses along her waist and the curve of her thigh. I stay near her shoulder, my mouth caressing the curve of her neck, feeling the thrum of her pulse beneath my lips.

She moans, hips rocking gently, her body sensitive and burning, already attuned to us. The tension coils tighter. We surround her and prepare to seal the bond.

"Are you ready?" I ask softly.

"Yes," she whispers. "Please."

And we bite, my teeth breaking skin, the coppery taste of blood on my tongue.

Three sets of teeth sink into her skin—River at her

inner thigh, Levi at the swell of her breast, and me at her throat.

She cries out, sharp and high, her whole body bowing between us, but her next breath is a gasp of need, a whisper of *Don't stop.*

I feel the change instantly.

It's like a wire threads through my soul, locking me to her. A flash of heat, of belonging, courses through my chest and down to my very bones. My knot throbs, still locked inside her, but now it feels more than physical. Spiritual. My body knows hers in a way I can't explain, every heartbeat syncing, every thought drowned in Emma.

I pull back from her throat, panting, and stare down at her like I've never seen anything more beautiful in my life.

I'm hers.

And I'll never survive being without her now.

River groans as he lifts his head, licking blood from his lips. "That's beautiful," he mutters, then kisses her hip like a vow.

Levi licks a smear of crimson from her breast, then rests his forehead on hers. "You're ours now."

Emma huffs a wet, teary laugh. "You three can still joke around during the most emotionally intense moment of my life?"

"We're Alphas," Levi says smugly. "Multitasking is a specialty."

"I'm stuck under your collective body weight," she adds with a grin. "And also full of knots and cum."

"Flatter us more," River murmurs, nuzzling against her legs.

We collapse again, still tangled. Levi and I are still knotted deep inside her, pressing her snugly between us, as though we're guarding her from the world. River lies sprawled across her lower half, his head near her hip.

Her fingers thread through mine, and when she speaks, it's soft, full of something real.

"That was... incredible, and I don't think it's over."

I lean forward to reach her better and press a kiss to her damp temple. "We'll go again."

Emma laughs, and I swear I could die happy right here, inside her, claimed by her, wrapped around everything I never thought I'd have.

Home.

"Once you're ready," I add, grinning into her neck.

She huffs a laugh, completely relaxed between us. "Right. Just as soon as your knots decide to calm the hell down."

River chuckles from near her hip, kissing her skin. "You love our cocks."

She hums, smug and sweet. "I really fucking do."

18

EMMA

Three days of heat-induced passion blur together in a haze of hands, mouths, cocks, and overwhelming pleasure. Three days of being filled in every possible way, of coming so many times that I lost count, of being covered inside and out with more slick and seed than I thought humanly possible. Three days of surrendering completely to three Alphas who worshipped my body like it was their personal temple.

And now, finally, I feel normal again. More than normal. I feel incredible, as though I'm vibrating at a frequency I've never experienced before. My skin practically glows, my hair is shinier, and there's a contentment in my bones that goes deeper than mere satisfaction.

But with that contentment comes a terror that threatens to choke me.

They bit me at my request. All three of them.

Claimed me with marks that still throb gently over my body, a constant reminder of what we've done. Does this mean it's forever? The rational part of my brain knows that plenty of couples have broken up after bonding bites, even though it comes with agonizing longing and pain that can last for years.

Please, universe, don't let that happen to me. I've gone ahead and trusted again. I want to be right this time.

The thought of losing them has my chest tightening with panic. I've been hurt before, rejected and discarded like I was nothing. The scars from Chad's betrayal are still fresh, and the idea of experiencing that kind of devastation again, but magnified by three and intensified by the biological bond, is almost paralyzing.

Stop it, I tell myself firmly. *They chose you. They marked you. They're taking you out tonight to celebrate.*

Dinner at Starlight & Sage, the new restaurant that opened in Whispering Grove last month. According to River, it's supposed to be an amazing fusion of rustic mountain cuisine with sophisticated presentation, the kind of place where people get dressed up but not stuffy, where the atmosphere is cozy rather than intimidating.

The guys insisted on buying me something special to wear, and when I protested that I didn't need new clothes, Atlas simply said, "You deserve beautiful things, Emma. Let us give them to you."

How do you argue with that?

The dress they chose hangs on the back of my door,

and every time I look at it, I can't quite believe it's mine. Midnight-blue silk that seems to contain entire galaxies, with tiny crystal beads scattered across the fabric like stars. It's the most beautiful thing I've ever owned.

I slip out of my robe and carefully lift the dress from its hanger. The silk whispers against my skin as I pull it on, settling over my curves like it was made specifically for my body. The neckline dips low enough to show the swell of my breasts without being indecent, while spaghetti straps leave my shoulders bare, displaying one of my healing bite marks. The skirt fits snugly over my hips before falling in a graceful line to my ankles, with a slit up the side that reaches higher than mid-thigh.

Every step I take, the fabric slides against my legs with a whisper of sound, the slit revealing flashes of thigh that make me feel powerful, feminine, and desired all at once.

I turn to face the full-length mirror and barely recognize the woman staring back at me. My hair falls in loose waves around my shoulders. My skin has that post-heat glow that makes me look radiant and healthy. The dress transforms me from the girl next door into someone sophisticated.

Is this what real happiness feels like? This bubbling effervescence in my chest, this sense that the world is full of infinite possibilities?

A soft knock at the door interrupts my thoughts. "Come in," I call.

River slides through the doorway, and I smile instantly at seeing him. He's dressed in dark jeans and a button-down shirt the color of forest shadows, the sleeves rolled up to reveal those powerful forearms. His golden hair is styled with just enough product to look deliberately tousled, and his usual easy grin is replaced by something darker and sexier.

"I brought your—" He stops mid-sentence, his eyes going wide as he takes in my appearance. "Fuck me," he breathes, the shoes he was carrying forgotten as they dangle from two fingers.

I feel heat rush to my cheeks under his obvious appreciation. "Do I look okay?"

"Okay?" He adjusts his cock through his jeans with his free hand, not even trying to hide his reaction. "Sugar cube, you look like every wet dream I've ever had wrapped up in designer silk."

A giggle escapes me at his crude but flattering assessment. "River!"

"What? I'm being honest." He sets the shoes, strappy heels that perfectly match the dress, on the dresser and moves closer, his eyes never leaving mine. "Twirl for me."

I do as he asks, spinning slowly so the skirt flares around my legs, the slit revealing more of my thigh. When I face him again, his smile stretches wider.

"I've never worn anything like this," I admit, suddenly self-conscious under his heated stare. "I feel like I'm playing dress-up."

"It suits you so perfectly," he murmurs, reaching

out to trace the line of my collarbone with one finger. "We may need to get you an entire wardrobe of dresses if this is how you look in them."

"I don't need a whole wardrobe."

"We'll see about that," he says with a wicked grin that tells me this argument is far from over.

I roll my eyes, but I can't help smiling. This easy feeling of being cherished and desired is everything I never knew I was missing.

"I still can't believe how things are turning out," I confess, my voice softer now. "More than a week ago, I was heartbroken and alone. Now..."

"Now you're ours," he finishes, his hands coming up to frame my face. "And we're yours. However you want us."

Before I can respond, he steps closer, his palm sliding around the back of my neck to pull me toward him. His lips meet mine in a kiss in slow, deliberate motion. His tongue slides inside to tangle with mine in a dance that makes my knees weak.

When we finally break apart, I'm breathless and clinging to his shoulders for support.

"We should go," I manage, though the words come out husky and unconvincing. "The reservation..."

"In a minute," he says, his eyes sparkling with mischief and something darker. "First, let me help you with your shoes."

He retrieves the heels from the dresser and kneels before me in one fluid motion, his hands gentle as he guides my foot onto his bent knee. "Hold on to me," he instructs, offering his head and shoulders for balance.

I rest my hands on his broad shoulders, feeling the warmth of him through his shirt as he carefully slips the first shoe onto my foot, his fingers surprisingly deft with the delicate strap. The simple act of him kneeling before me, attending to such an intimate task, sends a flutter of arousal through me.

"Other foot," he murmurs, switching my feet on his knee. As he secures the second shoe, his hands linger on my ankle and my calf, his touch sending sparks up my leg.

Once both shoes are on, I move to step back, but he doesn't rise. Instead, he lifts his gaze to mine, and I notice the familiar twinkle of danger and trouble in his bright blue eyes—the look that usually means I'm about to be thoroughly ravished.

"River, we don't have time," I whisper.

His hands slide up my thighs, taking advantage of the dress's high slit to push the silk aside. Cool air hits my skin, and I realize exactly how exposed I am in this position.

"Lacy thong," he observes with obvious approval, his fingers tracing the edge of the delicate fabric. "I can see right through it."

Heat floods my face, but I can't deny the thrill that runs through me at his appreciation. "You like it?"

"You have no idea," he growls, leaning forward to press tiny kisses along the edge of my underwear, his breath hot against my skin. "I can't get enough of you, of this."

His fingers hook into the elastic at the bikini line of my thong, peeling the fabric aside. I should protest, but my body betrays me by leaning into his touch. "We have to go. The others are waiting."

"I can't," he says, his voice rough with desire. "I just need—"

His words are cut off as his tongue finds me, drawing a gasp from my lips that echoes in the quiet room. My legs immediately turn to jelly, threatening to give out as he begins to work me with single-minded determination.

I breathe, my hands flying to his hair as he pushes deeper between my thighs, his tongue dragging long, hungry strokes through my slick folds. He finds my clit, circling it once, then again, firmer, wetter, until I can't think, can't breathe. My back arches as heat coils low and tight in my belly.

"We're not going to make it to dinner."

He doesn't respond with words, but his low, amused chuckle hums against my pussy, and the vibration sends a jolt straight through me. My thighs try to snap shut, but he's already there, already locked in, holding me open with a grip that says *You're not going anywhere*.

His hands slide under my thighs, pulling them slightly wider as he devours me like I'm his favorite ice cream, licking, sucking, tongue-fucking me. I moan, broken and high, fingers tugging his hair as my body trembles beneath him. He groans against me like he can't get enough, like tasting me is driving him mad, and I swear I can feel the heat of his need bleeding into my skin.

Tears prick at the corners of my eyes from how overwhelming it is, pleasure flooding me, wave after wave, each one threatening to break me open.

He's not just eating me out. He's claiming me.

This is feral, hungry, desperate, River consuming me with a savagery that steals my sanity.

My legs wobble dangerously, the muscles trembling as pleasure coils tighter and tighter, threatening to snap. I'm completely at his mercy, helpless under the weight of his mouth and the ruthlessness of his tongue. The only thing keeping me upright is his grip, hands like iron on my thighs, keeping me in place as he devours me like he owns me.

"River," I gasp, voice raw, shaking. My fingers twist in his hair, desperate, needy, pulling without realizing it as my climax builds with terrifying speed. "I can't... I'm going to..."

He doesn't let up.

If anything, he doubles down, tongue working deep, relentless strokes, lips sliding against my clit. His fingers dig into my skin hard enough to bruise, but the pain only sharpens the pleasure, grounding me as everything else spirals out of control. It's too much. The drag of his tongue. The heat of his mouth. The possessive grip on my flesh. It's like my body doesn't belong to me anymore; it's his.

Then the orgasm hits me unrelentingly. I cry out, and it rattles me. My body convulses, hips jerking, thighs clenching around his head as wave after wave of pleasure tears through me. He doesn't stop, doesn't let up, not for a second. He wrings every last tremor from me, tongue running over my slick, oversensitive flesh until I'm shaking, sobbing, half laughing as I beg him to stop.

Only then does he pull back, slowly and deliberately, his tongue making one last possessive pass between my folds—cleaning me, claiming me. When he finally lifts his head, his eyes are dark and feral with satisfaction. His lips are glistening, and he licks them clean with a slow swipe of his tongue, not breaking eye contact.

Then, like it's nothing, he carefully adjusts my thong back into place, like a man tucking away a secret he plans to savor later.

"Just wanted to make sure you're properly sated before we go out," he says with a wink, rising to his feet. "So you only think of me. Of us."

I lean against him for support, my legs still unsteady from the intensity of my release. "As if anyone else could ever drag my attention from you three," I manage, still breathless.

"Ready to go, you two?" Levi's voice comes from the doorway, followed immediately by a sharp intake of breath. "Fuck, it smells incredible in here."

River glances over at him with obvious satisfaction. "Had a quick pussy snack to keep me going through dinner," he says with a grin that's pure masculine smugness.

Levi's eyes widen with desire and what looks like jealousy. "We have time in the car for another snack," he suggests in my direction.

I burst into giggles at his expression, the absurdity of the situation breaking through my post-orgasmic haze. "You're all insatiable," I accuse, though there's no heat in my words.

"Only with you," River says, taking my hand and pulling me toward the door.

The drive to the restaurant is relaxing—Atlas's hand on my thigh, Levi's fingers playing with my hair from the back seat, River stealing glances at me whenever I turn to stare at him.

"I have to get back to writing tomorrow," I mention as we navigate the town roads and traffic. "My deadline is coming up fast, and I've been... distracted for the past few days."

"We'll make sure you have everything you need," Atlas assures me from the driver's seat. "Coffee, food, complete silence if that's what helps you work."

"Though we might need to head back to work ourselves," Levi adds apologetically.

"For sure," I say, though the thought of being alone after three days of constant companionship sends a little pang through me. "I'm a big girl. I can manage a few hours without you."

"Can you, though?" River teases. "Because the withdrawal might be pretty severe after this weekend."

I turn to him, eyeing him and giving him a smirk, but I'm hoping he's wrong. The bond between us is still new, still strong, and I've heard separation anxiety is a common side effect in the first few weeks.

When we arrive at the restaurant, Starlight & Sage turns out to be everything River promised and more. The building occupies a restored Victorian house on the edge of town, its wraparound porch strung with fairy lights that twinkle like stars against the darkening sky. Through the windows, I can see warm golden light and glimpses of exposed brick and dark wooden beams.

Inside, the atmosphere is exactly what I hoped for—elegant but welcoming, with white tablecloths and flickering candles creating intimacy without stuffiness. Our table is perfectly positioned near a large window that offers a view of the street below.

"This is beautiful," I murmur as Atlas pulls out my chair with old-fashioned chivalry, leaving me grinning.

"Not nearly as beautiful as you," he replies, pressing a kiss to the top of my head before taking his own seat.

The menu is an adventure in itself with dishes that include fresh game from the surrounding mountains.

"I'm getting the trout," Levi announces after careful consideration. "The description mentions herbs that grow wild in these mountains."

"Of course you'd choose based on botanical research," River teases, nudging him with his elbow. "I'm going for the bison short ribs. Go big or go home."

"What about you?" Atlas asks, turning his attention to me.

I scan the menu, overwhelmed by the choices. "Maybe the... actually, I need to use the restroom first. Can you order me something if the server comes by? I trust your taste."

"You got it," Atlas states, rising slightly from his chair as I stand—another gesture of old-fashioned courtesy that never fails to charm me.

I make my way across the restaurant, weaving between tables filled with couples and families enjoying their evening out. The atmosphere is relaxed and convivial, the kind of place where everyone seems to be having a wonderful time.

I'm almost to the restroom when I see them.

Chad and Megan, sitting at a corner table. Her hand covering his across the white tablecloth has my stomach lurching with disgust. With anger.

What the fuck!

I freeze mid-step. Of course. Of fucking course, he lied when he called me during my heat, claiming that things with Megan weren't what I thought, that they were over, that she was too complicated. But here he is, in my town, with her, looking perfectly content with his betrayal.

The sight of them together ignites a rage in me that I haven't felt since the day I found Megan's message on his iPad. How dare he come here?

My sharp intake of breath must have been audible because Chad's head turns in my direction. Our eyes meet across the restaurant, and I watch his expression shift from surprise to something far darker—predatory.

He looks exactly the same. Too polished. Too perfect. The light brown hair with those ridiculous, expensive highlights is still styled as if he stepped out of a men's grooming ad. Designer everything, right down to the Italian leather shoes and that oversized watch he never shuts up about.

He's on his feet immediately, abandoning Megan without a word as he strides toward me with that confident swagger that used to make my heart race. Now, it just turns my stomach.

Panic floods my system, fight-or-flight instincts screaming at me to run. I whirl around and rush back toward our table, my heart hammering in my throat and my hands shaking with adrenaline.

Atlas is out of his chair before I even reach the table, his protective instincts obviously triggered by whatever he's reading in my body language.

"Emma?" he says, his voice sharp with concern. "What's wrong?"

I can't speak, can't find the words to explain. I glance back over my shoulder and see Chad approaching, his chest puffed out with false bravado, that familiar sneer on his face that I used to mistake for confidence.

"Emma!" he calls, loud enough that other diners begin to turn and stare. "What the fuck are you doing here with them?"

I try to answer, try to tell him exactly where he can shove his questions, but my voice has vanished. All the old emotions come flooding back—the humiliation, the betrayal, the crushing sense of not being enough. I hate him for still having this power over me, hate myself for letting him affect me this way.

Finally finding my voice, I say, "Last time I spoke with you, I told you to fuck off, Chad."

River and Levi rise from their chairs with predatory grace, flanking Atlas as he steps slightly in front of me. The guys seem to catch on immediately.

"Oh, this is Chad," Atlas states, his voice deceptively calm as he turns to face my ex. "How... interesting."

For the first time since approaching our table, Chad's eyes widen, taking in the three Alphas, and perhaps he is finally registering that he might be in over his head. Three large, clearly fit men have turned their attention to him, and none of them look particularly friendly.

"I'll see you soon, Emma," Chad snarls, but I can hear the uncertainty creeping into his voice.

Atlas moves faster than I expect, his hand shooting out to grip Chad's arm with enough force to make him wince.

"Actually," Atlas says, his tone conversational despite the steel in his eyes. "You're going to join us for a moment."

In the same instant, Levi swoops me from my seat

by my arm. "Come," he murmurs in my ear. "Let's give them some privacy to talk."

He guides me to an empty table nearby, far enough that we won't be in the immediate blast zone but close enough that I can still see what's happening. Other diners are staring now, sensing drama. Shit!

"I don't want to cause trouble," I whisper to Levi, guilt and anxiety warring in my chest.

"You're not causing anything," he assures me, his hand warm and steady in mine. "This is his doing, not yours."

Back at our table, Atlas shoves Chad into my abandoned chair. River takes the seat across from him, leaning back with deceptive casualness while Atlas looms over Chad's shoulder. To anyone watching, it might look like a friendly conversation, but I can see the tension in their bodies, the primal stillness that speaks of barely leashed aggression.

Chad glances between Atlas and River like a cornered animal, finally seeming to understand that he's made a serious miscalculation.

"She's a dumb Omega," he states, his voice carrying clearly across to us. "You're idiots if you think she'll be anything good for you. But I accepted her, and she's mine, so you'd better fuck off."

The words strangle me, each one designed to cut deep and remind me of every cruel thing he ever said during our relationship. But this time, instead of crumbling, I feel a fierce surge of pride. Because this time, I'm not alone.

One moment, River is lounging in his chair, all lazy smirk and relaxed limbs—then he moves. In a blink, he's out of his seat and on Chad, slamming him face-first into the white tablecloth, a fist tangled in his perfectly styled hair.

My eyes widen. Oh my God. That was fast. Like, blink-and-you-miss-it, apex predator speed.

Chad lets out a strangled noise, more indignation than pain, but he doesn't even get the chance to recover before River leans in, low and dangerous, holding his head flat to the table.

"Let's try that again," River growls, his usual playful tone replaced by something deadly calm. "But this time, show some respect when you talk about our Omega."

The restaurant has gone completely silent now, all pretense of normalcy abandoned as the drama unfolds. Nobody moves to intervene—perhaps sensing that these Alphas are not to be trifled with, or maybe simply recognizing that Chad brought this on himself.

Atlas leans in. "Emma doesn't exist for you anymore," he says, but his voice carries in the stillness. "In fact, after tonight, you're going to forget you ever knew her name."

"You can't—" Chad begins, but River increases the pressure on his skull, cutting off his words.

"Here's what's going to happen," Atlas continues with lethal calm. "You're going to finish your dinner. You're going to pay your check. And then you're going to leave Whispering Grove and never come back.

Because if I see you near Emma again, if I hear you've tried to contact her, if you so much as breathe her name in public, I will make you disappear. Are we clear?"

Chad tries to nod, limited by River's grip on his hair. "Crystal," he gasps.

"Good." Atlas straightens, and River releases his hold, allowing Chad to sit up. But they don't back away, keeping him trapped between them like wolves circling wounded prey.

"One more thing," River adds, his cheerful mask sliding back into place with terrifying ease. "That wasn't a threat. It was a promise. And we always keep our word."

Chad scrambles to his feet, his face flushed with humiliation and what looks like genuine fear. "You're all fucking insane," he mutters, but he's already backing toward his table.

"Maybe," Atlas agrees with a cold smile. "But we're her kind of insane. Run along now."

Chad doesn't need to be told twice. He practically flees back to Megan, who's been watching the entire confrontation with wide, horrified eyes. They have a brief, heated discussion before Chad throws money on the table, and they make a hasty exit, Chad casting one last fearful glance in our direction before disappearing into the night.

The restaurant slowly comes back to life, conversations resuming in hushed tones as people try to process what they just witnessed. Atlas and River make their way over to where Levi and I sit, their expressions immediately softening when they see me.

"I'm sorry," Atlas says, settling into the chair beside me. "We didn't mean to make a scene."

"Are you kidding?" I ask, looking between the three of them with something approaching awe. "That was the most incredible thing I've ever seen. Nobody has ever stood up for me like that."

"Then get used to it," River says with a grin that's equal parts dangerous and affectionate. "Anyone who hurts you answers to us now."

"But our dinner... and everyone is staring at us," I protest weakly, gesturing toward the table they've abandoned.

"Fuck the fancy dinner," Atlas states, offering me his hand. "Let's get out of here."

They huddle around me as we leave the restaurant, Levi leaving some money on the table for our troubles, I assume.

Thirty minutes later, we're parked at a scenic overlook outside town, the city lights twinkling below us while we feast on tacos and burritos from a food truck. The dish is simple but delicious, and the company is infinitely better than any fancy restaurant could provide.

"This is my kind of going out," I say around a bite of carne asada.

"Ours too," Levi agrees, carefully folding his burrito to prevent spillage. "Though perhaps next time, we should start with the food truck and skip the drama."

"I really appreciate you standing up for me with Chad," I say, setting down my taco to look at each of them seriously. "God, he's such a fuckhead."

The crude assessment makes all three of them burst into laughter.

"There's our Emma," River says with delight. "I was worried Chad might have scared away your sass."

"Never," I assure him. "Though for a minute there, I felt like I was with him again, all tongue-tied and intimidated. I hate that he still has that effect on me."

"It's natural," Atlas explains, his arm coming around my shoulders to pull me closer. "He was designed to hurt you. But you're stronger now, and you're not alone."

"We'll always protect you," Levi adds. "That's what packmates do."

Packmates. The word settles over me like a warm blanket, filling spaces inside me I didn't even know were empty. For so long, I've been independent by necessity, convinced that needing someone was a weakness I couldn't afford.

But sitting under the stars with three Alphas who would literally fight for me, who make me laugh, drive me crazy, and worship my body like it's their religion, feels like home in a way nothing ever has before.

"So, what happens now?" I ask, voicing the question that's been nagging at me since we left the restaurant. "What if he comes back?"

"He won't," Atlas says with absolute certainty. "And if he does, we'll handle it."

"I don't want to cause you problems—"

"Emma," River interrupts, leaning over to silence me with a gentle kiss. "Stop borrowing trouble. Chad is a coward and a bully, and bullies run when they meet real resistance. He's already halfway back to whatever rock he crawled out from under."

"And even if he isn't," Levi adds, "we meant what we said. You're ours now. That means your problems are our problems, your fights are our fights. No exceptions."

I look between the three of them and feel something click into place inside me. These are my Alphas. This is my pack. This is my future.

"Okay," I say simply and mean it. "Okay."

We sit in comfortable silence after that, finishing our impromptu dinner while the stars come out overhead.

Chad tried to make me feel small, tried to drag me back into the darkness of self-doubt and insecurity. Instead, he gave my Alphas a chance to show me exactly where I stand with them. He reminded me how far I've come from the broken woman who fled to Whispering Grove less than two weeks ago.

I lean back against Atlas's chest, River's hand warm on my waist, Levi's fingers gentle in my hair, and smile up at the infinite sky above us.

This is what real happiness feels like. This is what home feels like.

And no one—not Chad, not anyone—is ever going to take it away from me again.

19

EMMA

The cursor blinks mockingly at me from my laptop screen. I've just finished another chapter. Fourteen pages. Damn amazing for a morning's work. I lean back in the wooden chair I've claimed as mine here in the watchtower, stretching my arms above my head until my spine pops. A week of this routine and I'm finally hitting my stride again. The words are flowing like they haven't in months—hell, maybe years.

If I keep this pace, I'll have the manuscript finished by the end of next month. The thought sends a thrill through me. For the first time since Chad's betrayal, I feel like myself again. Like the writer I was meant to be, not some broken shell of a woman questioning every word she puts on paper.

The morning sun streams through the windows, casting everything in golden light. I dive into plotting the next chapter, when heavy, deliberate footsteps thump on the wooden stairs outside.

"Don't mind me," Atlas's deep voice rumbles as he steps into the watchtower, his full attention on me. "Just enjoying the scenery."

I twist in my chair to face him, and sweet Jesus, the man should come with a warning label. He's wearing jeans that could be classified as a public hazard for how perfectly they hug every inch of his powerful thighs. The sleeves of his navy button-up shirt are rolled to his elbows, revealing those corded forearms that make my mouth go dry, and he's got that slow, knowing smile that makes my heart perform Olympic-level gymnastics.

"The scenery of the forest is pretty spectacular from up here," I manage, though my voice comes out breathier than I intended.

"I wasn't talking about the forest." His gaze sweeps over me, taking in my messy bun, my oversized sweater that's slipping off one shoulder, and the way I'm curled up in this chair like it's my personal throne.

"Oh?" Heat blooms in my cheeks, spreading down my neck. "What scenery were you referring to, Chief?"

He strides toward me with powerful shoulders, chest out, lips pulling into a devious grin. My skin prickles with awareness.

"A brilliant woman lost in her creative world, completely in her element." He stops close enough that I inhale his intoxicating scent of woodsmoke and maple, and the heat radiating from his body has me leaning into him. "That's one hell of a view, Emma."

My cheeks burn hotter, and I tuck a strand of hair behind my ear. "Keep talking like that, and you're going to give me a complex."

"Good. I like making you blush." His voice drops to that gravelly tone that does inappropriate things to my insides. "Makes me wonder where else you blush."

"Atlas," I tease.

He chuckles. "How's the writing going, sweetheart?"

I gesture to my laptop, trying to ignore how the endearment makes my heart flutter. "Better than it has in months. I think being up here helps. Something about the isolation, the quiet... It's like my brain finally has space to breathe again."

"I'm glad." There's something almost tender in those dark eyes. "You looked so defeated when you first got here. Seeing you like this, passionate about your work again, alive, is incredible."

My chest tightens. "You really noticed that?"

He opens his mouth to answer, then stops, his gaze shifting to stare past me toward the windows. "Hold that thought. Look." I turn in my chair, but he's already moving, stepping back outside onto the balcony that wraps around the watchtower. "Come here," he calls softly.

I follow him outside. The wood balcony is warm under my bare feet, and the morning air carries the scent of pine and wildflowers. Atlas is standing at the railing, his body tense with stillness.

"What are we looking at?" I whisper, moving to stand beside him.

He points toward the tree line below. A doe and her fawn are grazing peacefully in the clearing, the baby all legs and spots, staying close to its mother as they move through the tall grass with careful, graceful steps. The morning light makes their coats gleam like burnished copper.

"They're beautiful," I breathe, not wanting to startle them.

"They come here most mornings," Atlas murmurs, his voice low and intimate. "This is their safe space."

Something about the way he says it makes me look at him instead of the deer. "Is that what this place is for you? A safe space?"

"Yes." His arm comes around my waist, pulling me against his solid warmth. "But lately, safe spaces include wherever you are."

My body melts into his without hesitation, fitting against him like we were designed for this. I tilt my head back to gaze up at him, and the sweet smile on his face leaves me swooning. There's something raw there, vulnerable beneath his Alpha confidence.

"Atlas," I whisper.

Then he's kissing me, and every coherent thought evaporates.

This kiss is soft and loving. His lips are warm and sure against mine, tasting like coffee and honey, and

I'm addicted. The cool morning breeze whispers around us, carrying the scent of pine and earth, and for the first time in longer than I can remember, I feel completely free.

Like I could float away on this feeling and never come back down.

When we break apart, I'm dizzy and breathless, my hands fisted in his shirt.

"You came here to distract me," I accuse, though my voice is husky with want.

His grin is pure sin. "Is it working?"

"You know it is." I try to step back, but his arm tightens around my waist. "But if we stay here, I know where this will lead... with me bent over my desk and my laptop crashed on the floor."

His pupils dilate. "Now, there's a thought."

"Down, boy." I press my hand against his chest, feeling his heart thundering beneath my palm. "Some of us have deadlines."

He laughs, and my knees weaken. It's rich and uninhibited, the kind of sound that has me wanting to spend my life trying to hear it again.

"Well, speaking of distractions... I want to take you out."

"Oh?" I cross my arms, which makes his gaze drop to my cleavage for a split second before snapping back to my face. "What's the occasion? Did I win the lottery? Get nominated for a Pulitzer? Finally master the art of not burning toast?"

"Do I need an occasion to want to spend time with my gorgeous Omega?"

The possessive pronoun makes heat spike through me, but I'm not about to let him off that easily. "Flattery will get you everywhere, Chief, but it won't answer my question. Spill it."

His hands find my hips, and his thumbs rub small circles through my sweater, making it hard to think straight.

"Levi and River are getting ready to go join the police for a thorough investigation of the burned cabin. Figured you could use a distraction, and I may have planned something special."

The mention of the cabin sends ice through my veins. "You think they'll find something?" The words come out smaller than I intended, and I can't help wringing my hands.

Atlas takes my hands, gently prying them apart and wrapping them around his waist instead. His touch is warm, grounding. "It'll all be fine. You'll see. I promise."

The words are burning on my tongue before I can stop them. "So, once it's all done and the police no longer require me to stay here, you want me to—"

"Nope." His voice is firm, but there's amusement dancing in his eyes. "Don't say it."

"You don't know what I was going to say." My voice has that stubborn edge it gets when someone tries to tell me what I'm thinking.

"I do." He leans down and kisses the tip of my nose,

and I scrunch my face. "You were going to ask if we're going to want you to leave and go back to your boring little town where nothing happens and no one appreciates how fucking incredible you are."

My mouth drops open. "How did you...? That's exactly what I was going to say, you smug bastard."

He throws his head back and laughs, and the gorgeous sound turns my insides to liquid fire again. That three-day scruff has him resembling some sort of rugged wilderness god. I want to trace every line of his jaw with my lips.

"I know you better than you think," he says, still grinning. "I can practically see your brain working, calculating exit strategies and worst-case scenarios. But here's the thing, Emma—you're not going anywhere. You're ours now, and we want you to move in with us for good. Bring your things from your town. This is your place now."

"Are you serious?" My voice comes out barely above a whisper.

"Dead serious." His expression turns fierce, possessive. "We marked you with our bites, Emma. You belong to us now. All of us. And we're not letting you go."

Joy bubbles up in my chest, bright and effervescent. I can't help the smile that spreads across my face as I throw my arms around his neck and hug him hard, pressing my whole body against his.

"You have no idea how happy that makes me."

He kisses the top of my head, his arms tightening around me like he's afraid I might disappear.

I freeze for a beat, still holding on to him, heart thudding in my chest. Did he really just ask me to move in with him?

God. This is happening.

Am I ready for this?

I mean, yes, technically, I don't have a place right now. So moving in sounds perfect in theory. Logical, even. But moving towns? Starting over? Putting my toothbrush next to theirs and waking up in the same bed every day? That's not nothing. That's... big. Huge.

And what if I mess it up?

I pull back just enough to meet his gaze, nerves suddenly jamming in my throat.

His eyes soften as he lifts his hand, his thumb brushing slowly across my lower lip.

"Hey," he says, voice low and steady, like he's trying to tether me to the ground. "Don't overthink it."

I blink at him, caught between laughter and tears.

"Let's just have fun today, okay?" he continues. "We've got time to figure everything else out."

And somehow, I believe him.

"So then... day out?"

"Absolutely." I grin up at him. "Lead the way, Chief."

We head downstairs, and I hear Levi's and River's voices before we even reach the bottom. They're in the kitchen, gathered around the coffeepot as if it holds the secrets of the universe.

"Morning, sweet thing," Levi says when he spots me, abandoning his coffee to cross the room. His eyes are warm and appreciative as they sweep over me. Before I can say a word, he takes my hand and spins me away from Atlas.

"Hey!" I laugh, stumbling slightly as Levi pulls me against his chest.

"My turn," he murmurs, one hand sliding into my hair while the other settles at the small of my back. He kisses me, slow and thorough, as though he has all the time in the world to explore my mouth. When he finally releases me, I'm breathless and flushed.

"Good morning to you too."

"Don't hog her, Wolfe," River complains, but there's laughter in his voice as he appears on my other side. "Some of us haven't had our Emma fix today."

"Wolf?" I look sideways and smirk at Levi, who just shrugs.

"Wolfe by name, Wolf by nature," River explains, then grins wickedly. "He's got that whole lone-wolf brooding thing down to an art form."

"I don't brood," Levi protests.

"You absolutely brood," River and Atlas say in unison, making me giggle.

River takes advantage of my distraction to spin me into his arms, dipping me dramatically as if we're in some old Hollywood movie. "Hello, gorgeous," he says.

"You're too adorable," I tell him, but I'm grinning.

"Adorably handsome," he agrees, then kisses me senseless.

When he sets me upright, I have to grab his shoulders to keep from swaying.

"We should have a competition," River announces, winking at me. "See whose kiss Emma loves the best."

"Absolutely not," Levi states, but there's a smirk on his lips. "We all know I'd win."

River gasps in mock outrage. "Them's fighting words, pretty boy."

"Nope, I'm out of this one," I declare, holding up my hands. "I plead the Fifth, Sixth, and Seventh Amendments."

"That's not how amendments work," Levi points out with a small smile.

"Don't care. I refuse to choose between you beautiful Alphas."

Atlas clears his throat. "If you two are done molesting our Omega..."

"Actually," Levi interrupts, checking his watch, "we should get going. The police want to meet us there in fifteen."

River's expression grows more serious. "Right. The cabin investigation."

Atlas's hand settles on my lower back. "You two be careful, okay? And call if you find anything."

"We will," Levi promises, then comes over to kiss my forehead. "Try not to let this one corrupt you too much while we're gone."

"No promises," I say with a grin.

River bounds over, stealing one more quick kiss.

"Save some energy for when we get back," he murmurs against my lips, making me blush.

They finally leave, and the sudden quiet feels strange after their boisterous energy. Atlas turns to me with a white box in his hands.

"This is for you," he says, and for the first time since I've known him, he looks almost shy. "Go upstairs and change into it."

I take the box, eyeing him suspiciously. It's surprisingly light, which could be good or very, very bad. "Should I be worried?"

"Go," he says, smacking my ass playfully, making me yelp and laugh.

"You're lucky I like you," I tell him, heading for the stairs.

"I'm counting on it," he calls after me.

Upstairs, I sit on the bed and carefully unwrap the box. Inside, nestled in tissue paper, is a bikini. The world's smallest, most scandalous bikini I've ever seen, in bright yellow that will probably glow against my skin.

"Holy shit," I breathe, holding up the scraps of fabric. There's barely enough material here to cover a postage stamp, let alone my assets.

"Really?" I call down to him. "And what exactly are you wearing for this mysterious adventure?"

"Quit stalling," his voice drifts up from downstairs.

I hold the bikini up to myself in the mirror, trying to figure out how it's even supposed to work. The top is basically two tiny triangles connected by strings, and the bottoms... well, calling them bottoms is generous. They're more like strategically placed patches of fabric held together by more strings.

"What the hell," I mutter, stripping out of my clothes. "When in Rome..."

Getting into the bikini is like solving a puzzle. There are strings everywhere, and I'm not entirely sure I've got them all in the right places. When I finally look at myself in the full-length mirror, I barely recognize the woman staring back at me.

The yellow fabric is practically neon against my skin, making my hair look like spun gold and bringing out the amber flecks in my hazel eyes. But more than that, I look... sexy. Dangerously, devastatingly sexy. The kind of sexy that stops traffic and starts wars.

The top pushes my breasts up and together, creating cleavage that could probably be seen from space, while the bottoms sit low on my hips and high on my thighs, showing off legs that look endless. The back is basically nonexistent—just a string that disappears between my ass cheeks.

I feel exposed and powerful all at once, as if I could conquer the world or at least reduce a certain fire chief to a puddle of want. The thought makes me grin wickedly.

I quickly pull on denim shorts and an oversized T-shirt over the bikini—no way am I walking downstairs dressed like a centerfold model—and head back down to find Atlas closing the tailgate of his truck.

"Ready?" he asks, opening the passenger door for me.

"Such a gentleman," I tease, climbing in.

He starts the engine, and country music fills the cab.

I reach over to squeeze his thigh, then slide upward. The muscle jumps under my touch.

"Keep touching me like that, and we're never leaving this driveway," he warns, his voice rough.

"Promises, promises," I say, but I move my hand back to my own lap. For now.

We're barely out of the driveway when his phone rings through the truck's speakers. The caller ID shows Claire's name, and Atlas glances at me with an apologetic grimace before answering.

"Atlas here."

"Hey, boss!" Claire's voice is bright and cheerful, clearly not knowing she's on speaker. "How are you doing today? I hope I'm not interrupting anything important."

"What do you need, Claire?" Atlas's voice is clipped, professional in a way that makes me bite back a smile.

"Oh, just checking in! We got some new volunteers today, and I have the team showing them the ropes. Everything's really quiet here, but don't worry. If anything happens, I have you on speed dial." There's a pause. "So, where are you off to today? Anywhere special? Anywhere you might want some company?"

She giggles, and I have to cover my mouth to keep

from snorting. The audacity of this woman is almost impressive.

"Just kidding!" she adds quickly, but the damage is done. "But seriously, if you need anything at all, and I mean anything, I'm here for you. You know that, right?"

I can see Atlas's jaw tightening, the muscle ticking in a way that means he's reached his limit. "Claire, we need to talk."

"Oh?" Her voice perks up hopefully. "About what?"

Atlas glances at me, and I nod encouragingly. It's past time someone put a stop to this.

"Your behavior," he says bluntly. "The flirting, the inappropriate comments, the way you've been treating Emma. It needs to stop."

The silence stretches so long that I wonder if she hung up. Then she gasps, and I can practically hear her scrambling for words.

"I... What do you mean? I haven't been—"

"Yes, you have," Atlas cuts her off. "We've all noticed it. Me, River, Levi. We've made it clear that we're not interested in anything beyond a professional relationship, yet you keep pushing. And your attitude toward Emma has been unacceptable."

"But I—"

"This is the only warning you're going to get," Atlas continues, his voice as hard as granite. "Either you pull yourself together and act like the professional I hired, or you can pack your things and leave. We have plenty of volunteers who would be happy to take over your duties. Are we clear?"

Another long silence, then the sound of sniffling. "Oh God, I'm so sorry. I didn't realize I was being so obvious. You're right, and I'm mortified. I know my behavior has been inappropriate, and that's completely on me." Her voice breaks slightly, and despite everything, I feel a pang of sympathy for her.

"I think... I think I need to join a dating site or something, move on properly. I've been stuck for so long, and it's not fair to any of you. Especially not to Emma. I owe her an apology."

Atlas's expression softens fractionally. "Look, you've been incredible at the station, Claire. I don't want to lose you as an employee, but this behavior can't continue."

"It won't. I promise. I'll apologize to Emma when you get back, and I'll keep things strictly professional from now on. Thank you for being direct with me. I needed to hear it."

The call ends, and I say, "That was intense."

He runs a hand through his hair, sighing. "Probably overdue. But she sounded genuine."

"She did," I agree. "I actually felt kind of bad for her."

"You would," he says with a small smile. "You've got too big a heart."

We drive in comfortable silence for a few minutes.

"Everyone's got tragedy in their past," he says quietly. "Claire's Alpha died two years ago. Car accident. She's been struggling to move forward ever since."

I gasp, pressing a hand to my chest. "Oh, that's awful. I didn't know."

Atlas nods. "Losing your mate... it breaks something fundamental in you. I can't imagine."

"Is that why you three found each other as a pack?" I ask softly. "Because you were all needing a bond from your pasts?"

He's quiet for so long that I think he won't answer.

"River was kicked out by his parents. They wanted him to be a perfect Alpha, and when his pheromones didn't match their expectations, they sent him to a corrections facility. Spent years trying to fix something that wasn't broken."

My heart clenches. "He told me, and I hate that his parents did that to him."

"Then Levi lost his parents in a house fire when he was fifteen. Faulty wiring. He was at school when it happened and couldn't save them. That's why he's so obsessed with fire prevention—it's his way of making sure no one else goes through what he did."

My stomach hurts so much at hearing the heartbreak Levi must have gone through.

Atlas's knuckles are white on the steering wheel. He said nothing, and my heart hurt for him.

I reach over and take his hand, threading our fingers together. "I'm sorry. All of you have been through so much."

"We found each other when we needed it most,

when we were all broken," he says. "Formed our own pack, our own family. And now…"

"And now?"

He brings our joined hands to his lips, pressing a soft kiss to my knuckles. "Now you fit right in with us. Like you were always meant to be part of our little family."

"Fate," I whisper, leaning closer to him across the console. "You really believe that?"

"With you? Hell yeah, I do." He glances at me, and the raw honesty in his eyes has me close to losing my breath. "I've never believed in fate before, but then you stumbled into our lives, and suddenly, everything makes sense."

I can't find the words for the emotion swelling in my chest, so I just squeeze his hand tighter and rest my head against his shoulder. "I love that," I murmur. "I love being part of your family."

"Me too."

Twenty minutes later, we turn down a dirt road I didn't even know existed. It winds through dense forest, branches creating a canopy so thick that it's like driving through a green tunnel. When we finally emerge into the sunlight, I gasp.

It's paradise.

A rolling meadow stretches down to a crystal-clear river that sparkles like diamonds in the morning sun. Ancient trees flank a walking path, their branches reaching toward a sky so blue it almost hurts to look at. Wildflowers dot the grass in splashes of color—purple lupines, yellow buttercups, and white daisies that dance in the gentle breeze.

I climb out of the truck on unsteady legs. "This is…"

"Beautiful," he finishes, pulling a large wicker basket from the truck bed along with a thick quilt. "Not many people know about this place. It's been in my mentor's family for generations. He showed it to me."

I spin in a slow circle, trying to take it all in. The peace here is almost unbelievable. "I might cry or faint, or both. How is this my life right now?"

He chuckles. "Come on, let's get set up."

He spreads a quilt under the shade of a massive oak tree, close enough to the water that we can hear it babbling over the rocks. Then he starts to pull out food from the basket, and I'm close to drooling.

Flaky croissants that smell like butter and heaven, fresh strawberries and grapes, sliced peaches. There's a small container with various cheeses—Brie, aged cheddar, something with herbs. Crackers, sandwiches that seem professionally made, pastries that belong in a French bakery window. And what looks like home-made lemonade in mason jars.

"Did you rob a gourmet market?" I ask, sitting cross-legged on the blanket.

"Maybe." He kicks off his boots and settles beside me, close enough that I can sense the heat radiating from his body. "Try the strawberries. They're from a farm about an hour from here."

I bite into one, and juice runs down my chin. It's so

perfectly ripe and sweet that I can't help the little moan that escapes me. "Oh my God, that's incredible."

He reaches out to catch the drop of juice with his thumb before it can drip onto my shirt. "Messy girl," he murmurs, and the way he says it turns me on slightly.

We sample everything, and I have to admit, whoever helped him plan this has excellent taste. The cheese melts on my tongue, the croissants are buttery perfection, and the sandwiches, turkey and avocado with some kind of herb spread, are restaurant quality.

He's watching me eat. "You've got a little..."

He reaches out to brush a crumb from the corner of my mouth, and the simple touch sends electricity shooting through me. When I automatically lick my lips to catch any other crumbs, his pupils dilate.

"Emma," he says, his voice rough.

"Yeah?"

Instead of answering, he stands up, and I find myself transfixed by the way he moves so powerfully, as if he's constantly aware of his body and its capabilities. He reaches for the hem of his shirt, and I forget how to breathe.

"What are you doing?" I ask, though my words come out breathy and distracted.

"Going for a swim." He pulls the shirt over his head, and sweet mother of God, the man is a work of art. Broad shoulders, defined chest, abs that look like they were carved from marble.

"Is it legal for you to be this attractive?" I blurt out, then immediately want to hide under the blanket. "I mean, you could cause accidents. Traffic pileups. Mass hysteria."

He laughs. "Only if you're watching."

His jeans join his shirt, leaving him in black boxer briefs that are clearly designed for swimming. They sit low on his hips, and the way they cling to his thighs and ass has me gawking.

"Coming in?" he asks, almost at the water's edge.

He wades in until he's waist-deep. He is devastatingly gorgeous. "The water's perfect," he calls.

I stand up on unsteady legs and start stripping out of my shorts and T-shirt. The moment the fabric hits the blanket, Atlas goes very still in the water.

"Jesus Christ," he breathes.

I glance down at myself, at the way the yellow bikini barely covers me. I feel exposed and powerful at the same time, as if I could bring this Alpha to his knees with nothing but a smile.

"Wait," he says as I start toward the water. "Turn around. I need to see..."

Heat floods my cheeks, but I do as he asks, executing a slow turn that I know shows off the practically nonexistent back of the bikini.

"Fuck me," he groans. "Emma, you have any idea what you look like right now? Like every fantasy I've ever had come to life."

The raw want in his voice makes me bold. "Just fantasies?" I ask, stepping into the cool water. "That's disappointing."

"Oh, sweetheart," he says, moving toward me like a

predator stalking prey. "I'm going to show you exactly how much more than fantasies you inspire."

The water is perfect, cool enough to be refreshing without being shocking. It's crystal clear, and I can see smooth rocks on the bottom and small fish darting between the shadows. But all of that fades into background noise when Atlas reaches me.

His hands settle on my hips, and he lifts me effortlessly until my legs wrap around his waist. The position presses us together, his hardness against me, and I can feel exactly how much the bikini affects him.

"Hi," I whisper, suddenly shy despite the scandalous swimwear.

"Hi yourself." His voice is rough, his eyes dark with want. "You're so fucking beautiful that it hurts to look at you."

"You keep making me blush."

"I'm obsessed with you." His hands slide up my sides, his thumbs brushing over my erect nipples. "You know that? The way you bite your lip when you're thinking, the little sounds you make when you're writing, how you get that crease between your eyebrows when you're concentrating. I watch you, and I can barely think straight."

His confession makes my heart race. "You do the same thing to me. All of you do. I've never felt anything like this before."

"Good," he growls, then his mouth is on mine.

This is all heat and demand, his tongue sliding against mine with devastating skill. I can taste the strawberries we shared and the faint hint of tea from this morning.

My hands fist in his hair, and I arch against him, seeking more contact. The movement presses my barely covered breasts against his chest, and we both groan at the sensation.

"You're my complete undoing," he whispers against my lips. "Do you know that? I've spent years keeping control, being the responsible one, then you walk into my life, and I can hardly remember my own name."

"Good," I whisper back, nipping at his lower lip. "I like having that effect on you."

He kisses me harder, one hand at the back of my neck while the other explores the minimal coverage of my bikini. His thumb brushes over my nipple through the thin fabric, and I gasp into his mouth.

"Oh, those nipples look so cold," he says with fake concern, though his voice is rough with want. "Show me. My mouth is so warm."

I laugh at him.

"So responsive," he murmurs, leaning me slightly back by his hand gripping my nape and somehow managing to slip my bikini aside on one breast. When his mouth closes over my nipple, I moan, arching into him. His tongue does wicked, flicking things to my nipple, and I hiss at the sensation. "Fuck, Emma, I could spend hours just learning what makes you gasp like that."

"Please…"

"Please what, sweetheart?"

Before I can answer, his phone starts ringing from the shore, shrill and insistent in the peaceful quiet.

"Ignore it," he murmurs against my throat, his lips taking more of my breast into his mouth.

But his phone rings again and then again, cutting through the moment like a knife.

"Shit," he groans, reluctantly releasing me. "I have to get that. Could be the station."

He wades toward shore, and I follow, fixing my bikini, suddenly feeling the chill of the water without his warmth. I grab a towel from the basket and wrap it around myself while he answers the phone, water still dripping from his hair.

"Levi, what's up?" His voice is tense, immediately shifting into work mode.

I settle on the sunny part of the blanket with some cheese and crackers, but my appetite has vanished. There's something in Atlas's posture that makes my stomach clench with anxiety.

The silence stretches, and I study his expression growing more serious with each passing second.

"Are you sure?" he asks, his voice clipped. "And the owner wants to— Fuck. Yeah, I understand."

That's when I know this is about the burned cabin. The cheese turns to sawdust in my mouth, and my hands start to shake.

Atlas is quiet for a long moment, listening to whatever Levi is telling him. I can see the muscle in his jaw ticking, the way his free hand clenches into a fist.

"We'll head back now," he finally says. "Don't let them do anything until I get there."

He hangs up and turns to me, his expression carefully controlled in that way that means he's trying not to scare me. Which, of course, scares me more than if he'd just looked panicked.

"It's bad, isn't it?" I whisper, setting down the crackers with trembling fingers.

He's beside me in an instant, pulling me against his chest despite the fact that we're both still damp from the river. "We have results from the cabin investigation."

"And?" My voice is barely audible.

"It was started by a candle. Accidentally, probably... but..." He hesitates, and I can feel him choosing his words carefully.

"But what, Atlas? Just tell me."

"The owner was contacted about the findings. He wants to sue for damages."

The world tilts sideways, and I can't breathe. Sue. The word echoes in my head like a death knell, bringing with it images of lawyers and court dates and my name splashed across headlines. Everything I've worked for, everything I've built—gone.

"Emma." Atlas's voice sounds like it's coming from underwater. "Hey, look at me."

But I can't. I'm drowning in panic, my chest hurting like someone is sitting on it. My vision starts to gray at the edges.

"Sweetheart, breathe. Just breathe for me."

His hands frame my face, forcing me to meet his eyes.

"I can't," I gasp. "I'm scared."

"You're going to get through this with us by your side," he says firmly. "We'll figure this out. I promise you, Emma."

"How?" The word comes out as a sob. "He's going to sue me for everything I have. My career, my reputation, it'll all be gone. I'll be that author who burned down someone's cabin. No publisher will touch me."

"Stop." His voice is sharp enough to cut through my spiral. "That's not going to happen."

I want to believe him, but the fear is too strong, too familiar. This is what happened with Chad, everything falling apart, my world crumbling around me while I stood helpless to stop it.

"You don't understand," I whisper. "This is what I do. I ruin things. I trusted Chad, and he strangled my creativity. I come here, and I burn down someone's property. Everything I touch turns to ash."

"That's bullshit, and you know it." His voice is gentle but strong. "Chad was a bastard who took advantage of you. The cabin was an accident, a fucking candle, Emma. You didn't burn anything down on purpose."

"But the lawsuit—"

"We'll deal with that. Together." He pulls me closer, and I feel his heart beating steady and strong against my cheek. "You're not alone in this anymore.

You have us—me, River, Levi. We're not going anywhere."

I want to believe him, but the fear is a living thing in my chest, clawing at my ribs. "What if you change your minds? What if this gets too complicated, too messy? What if—"

"Emma." He tilts my chin up, forcing me to meet his eyes again. "Do you remember what I told you earlier? About us being broken?"

I nod, not trusting my voice.

"We found each other because we needed family. Real family. The kind that doesn't abandon you when things get hard." His thumb brushes away a tear. "You're part of that family now. Which means when you hurt, we hurt. When you fight, we fight beside you. That's what pack means."

"You barely know me," I whisper.

"I know enough." His voice is fierce, possessive. "I know you're brave enough to leave everything behind and start over. You're strong enough to build a career. You're loyal enough to put up with Chad's shit for months. And you're generous enough to worry about some stranger's property even when you're the victim here."

His words chip away at the panic, replacing it with something warmer. Hope, maybe. Or just the desperate need to believe that this time will be different.

"We should go," I say finally, my voice still shaky. "If there's going to be a legal battle, I need to start preparing."

"There's not going to be a legal battle," Atlas says. "Trust me on this."

I look up at him. "Why not?"

He's quiet for a moment, then sighs. "The cabin owner, Martin Greene, is a local businessman, owns a few rental properties around the county. He's also got a reputation for being litigious—sues at the drop of a hat, usually settles out of court for nuisance money."

"So, he's going to bleed me dry."

"No, he's not." Atlas's smile is sharp and predatory. "Because Martin also has a habit of cutting corners on his rental properties. Faulty wiring, broken smoke detectors, expired fire extinguishers. Levi's already found three code violations in the preliminary report."

For the first time since the phone rang, I can breathe properly. "So if he tries to sue me..."

"We counter with negligence. Failure to maintain safe premises. A dozen building code violations that put his tenants at risk." Atlas's grin is all teeth. "Trust me. Martin is not going to want this to go to court."

Relief floods through me, so intense that it's almost painful. I throw my arms around his neck, pressing my face against his throat. "Thank you," I whisper. "Thank you for not letting me face this alone."

"Never," he murmurs into my hair. "You're ours now, Emma. We protect what's ours."

The possessive words should probably bother me, but instead, they make me feel safe in a way I haven't felt in years. Protected. Cherished.

We pack up the picnic. When Atlas loads the basket into the truck, I catch his hand.

"This was perfect," I tell him. "Before the phone call, I mean. This whole day... it's been perfect."

"The first of many," he promises, then kisses me softly. "Come on. Let's go home and deal with this Martin situation. Together."

Home. The word settles into my chest like a warm glow. For the first time in longer than I can remember, I actually have one that feels like it did when my parents and my grandmother were still alive.

And I believe every word Atlas said about sticking by my side.

20

I'm back in my shorts and T-shirt, the memory of our perfect morning at the river feeling like a lifetime ago as I pace the length of the watchtower. The wooden floorboards creak under my restless steps, and I can't stop wringing my hands despite knowing it betrays every anxious thought spiraling through my mind.

Atlas is outside on the balcony when the grunt of a vehicle sounds from down below. In no time, Levi and River join us, and with Atlas, they all move indoors with me.

"Sit down, sweet thing," Levi says softly, gesturing to the chair I've claimed as my writing throne.

"I don't want to sit down." The words tumble out sharper than I intended, edged with panic. "Just tell me. How bad is everything?"

River runs a hand through his golden hair, leaving it even more tousled than usual. "It's… complicated."

"The fire was definitely started by a candle," Levi begins. "The burn patterns, the point of origin, everything confirms it, including part of the candle remnants."

My knees nearly buckle, and I have to grab the edge of my desk to stay upright. "I knew it. I fucking knew it was my fault."

"Emma, wait—" Atlas starts, but I'm already drowning.

"God, I'm such an idiot. I should have checked it twice, three times. I should never have lit the damn thing in the first place. Now some poor man's property is destroyed, and I'm going to lose everything I've worked for, and—"

"Stop." River's voice cuts through my spiral like a blade. "Just stop for a second and listen to what we're actually telling you."

Something in his tone, urgent but not panicked, penetrates the fog of my anxiety. I press my lips together, wrapping my arms tighter around myself like I can physically hold the pieces together.

"We found the candle," Levi continues. "But there's something very strange about where it was located."

He pulls out his phone, clicks it a few times, then hands it to me with a photo. My hands shake as I accept the phone. It takes me a moment to make sense of what I'm seeing—the charred remains of what used to be the cabin's blackened fireplace beams and ash-covered debris creating a hellscape of destruction.

"I don't understand what I'm looking at," I admit, squinting at the image.

"Look closer," River says, moving to stand behind my chair. His hand settles on my shoulder. "See that area under what used to be the far wall?"

I follow his pointing finger to a section of the photo where fallen timber has created a sort of cave. Nestled in the shadows, almost hidden from view, is a partially melted glass jar surrounded by debris. Atlas is studying it over my shoulder too.

"That's the candle," Levi explains quietly. "Or what's left of it."

"But that's..." I frown, trying to reconcile what I'm seeing with my crystal-clear memory of that night. "That's not where I put it when I had it lit."

"Where should it have been?" Atlas asks.

I close my eyes, forcing myself to relive those final moments in the cabin. "On the coffee table. Right in the center, on one of those little wooden coasters shaped like leaves. I remember being so careful about it, worried about wax dripping onto the wood."

"The coffee table was on the complete opposite side of the room," River says quietly. "Nowhere near where we found the candle."

My eyes snap open, and the world tilts sideways. "What are you saying?"

"We're saying the candle didn't start the fire from where you left it," Levi explains, reaching over to the phone still in my hand and flicking to the next image. "Someone moved it."

"But who would... why would...?" The words come out as barely a whisper.

"That's what we're trying to figure out," Atlas says.

I glance down at the photo, and this one is a close-up of the melted candle jar. The glass has partially fused with whatever surface it was sitting on.

"But there's something else," Levi continues. "Something that doesn't make any sense."

I study the image, noting how the heat has warped everything beyond recognition. "What am I supposed to be seeing?"

"Look at what's underneath it," River says.

I squint at the photo, holding it closer to my face. There's definitely something beneath the melted remains of the candle—fabric, by the look of it. The fire has partially fused it to the glass and whatever surface it was sitting on.

"Is that...?" I start to ask, but Levi is already reaching for his laptop.

"We managed to get a clearer shot before the investigators moved everything," he says, flicking to the next image on the phone.

Even charred and partially melted, the pattern is unmistakable—tiny gold moths swirling through inky blue fabric, their delicate wings caught in mid-flight.

"That pattern looks familiar," I whisper, staring at the screen in growing confusion.

"From where?" Levi asks.

I shake my head, studying every detail of the design. "I've never owned anything with that pattern, but I've seen it before. Those moths, that specific shade of blue…"

"Could it have been something that was already in the cabin?" River suggests. "Maybe curtains or a throw pillow?"

"The investigators would have documented everything that belonged to the property owner," Levi says, scrolling through his notes with methodical precision. "This fabric isn't listed in their inventory."

"So, if you didn't leave the candle there, someone else was in the cabin," Atlas says, his voice going hard and dangerous. "Someone who moved Emma's candle."

I sink into my chair, my legs suddenly unable to support me. "You think someone did this on purpose? You think someone actually wanted to frame me?" I keep studying the screen, at those golden moths frozen in their final dance, and suddenly the memory flares over me.

"Oh my God," I breathe, my hand flying to my throat.

"Emma?" Atlas straightens immediately, his Alpha senses picking up on my distress. "What is it?"

"I know where I've seen that pattern before." My voice comes out hoarse, shocked. "It was Megan. Chad's new girlfriend. She was wearing a scarf with that exact design when I bumped into her at the grocery store."

The silence that follows is deafening. My heartbeat thumps in my ears.

"When did you last see her?" River finally asks.

"Megan Sloane." I'm already pulling out my phone from my pocket, my fingers trembling as I navigate to her social media profiles. "She was wearing it on the day I checked into the cabin. A silk scarf around her neck. I remember thinking it was beautiful, even though I hated her guts."

I find her Instagram account and hold up my phone, showing them a photo from just two weeks ago. There she is, brown hair, perfectly made up, wearing that same scarf with the gold moths dancing across blue silk.

"This is her," I say, my voice gaining strength as the pieces start falling into place. "But why would part of her scarf be in that cabin?"

Atlas leans forward, studying the photo intently. "Do you have any other information about her?"

"Megan is from Moonshell Bay. She works at *The Tideline Tribune*, sent here to cover one of the many festivals this town holds." The memory tastes bitter in my mouth.

River suddenly goes very still, his eyes widening with recognition. "Wait. Hold on."

He pulls out his own phone, scrolling through what looks like photos, then pauses. "Holy shit. Guys, look at this."

He shows us a picture that makes my blood run cold. It was clearly taken at the burned cabin, revealing the crime scene tape and investigative equipment. But in the front yard is a figure, Megan, seeming to search for something on the ground.

"That's the woman who was snooping around the crime scene the other day," River states. "She claimed to have just lost something on the grounds when I questioned her, but something felt off. I thought nothing more of it. There are weirdos everywhere."

"She was there?" I stare at the photo.

"Gets better," Levi says grimly, taking his phone back from Emma, staring at River. "I got a message this morning from my contact about that sedan, the one you saw her leaving in at the scene." He reads the email. "Rental vehicle, hired by one Megan Sloane of Moonshell Bay. Still on rental for a couple more days."

The world stops spinning. Everything goes silent except for the rushing of blood in my ears.

"She broke in," I whisper, the words feeling foreign on my tongue. "She actually broke into the cabin and tried to... tried to... What was she doing? Trying to start a fire and kill me?" My stomach churns with nausea and fear. "Am I still going to get sued? Even with this evidence?"

Before anyone can answer, my Alphas approach. Atlas crouches in front of my chair, his hands settling on my knees with gentle firmness. River moves to stand behind me, both hands on my shoulders now. Levi settles on the arm of my chair, close enough that I can feel his warmth.

"We're going to find out the truth. And now we

know that it has something to do with Megan, that the fire is connected to her," Atlas says.

"River," he continues without taking his eyes off me, "call the police station. Get the investigating cop on the line and tell him about our discovery."

"On it," River says, already dialing.

Levi's hand finds my back, rubbing slow, soothing circles. "It's going to be okay," he murmurs. "You see? We have contacts, legal resources, and we're going to fight this every step of the way. You have us in your corner now."

The gentle certainty breaks something loose in my chest, and tears burn behind my eyes. My whole body is shaking, the full magnitude of what we've discovered crashing into me like a freight train.

I stumble to my feet, needing to move, needing to do something with the adrenaline coursing through my system. But my legs are unsteady, and I barely make it to the small couch before collapsing.

Atlas and Levi follow, flanking me on either side like bookends. I curl up between them, pulling my legs against my chest in a defensive ball.

"If she really did this, if she actually framed me..."

"Hey." Levi's arm comes around me, pulling me against his side. "This sort of thing happens more often than you'd think, especially in our line of work. We've been sued multiple times—occupational hazard of being first responders. Our lawyers have won every single case."

"But this is different," I protest, even as I let myself

sink into his warmth. "This is criminal. This is someone deliberately trying to destroy my life."

"Which makes it even easier to fight," Atlas says firmly. "It's clear that Megan did something. The evidence is right there."

River finishes his call and joins us, somehow managing to squeeze onto the couch, so I'm completely surrounded by solid Alpha warmth. "Detective has the photos from his team, and he's also putting out an APB on Megan to bring her in for questioning."

I lean back against the couch, trying to process everything. "It must have something to do with Chad, right? Why else would she do this? What could she possibly gain from breaking in?" A thought strikes me suddenly, and I sit up straighter. "You know, I accidentally brought Chad's duffel bag with me on this so-called vacation. It got burned in the fire, but... could that be what she was after? Could she have broken in to look for that bag?"

"What was in it?" Atlas asks immediately.

"Just clothes and toiletries," I trail off. "That would make sense, right?"

"So, she breaks in looking for the bag," River muses, "finds you asleep instead, and decides to what? Burn the place down with you in it?"

"Maybe she panicked," Levi suggests. "Maybe she moved the candle to create a distraction while she searched, not realizing it would cause a fire."

"With fabric from her own scarf as kindling?" I shake my head. "That doesn't seem right."

Atlas stands abruptly, his jaw set in that way that means he's made a decision. "I'm making you some hot chocolate," he announces. "With an obscene number of marshmallows."

"Oh, you don't have to, but I can't say no."

"You're in shock. You need sugar, and taking care of you gives me something to do besides fantasizing about strangling your ex-boyfriend with my bare hands."

Despite everything, his protective fierceness makes me smile slightly. "Thank you."

While Atlas clatters around downstairs, River disappears briefly and returns with a plate of cookies, the chocolate chip ones.

"Here," he says, settling back beside me and offering the plate.

I take one with trembling fingers, not because I'm hungry but because the gesture is so sweet that it makes me want to cry. The cookie is perfect—soft and chewy with just the right amount of salt to balance the sweetness.

"How did you even remember I liked these?" I ask.

"We noticed that you enjoyed eating them when you stayed at the fire station," Levi says simply, his arm tightening around me. "Every little detail, every preference, every story you've told us. That's what you do when you love someone."

The casual way he drops the L-word makes my

heart skip, but before I can process it fully, Atlas returns with a mug of hot chocolate that looks more like a marshmallow sculpture than a beverage.

"Damn, Atlas." I laugh despite myself. "Did you leave any marshmallows for the rest of the world?"

"Nope," he says unrepentantly, settling on my other side and pressing the warm mug into my hands. "You need spoiling, and I need to spoil you. Win-win."

The hot chocolate is rich and sweet and comforting in a way that makes me feel like a child being cared for after a nightmare. Which, I suppose, isn't far from the truth.

"You know what the worst part is?" I ask after a few sips, the sugar already starting to calm my shattered nerves.

"What?" River asks, his fingers threading through my hair in a soothing rhythm.

"I came here to get away from Chad's bullshit. And somehow, the bastard still managed to impact my life in the worst possible way." My voice cracks on the last word. "Even when he's not here, even when I think I've escaped, he's still finding ways to destroy everything good that happens to me."

"No," Atlas says firmly, his hand finding my free one and squeezing tight. "He's not destroying anything. We won't let him."

"But he already has," I protest. "Look at this mess. Look at what I've dragged you all into."

"Emma, listen to me." Levi's voice is gentle but

implacable. "You didn't drag us into anything. Someone else did... Megan, Chad, or whoever created this situation. You're the victim here, not the perpetrator."

"And you're not alone anymore," River adds, pressing a kiss to the top of my head. "This isn't just your fight. It's ours now. All of ours."

"We protect our pack," Atlas says simply. "And you're part of our pack now. Completely and utterly part of our family."

Suddenly, I'm crying, not the panicked, desperate tears from before, but something deeper. Relief, maybe. Gratitude. Love.

"I don't know what I did to deserve you guys," I whisper through my tears.

"You don't have to deserve us," Levi says softly. "You just have to let us love you."

I set down my hot chocolate with shaking hands and turn to bury my face against his chest, letting myself be held and comforted and protected. For the first time since this nightmare began, I actually believe that everything might be okay.

"We're going to figure this out," Atlas promises.

"I love you guys so much," I murmur, the words slipping out soft and breathlessly. It surprises even me how easily they come, words I thought I'd have to choke out, or hide forever behind fear. But here, in their arms, they feel natural. Real. Safe.

There's a pause, like the world holds its breath.

Atlas stills beneath me. Levi's hand on my hair

pauses, fingers tangled in the strands. River's entire body tenses at my side.

Levi lets out a shaky breath, his voice a whisper against my scalp. "We love you too, sweet thing." He presses a kiss to my head like he's trying to memorize the moment.

"Love you more than you'll ever know," River says, his voice low and reverent, his fingers tightening around mine.

Atlas pulls me in closer, like he could somehow fuse me to him. "You are my world," he adds. "And I love you."

My throat tightens, and I blink fast, overwhelmed by the sudden wave of warmth, of being seen, of being loved. I didn't realize how heavy that word was until I let it out, and how light I feel now that it's returned to me, multiplied.

They don't just love me. They heard me. Felt it. And it means everything.

As I am surrounded by their warmth and protection, letting their love wash over me like a healing balm, I can't help but think that I just told the guys I loved them, and they said it back.

And just like that... I wasn't alone anymore.

21

RIVER

I spot Megan, a flash of sleek dark brown hair and a blue summer dress against the brick backdrop of downtown. She has a professional camera slung around her neck and a small backpack. I recognize her immediately from the photos Emma showed us earlier and from catching her snooping around the burned cabin.

Megan Sloane. Chad's girlfriend. The woman who was supposedly just an innocent bystander in Emma's nightmare.

"There," I murmur to Zak, nodding toward where Megan is talking to what looks like a shop owner outside a small boutique. "That's her."

Detective Zak Morrison follows my gaze, his sharp hazel eyes immediately locking on to her. We've worked a few cases together over the years, so it feels natural to head out with him whenever something we've reported gets passed on to him.

Zak's good people—one of the few authorities I genuinely like grabbing beers with every now and then. Met him three years ago during a warehouse fire that turned out to be insurance fraud, and we've been friends ever since. Plus, he's got a twisted sense of humor that matches mine when we're not in full professional mode.

Glancing back at Megan, she has a brittle quality to her, as if she's holding herself together through sheer willpower.

We approach her casually. No point in spooking her into running before we get what we need.

"Excuse me, miss?" Zak says, his voice carrying that particular cop authority that immediately gets people's attention.

She glances up from her interview, and I see the exact moment recognition flickers across her face. Her dark brown eyes widen as they fix on me.

"Wait," she says, her voice pitched higher than it should be. "You're... from the restaurant. The other night."

So, she noticed me. I hadn't even registered her being there, seeing as I was too busy trying not to smash Chad's head through the table.

"Small world," I say with a grin. "Funny how you keep turning up in places connected to my Omega."

"I don't know what you're talking about."

"Detective Morrison," Zak says smoothly, pulling out his badge. "We'd like to ask you a few questions."

"About what?" She's already taking a step backward. The person she was speaking with stepping back into the store.

"About the Pinecrest Cabin fire," Zak continues. "What do you know about it?"

"Just that it burned down," she says too quickly.

I tilt my head, studying her with the kind of focus I usually reserve for analyzing burn patterns. "So, did you find whatever you dropped on the front lawn of the cabin when I found you there?"

The color drains completely from her face. "I think I need a lawyer."

"That's your right," Zak agrees. "But once you lawyer up, things get complicated. Makes you look guilty as hell. And you're less likely to receive a bargaining deal from me. Right now, we're just having a conversation. You help us understand what happened, and maybe we can help you avoid the worst of what's heading your way."

She blinks a lot, gnawing on the corner of her lower lip. She must know she's completely fucked either way.

"There's a café across the street," she says finally, her voice barely above a whisper. "Can we... can we talk there?"

The café is one of those trendy places with exposed brick and furniture that resembles a vintage-store explosion. We claim a corner table, and I notice Zak positions himself so he can see the whole room while I keep an eye on the exits.

Megan clutches her backpack like it's a shield, her camera forgotten on the table between us. Up close, I can see the fine stress lines around her eyes and the way her hands shake slightly as she reaches for her water. She looks like she's about to bolt any second.

"I'll help, okay?" she says before Zak can even start. "But I'm not going to get in trouble for this. I didn't do anything wrong."

Zak sets down his pen carefully. "I can't promise you won't face consequences, Megan. But cooperation can definitely lessen the severity of any charges. And if you're covering for someone else, you need to ask yourself, would they do the same for you?"

She bites her lip, and I can practically see the wheels turning in her head.

"You were at the Pinecrest Cabin crime scene earlier in the week," Zak continues. "Why?"

"I can't..." She shifts uncomfortably, wrapping her arms around herself. "This is so fucked up."

"Megan," I say, letting steel creep into my voice. "I watched you pick through burned debris like you were searching for something specific. We're way past pretending you weren't there."

Her face crumples slightly. "God, I never wanted to do this," she whispers, and tears start forming in her eyes. "But he made me. Fucking Chad said if I did this one thing, he'd... he'd share everything fifty-fifty with me. But really..." She takes a shuddering breath. "Really, he threatened to leave me if I didn't prove how much I loved him."

My jaw tightens. Another woman manipulated by

that piece of shit. The pattern is becoming crystal fucking clear, and it's making my blood boil.

"What were you searching for?" Zak presses gently.

She hesitates, glancing between us nervously. "A... a bag."

"What kind?"

"A duffel bag," she admits reluctantly.

The anger starts building in my chest like a wildfire. Every instinct I have is screaming that this is about to get so much worse.

"Whose bag?" I need to hear her say it.

"Chad's." She won't meet my eyes. "Emma took it by mistake when she left for her vacation."

"How did you get inside the cabin?" Zak asks.

"Technically, it wasn't breaking in," she says quickly, defensive. "The place was rented under Chad's name, and he gave me permission to enter. He gave me the access code."

"And you have proof of him giving you the access code?" Zak asks.

She nods and pulls out her phone, showing him the conversation. Zak quickly takes photos with his phone.

"What was so special about this duffel bag?" I ask, though I'm already dreading the answer.

She hesitates again, appearing genuinely distressed.

Zak leans forward slightly. "Megan, remember what's at stake for you here. Being charged and sued by the cabin owner for fire destruction, plus anything else that might come to light that we aren't aware of yet."

"I had nothing to do with planning this!" she bursts out, eyes wide with fear. "Chad only just told me about it recently. I didn't even know what I was really doing!"

"Okay," Zak says calmly. "Go on."

She takes a shaky breath. "He said he had a signed contract he needed urgently from the bag. That Emma had taken it by accident, and he needed it back."

"What sort of contract?" I ask.

Her face turns even paler. "A management agreement. He said Emma had signed it, giving him full control over all her book royalties going forward." Her voice drops to almost a whisper. "He said once it was notarized, he'd be legally entitled to everything she earned from her writing. Forever."

The rage that floods through me is so intense I have to grip the edge of the table to keep from lunging across it. "That's bullshit. Emma would never sign something like that."

"He said she did," Megan insists, but there's uncertainty in her voice now.

"How exactly did this alleged signing happen?" Zak asks.

Megan squirms in her seat. "At a bar. He said she'd had a few drinks and was really relaxed. That she didn't read it too carefully."

The euphemism makes my skin crawl, and I feel my hands clench into fists under the table. "He drugged her."

"I don't know!" Megan cries, genuine distress in

her voice. "Maybe? I don't know what he did. He just said she was... cooperative when she signed it and had a witness sign to agree she wasn't under duress."

I want to put my fist through Chad's face. The thought of him slipping something into Emma's drink, taking advantage of her, makes me see red.

"You knew Emma was staying at the cabin," Zak states. It's not a question.

Megan nods reluctantly. "Chad told me she might be there. He said to be really quiet, not to wake her up."

"Walk us through exactly what happened," Zak continues.

Megan takes a shuddering breath. "I got there around midnight. Used the code Chad gave me. The house was dark and quiet."

"Go on," Zak encourages her.

"It was so dark I could barely see anything. I found some candles in the living room and matches, so I lit one and carried it around to help me look for the bag."

Zak and I exchange glances.

"You lit the candle?"

"Just to see," she says defensively. "I was trying not to wake up Emma while searching for the duffel bag. But then I heard footsteps upstairs, like Emma was getting up. I panicked."

"What did you do?" Zak asks.

"I blew out the candle and ran," she admits. "Got in my car and drove away as fast as I could."

"Without the bag," I observe.

"I never found it," she says miserably.

Zak pulls out his phone and shows her the crime scene photo of the melted candle with the fabric underneath. "Your scarf?"

Her hand flies to her throat instinctively. "I... I lost it that night."

"This is yours, right?" Zak zooms in on the gold moth pattern.

Her face turns white as milk. "Yes, but I don't understand..."

"I'm guessing you were using the scarf to hold the candle," Zak explains patiently. "Maybe to avoid leaving fingerprints or because the glass was hot. Then, when you heard Emma moving around upstairs, you panicked. Set the candle down with the scarf still wrapped around it, maybe even knocked it over in your rush to get out."

"I... shit." She blinks rapidly, and I can practically see the pieces falling into place in her mind. "I didn't know. I would have put out the flame if I'd realized... Fuck, I didn't do it on purpose. I didn't go there to start a fire. I just wanted the damn bag for Chad."

The casual way she talks about breaking into the place where Emma was sleeping makes my anger spike even higher.

"I thought I blew it out!" she protests, almost as an afterthought.

"But you're not sure," Zak presses.

"No," she admits quietly. "I was scared. I just ran."

This woman nearly killed Emma over a fucking contract that probably wasn't even legal.

"Let's talk about Chad," Zak says. "He promised you fifty percent of Emma's royalties for doing this?"

"I guess," she says, tears starting to stream down her cheeks. "I just... I thought he might be 'the one,' you know? He said Emma was trying to destroy his career, that she'd stolen from him. I believed him."

My hands are curled so tightly my knuckles are white. The idea that this woman was so desperate for Chad's approval that she'd risk Emma's life makes me sick.

"Are you willing to testify against him?" Zak asks. "Tell us exactly what he asked you to do and why?"

"Will that keep me from getting sued and charged?" she asks hopefully.

"That depends on a lot of factors," Zak says, and I know he sometimes stretches the truth to scare someone into working with him. "But cooperation goes a long way toward showing good faith."

"I'll testify," she says quickly. "I'll tell you everything. It's all his fault."

"Where is he now?" I ask, trying to keep the violence out of my voice.

"I don't know," she admits. "He said he had business to take care of this morning and he would meet me in town a bit later."

Zak closes his notebook and glances at Megan seriously. "Here's what happens next. You're coming with me to the station to give an official statement. Everything you just told us, on the record."

"And Emma?" Megan asks. "What happens to her?"

"This should put an end to any legal issues she might have faced," Zak confirms.

Relief floods through me, though it's mixed with a healthy dose of rage at what Chad put Emma through.

We're on our feet, leaving the café, when I spot the asshole.

Chad is standing across the street, partially hidden behind a parked SUV, but I recognize him immediately from the restaurant. Same bland, corporate look, same entitled posture that screams middle-management asshole, even from a distance.

His gaze finds Megan first, and I watch his face go through about five different emotions in rapid succession. Then he stares at me, and the recognition is instant.

He runs.

"Zak!" I shout, already moving.

"River!" Zak yells, but I don't hear the rest of what Zak is calling out. I'm running madly.

Chad's fast for someone who probably spends most of his time behind a desk, but panic makes people sloppy.

He darts between parked cars, probably thinking the obstacles will slow me down. Instead, I vault over a Honda Civic without breaking stride, which seems to panic him even more. People move out of our way.

The stupid bastard cuts into an alley, and I'm furious, thundering behind him. The alley is narrow, lined with dumpsters and loading docks that create perfect choke points. Chad stumbles over some loose debris, and that's all the opening I need.

I tackle him hard, driving my shoulder into his lower back and sending us both crashing to the asphalt. He tries to roll away, but I'm already on top of him, with him facing me.

My first punch connects with his jaw, snapping his head to the side.

"You piece of shit," I snarl, hitting him again. "You drugged her."

"Get off—" he starts, but I cut him off with another punch to his ribs.

"You tried to steal everything she worked for," I continue, punctuating each word with another hit. "Had your psychotic girlfriend nearly burn her alive."

"She's lying!" he gasps, blood running from his split lip. "Whatever that bitch told you—"

I hit him harder, rage flooding through me at his casual dismissal of both women he'd manipulated.

"Lying about what, exactly?" I demand. Another punch, this time to his stomach.

"River." Zak's voice cuts through my anger. "That's enough."

I force myself to pull back, though every instinct screams at me to keep going until Chad stops moving entirely.

"He assaulted me!" Chad wheezes, trying to sit up. "You saw him attack me!"

"Didn't see a thing," Zak says calmly, hauling Chad

to his feet and cuffing him. "You must have tripped down those loading dock stairs over there. Dangerous things, concrete steps."

"You can't—"

"Chad," Zak interrupts. "You're coming to the station with me for questioning."

I step back, flexing my bruised knuckles with deep satisfaction. It's not nearly enough payback for what he put Emma through, but seeing him with blood on his face is a pretty good start.

As Zak leads Chad toward his cruiser, where Megan is waiting in the back seat, I can't help but grin. Martin Greene, the cabin owner, is going to eat him alive in civil court.

I give my thanks to Zak, and he's off. Catching an Uber back to the watchtower gives me time to process everything. Emma's been torturing herself with guilt over an accident she didn't cause, while the real architect of this clusterfuck was planning to profit from her misery.

Not anymore.

I take the stairs to the watchtower two at a time as I spot the three of them up there, practically bouncing with anticipation.

"Holy shit, do I have news for you," I announce as I burst through the door.

Emma glances up from where she's curled up on the couch between Atlas and Levi, her eyes shadowed with worry.

"What is it?" she asks, and there's so much

desperate hope in her voice that it makes my chest tight.

"Baby, you are completely, totally, one hundred percent not to blame for any of this cabin fire shit," I tell her, crossing the room in quick strides. "Chad set the whole thing up, and we've got his ass with the police."

She launches herself at me before I even finish speaking, and I catch her easily, spinning her around as she wraps her arms and legs around me like I'm her personal lifeline.

"Tell me everything," she demands against my neck, and I can feel her trembling with relief and residual fear.

"Oh, I'm going to," I promise, setting her down but keeping my arms around her. "But first, you should know that your ex-boyfriend is probably going to be very, very poor by the time Martin Greene gets done suing him."

The relief and vindication on her face make every bruised knuckle worth it.

Levi and Atlas are grinning.

I guide her back to the couch, where Atlas and Levi are waiting. "Now, let me tell you the story of how we caught the world's dumbest criminal mastermind..."

22

The evening air out on the watchtower balcony is absolute perfection. Warm enough that I'm comfortable in just my sundress, but with that mountain coolness that makes me want to curl up against someone. Lucky for me, I have three someones who are more than happy to oblige.

I'm in an outdoor lounge seat with Levi sitting behind me, my back pressed against his solid chest while his arms circle my waist. Every time I shift even slightly, I sense his heart racing, the hardness against my lower back throbbing.

"Stop squirming," he murmurs against my ear, his voice rough in the way that curls my toes. "Unless you want me to drag you inside right now."

"Maybe I do," I tease, deliberately wiggling my ass against him and grinning when he groans softly.

"Behave," he warns, but his hands tighten on my

waist in a way that suggests he doesn't really want me to behave at all.

The deck around us looks like a food bomb went off. Paper plates smeared with barbecue sauce from River's perfectly grilled ribs, empty containers that once held Atlas's potato salad, and the completely demolished remains of what used to be an entire watermelon. My homemade apple pie sits mostly destroyed on the side table, with only two stubborn slices left after River declared it better than his mother's and proceeded to have four pieces.

"I still can't believe you ate four slices of pie," I say, shaking my head at him where he's sprawled in one of the Adirondack chairs like some sort of golden god, beer in hand and feet propped up on the railing.

"What can I say? I'm a growing boy." He grins, patting his perfectly flat stomach. "Besides, when a woman makes me a pie, I show proper appreciation."

"Proper appreciation would have been leaving some for the rest of us," Atlas grumbles, though he's fighting a smile as he settles into the chair beside River with a fresh beer.

"You snooze, you lose, Chief," River shoots back. "Should've moved faster."

"I was cleaning up your mess from the grill," Atlas points out. "Someone left barbecue sauce on literally every surface within a ten-foot radius."

"That's called flavor enhancement," River says with completely fake dignity. "I'm an artist."

"You're a disaster." I laugh.

River clutches his chest like I've wounded him. "Emma, baby, you're breaking my heart here."

"Your heart will survive," Levi says dryly, his chin resting on top of my head. "Your ego, on the other hand…"

"My ego is bulletproof, Wolf Boy. Nice try, though."

I crane my neck to stare up at Levi. "Wolf Boy?"

"River thinks he's clever," Levi explains, rolling his eyes. "Apparently, having the last name Wolfe makes me fair game for terrible nicknames."

"I think it's cute," I tell him, reaching up to trace the sharp line of his jaw. "Very fierce and mysterious."

"See?" River points his beer at us triumphantly. "Emma gets it. She appreciates my comedic genius."

"I appreciate many things about you," I say sweetly. "Your cooking, your laugh, the way you look in those jeans…"

River preens under the praise while Atlas snorts with amusement.

"Don't feed his ego, sweetheart," Atlas warns. "We'll never hear the end of it."

"Too late," River announces. "Emma thinks I'm irresistible. It's official."

"We all think you're irresistible," I point out. "That's why we're together."

"Fair point," Levi concedes, pressing a kiss to my temple that makes me shiver. "Though some of us are more irresistible than others."

"Are you starting a competition?" River asks,

eyebrow arched. "Because I will destroy you all in any contest of irresistibility."

"Really?" Atlas leans forward, clearly ready to rise to the challenge. "Because I seem to remember being the one who could bench-press you both at the same time last week."

"Only because River was distracted by Emma in those tiny yoga shorts," Levi points out dryly.

River smirks sinfully. "I was... loving the view. There's a difference."

I'm laughing at the banter, which I'm convinced can continue for hours without pause.

"Sure there is," Atlas states with a smug grin.

"Actually," River counters, "I'm pretty sure I won the last three poker games, so technically, I'm the superior Alpha here."

"You cheated," Levi accuses.

"I used strategy," River corrects. "Not my fault you can't read my poker face."

"Your poker face is terrible," Atlas snorts.

"You were doing that thing where you bite your lip when you're trying not to laugh," Levi says, his arms tightening around me. "Dead giveaway."

"Okay, okay." I laugh, holding up my hands. "Before this turns into some sort of Alpha pissing contest about who's the most competitive, can we agree that you're all equally ridiculous?"

"Diplomatic," Levi murmurs approvingly. "Though we all know I'm the most irresistible."

River nearly chokes on his beer. "You? Mr. Silent-and-Brooding?"

"I prefer mysterious and sophisticated," Levi corrects. "Some women appreciate a man of depth."

"Some women appreciate a man who can make them laugh," River counters.

"Others prefer a man who can protect them," Atlas adds.

"And some women," I interrupt, "appreciate having all three in one convenient package deal."

The silence that follows is filled with the kind of heat that tingles my skin.

"Best seat in the house up here," River says, breaking the sudden quiet and gesturing toward the valley below with his beer. "I still can't believe people fight for parking spaces in town when we've got front-row seats to the whole show."

He's absolutely right. The watchtower's elevation gives us an unobstructed view of the valley, where Whispering Grove spreads out like something from a postcard.

"Five minutes to showtime," Atlas announces, checking his watch.

"Speaking of shows," River says with a wicked grin that immediately puts me on alert. "Remember last year's Fourth of July disaster?"

Atlas groans and covers his face with his hands. "We swore we'd never speak of that again."

"What happened last year?" I ask, settling back

against Levi's chest. His arms tighten around me, and he kisses the top of my head.

"Oh, this is good," Levi chuckles. "These two geniuses decided to throw a barbecue for half the fire station."

"It was Atlas's brilliant idea," River says, pointing an accusing finger. "He said, and I quote, 'How hard can it be to grill for fifty people?'"

"I still maintain that the grilling wasn't the problem," Atlas says defensively. "The grilling was perfect."

"It was fine," Levi agrees. "Everything else went to absolute shit."

"Details," I demand, getting comfortable. "I want the full story."

"Well, it started when our fearless leader decided we needed not one, not two, but three different grills going simultaneously."

"For efficiency," Atlas interjects, as if this explains everything.

"Right. Except Captain Organized over there set them up too close to the house, and when the wind picked up—"

"The awning caught fire," Levi finishes. "Small fire, easily contained, but enough to send fifty people into full panic mode."

"Wait, you guys started a fire at your own Fourth of July party?" I'm laughing so hard I can barely get the words out. "You're firefighters!"

"The irony was not lost on us," Atlas says dryly. "But that wasn't even the best part."

"That's when our uninvited guests showed up," River continues, taking a dramatic pause to sip his beer.

"Who?"

"Mama bear and two cubs," Atlas confirms. "Apparently, the smell of grilled meat carried far into the woods."

I sit up straighter in Levi's arms. "Oh my God, seriously?"

"Picture this." River gestures wildly, nearly spilling his beer. "Fifty grown adults screaming and running for the house while a three-hundred-pound black bear and her adorable little babies help themselves to our entire buffet spread."

"We all ended up crammed inside like sardines," Levi adds. "We were watching through the windows while the bears systematically demolished everything we'd spent hours preparing."

"Everything?" I ask, though I'm laughing so hard I can barely breathe.

"Potato salad, corn on the cob, an entire sheet cake that spelled out 'Happy Fourth of July,'" Atlas lists.

"The cubs were actually pretty cute, though," River admits. "One of them got its head completely stuck in the watermelon. We were all pressed against the windows, taking pictures while it stumbled around blind."

"So, what did you do? Just... wait for them to leave?"

"We watched through the windows for about two hours," River says, gesturing wildly. "Fifty people crammed into the house like sardines, trying to stay quiet while mama bear and her cubs had the feast of their lives."

"Two hours?" I gasp.

"They were very thorough," Atlas says dryly. "Ate everything, then took naps on our lawn furniture."

"The cubs curled up in our hammock," Levi adds with reluctant fondness. "It was actually pretty adorable."

"Finally, around sunset, they wandered back into the woods," River continues. "But by then, everyone was starving, and we had zero food left."

"That's when we ordered twenty-seven pizzas," all three of them say in unison, which sends me into another fit of giggles.

"Twenty-seven?" I gasp.

"We had a lot of hungry, disappointed people to feed," Atlas explains. "Plus, by that point, we were all pretty drunk from stress-drinking while watching bears destroy our barbecue."

"The pizza delivery guy was not happy about driving all the way out here with that many boxes," River adds.

"Did you tip him well?" I ask.

"We gave him a fifty percent tip and a beer," Levi says. "He earned it."

"We spent the rest of the night in the basement playing pool and darts," River continues. "We occasionally checked to see if our furry party crashers had returned."

"Hey, wait," I say, suddenly remembering something. "You have a game room downstairs? I haven't seen it yet."

"Had," Atlas corrects. "We're converting it into a home gym now."

"Though we'll probably turn it back into a family room eventually," Levi says, his voice casual but his arms tightening around me. "You know, for when we need space for the baby."

"Babies, plural," River clarifies with a grin that's pure mischief. "At least five."

I nearly choke on my own laughter. "Five? You guys are getting way ahead of yourselves here. I'm in no rush for babies. I want to enjoy being thoroughly corrupted by you three for a while first. Besides, I'm on the birth control shot. Good for three months at a time."

River nearly spits out his beer. "Sweetheart, you do realize that sometimes an Alpha's seed is potent enough to override even the strongest birth control, right?"

"That's not actually true," Levi murmurs near my ear. "Though there have been documented cases in medical literature."

My eyes widen. "Are you guys serious?"

"Dead serious," Atlas confirms. "My cousin's mate was on the pill, had an IUD, and was using spermicide when she got pregnant with their first."

"Holy shit," I breathe. "Well, maybe we should invest in some condoms, then."

The suggestion sends all three of them into hysterics.

"That's adorable," River manages between fits of laughter. "You think condoms would survive us and our knots?"

"Okay, okay," I say, though I'm still giggling. "Let's just take things one step at a time. No need to plan the entire nursery just yet."

Before anyone can respond, the first firework explodes across the sky in a brilliant cascade of gold and red that makes me gasp in pure delight.

"Oh my God," I breathe, craning my neck to get a better view. "It's incredible from up here."

The fireworks bloom directly in front of us, so close it feels like I could reach out and touch the trailing sparks. The sounds are crisp and clear—the whistle of rockets launching, the deep boom of the larger shells, the crackling hiss as sparklers scatter across the night sky in showers of light.

Atlas scoots his chair closer, and River does the same until I'm completely surrounded by warm, solid Alpha bodies. Levi nuzzles my neck, and I can feel his chin resting on top of my head as we all tilt back to watch the show.

"This is perfect," I murmur, letting myself sink completely into the moment. "I've never had a view like this for fireworks."

"Wait until you see the grand finale," River states. "They always save the best for last."

A particularly spectacular firework explodes in a shower of blue and white, and I tip my head back against Levi's shoulder with a contented sigh. His lips brush against my temple, and I shiver at the contact.

"You know," I say softly, "I never really felt like I had a home after my parents died. Even living with my grandmother, as much as I loved her, it always felt temporary. Like I was just waiting for real life to start."

The words slip out, riding on the magic of the moment and the safety of being held by these three incredible men.

Atlas reaches over to take my hand.

"Here," I continue, my voice barely audible over the fireworks, "with you three, for the first time in so long... I actually feel like I'm home."

The silence that follows is heavy with emotion.

"For the first time in years," I whisper. "I feel completely loved."

"That's because you are loved," River murmurs. "So fucking loved it's not even funny."

"I fell in love with your smart mouth first," Atlas admits, his thumb stroking over my knuckles.

"I fell in love with your laugh first," River says, setting down his beer to give me his full attention. "But it was your courage that sealed the deal. The way you trusted us even when you were terrified, the way you let us see all your broken pieces."

Levi kisses my cheek. "I fell in love with every inch

of you," he says quietly. "The way you create entire worlds with words, the way you see beauty in everything. But mostly, I fell in love with your strength."

Tears stream down my face, but they're good tears, filled with gratitude.

"I love you too," I manage through my tears. "All of you. I know it's crazy fast, but it feels like this is what I've been waiting for my entire life."

Another massive firework bursts overhead, bathing our faces in golden light. And I'm awed. The entire sky explodes in cascades of every color imaginable.

I'm surrounded by warmth and love and the absolute certainty that this is exactly where I belong.

"My parents would have loved you three," I say, the words carrying a wistfulness that sends a sharp ache in my chest. "They always worried I was too stubborn to let anyone take care of me, but they would have seen how happy you make me."

"They'd be proud of you," Atlas says firmly. "At everything you've accomplished, everything you've survived. You're incredible, Emma."

"My grandmother used to say that love finds you when you need it most, not when you're searching for it," I continue. "I wasn't looking for this... for you three. I was just trying to survive. But somehow, you found me anyway."

The grand finale begins, and the sky becomes a canvas of light, color, and sound. I gasp in wonder as burst after burst illuminates the night, each one more spectacular than the last.

"Have you ever been skinny-dipping?" River asks suddenly, completely out of nowhere.

I nearly fall off Levi's lap. "What? No! Why would you...?"

"Well, what are we waiting for?" Atlas grins, already standing up.

"Wait, what? Now?" I sputter as River jumps to his feet with far too much enthusiasm.

"Perfect night for it," Levi says. "Warm air, secluded spot..."

"Are you guys insane?" I protest as they start hauling me toward the stairs. "You just told me about bears! Literal bears that crashed your party!"

"The fireworks will keep them away," River assures me, though he's grinning like a maniac. "They don't like loud noises."

"This is madness." I laugh, but I'm not really fighting as Levi guides me down the stairs with his hands on my waist. "Complete and utter madness."

"The best kind," Atlas agrees, already grabbing keys and towels.

Twenty minutes later, we're at our secret spot by the river, and I'm having serious second thoughts as I watch all three of them strip out of their clothes with zero hesitation or modesty.

"Holy shit," I breathe. Even after all these weeks together, seeing them naked in the moonlight never gets old. Atlas's broad shoulders and powerful chest, River's lean muscle and golden skin, Levi's tall frame and those abs—they're like something out of a fantasy.

"Your turn, gorgeous," River calls from where he's already waist-deep in the water. "Don't leave us hanging."

"The water's perfect," Atlas adds, though the way his gaze is devouring me suggests the water temperature is the last thing on his mind.

"Come on," Levi coaxes, though he hasn't moved from where he's standing on the shore, clearly content to watch the show.

With a deep breath and a muttered prayer to any deity who might be listening, I reach for the hem of my sundress.

The wolf-whistles and appreciative sounds that follow as I strip make my cheeks burn but also send heat shooting straight through me. There's something incredibly powerful about being looked at the way these three men check me out, as though I'm the most beautiful thing they've ever seen.

"Fucking gorgeous," River groans from the water.

"Perfect," Atlas agrees, his voice rough with want.

"Get in here," Levi calls as he wades in the water.

The water is shockingly cold against my feet, but I force myself to wade in quickly, knowing that hesitation will only make it worse. The moment I'm deep enough, I dive under completely, letting the cool water envelop me.

When I surface, gasping and laughing, all three of them are surrounding me like sharks who've scented blood.

"Better?" Atlas asks, his hands sliding around my waist.

"Much," I gasp. I'm very aware of how close they all are, how the water makes everything more intimate somehow.

River moves behind me, his chest pressed against my back, while Levi positions himself at my side. I can feel all of them.

"This was your plan all along, wasn't it?" I accuse, though I'm laughing. "Get me naked and defenseless."

"Defenseless?" River murmurs against my ear, his hands skimming over my sides underwater. "Baby, you're the most dangerous thing in this river."

"Definitely," Levi agrees, his lips finding my shoulder. "You have no idea what you do to us."

Suddenly, Atlas leans in and kisses me. I melt into him completely. When we break apart, I'm breathless and wanting and completely surrounded by everything I never knew I needed.

"I love my life," I whisper against Atlas's lips.

"Our life," Levi says, and the words sound like a vow.

I find myself glancing up at the stars with a smile I can't contain. The fireworks are over, but the magic of the night lingers, wrapping around us like a warm blanket.

"Thank you," I whisper to the night sky. I know my parents and my grandmother would be so happy to see me loved, protected, and completely, utterly home.

As they begin kissing me all over, hands exploring

my body, I curl against my three Alphas and think about how, sometimes, the best things in life happen when you're not looking for them.

I came to Whispering Grove broken and alone, just trying to survive.

Now, I'm staying as their mate, their family, their forever.

And for the first time in longer than I can remember, everything feels exactly as it should be.

EPILOGUE

EMMA

I stand outside the Flour & Fable Bakery, my hands trembling slightly as I stare at the transformed storefront. Three months ago, I stumbled into this quaint little bakery as a broken woman fleeing from the wreckage of my old life. Now, the windows are decorated with banners featuring my name and the cover of *Moonfire's Daughter: Book Five*, and people are moving around inside.

My fifth book. My baby. The culmination of everything I've learned about writing, about love, about finding your place in the world. After everything Chad tried to destroy, here I am with a story I'm genuinely proud of.

"You look like you're about to hurl all over those pretty decorations," Jess observes from beside me, her flame-red hair practically glowing in the late afternoon light. She's got curves that could stop traffic and the kind of confidence that makes her seem taller than her actual five-foot-six frame. Her emerald-green eyes are sparkling.

"I might," I admit, pressing a hand to my stomach. "This is so much bigger than I expected. Why did I let them talk me into this?"

"Because you're a badass author who deserves to have people celebrate her badass books." Jess bumps my shoulder with hers. "I flew my ass all the way out here to see you in your natural habitat. You'd better not chicken out now."

She's been planning this visit for weeks, timing it perfectly with my book launch. Having her here feels like bridging two worlds, my old life and my new one, balanced.

"Besides," she continues with a wicked grin, "I'm dying to finally meet these Alphas of yours in person. The FaceTime calls are great and all, but I want to see if they're as stupidly attractive in real life as they are on camera."

"They're going to love you," I tell her, though part of me is terrified they'll team up and share embarrassing stories about me. "They already do, actually. River keeps asking when you're going to move out here permanently."

"Smart man. I like him already." She strikes a dramatic pose that makes me snort with laughter. "Now, come on, before I have to physically drag you inside. Your boys told you to arrive with me so they could help set up, remember? They're probably wondering where the hell we are."

Right. The plan. Something about wanting to surprise me. Though, knowing them, they probably just wanted to make sure everything was perfect.

The moment we push through the door, I'm immediately overwhelmed by warmth, laughter, and the most incredible smells. The bakery has been completely transformed. Lily and Hannah have outdone themselves. No, they've basically created magic.

The usual bakery display cases have been moved to create an open space with a small stage area, complete with a podium and microphone. Tables are scattered throughout with the most beautiful spread of food I've ever seen in my life.

There are Lily's famous croissants, delicate petits fours decorated with tiny edible flowers that seem too pretty to eat, chocolate-dipped strawberries arranged like actual bouquets, and what appears to be an entire architectural marvel made of macarons in every color of the rainbow.

Ruby's contribution is obvious from the professional tap system she's installed along one wall, flowing with what I know is her award-winning craft beer alongside pitchers of cocktails.

But what actually makes me want to cry are the decorations. My book cover, a stunning fantasy landscape with a badass female warrior silhouetted against a magical sunset, is blown up and displayed behind the stage as though I'm some kind of real author or something. Smaller versions are scattered throughout the space, along with fairy lights that make everything feel like we're inside one of my fantasy novels.

And there, in the center of it all, is a table set up with stacks of my books and a sign that reads *Meet the Author — Emma Collins.*

"Holy shit," I breathe, my eyes filling with tears. "This is…"

"Fucking incredible?" River appears at my elbow like he's been summoned, sliding his arm around my waist and pulling me against his side. "You deserve incredible, beautiful."

"More than incredible," Atlas adds, materializing on my other side with that satisfied smile that means he's particularly pleased with himself.

"Thank you. I'm nervous as hell. So, where's Levi?" I ask, craning my neck to look around while trying not to cry and ruin my makeup.

"Arguing with Archer about optimal book positioning," River says with a grin. "Apparently, there's a whole science to author-signing-table arrangements, and they both have very strong opinions."

"Of course there is." I laugh, some of my nervousness melting away just from having them close. Archer is one of Lily's Alphas and possibly the biggest book nerd on the planet, so of course he and Levi would bond over proper literary presentation.

"The infamous Jess," Atlas states, turning to my

best friend with that charming smile. "It's amazing to finally meet you in person."

"The one and only," Jess replies, grinning as she hugs him. "And you're even more ridiculously handsome in person, which I didn't think was possible. The camera really doesn't do you justice."

River snorts with laughter. "She's exactly as advertised," he tells me, dragging Jess into a hug.

"Oh, you sweet talker," Jess says, but she's blushing slightly. "I can see why Emma keeps you around."

"We keep her around, actually," River corrects with a wink. "She's the one doing us the favor."

"Damn right I am," I interject, making them all laugh.

Before the Mutual Admiration Society can continue, I'm swept away by a whirlwind of enthusiastic hugging.

"Emma!" Lily practically bounces as she wraps me in her arms. "You're here! How does it look? Is it too much? I worried it might be too much, but Hannah said—"

"Lily," I interrupt, hugging her back just as tightly. "It's perfect. It's beyond perfect. I can't believe you guys did all this."

"We did all this," Hannah corrects, appearing with her own hug. She has the same warm smile as her sister, but where Lily is all chaotic energy, Hannah has a calm confidence that probably keeps the bakery from burning down on a daily basis. "When we have a best-selling author in town, we pull out all the stops."

"I'm not a bestselling—"

"You're number two on the fantasy romance list and sitting at fifty in the entire Amazon store!" Hannah interrupts with a grin. "I checked this morning. That's huge."

"Holy shit, really?" Jess squeaks. "Emma! You didn't tell me!"

"I didn't want to jinx it," I mumble, feeling my cheeks heat up, but I've been crazily refreshing the page all day to watch my rank improve.

"Well, after tonight, you'll probably climb even higher," comes a familiar voice, and I turn to see Detective Morrison holding a beer and appearing surprisingly relaxed in civilian clothes.

"Zak!" I say, genuinely surprised to see him here. "You came!"

"Wouldn't miss it," he says with a smile. "And I wanted to let you know that Chad is being sued by Martin Greene, and he's gone back home to sort things out. I don't think we'll be seeing him again. And Megan has returned home too."

I can't smile hard enough at hearing about them running to lick their wounds.

"Plus, I wanted to see how the story ended. You know, metaphorically speaking."

"Much better than the beginning," I assure him.

"Speaking of stories," Ruby says, appearing with a cocktail that's the most beautiful shade of purple I've ever seen. "We should probably start thinking about the reading. People are getting settled."

"Right." My stomach immediately ties itself in knots. "The reading. In front of all these people who probably have better things to do on a Tuesday night."

"Hey." Levi appears at my side as if summoned by my anxiety, his calm presence instantly soothing my frazzled nerves. "You've got this, sweet thing. These people are here because they love your work."

"And because they love you," Atlas adds, his hand settling on the small of my back in that protective way that always makes me feel grounded.

"Plus, if anyone gives you trouble, we'll kick them out," River adds helpfully, making Jess snort with laughter.

"That's actually not helping," I tell him, but I smile despite my nerves.

"You know what? I think I need a drink before I do this," I decide aloud. "Something strong enough to make me forget that I'm about to make a fool of myself in front of half the town."

"Ruby's got you covered," Lily says, "She made a special cocktail just for tonight and calls it *Liquid Courage*."

"I love her already," Jess says, "What's in it?"

"Gin, elderflower, champagne, and a dash of magic," Ruby says mysteriously, handing me the purple cocktail.

"The magic is lavender simple syrup," Hannah stage-whispers, making Ruby roll her eyes.

"Spoilsport," Ruby mutters, but she's grinning.

I take a sip and immediately feel some of the

tension leave my shoulders. It's floral and bright, with just enough alcohol to take the edge off without making me tipsy enough to accidentally read the sex scenes out loud.

"This is incredible," I tell Ruby. "You're seriously gifted."

"Says the woman who creates entire worlds for a living," Ruby replies with a grin.

"Worlds where everyone is ridiculously attractive, and the sex is always amazing," Jess adds helpfully, making me choke on my drink.

"Jesus, Jess!"

"What? It's true! Your love scenes could melt paint off walls."

I look around the room, taking in all the faces. Some I recognize—people from town I've gotten to know over the past months, firefighters from the station, regulars from the bakery. Others are strangers, but they're all here for the same reason—to celebrate something I created with my own hands and stubbornness.

"You know what the crazy part is?" I say, mostly to myself. "Three months ago, I thought coming here was the end of everything. Turns out it was just the beginning."

"The best kind of plot twist," Jess says, and when I meet her green eyes, they're suspiciously bright. "And it's definitely going in my maid-of-honor speech, so remember you said it."

"Maid-of-honor speech?" Atlas perks up immediately. "Are we talking about weddings? Because I have very strong opinions about weddings."

"Down, boy," I say with a laugh. "Nobody's getting married. Yet."

"Yet," River repeats with a satisfied grin that causes my stomach to flip.

"Yet," Levi agrees, pressing a kiss to my temple.

Before I can process that particular revelation, Lily is clapping her hands to get everyone's attention.

"If we could gather around and take a seat," she calls out, "Emma is going to read from her work!"

The butterflies in my stomach immediately multiply by about a thousand, but as people start moving toward the stage area, I see nothing but smiling, supportive faces. Mrs. Chen from the flower shop gives me an encouraging thumbs-up. Jake from the hardware store raises his beer in a toast.

This is my community. These people have watched me settle in over the past three months.

"You ready for this?" Jess asks, squeezing my hand and handing me the notebook I asked her to bring for me to read from.

"As ready as I'll ever be," I reply, my voice steadier than I expected.

My three Alphas position themselves where I can see them easily as I make my way to the small stage. Atlas gives me an encouraging nod, River flashes me a thumbs-up and a wink that makes me grin, and Levi just smiles that quiet, proud smile that never fails to make my heart skip.

"Hi, everyone," I say into the microphone, and my voice only shakes a little. "I can't believe you're all here. When Lily first suggested doing this, I thought she'd lost her mind. I mean, who wants to listen to some random woman read made-up stories about people who don't exist?"

There's gentle laughter from the crowd, and I feel some of my nerves settle.

"But staring around this room, seeing all your faces, I realize how incredibly lucky I am. Not just to have readers but to have a community. To have friends." My eyes find Jess in the crowd. "To have my best friend, who flew across the country just to embarrass me in public."

"That's what I'm here for!" Jess calls out, making everyone laugh.

"And to have the most amazing, supportive, absolutely ridiculous Alphas a woman could ask for." I stare at Atlas, River, and Levi, feeling my chest tighten with emotion. "I honestly wouldn't be here without them. They believed in me when I didn't believe in myself."

"We love you too, sweetheart," River calls out, making me blush and the crowd *aww* in unison.

"So, tonight," I continue, "instead of reading from *Moonfire's Daughter*, I'm going to share something new. Something I've been working on—a never-before-seen story from a series I'm just starting. I want you to be the first to hear it. And it's dedicated to the three men who turned my world upside down in the best possible way." I grin at them. "This is for you."

I open the notebook in my hands, finding the pages I've been working on in secret.

"This is from *Wild Hearts Ranch*," I announce. "The first draft of chapter one."

I take a deep breath and begin:

I should have known the GPS was lying when it told me to turn down a dirt road that looked like it hadn't seen maintenance since the last ice age. But after twelve hours of driving through the Texas heat with a broken air conditioner and a car that made more noise than a dying whale, I was desperate enough to follow Siri into the gates of hell if it meant finding civilization.

What I found instead was a massive bull standing in the middle of the road, staring at my rental car as if I'd personally offended his ancestors.

"Okay, big guy," I said through the windshield, as if reasonable conversation would work on a two-thousand-pound animal with an attitude. "I'm just trying to get to Wild Hearts Ranch. You know, the place that's supposed to help city girls like me find their inner cowgirl?"

The bull snorted and pawed the ground.

That was when I made my huge mistake: I honked the horn.

The bull's head shot up, and for one terrifying moment, we stared at each other through the windshield. Then he lowered his massive head and charged.

"Oh, shit!" I floored the gas pedal, hoping to speed past him, but the rental car's tires hit the loose dirt and immediately lost traction. The wheel spun in my hands as the car fishtailed wildly across the road.

I was going too fast on ground that was basically powdered dust. The car skidded sideways, completely out of control, and I had just enough time to think, "This is how I die," before the passenger side slammed into a massive oak tree.

The impact threw me against the driver's-side door, and the engine died with a pathetic wheeze.

"No, no, no!" I turned the key frantically, but all I got was a horrible clicking sound. Through the rear window, I could see that the bull had found my car's new location and was expressing his displeasure by ramming his horns into my trunk.

The entire car shook with each impact. BANG. The rear window spider-webbed. BANG. Something that sounded expensive fell off the undercarriage. Shit!

I had two choices—stay and become the filling in a car-bull sandwich or make a run for it.

Glancing around the area, I spotted an enormous, fancy ranch house, which looked exactly like the one in the photo that I'd been searching for. That had to be my destination. It sat about fifty yards away, a sprawling wooden structure that screamed salvation. I grabbed my purse, said a quick prayer to whatever deity protected idiotic city girls, and bolted from the car.

The bull noticed immediately.

"Shit, shit, shit!" I sprinted across the dirt yard, my designer flats slipping on loose gravel. Behind me, I could hear hoofbeats gaining ground.

I hit the wooden steps at full speed, taking them two at a time, and threw myself against the front door. It swung open, and I tumbled inside, slamming it shut behind me just as something heavy crashed against it from the outside.

The door shuddered.

"Um, excuse me?" a woman asked from behind me.

I turned around, still breathing hard, and found myself staring at the most confusing scene of my entire life.

Three men were positioned around a rustic living room, each one holding a tiny, fluffy kitten and wearing no shirt. Not just holding—posing. One man sat in a leather armchair with an orange tabby kitten perched on his broad shoulder. Another leaned against the fireplace mantel, cradling a black-and-white kitten like it was made of spun glass. The third knelt on the floor with a gray kitten tucked against his chest, his expression as serious as death.

A woman with purple hair and enough camera equipment to shoot a movie stood in the center of it all, looking like I'd just ruined her masterpiece.

"Who are you, and why are you interrupting my shoot?" she demanded.

The door shuddered again behind me, and I pressed my back against it. "There's a bull outside trying to murder me, and your models are holding kittens."

"They're not models," the woman said with exaggerated patience. "They're cowboys. And this is a calendar shoot for the local animal shelter. 'Cowboys and Kittens—Adopt Love.'"

The cowboy with the gray kitten, who had dark hair and shoulders that belonged in a lumberjack competition, stood up slowly. "Ma'am? Are you hurt?"

"Only my dignity," I managed. "And possibly my rental car. Brutus wasn't interested in negotiations."

"Brutus?" The man by the fireplace had sandy-brown hair and laugh lines that suggested he found most of life amusing.

The third cowboy, still seated with his orange kitten, had the kind of steady presence that made you think he could handle anything. "We should probably go wrangle him before he decides to redecorate the truck."

"But we're not finished!" the photographer protested. "I need at least twelve more shots for the calendar, and the lighting is perfect right now!"

The door behind me gave another ominous thud.

"I think Brutus might have other plans," I said weakly.

The three men looked at each other, then at their kittens, and then at me.

"Then," said the one with the gray kitten, gently transferring the tiny ball of fluff to my arms, "looks like you're our emergency kitten-sitter."

Before I could protest, I was holding three kittens while watching three honest-to-God cowboys grab lassos from hooks by the door like this was just another Tuesday at the ranch.

The photographer threw up her hands. "This is exactly why I don't work with animals or children!"

I was wrangling the kittens as the orange one kept trying to climb up my shirt.

Through the front window, I watched the three men approach the bull with the kind of calm competence that suggested they'd done this before. A lot.

"*So, does this happen often?*" *I asked.*

"*Which part? The bull attacks, the ruined photo shoots, or random women falling through the door to hold kittens?*"

I glanced down at the three tiny faces staring up at me with complete trust. "All of the above?"

"*Welcome to Wild Hearts Ranch,*" *she said dryly. "Where chaos is just another word for Tuesday.*"

Outside, one of the cowboys had gotten a rope around Brutus's neck and was having what appeared to be a very serious conversation with him about appropriate social behavior. The bull looked thoroughly unimpressed.

"*I'm Sophia, by the way,*" *I said with my armful of kittens. "And I'm not supposed to be here for a relaxing vacation. I inherited this place from Rose Martinez's grandson.*"

The photographer's eyebrows shot up. "Oh, this is going to be interesting."

My shoulders pulled back at her loaded tone. "Why do you say it like that?"

The photographer let out a bark of laughter. "Sweetie, good luck telling those three men out there that this place actually belongs to you."

"*What do you mean?*" *I asked, though something cold was settling in my stomach.*

"*Because those three out there? They think this ranch is theirs. They had some agreement with Rose about buying it after working here for five years. And, well, she passed before the five years were up. They've been paying all the bills, maintaining the property, handling the livestock.*" *She gestured toward the window, through which I could see that the cowboys were still dealing with the bull. "Far as they know, Rose left them the ranch in her will."*

I stared at her. "But it was left to me. I have the paperwork."

"Well then, honey, you're about to have one hell of an awkward conversation."

Looking out at the three cowboys, who were now successfully leading a very grumpy bull away from the remains of my rental car, I felt sick.

But as the gray kitten purred against my chest and I watched the man who'd handed him to me tip his hat in my direction through the window, I realized that maybe complicated was exactly what my life needed.

Even if it meant fighting three gorgeous cowboys for my own ranch.

I look up from my notebook to find the entire room completely silent, hanging on every word. There's something magical about sharing a story like this, about watching people get lost in the world you've created.

Before I can say anything else, my three Alphas are suddenly on the stage with me, wrapping me in a group hug that makes the audience burst into applause.

"Please tell me those three cowboys are us. I love it," Atlas murmurs against my ear.

I am nodding crazily. "Of course."

"Are there going to be hot sex scenes in this one?" River whispers, loud enough that several people in the front row start laughing.

"River!" I gasp, mortified.

"Everyone can hear you," Levi points out dryly, gesturing to the microphone that's still picking up every word.

The laughter that erupts from the crowd is immediate and delighted, and River has the grace to look sheepish for about half a second before grinning unrepentantly.

"Well?" he asks, still loud enough for everyone to hear. "Are there?"

"Oh my God," I bury my face in my hands while the entire room dissolves into laughter and cheers.

"That's a yes!" Jess shouts from the crowd. "I've read her rough drafts!"

I'm laughing too hard to be genuinely mortified.

As the laughter dies down and we move to the signing table, I'm struck by how natural this feels. How right. I'm surrounded by love, laughter, and the kind of community I never knew existed.

"You know," I tell my Alphas as they hover protectively while I sign books, "I never thought I could ever be this happy."

"Could be?" Levi raises an eyebrow.

"Okay, fine. I'm ridiculously, stupidly, completely happy."

"Good," Atlas says, pressing a kiss to the top of my head.

"And we're just getting started," River adds.

As the real party is just beginning, I find myself standing in the middle of the room, surrounded by the warmth of laughter and conversation that shows no signs of slowing down.

Three months ago, I thought I was running away from my life.

Turns out, I was running straight toward it.

And the best part? This is just the beginning of our story.

ABOUT HARLEY KNIGHT

Hi, I'm Harley Knight! I'm a romance author from the USA who's absolutely obsessed with books, writing, and happily-ever-afters. I love creating stories filled with emotion, passion, and unforgettable characters that stick with you long after the last page. When I'm not writing, you'll find me lost in a good book or dreaming up my next big adventure. For me, there's nothing better than crafting love stories that remind us all why love is worth fighting for.

www.ingramcontent.com/pod-product-compliance
Lightning Source LLC
Chambersburg PA
CBHW062311200726

48292CB00006BA/1983